Trick or Treat

JACKSON SHARP

PENGUIN BOOKS

PENGUIN BOOKS

UK | USA | Canada | Ireland | Australia
India | New Zealand | South Africa

Penguin Books is part of the Penguin Random House group of companies
whose addresses can be found at global.penguinrandomhouse.com.

Penguin
Random House
UK

First published 2015
001

Copyright © Working Partners Two Limited, 2015

The moral right of the author has been asserted

Set in 12.5/14.75 pt Garamond MT Std
Typeset by Jouve (UK), Milton Keynes
Printed in Great Britain by Clays Ltd, St Ives plc

A CIP catalogue record for this book is available from the British Library

ISBN: 978–1–405–92026–1

www.greenpenguin.co.uk

MIX
Paper from
responsible sources
FSC® C018179

Penguin Random House is committed to a
sustainable future for our business, our readers
and our planet. This book is made from Forest
Stewardship Council® certified paper.

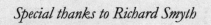

Special thanks to Richard Smyth

Prologue

Little Mouse awoke in the dark and jumped at the noise of a gunshot. It was followed by more, in staccato succession, and then by men's voices, raised in anger and alarm. There was also an oily smoke-smell, the smell of chicken or pork left too long in the oven. He swung his legs out of bed, rubbing at his face. Had Marek the Cook put a joint of meat on to roast for supper, and forgotten about it? Or, more likely, got dead drunk on raki and passed out in the kitchen chair . . .

But it was still dark! And this noise –

He pulled aside the hessian curtain at the dormitory's only window. He shivered and thumbed at his eyes, trying to smear away the fog of sleep.

Light, beyond the misted windowpane. Orange light. Firelight. More gunshots, shouting – and screaming, too, wild screaming. And the *smell* –

Something worse than a burned joint of meat, this. He wiped the glass with the heel of his hand and called over his shoulder: 'Radi? Mirko? Come and look at this. Something's going on.'

No answer. He turned. In the darkness he could see the three white oblongs of the other boys' beds. Blankets thrown aside. Empty.

The brothers of St Quintus had given him his name, Mali Miš, Little Mouse, when he had first entered the monastery as a half-starved child. Timid, twitchy, scrawny and wide-eyed – that was Little Mouse. Even now, at fifteen, he stood out among the boys at the monastery for his small size, his wary manner, his quietness.

His gut squirmed like a trapped animal.

A scream of pure terror pierced the windows and walls of the building.

Here in the dorm, Little Mouse thought, *there is no screaming and no smoke. There are no guns and no fire. Here in the dorm I am safe.*

His throat hurt. The fear in his gut threatened to burst loose. He swallowed down a sob.

Here in the dorm, I am alone.

He turned from the window. He ran for the door.

The monastery courtyard flickered white and black. Someone had turned on the big floodlight, but the generator that ran it from the basement was old and temperamental and the light could never be relied on.

Through the shuddering darkness Little Mouse looked upon the killing.

Men in uniform were everywhere. Not smart like the soldiers Little Mouse had sometimes seen parading through the town. These were shabby, desperate.

At the monastery gate he saw a soldier on one knee, holding another man flat to the floor with his arm bent up his back. The man on the ground had a black beard and was shouting something over and over. The soldier had a gun in his free hand. He put it to the man's head. Little Mouse looked away but he couldn't close his ears to the noise of the shot. Neither could he shut his mind to the terror of the silence that followed it.

In the shadow of the west wall, where Brother Vidić cultivated his bean plants, three soldiers with rifles stood around a woman who lay on her back. She was screaming, too. A headscarf and some other garments lay beside her. When one of the soldiers turned away Little Mouse saw first that he was laughing and then that his trousers were unfastened. There were dark stains down his front.

Beyond the walls a fire was raging.

Little Mouse thought that soldiers were supposed to protect people, but these men had brought nothing but violence and fire and death.

Little Mouse took a few steps down into the courtyard. Through the gates he could see more flames, roaring from the houses and shops of the village's main street. Gunshots rattled like hailstones on an iron roof.

Two men, running fast, hurtled round the corner of the street, headed for the monastery gates. There was a series of quick booms, like angry rapping at a door, then the men tumbled, one after the other. Both crashed face first to the concrete.

Little Mouse winced. Then he saw the blood pooling under their heads, more blood than you would ever get from a broken nose or a grazed elbow. A man in uniform, with no cap and his jacket open, jogged up behind them and fired his rifle three more times into their still bodies.

The soldiers were Serbs, Little Mouse understood. Vicious enemies from another country with another religion.

Heathens, some of the brothers said they were. But Abbot Cerbonius only called them 'children of another god'. The abbot could sometimes be hard to understand.

Subtle, Little Mouse had heard the others call him. He could tell they didn't always mean this description as a compliment – but Little Mouse loved the abbot anyway.

Where was he now? Little Mouse wondered. The abbot was the wisest and bravest man Little Mouse knew. He would put a stop to this horror. He would tell Little Mouse what was happening and how they could put an end to it. Little Mouse looked around, craning for a glimpse of the familiar tall, cassocked figure.

At the eastern end of the yard, in the shadow of an arcade of brick arches, he glimpsed a hunched figure; the flickering light revealed the steel-blue of his cassock, and Little Mouse's heart leapt –

But in another moment he realized that it was not the abbot but Brother Markus, the stony-faced schoolteacher. And Brother Markus wasn't alone: with him, being shepherded cautiously through the dark arches towards the rear gate, were the monastery's other boys – Mirko, Radi, Nema – his friends!

Little Mouse called out. But it would take a miracle to be heard over the uproar of guns, flames and terrified screams. The sounds of hell itself, it seemed to Little Mouse. But the abbot taught that God watches over us even in the darkest places – especially in the darkest places – so Little Mouse kept his faith. 'Brother Markus,' he called again. Again his words were whisked away by the shrieks of the tormented and the howling laughter of demons. Little Mouse whispered a prayer to Jesus, and called a third time, 'Brother Markus!'

The monk turned his head. He looked directly towards Little Mouse. *A miracle,* Little Mouse thought fleetingly.

Christ protects the meek and Little Mouse was the meekest of all his children. He felt sick with relief – he would escape with the others and Brother Markus would take him far from the vicious Serbs.

But then Brother Markus's face hardened. The monk turned away and followed the boys into the shadows, and none of Little Mouse's calls or prayers brought him back.

You saw me, Little Mouse thought, tears blearing his vision. *You saw me, an idiot boy, a half-witted kitchen lad. Christ turned your head towards me,* he thought, bitterly, angrily. *Christ gave you the choice: save me, or desert me. And it was the man in you that made the choice. God forgive you, brother!*

Little Mouse took a few hopeless steps towards the gates. He blinked in the smoke. Two soldiers hammered at the unmoving body of a man with their rifle butts. A woman knelt on the ground with her face buried in her hands while a soldier postured behind her with a hunting knife.

Across the wide concrete street he saw frantic cassocked figures silhouetted against the flames that played against the windows of the monks' quarters. Soldiers drank and smoked cigarettes in the street outside while the building burned. When one of the figures smashed the window and began to climb through to escape the fire, one of the soldiers raised a gun and shot him dead. His body hung as limp as a doll's, half in and half out of the broken window.

There was laughter from the soldiers, and a shout: '*Goreti, goreti.*' Burn, burn.

Flames consumed the still body of the fallen monk.

Little Mouse thought of that smell, that inescapable

smell, the smell of oily kitchen-smoke, of something left too long in the oven –

'Little Mouse!'

He spun round, whimpering in dread, to see a huge figure bearing down on him, arms outstretched. He flinched, raising his hands to protect himself – but then, shadowed against the flickering floodlight, he made out a shock of untamed white hair, and heard the apparition again say his name, 'Little Mouse,' in a familiar deep-chested voice, and knew that the abbot had come back to save him.

Little Mouse sobbed out a noise as Abbot Cerbonius grabbed him and clutched him to his chest. The abbot's crucifix dug into the boy's cheek but he cherished the pain.

'We must act quickly,' the abbot said. He loosened his embrace and gripped the boy sternly by his shoulders. The old man's grey gaze was steady and calm but his voice betrayed overpowering emotion. 'Only we remain, do you understand? When the devils grow weary of murder they will plunder our treasures. The glories of our Church. They are coming *now*, Little Mouse, do you understand me?' He straightened, looking around wildly. 'The treasures are the sacred responsibility of our order, and we must protect them. We are the only ones left who can stop the devils, child. Praise be to Christ Jesus. We are the only –'

He broke off. Little Mouse watched him, puzzled. The abbot stared at something above Little Mouse, his jaw hanging open. Something in the sky. *A vision!* Little Mouse thought. He knew that only the most faithful of God's servants were blessed with such a gift.

Then he saw the dark-red coin appear on the abbot's high forehead, a circle the size of a dinar piece, then a five-dinar piece, then a heavy tear of dark blood rolled from the coin and down the abbot's face, painting a red stripe across his open eyeball.

The abbot crumpled to the floor. Behind him stood a soldier, chewing gum and gripping the butt of a revolver with both hands. He began to lower the gun – but then he saw Little Mouse and the black eye of the revolver's muzzle lifted again.

'Fucking stinking Croat shits living in filth like rats in a sewer,' the soldier said in a dull voice. 'And you bastards here with your cellars stuffed with gold. Living like fucking kings, huh?' He cocked the gun. 'Don't remember when I last got paid. And we should've got extra for all the overtime we put in at Hrasnica.'

Little Mouse's throat was dry. He looked at his beloved abbot's still body.

I have nothing, he wanted to say. *No gold. No friends. No family. I have nothing in the world.*

'I'll give you five seconds for one last prayer,' the soldier said. He smiled with just his mouth. 'Better make it a quick one.'

I have nothing, Little Mouse thought. *You have taken from me the only father I ever had.*

He looked into the eye of the gun and swore to God that he wouldn't blink.

'Crazy little bastard,' the soldier said. His finger tightened on the trigger.

Chapter One

4 October

White face. Staring eyes, red-rimmed in the car's head-lamps. A trembling hand holding a half-empty bottle of water.

Christ, Rose thought. The things that call themselves coppers nowadays.

She killed the engine, got out of the car. It was cold – it was always a few degrees colder out here in the bloody cabbage fields. She pulled on leather gloves as she crossed the road to where the PC waited by his patrol car.

'M-ma'am,' he stuttered.

She flexed her fingers into the gloves and looked him up and down.

'What are you?'

'PC Ganley, ma'am.'

'Where's Conners?'

'Qu-questioning the lad who found the b-body, ma'am.' Ganley gulped. She almost felt sorry for him. Made damn sure not to show it.

'Then who's guarding the body, Constable Ganley?'

The constable looked out into the darkness of the field. His Adam's apple bobbed.

'I wouldn't w-worry, ma'am.' He looked her in the eye briefly, then looked away. 'She's not going anywhere.'

She could have slapped him. He knew as well as she did that that wasn't the bloody point. Instead she said: 'Next time you throw up on duty, Ganley, be sure to turn your back to the wind. Find a tissue and get that puke off your shoes. And I'll be mentioning this to Sergeant O'Dwyer.'

She turned away. She saw Pete Conners, notebook in hand, talking to a man who had his back to her. Conners gave her the slightest of nods. Solid man. Ex-Met. She looked at the man he was talking to. Tall. Shock of hair under a woolly hat. Narrow trousers, corduroy coat. Student? Long way out of town for four in the morning. But then, they get everywhere, students, Rose thought – like woodlice.

Conners and the suspect – because that was what he'd end up being, whatever his story was – stood at the edge of a broad sweep of grassy field that vanished into darkness beyond the glow of the patrol car's headlamps. A row of black trees about a mile away screened the weak crown of light that marked Oxford town.

Rose clicked on her torch and stepped into the darkness. The waist-high grass sighed. She looked back over her shoulder.

'Are you in any state to help, Constable,' she called out, letting a twang of impatience enter her tone, 'or do you want me to just wander around in the dark till I stumble across a corpse?'

She knew Conners and the suspect were looking at her, but a bit of theatre never did any harm. Let the suspect know he wasn't going to get an easy ride. Give Conners something to grin about – he'd need it, what with this coming at the end of an eight-hour night shift. And get this young lad Ganley's mind off – well, off whatever it was he'd seen out there.

Ganley jogged awkwardly down the verge – 'Yes, ma'am. Sorry, ma'am.' – and pointed his torch beam along a faint diagonal pathway someone's feet had made in the grass.

'Along there,' he said, making the torch beam wag. 'A hundred metres or so. You can't miss it,' he added, in a sick voice.

'Who made the path?'

'Here when we got here, ma'am. Could've been the killer, or maybe the lad Conners is talking to.'

'Or a curious passer-by. Or the press. Or a coachload of Japanese tourists for all you'd know.' She breathed out hard through her nose. 'Jesus, Ganley. *Never* leave a crime scene unattended.'

'No, ma'am. Sorry, ma'am.'

'Now piss off out of it. Go see if Conners has got any sense out of our friend over there.'

'Yes, ma'am.'

She waited till his clumping footsteps had faded – heard the murmur of him and Conners talking by the car. The tips of the grass stems bristled against her bare wrist. Then she moved forwards, into the field.

It was like stepping into the sea. The dark grass, petrol-blue in the gloom, moved with the wind in soughing waves. It felt cold and heavy about her legs as she walked. Her torch beam danced, neurotically alert, a narrow beam, designed to pick out detail.

A hundred metres, he'd said. She'd see it soon. She forced herself to breathe.

She'd never liked going in the sea, as a kid. Too much you couldn't see, too much mystery. Too many monsters.

A little way ahead the grass path widened into a clearing of stamped-down grass. She paused, tracking the torch beam carefully, right, left, right, left. The crime scene might not yet be a completely lost cause, in spite of stupid young Ganley's best efforts. She moved forwards carefully, peering into the darkness. There'd be a body, sure, she was ready for that and God knew what else, but a crime scene was about so much more than a body. Even in her granddad's day they'd known that, and now, with DNA fingerprinting, forensic serology, blood-spatter analysis – now you could build a prosecution case on a quarter-inch of a blade of grass, and make it stick.

A body at a crime scene is a cry in the dark. But when you're a copper you have to listen for the whispers, too.

The narrow torch beam picked out a foot. A small foot, a woman's bare foot. Rose squinted. The body wasn't lying on the ground. It was hanging, or pinioned. But there was a fresh breeze blowing from the north and the foot didn't move, the body didn't sway – and anyway, what was there for it to hang from out here in the middle of a field?

The leg, in some sort of hippy-type hessian trouser, was angled away from the vertical. Rose's torch beam crept upwards through the darkness. The folds of the hessian made vivid shadows. Legs loosely apart. No visible damage yet, no stains. It wasn't the horror-movie bloodbath Ganley's reaction had led her to expect.

Her top, too, was woven from coarse fabric. An inch of pale belly showed between the top and trousers. Ill-fitting *and* ugly. The round torch beam took in the dead woman's skinny torso, shoulders, hips. Her arms were spread. She was spreadeagled – on a hay bale, a stack of timber, something like that. Funny that her clothes were all intact, then.

It'll be the face that spooked Ganley, Rose thought. There's something about faces – and something about us, something that means we can't stand the sight of another human face that's been messed with, fucked up, made wrong.

The torch beam moved up the woman's splayed body. It didn't quiver. She wouldn't let it quiver.

Whatever you've done to her face, you sick bastard, she thought, I'm ready for it.

The neckline of the strange hessian top showed two pale collarbones and a small cross on a fine chain. The skin of the woman's neck was bleakly white. Then –

A cap of black blood. A cut edge of vertebra. The rotten timber behind. Nothing else.

'Jesus,' Rose murmured. Cleanly beheaded. *What the hell?*

She moved the torch beam to the right, tracking carefully down the woman's shoulder, her arm, to her clawed left hand.

To what was held in her clawed left hand.

Oh Christ. Oh Jesus bloody Christ.

Rose stepped reflexively backwards, caught her heel on a tussock of grass. Fell sprawling.

She lay on her back in the half-darkness, fighting for breath, staring up at the woman's body, fastened to a cross, holding her own severed head in her left hand.

Rose climbed to her feet, mind racing. She fought to get a grip on her thoughts, to master her heartbeat, her breathing – to contain the panic. For half a second, when the white torch beam had fallen across the lifeless face, she'd wondered if she was finally having that breakdown everyone said she had coming. It was, surely, an image from a nightmare, a psychotic's hallucination – that dangling, lifeless head, suspended by its pale-blonde hair.

But this is real, Rose told herself. *This. Is. Real.*

A real crime. A real murder, and a real murderer. A real body, that was once a real woman, with real friends, real family –

Time to do your bloody job, DI Rose.

Now she went over the body with the torch held close by her right temple. The woman wasn't tied to the cross – she was pinned to it, with neat iron pins pushed through the skin of her calves and wrists. She hadn't bled. The cross itself *wasn't* a cross but a section of an old wooden cartwheel, propped up with scrap timber.

The hair of the woman's head was knotted intricately to the dead hand. Her eyes were closed. She'd been pretty, Rose noted – pale as paper in the torchlight, with striking dark brows and an accentuated upper lip. Her chin was pointed and her cheekbones were high and flat.

Rose pulled off her leather gloves and snapped on a pair of latex disposables. She knelt to examine the severed throat. Wasn't sure what she was looking for – Christ, she wasn't a pathologist, and wouldn't want to be – but you never knew. She gently touched her fingertips to the cut edge of flesh, suppressing a shiver at its coldness. So tidy, she thought. A neat job. One of *those*. She'd read about the type: the retired accountant running women's skins through his Singer sewing machine and never missing a stitch; the model-plane enthusiast with a shelf full of severed human ears, each one neatly bottled, pickled, labelled and filed. OCD psychos. As if it was somehow better, neater, because you didn't leave a mess.

Every murder leaves a mess, Rose knew.

The man – yes, it was a man, must be a man – had done a clean, tidy job with the neck, too. Rose had had to climb on to the cartwheel-cross to take a look. It had taken everything she had to turn the torchlight once again on the black blood of the stump. Something about the stark inhumanity of it made her gut turn to ice-water.

It looked like a cord had been used to tie off the blood vessels. This had probably reduced the bleeding. And Rose noticed something else – a hint of purple-blue, a sad, crocus colour, in the skin of the woman's throat. Bruises. The hard touch of the killer's fingers. Just another brute, Rose thought. Just another woman-killer.

It took her a long time to finish her examination. The boys in the patrol car would be cursing her name. But it was what they owed her, this poor bloody woman, whoever she was. To do their bloody jobs. To do everything they could.

Peeling off her latex gloves, Rose cast the beam of her torch once more over the body, and felt bile rise nauseatingly in her throat. She was a copper, born and bred; she'd always thought that good coppers could turn their feelings off and on like a tap, could choose what to feel and when to feel it. They could simply decide not to be horrified, not to be frightened, not to feel vulnerable, not to feel sick –

Her dad would've said so. His dad, too. But they'd never seen anything like this. Had anybody?

The torchlight glimmered on something in the grass, below the dead woman's feet. Something plastic. Rose knelt, pulling on a glove. The plastic was a clear wallet for a bus pass or travel card; it had half fallen from its place in a woman's purse.

Rose glanced up.

'This yours, love?' She thumbed a driver's licence from its slot in the leather. 'Let's see who you are.' *Or were,* she added silently.

She had to catch her breath when she saw the woman's picture. The full top lip, the dark brows – the same face, of course, in a way, but Christ, what *life* there was in it then. The woman's blonde hair was tousled into a loose pile on top of her head and she was smiling broadly in the photo booth. Must have been having a good day, that day.

Rose bent her head. *Jesus.*

She wiped her eye with a knuckle and blinked at the name on the licence. Katerina Zrinski.

'*This* was you, Katerina,' she said firmly, out loud. She tapped the photograph with her fingertip. Scowled up at the body on the wheel, the stark neck-stump, the horrendous burden knotted to the left hand. Nothing but evidence for the lab, that, now, she told herself. Just a body, a thing of bones and cold flesh. Not a person, not a woman – not Katerina Zrinski. You were long gone, Katerina, Rose thought, before he did that to you. She took a last look at the photo before she sealed it into a ziploc bag.

She bagged the purse, pushed it into the inside pocket of her coat and turned away from the monstrosity that had once been Katerina Zrinski.

A flash of movement caught Rose's attention. Something moved in the deep, dark grass.

Rose spun round, bringing the torch up sharply. Swaying grass and distant trees. An insect danced fitfully across the beam.

Dawn had begun to show faintly, smudgily, above the horizon to the east; the fields, black when she'd arrived, were blues and greys now. But where Rose stood it was still dark, the meadow still a murk of shifting shadows.

There was someone out there.

Katerina's body was a display, an exhibition, Rose thought as she played her torch over the swaying grass-tops. The killer had *wanted* someone to see this – otherwise, what was the point? He wanted to shock, to frighten – who knew what exactly went through a twisted mind like this – but he certainly wanted *something*, some sort of reaction. And surely there was no fun in getting a reaction if you weren't there to see it . . .

He's here, she thought. He's watching.

She turned to look back to the lonely lane where the two cars were parked. The patrol car was a little island of off-white light in the darkness. It seemed a long way away. She flashed her torch on and off to catch their attention. The patrol car's headlights blazed and faded as a response. They were still awake: that was something. Rose made a sharp gesture.

After what must have been a short debate, the younger

PC, Ganley, climbed out of the car and started warily down into the field.

Again the noise behind her. Again Rose spun. Again nothing.

Then the night exploded.

A crash in the grass followed by a blinding white flash – Rose threw her arm across her eyes. After so long in darkness, so long in silence, the sudden burst of noise and light hit her like a blow to the face.

But it didn't take her long to recover her senses. *Light. Flash. Camera. Photographer. Go!* Three generations' worth of policing instinct kicked in in half a second, and DI Lauren Rose was sprinting full tilt through the grass, chasing the clunk of a camera-bag and the flicker of white trainer soles in the night.

She was a fast runner, always had been: good balance, a strong core, muscular legs – legs made for sprinting, not short skirts, she'd always thought. That had bothered her when she was younger. Not now.

The photographer veered left, probably hoping to lose Rose, but not factoring in the fraction of a second's advantage his clumsy sidestep would give her – if she was quick enough.

But this wasn't Rose's first foot pursuit, and she'd read the move. She plunged forwards, straw-like grass stems raking across her face, and felt the edge of her shoulder thump into the man's lower thigh. He made a grunt of pain and crashed to the floor. Dead-legged him, she thought, rolling swiftly to her feet. *Good.*

The man was face down in the grass, swearing a blue streak. She dropped a knee firmly into his lower back and dragged her cuffs from her pocket. *Clunk, click, off to the nick.* Pure muscle memory, this – she could've done it blindfold.

She straightened up, breathing hard. Rubbed her shoulder and looked down at the man groaning at her feet. His camera-bag – a swish one, it looked like – had fallen a few feet away from him. His head was turned to the side; he was grimacing with pain.

He blinked and swore when Rose turned the torch beam on his face. He couldn't have been more than eighteen. Sharp cheekbones, eyes pale and close together, nose long and slightly indented at the tip. A spatter of acne under his raw-shaven jawline.

Rose dug the angular toe of her boot into his ribs.

'Who are you?' she asked shortly.

'Let me up.'

'Give me your name.'

'Olly. Olly Stevenage.'

'What were you –'

'I mean *Oliver.* Oliver Stevenage. Put Oliver.'

'What were you doing here?'

'I'm a student.'

'Agriculture student? What were you doing in the middle of a field at five in the morning?'

'English Lit, actually. I –'

'*What were you doing here?*'

The young man paused. His expression was somewhere between 'afraid' and 'affronted'. Whoever the hell he was, Rose saw the lad wasn't used to being spoken to like this.

'I think I should have a solicitor,' he said. 'I'm allowed a solicitor.'

Rose swallowed, pushed her hair behind her ears. *Turn it on, turn it off. Going postal on this toerag isn't going to help Katerina.*

A voice in her head added dully: *Nothing's going to help Katerina. Not now.*

She dropped to one knee beside Stevenage, grabbing a handful of the student's plaid shirt.

'What did you see?' she said, forcing her voice to remain level. It was like trying to get a grip on a snapped steel hawser. 'Back there. What did you see? What did you take a photograph of?'

'Nothing.'

'Mr Stevenage, do you think the university will let you complete your degree once you've got a criminal record?'

'I'm serious, I didn't see anything. I took a shot in the dark – to coin a phrase.' He smirked unpleasantly. 'I saw the cop car, and someone with a torch. You, I guess. I pointed and clicked. Who knew what the flash might show up?' A shrug. 'I'm a journalist,' he said. 'I take chances.'

'Actually, Mr Stevenage, you're a student, and what you're *doing* is trespassing on a crime scene and interfering with a police investigation.' She bent closer. 'So I suggest you cut out the wisecracks and start taking the situation you're in a bit more seriously.'

The student squirmed and made an indignant face.

'Look, it was Rob, all right?'

'Rob?' She shook him by his shoulder. 'Rob who?'

'Rob, my housemate. The guy your mates have got in the car. The guy who found – whatever it is out there. The body, right? He's an astronomer – he was out here looking for, I don't know, planets or whatever. I got a message from him saying he'd turned up something bloody weird, so along I trotted. I'm a –'

'A "journalist". Yes. You said.'

Rose turned as Ganley came galumphing through the grass. She looked up at him. The run had restored a bit of colour to his face, at least.

'In your own time, PC Ganley.'

The young constable swallowed.

'You all right, ma'am?'

'Yeah.' She stood, brushing grass from her charcoal trousers. 'This is Oliver Stevenage, or so he says. The man who found the body – what's his story?'

'He was in the field making astronomical observations,' Ganley said, falling automatically into the stiff, just-the-facts manner of the copper in court. 'Apparently there was due to be an excellent view of the Orion nebula between two and five a.m., ma'am.'

'Did he have the kit? Telescope, whatever?'

'Yes, ma'am. Looked like a good one, too. And Conners reckons he's kosher.'

'Hm.' She looked down at Stevenage, whose face, still pressed into the grass, was twisted into a self-righteous scowl. 'All right. Get this one up and checked out. I want a full statement – and I mean full, Ganley. And get hold of that camera –'

Olly Stevenage set up an indignant babble of protest. She ignored it.

'– and find out what's on it. I want print copies of everything. All right? All right.'

She left the constable helping the complaining student

to his feet. When she looked back to the lane, she saw that three new cars had arrived. She narrowed her eyes against the dawn light: couple of uniforms, half a dozen suits.

Major Crime Unit. Her *colleagues*. Great.

Rose swore crisply, and began to walk back along the faint path of broken stems.

'What's she got on? Potato-sack chic, is it? Alternative type – eco-warrior. Reiki classes, quinoa for breakfast, that sort of thing.' DI Leland Phillips, tall, willowy, with a weak chin and lazy-lidded brown eyes, sniffed. 'The papers are going to be all over this like flies on shit.'

You needn't sound so happy about it, Rose thought.

'Shame about the scene,' grunted DS Mike Angler. He was a thickset man in his thirties with thinning hair and a permanent fuzz of stiff grey-black stubble. Unambitious, dim, bone idle. Phillips's man, through and through. He scratched his fat chin. 'SOCO ain't gonna be happy, ma'am.'

Phillips made a self-satisfied humming sound through pursed lips.

'Ye-es,' he said, rocking on his heels. 'Pity you couldn't keep on top of the housekeeping here, Rose.'

She bristled. Couldn't help it. These Major Crime Unit bastards – they knew how to push her buttons, all right. And a case like this – 'juicy', they'd call it – was right up their street. If she didn't watch it, they were liable to take the case – and Katerina – away from her.

'If SOCO can't find enough here to give us something to work with, they're in the wrong bloody job,' she said.

Phillips crossed his arms in unimpressed silence. Angler emitted another grunt and sipped from his cup of takeaway tea.

The horror on the cartwheel-cross looked no better in the ghastly pale light of early morning. The body in its strange garments was horribly, unnaturally splayed. The blood-cap of the stump, now showing dark red, made a sickly contrast with Katerina's white skin. The severed head knotted to the bony dead hand was an appalling violation.

'Least there's no mystery about how she died,' said Angler.

That's coppers for you, Rose thought. Mask your horror with a joke. Make an off-colour remark when you feel like crying with fear. *Turn it on, turn it off.*

She was closest to the body, resting a latexed hand on the wood of the cartwheel. Angler and Phillips stood a safe distance away – like spectators at a bonfire. She sniffed. The stale smell of the body caught at the back of her throat, but there were notes of fragrance there, too. Katerina had been wearing scent, something simple, rosewater maybe – and then something else more delicate, woody, complex –

'Fuck me. This is a fucking nightmare, isn't it? Christ Almighty. The state of it.' DCI Morgan Hume, arriving late, pushing past Phillips and Angler to stand before the body with his hands on his hips. 'Where are we at?'

Phillips opened his mouth to speak but Rose beat him to it.

'DS Angler was just about to tell us how she died,' she said quickly.

The tubby sergeant glared at her.

Hume, looking at Angler over his shoulder, prompted: 'Go on, then, Poirot. Let's have it.'

'A knife-cut to the throat,' Phillips cut in. 'Rapid blood loss from the carotid artery. Over in seconds. The way they do it in slaughterhouses. Highly efficient, in a grue-some sort of way.'

Hume raised his unkempt eyebrows.

'That so?' He turned back to the body. 'The thing about slaughterhouses, Phillips, the first thing you notice about them, is that there tends to be a lot of *blood*. On account of the bleeding.' He snorted, shook his head. 'Fucking hell.' His foul-tempered gaze fell on Rose. 'Your turn,' he said. 'Let's have it.'

'The beheading was clearly post mortem. Look here.' She reached up and touched the woman's skin by the bruised cut-line. Phillips winced. She took a grim satisfac-tion in that. 'Barely any blood seepage round the cut, sir. Her skin's been wiped down, but not thoroughly. I can smell her perfume. Without a proper scrubbing there'd be blood in the grain of her skin and you can see there isn't, sir – if you look closely.'

'Okay.' Hume nodded. 'So what was it, then? Natural causes? Ebola? Fucking bird flu?'

Phillips guffawed.

'I'd guess beating and strangulation, sir,' Rose said. 'There's faint bruising, maybe fingermarks, on her neck. No damage to her face, but you can see the edges of some serious contusion here, at her collar. Presumably a lot more under her shirt. Internal injury. That's my guess, if I had to call it.'

24

'Well, that seems pretty conclusive,' Phillips said loudly. 'Guess we can all go home now.'

The DCI ignored him. Looked up at the body, blinked, swore, scratched his jawline.

'All right,' he murmured.

'Sir?'

'Stick with it, Rose. It's yours for now. Look her up, go dig out some family, friends, whatever you can find. I want to know who this Miss Zrinski was, what she did, who she knew, where she worked, who she was fucking – especially that. I'll be at the station. Keep me posted.' He turned away. 'Phillips, give her whatever she needs,' he said as he stumped past them, heading back to the lane.

Rose momentarily locked eyes with the tall, arrogant DI. Fat bloody chance of that, she thought.

Phillips was holding the woman's bagged-up driver's licence. He glanced down at it, smoothed the clear plastic of the bag to read the details. His face creased as if he'd smelled something rancid.

'Have fun in the Leys,' he said. Tossed the bag to Rose, then smoothed the parting in his hair. 'Take an interpreter.'

But Rose was looking up again at the brutalized ruin of Katerina Zrinski. Was it someone you knew, Katerina? she wondered. It nearly always was. A lover, a neighbour – even a father or a brother.

The Leys was an immigrant district. She wondered where Katerina had come from, how far she'd travelled – just to end up here, to wind up like this. Poland, Lithuania, Russia?

The family would be hard. Family was always hard. She

should know: it was a job the male coppers always ducked out of, turned over to the only woman of the team. 'Job for a female officer, this.' That was the formula. 'Needs, y'know, a woman's touch.'

Rose reached up to brush the fingertips of the dead woman's right hand with her own.

This is going to be tough for your family, Katerina, she thought, and I'm sorry for that – more sorry than I can say.

Dropped her hand to her side, snapped off the glove, turned away. *But not as sorry as this sick bastard will be when I catch up with him.*

Everything is steeped in the vivid red of the abbot's blood. Little Mouse looks down at his hands: they, too, drip with blood. The dead abbot, sprawled on his back, mouths Little Mouse's name, over and over. Little Mouse is on his knees. The Serb has made him kneel. The muzzle of the soldier's gun fills the world. The soldier presses it to Little Mouse's forehead. The touch of it burns him like a ladle handle left over a gas flame, and he howls. He smells the oily smoke-smell. The monastery is burning, the village is burning – and now Little Mouse is burning, with flames of blood-red that dance and roar and rise and rise –

His own scream woke him. He jerked upright, wheezing for breath.

'Child. You are awake.' A voice he didn't know. A man's voice. Slow and old and thick with saliva.

'Who's there?'

Little Mouse's head thundered to the pounding rhythm of his heartbeat. He blinked. Was it dark – or was he blind?

'I am here, child. You have found . . . salvation.'

Little Mouse jumped with alarm as a match flared in the darkness and the swelling light of a candle illuminated a black-robed figure. He seemed out of focus, blurred. Little Mouse realized that his vision was fogged, a ragged ring of flickering shadow with a small, clear spot in its centre.

The figure approached, and settled with a murmur of discomfort on the foot of the bed.

'Who are you?'

'You will call me Father.'

'I was shot,' Little Mouse mumbled. 'Wasn't I? I was shot.'

'You were. Is there pain?'

'I – I can't see right. My eye, my left eye is like looking through smudged glass. And my head hurts.'

The figure made a disapproving growl. 'These are small things, beside the sufferings of Christ.'

'Yes,' said Little Mouse hesitantly. The figure seemed to be waiting. He did not want to anger the figure. He felt that something terrible would happen if he did. 'Father,' he added, in a small voice.

The figure let out a wet breath of satisfaction. Little Mouse shivered at the sound.

He shrank under his blanket as the candle began to move waveringly towards him. He saw its hooked black wick, the stub of dirty wax and the stained saucer the candle stood in. He stared at the gnarled thumb that gripped the saucer, deeply ridged at the knuckle, the thumbnail an inch long and rimmed with grime.

Then the candle lifted and illuminated a face straight from hell.

A pockmarked white brow. Bald head beneath a filthy skullcap. Long black shadows, the shape of graves, beneath high cheekbones. A damp, tangled white beard that clung to the chin and ropey throat. Spit glimmered on a tremulous lower lip the colour of over-boiled liver.

And his eyes – Little Mouse caught their pale gaze for a brief second and had to hide his face behind his hands.

'How – how did I survive?' Little Mouse whimpered. He thought of the man with the gun and the dead black eye of the revolver. He

thought of the other children, Radi, Mirko, and all the brothers of St Quintus. He thought of the abbot with the coin of blood on his forehead. How many of them still lived? Of all the monastery's faithful, was he the only one to escape the Serbs? 'How can it be?' he wailed.

The man – Father – didn't answer. Instead he leaned closer to Little Mouse and said: 'Are you of the True Church, child?'

Little Mouse nodded quickly. 'Hail Mary, full of grace. The Lord is with thee.'

'You are baptized and truly penitent?' the man pressed. 'Do you love the body of Christ?'

'I am – I do, Father.'

He glanced up at the man's face. The terrible pale eyes were wide and seemed to burn like the sun through cloud.

'You will say the Roman catechism.'

Little Mouse gulped.

'I believe in God, the Father Almighty, creator of Heaven and Earth,' he recited, numbly.

'Again.'

'I believe in God, the Father Almighty, creator of –'

'Why did God become man?'

Little Mouse stumbled. 'That, that m-man might become God.' Even in the strange hut and under the intense stare of the priest, there was a comfort in these questions.

'Who showed to mankind the path from damnation to salvation?'

'My lord Jesus Christ.'

'Who is your saviour, child?'

The sob broke, rolling thickly, achingly up through Little Mouse's throat, and spilled chokingly from his mouth. God is here, Little Mouse realized. Even in this darkest of times and most frightening of places.

'M-my, m-my l-l-lord —'

The priest bared his brown teeth and leaned closer, his ravaged face so near that Little Mouse could smell onion and black tea on his breath.

'I said who is your saviour?' the priest demanded.

'My lord Jesus Christ, Father! My lord Jesus Christ!'

And then Little Mouse was lost in tears. For what, exactly, he couldn't say. He wept with grief, despair, as a lost child weeps — but he felt a strange happiness, too. Despite how harshly it had been tested, his faith remained true. Through his losses, Little Mouse had found his salvation in Christ's love.

He pressed his face into the coarse, unwashed blanket and sobbed in gratitude. Was every brother and boy of St Quintus dead? Of all the flock of the monastery, had the Lord saved only him? He felt a hand on his shoulder. The touch of it was as hard, as strong as yew wood.

'You asked why you are still alive,' he heard the man say. 'I will tell you. It is God's doing. The demon Serb's bullet is still lodged in your head, but by the grace of the Lord you live. Are you listening to me, child? The Lord spared you so that you may do his bidding, and serve as his instrument. You are blessed, truly blessed.' The man's voice had fallen to a hoarse whisper, clotted with emotion. 'You belong to the True Church now,' he rasped. 'Do you hear? You belong to God now.'

Chapter Two

The kid slammed into the side of the car before Rose even saw him. She jumped at the juddering impact, swore, flung open the driver's door –

'Are you okay? What the hell were you playing at?'

The kid – stick-thin in a hoodie and cheap trainers – gawped at her, swaying against the car's offside wing. Hollow-cheeked face spattered with angry pimples. Pupils swollen, the rims of his eyelids a jaundiced yellow. He said something: 'Yurrhh' or 'Yohh'.

What was he, fifteen, sixteen? And high as a bloody kite at seven-thirty in the morning.

She flashed her badge wearily. 'You want to watch it,' she said, giving him a steady look. 'You never know who you might run into.'

The kid laughed and shouted a few words of gibberish. Reeled off down the street, vanished into the shadows of a rotten-looking tower block.

Rose slumped back into the driver's seat and sighed. The Leys. Yeah, this was Oxford, not South London – yeah, her dad would've said it was a bloody kiddies' playground next to the arse-end of Peckham, Bow, Brixton Hill – but still. A bad place, a tough place. A place no one would live if they had a choice. A place full of people who ran out of choices a long time ago.

She drove on, taking it slow, keeping an eye out, and

pulled up in a side road by an estate of dingy-looking brown-washed housing blocks. Checked her notes. This was the address on the driver's licence. Katerina's home.

The usual crap littered the thinly grassed forecourt: a broken pane of glass, a stained, ripped mattress, a carrier bag of dirty nappies, a heap of damp cardboard. The lock on the main door was broken – the door moved sluggishly open at her push. Lobby stank of piss and skunk. Lift out of order, of course. Rose took the concrete stairs two at a time.

The landings were strewn with boxes, bags, rubbish. Graffiti coloured the grimy walls with a dozen languages. She found she knew the odd word, picked up here and there: *lopov*, Bosnian for 'thief'; *zeu*, Romanian for 'God'; *pyktis*, Lithuanian for 'fuck'.

And on every floor eyes watched her and voices muttered. Should've brought a sign to pin on my back, she thought: 'I AM NOT FROM IMMIGRATION' in nine languages. The place buzzed with suspicion. Christ, you couldn't blame them.

Rose knew she had to get a handle on this girl, this woman, who up to now had been nothing to her but a horror in an Oxford meadow and a name and a face on a laminated card. It'll be family she lived with, she thought as she neared Katerina's flat, not friends. Family's what matters in a place like this.

Family makes it harder. Family means real, bone-deep grief; family means tears, anger, denial, blame. But Katerina's family will be the ones who knew her the best. That's what Rose needed. No one knows you like your flesh and blood know you.

On the fifth floor she found the flat and knocked, a proper copper's knock that rattled the cheap door in its frame. That was for the benefit of whoever was watching from across the hall or lurking in the stairwell, it said *Don't dare fuck with me*, and said it loud and clear – but she regretted it the moment the door opened.

A girl with Katerina's eyes stood in the doorway, her hand trembling on the latch.

Rose let her hard front slip a little. Kept her badge in her pocket for now.

'Hello,' she said. The girl didn't answer. Just kept on chewing her lip. Rose pressed on: 'My name's Detective Insp– I mean, my name's Lauren Rose. I'm from the police.' A brief smile to offset the force of the word. 'Do you – do you speak English?'

The girl, shivering in her faded pink dressing-gown, said nothing. Her eyes – so palely blue they seemed almost to have no colour at all – shone with tears.

As if she already knew.

'Are you all right?' Rose prompted.

A door opened in the flat and another young woman stepped out into the hallway. Older, this one; a little darker. Less afraid, maybe – but not by much. She was in a thin dressing-gown too. It made Rose cold to look at them.

The new girl put her hand on the younger one's shoulder. Sisters: there could be no doubt when you saw them side by side. She looked at Rose as if reading something written in her face. Rose was about to ask her if *she* spoke English when the girl said a word that was the same in any language.

'Katerina?' she whispered.

And in answer Rose could only shake her head.

There was a moment of perfect silence when the girls' eyes widened and their faces went taut. Shock? Horror? No, Rose thought as she watched the body blow of this terrible news crash into them. It was despair. Pure despair. When the moment passed the two young women collapsed, wailing, into each other's arms.

Rose stepped into the flat and softly closed the door behind her.

Phillips, damn him, had been right – she should've brought an interpreter. Rose perched on the drab sofa while the girls talked between themselves.

She could guess roughly at what they were saying – grief is grief, wherever you come from – but at best she was getting the message in broad brushstrokes; what she needed was the fine detail. Not just the words, though that would have helped, but the inflections, the emphasis, the nuance – and the words *not* spoken: the ones that should have been there but weren't.

Rose stuck at it for a few minutes. She pegged the language as Slavic, maybe Serbian, Croatian – but she couldn't make much of it. Besides, after a while, it seemed to her that everything the girls said was overwhelmed by that one repeated word: *Katerina*.

Listening not just to what people said but how they said it was an unofficial branch of forensics, and part of every good copper's toolkit. Here, barely understanding a word, Rose felt as though she'd been deprived of her sense of touch or smell. Lost.

She got up and walked to the kitchen counter. It barely took her a dozen paces to cross the flat. There was a chunky electric kettle with a frayed lead, a glass jar of tea-bags on a shelf over the sink. She filled the kettle as behind her the girls talked on.

They had an awful lot to say to each other, she thought. Of course, grief could take people in all sorts of different ways, but still –

Rose remembered her mother's death. It had been quick, as these things go; she died in a hospice three weeks after the first diagnosis of cancer. They were there with her at the end, Lauren, her three brothers, her dad. All coppers, or future coppers. Cracking jokes and swapping stories at the bedside – her mum, too.

Then after, she remembered, no one had said much. No one had given her a hug, even at the funeral. She remembered, not long after, seeing her dad in the back garden by himself, smoking a cigarette. She'd run to the door, to go out there, talk to him, play with him – but Michael, her oldest brother, had stopped her. 'Dad just needs a bit of time to himself,' he'd said, and winked, and sent her off upstairs to play with her toys. She was five years old.

And that was pretty much it. That was as close as the Roses had ever got to showing grief, real grief.

Did it mean they cared any less? Did it mean they didn't love one another, wouldn't have died for one another, killed for one another? Did it hell. Different people had different ways of dealing with things. That was all.

She remembered the ache, though – the ache of losing

the most loved, the most important person in her life. Of course she remembered it. It had never gone away.

The click of the kettle switching itself off was unexpectedly loud. The girls stopped talking. Rose turned to look at them. Whatever the detail, whatever the fine print, these girls were feeling the first tremors of that same ache right now.

'I – I thought I'd make us tea. Then perhaps we can talk.'

The older girl, working her pale fingers together anxiously, took a step towards her.

'Katerina,' she said, hesitantly. 'How?'

A vision of Katerina's body – spreadeagled, decapitated, defiled, abandoned – flashed across Rose's vision and she turned back to the kitchen counter, fumbling for mugs in the cupboard, fishing three teabags clumsily from the jar.

'We're – investigating,' she said.

'Was it – did she suffer?'

Turn it on, turn it off. Like a tap, remember. As she poured hot water into the cheap tin cups she carefully composed her face: calm, professional, neutral. She took up two of the mugs and turned again to face the girl.

'We're investigating,' she repeated, 'and believe me, we're doing everything we can to find out exactly what happened to Katerina.'

The older girl spoke decent English, it turned out. Her name was Sofia. She was Katerina's sister – the middle sister. She sat bent over on a broken cane chair and held her mug of tea cupped between both hands. Her mousy hair had partly spilled from its knot at the nape of her neck. Her face was sharper than either of her sisters', longer in the nose, with an upper lip that was peaked rather than full.

Rose sat on the sofa. The youngest sister, Adrijana, was curled beside her, silent, with her knees drawn up to her skinny chest. Her attention jumped from her sister's face to Rose's, but her gaze skittered away whenever Rose met her eyes.

'Can you think of anyone,' Rose asked Sofia gently, 'who might have wanted to cause Katerina harm? Who might have wanted to hurt her?'

A quick look passed between the two sisters. Rose made two mental notes: first, something's up; second, this pair know more English than they're letting on.

'No,' Sofia said. When she moved her left hand from her mug to push a stray hank of hair from her face Rose saw that the hand was trembling.

She changed tack.

'When I came to the door just now,' she said, looking first at Adrijana and then at Sofia, 'you knew something was wrong, didn't you? Something to do with Katerina?'

Silence.

'Was Katerina in some sort of trouble?'

Sofia sniffed, and shook her head.

'No. Never.' Another furtive glance at Adrijana. You must think I'm bloody daft, girl, Rose thought. 'We didn't know where she was,' Sofia went on. Her voice teetered on the brink of breaking. There was strain in it, like the groan of weak ice. 'Three days, we hadn't seen her. And we couldn't, we didn't —'

'No police,' interrupted Adrijana in a resentful voice.

'They say. People here. No police, *or else*. Who to tell? Who can help?'

'We asked Father Florian,' Sofia said.

'Who?'

'Our priest – at our church, Church of the Queen of Peace. The last time –' She broke off. Took a sip of tea, gulped, managed to master her feelings. 'The last time we see Katerina, she was going to church. For confession.'

'What did you think might have happened?'

'Katerina went away sometimes, with Father Florian, with the church – on missions. To help, to help people, you see? We thought maybe she had gone away on a mission and forgot to tell us –'

'But there was no mission?' Rose nodded sympathetically. 'I understand.' She looked curiously at the two sisters. Adrijana wiped her nose on the back of her wrist. Sofia returned her look, blankly, emptily. Rose could see a vein quivering rapidly in the girl's pale throat.

'I want you both to know,' Rose said carefully, 'that you're not going to get into any trouble. Do you understand? Not with me, not with the immigration people, not with anyone.'

Sofia lifted her chin at that.

'We have papers!' she said sharply. 'All of us. Passports. Papers, all legal!'

Then what the hell are you so scared of? Rose thought.

'You can tell me,' she said softly, 'if something's bothering you.'

Sofia looked at her sister. Out of the corner of her eye Rose saw Adrijana shake her head. At first she'd taken Adrijana's passiveness as a sign of shock and taken Sofia's greater openness as a sign of greater capability. She wasn't so sure now. There was a kind of wildness in the older sister – and perhaps a kind of strength in the quiet, thoughtful Adrijana.

Rose sipped her tea, pretended not to have noticed anything.

A bang on the door jolted her to her feet.

Not a copper's knock, this. This was a brutish thumping with the meat of the fist, the banging of someone who meant to come through the door one way or another, even if they had to smash it off its hinges. Three more heavy bangs, and a shout in a language Rose didn't know.

She looked quickly at the two girls. Both had their white faces turned to the door. Both seemed too petrified to move. Adrijana clutched her dressing-gown to her chest. Lukewarm tea slopped from the mug held in Sofia's shaking hands.

Rose stood and took her badge from her pocket. Nasty surprise for someone, she told herself. Pounding on a door loud enough to wake the dead expecting a terrified teenage girl, then coming face to face with DI Lauren Rose.

She'd seen what some sick bastard had done to these girls' big sister just hours before and Rose was in no mood to tolerate another inadequate excuse for a man taking out his anger issues on the Zrinskis. Not now. Not ever, come to think of it.

'Don't worry,' she told the sisters. 'I'll handle it. Don't worry.'

Wasn't sure *how* she'd handle it. She'd have to figure that out as she went along.

39

Three more thumps. Another yell. Aggressive, threatening.

Rose crossed the flat and pulled open the door. Led with her badge, flashing it at head height. It caught the man who stood there off balance. He'd been tilted forwards, prepared to press the advantage of his heavy shoulders, chest and beetling forehead. On seeing the badge he flinched backwards, had to shift his weight, shuffle his feet. It wasn't much, but it was something. An edge.

'Who are you?' Rose jabbed the question at him like a blade.

He raised his square chin, looked down at her. Rolled his muscular shoulders. You're wasting your time trying to intimidate me, pal, she thought. This sort of nonsense was bread and butter for any copper – especially a female DI who stood five-six in flats. Saw it every day.

'I asked you a question. Who are you?'

'Go,' the man said. He turned his head and spat. Then he said it again: 'Go.'

He was a little over six foot, naturally heavy, with fine black hair trimmed close to his scalp and a wisp of black beard beneath his lower lip. One tapered end of a blue-inked tattoo – serpent's tail, devil's horn? – showed over the collar of his white t-shirt.

'You're a charmer,' Rose said. 'What's your name?'

The man focused his close-set eyes on her. Not a lot of intelligence there. She moved forwards a fraction, trying to see if there was anyone further down the corridor or if he was alone. Couldn't see far enough past the bruiser's shoulder to tell.

'Name, not for you,' he said. 'Here, not for you. Zrin-ski, not for you.' He banged his fist on the door frame. 'Go,' he said. 'Now.'

There – just on the edge of her sightline, where the cor-ridor took a right-angled turn to the top of the stairway – Rose saw a man standing by an open window. There was something stacked at his feet. Pallets, or crates. Each one stuffed with plastic packets.

The tattooed man took a heavy step to his right, block-ing her view.

'Moving house?' she said. She swallowed hard, trying to wet her dry mouth. 'You know you could use the stairs. We're five floors up. Long drop. Wouldn't risk it myself. Specially if it's something – valuable?'

He narrowed his black eyebrows stupidly at her.

'Uh?'

Lights on, no one home, Rose thought. Waste of time trying to talk; she was getting nothing out of this bloody lunk.

'I think,' she said, in a clear voice, 'you should leave.'

The big man crossed his arms. Another tattoo – a flag, or a crest – bulged on his right biceps.

'*You* go,' he said. 'I stay.'

She was about to snap back with an arrest protocol – wondering, at the same time, what the hell good it would do – when the man again shifted his position, quite delib-erately, half-turning so that his left hip was towards Rose. She saw that his tight t-shirt was out of shape at the small of his back. Something was wedged in the waistband of his jeans.

A gun.

Her stomach lurched.

If he meant to frighten her, he'd succeeded. If he meant to frighten her *off* –

Rose grabbed for the weapon.

The man was slow. She had her hand on the butt of the revolver before he managed to twist his torso and take a savage grip on her upper arm. She yanked, but the gun was snagged in the fabric of the t-shirt. The barrel slipped loose. Then, sickeningly, the corridor seemed to come loose from its moorings as she was swung in a tight quarter-circle and slammed into the opposite wall. She grunted, fought to breathe, swung a crooked elbow fiercely upwards. Felt it connect with the man's soft, stubbled under-jaw. Heard his teeth clang together.

Don't let up, she thought. Don't give them a second. She linked both her hands together and swung them with a shriek of effort in a crosswise swipe towards the man's thick neck.

Not so slow this time. He whipped a hand upwards, closed it about both her wrists. Squeezed. Grinned.

Don't scream, she thought. Screaming just wastes breath. She bit her lip as her wrist bones ground together in his grip.

Her knee jerked up. This guy really *was* dumb – the first thing every woman learns about unarmed combat and the lunk wasn't ready for it. The contact was punishingly deep. He howled, doubling forwards, releasing her wrists, grabbing one-handed at his groin – but he didn't go down. Rose's clawed hand swept towards his face but he lurched at her and her grasping hand scraped uselessly through his hair. Stooping lower, he drove his shoulder forwards, upwards, ramming the thick-muscled bone hard into the base of her ribcage.

Everything vanished but the pain.

Rose retched. The corridor lights seemed to strobe. She felt paralysed, utterly helpless. Walls of featureless grey pressed in on her vision. As the man backed away she bent forwards, clutching at her chest, her gut. A noise she could never have imagined making – hoarse, shrill, inhuman – broke from her throat.

'Bitch,' she heard the man mutter. Through the mist she saw him turn his back.

He thought she was done with.

He thought he'd won.

Every muscle in Rose's body tightened in spasm. Never mind the pain, she thought. Pain can wait for later. What you're fighting for here is *control*. Breathe right. Let your muscles loosen. Hold it all together.

This is *your* body, DI Rose, her inner voice yelled. *Make it work.*

The man was yelling instructions to the man at the open window. Rose sank into a crouch, bunched her protesting muscles, then sprang for his broad back.

It was a wide target, but even then she almost missed as her knees buckled under her. Her hand, though, whipping out in desperation, found what she was after – her fingers closed around the exposed barrel of the gun.

The man turned, snarling a foreign curse. The gun came free. Rose's thumb caught in the belt loop of his jeans.

The gun clattered to the tiled floor. Rose fell heavily, painfully. Her vision fogged again as she reflexively cradled her twisted wrist. She struggled to stay conscious – fought to keep her grip on her beaten body.

She felt his brutish hands run from her neck to her waist. She thought of Katerina and the pale indigo bruises on her dead skin. Nausea overcame her and she closed her eyes, gasping for breath. *Stop,* she wanted to scream. *Whatever you're doing to me, stop.* Her head felt as though it was filling with hot, pounding blood. Her shirt-collar came sharply tight about her neck, choking her.

She opened her eyes. Five floors fell away dizzyingly beneath her. She became aware of hands gripping her shirt, her right ankle, the painful pressure of the iron stair-rail against her bruised midriff.

Poised over the deep stairwell, Rose fought to breathe, fought to think, fought – *oh God, oh God* – to keep still.

The man tilted her body an inch further towards the drop. She tasted vomit.

'You go,' the man said. 'Now.'

Rats trapped with snares of salvaged barbed wire. Thin stray cats and wild-eyed street dogs in narrow cages. The scalpel spotted with red rust. The sounds and smells of animal fear, animal panic.

The priest talked as he worked.

'What do you feel, Little Mouse?'

'I feel . . . thankful.' He had not been allowed up from the cot since he had woken.

The black-smocked priest bent over one of the dogs. Strung by its feet and neck, the animal struggled in its bonds. It was screaming. Terrible shadows were cast by the candlelight. Little Mouse could do nothing but watch.

'Thankful to me, for saving your life? Or thankful to Christ, for saving your soul?'

Little Mouse hesitated, groping for the right answer. Was there a right answer?

'To – to Christ, Father.'

'Good.' The priest nodded in the gloom. 'Good.'

There was the scrape of bone under the shrieks of the creature, then the dog's cries subsided. The priest whispered a prayer. There was the smell of blood.

And, afterwards, the relic, the icon – the thing of bones, tied with leather, greased with scented tallow.

Little Mouse feared the strange objects the priest fashioned from the poor beasts. He tried to see them as holy things, items to be revered, as the priest said they were. He tried to love them, as he loved Christ and the True Church. But he could not keep himself from being afraid.

'They will redeem you,' the priest said. 'Are we not ourselves mere things of bone and leather? They will redeem all of us.'

Chapter Three

'Some might say, Rose, that starting a ruck with an eighteen-stone Balkan bank robber in the flat of two grieving young girls was, I don't know, unwise? A misjudgement? Unprofessional, even?' DI Phillips smirked and smoothed his silk tie. '*I'm* not saying that, of course. I'm sure you had your reasons.' He looked down at her. 'Although I struggle to imagine what they were. Do you think you could enlighten me?'

Sitting on the front steps of the housing block, Rose scowled and rubbed at her aching ribs. Her head throbbed; she blinked irritably in the weak sunshine.

'He had a gun, Phillips. Highly aggressive, unpredictable. Probably juiced.'

'Oh well, in that case your conduct makes perfect sense. Page one of the police training handbook, isn't it? When confronted by a roid-raging gunman, don't call for back-up and try to defuse the situation – instead, start an impromptu UFC bout on the fifth floor.' He gave a stagey laugh of disbelief. 'Dear oh dear, Rose. Dear oh dear.'

Rose stared into the middle distance and paced her breathing. Footsteps and shouting reverberated in the lobby behind her, along with the crackle of radios. The place was busy with uniform, community liaison, CID. No translators, though. Just three of those worked the

47

whole Thames Valley beat, Rose knew. It wasn't enough –
but that was policing. Nothing was ever enough. Nothing
ever would be.

CID had had their eye on a smack-running racket out
of the Leys for months, it turned out. If things'd gone dif-
ferently, Rose would have been carpeted for getting in the
way of a major drugs investigation – but as it was she'd
shown her face at just the right time. Interrupted a big
stock transfer. CID had seen their chance and thrown
the kitchen sink at it.

Vanfuls of coppers turning over a housing block
full of illegals. The coppers with nothing but English,
the poor buggers up there with no English at all. The
place hummed with tension. The 'communication problem' it was called in the manuals – but if anyone put a
foot wrong, the communication problem wouldn't be the
half of it.

From the first floor, a yell, and the wrenching crash of
a door going through. Rose sighed. She tried to block out
the noise – tried to focus.

'A bank robber?'

'Uh?' Phillips looked round at her without much
interest.

'A bank robber, you said. The heavy up there.'

'Oh, him, yeah – we ran his name through the system.
Once we'd worked out how to spell it.' He snorted at his
own joke. 'Did time a few years back for knocking over a
building society in Cowley.'

'Background?'

'Some kind of Serbo-Croat-Boznoslavian.' Phillips
shrugged. 'A Mr Nitić. Been here about nine years, in

with the work gangs.' He did an if-you-knew-what-I-know face. 'And some other gangs,' he added in a murmur.

There were raised voices behind them: someone shouting furiously in a foreign language, and, over that, the familiar, deadening copper's intonation. 'All right, pal. Settle down. Calm down. All right, pal.'

It was him – the heavy who'd come about an inch from dumping Rose down the centre of the stairwell. Smear of blood drying on his cheek. Limping through the lobby between two thick-necked PCs.

'Speak of the devil,' said Phillips. Rose glanced up at him – it was almost gratifying to see the surprise on the DI's face when he took in the extent of the damage she'd done to the vicious lunk. There were advantages to growing up with a rugby front row for a family: being the little sister of three rough-arsed brothers taught you quickly enough how to break a wrestling hold and get in a telling blow or two of your own in reply.

'Uniform really did a number on him, didn't they?' Phillips said.

Rose's mind leapt back to the stiff-handed jab to the throat that had finally brought Nitić, grey-faced, to his knees. She'd happily have given Phillips the same treatment if she thought it'd be worth the paperwork.

The limping heavy – Nitić – saw her as he was being manhandled into the back of a police van. His thick-featured face twisted with fury. He opened his mouth to yell something, a threat, a volley of abuse – but the impassive PCs slammed the doors on his anger.

Rose grinned for the first time that morning.

But she wiped the smile when she saw blonde, fragile

Adrijana Zrinski standing hesitantly in the shadow of the building's stairwell. Rose stood painfully and waved.

'Adrijana! I'm here.' She stepped into the lobby and made her way towards the stairs. The girl swallowed nervously and lifted a packet of frozen peas.

'Face,' she said. 'For your face. *Modrica. Zamrznut.*' She hefted the dripping green packet again, smiled weakly. 'Birdseye. *Grasak.*'

Rose returned the smile, took the packet, pressed it to her pulsing cheekbone. A burst of pain from the cold – then numbing relief.

'Thank you,' she said, and meant it. A packet of frozen peas wasn't much – but in its way it was the first touch of true warmth she'd felt in days. She gestured for Adrijana to sit beside her on the bottom step. Phillips, bored with goading her, had wandered off to chat to a local reporter. An opportunity, then, to form a useful connection amidst all this mess – a living, human link with poor Katerina.

A sudden, saw-edged wailing broke from the floor above. Fat chance of that, Rose thought bitterly, jumping to her feet.

Adrijana stopped her with a hand on her forearm. She shook her head.

'No trouble,' she said. 'Grief. *Tuga*. Katerina.'

Rose sat down again. Through expressive broken English Adrijana made her understand that Sofia was sharing the news of Katerina's loss with the family's friends and neighbours. Many of them had known Katerina since she arrived in England – some since before then.

Adrijana stood.

'I should go to her,' she said.

Quickly, firmly, making it clear she wasn't asking permission, Rose said: 'I'll go with you.'

Back up the stairs. Back into the tense thrum of murmurs, whispers, urgent conversations behind closed doors.

While she still had Adrijana to herself, Rose took another stab at finding a chink in the Zrinski family's self-protective armour.

'Katerina was well loved, then?' she said, as they climbed together. 'Many friends here? In the community?'

Adrijana nodded gravely.

'Many,' she said. 'Katerina, always helping, helping others. She help at hospital, where she work. Help with benefit, immigrant, landlord. Help all the time. Problem, go to Katerina. Sometimes *too* help.' She smiled ruefully. 'What do you call? *Svetac*. A saint?' A nod. 'Katerina was a saint.'

Rose quickly joined the dots. Nitić. A criminal gang. A saint, a do-gooder. For the bad guys, a do-gooder was a troublemaker.

It didn't seem to fit, though. That horror, that *thing* out in the field – a gang hit? Hardly. Bullet in the back of the head and a splash in a canal, that was how the gangs dealt with troublemakers.

Keep going, Rose thought. Keep thinking.

'Saints have a habit of making enemies,' she said. At Adrijana's blank look she clarified: 'Bad people don't like it when people – people like Katerina, maybe – try to stop them doing what they want.'

Adrijana frowned.

'Bad people?'

'Nitić? Nitić's gang?' She watched the girl closely as she spoke. 'Nitic was very angry about something. Was he angry with Katerina?'

Adrijana gave her a sidelong look that was tinged with irritation.

'Nitić angry with *you*.'

You're not wrong there, Rose thought, conscious again of the deep ache in her ribs, the throb of her bruised face.

'But the gang,' she persisted. 'They work from here, they do their business here, don't they? Did Katerina know what they were doing? Did they try to frighten her?'

The grim stairwell rang unexpectedly with Adrijana's laughter.

'Katerina never frighten,' she said emphatically. 'Not frighten of anything. For sure not frighten of *gang*.'

Rose looked at her sharply. But her time was up – they were at the fifth floor, and the corridors were suddenly busy with people. It was, Rose thought, like being at the aftermath of an earthquake or a train wreck. The air trembling with sobs and cries. Face after face distorted by sorrow. A man with a pepper-grey beard seized her hand as she tried to pass him by, speaking words she couldn't understand through a creased mask of tears. A woman veiled and gowned in black sang a haunting song in a minor key. Rose lost Adrijana to the crowd almost at once. Pushing her way through to the door of the Zrinskis' flat, she saw the other sister, Sofia, leaning in the doorway. She wasn't weeping, or singing; her eyes were fixed on a distant point, her eyelids half-lowered. She had drawn a dark-blue headscarf over her brown hair and her pale hands anxiously knotted and unknotted the trailing loose ends.

'Sofia?' Rose pushed forwards, put a hand on the girl's shoulder. Sofia's eyes twitched, but she didn't look up. She said again, 'Sofia!' – nothing.

There was no sign, now, of the girl's earlier volubility. Shock setting in, Rose guessed. Grief taking hold.

A rattle of Croatian at her side: Adrijana, emerging from the embrace of a tearful young woman in jeans and a pullover. She shook Sofia by the shoulder, firmly but not unkindly. Sofia looked at her, blinked, murmured a syllable. Adrijana spoke again, jerked a thumb at Rose – Christ, she would have killed to know what the girl was saying.

'Could we go inside?' she interjected. 'I know it's such a difficult time, but –'

Sofia shrugged one shoulder and turned back into the flat. Adrijana went after her, followed by Rose. She left the door of the flat open – on balance, she thought, it was best not to give the Zrinskis' neighbours the impression that this was a matter of whispers and secrets. Besides – what was the old line about justice being done, and being seen to be done?

They stood awkwardly in the Zrinskis' sitting room. Rose's beaten body ached to sit down but she didn't want these girls to get too comfortable, not yet, not while there was still so much she didn't know – or, more to the point, so much they weren't telling her.

Time to target Sofia.

'I was asking Adrijana,' she said, 'about Nitić – about the gang? Do you know them?'

A dull stare in reply, and: 'Everyone knows them.'

'Did Katerina?'

'Of course.'

'Sofia, did she – was she frightened of them?'

Sofia didn't laugh as her sister had, but the ghost of a bitter smile passed over her face.

'Frightened? Katerina? Never. She was *fearless*.' Her sharp upper lip twisted in a momentary sneer and she added, as if talking half to herself, 'Katerina, frightened of Radovan Rakić and his friends? A joke.'

Rakić. Rose made a mental note of the name. Gang leader? Nitić's boss? The Leys gang had to be involved in all this, in Katerina's death – somehow. Rakić was a name she'd heard before. Never with anything good attached to it.

But the thing now was not to assemble data but to get at the truth, the human truth of Katerina's life.

'She knew them well, then? Rakić? Nitić?'

'Nitić is a clown,' Sofia snorted.

'The other man, then. Rakić. The leader? Was he – a friend of hers?'

Sofia's face gave away nothing. Rose glanced quickly at Adrijana – caught her looking questioningly at Sofia, as if to ask *Shall we tell?* or *Will you tell?* or *Dare I tell?*

'Adrijana? Katerina and Rakić – were they close?'

Then to the older sister: 'Sofia, I need to know about Katerina's life – who she knew, who she saw . . .'

Rose remembered DCI Hume's order: *I want to know who she was fucking – especially that.*

Deep breath. Then: 'Was Katerina seeing anyone?' No answer – but she was close. She could feel it. 'Sofia? Adrijana? Was she in a relationship?'

'No,' said Adrijana.

An answer – any answer – was a foothold, a wedge in the crack. Rose forced the girl to meet her eye. Turning up the tough-cop stuff.

'She was, wasn't she? Don't lie to me, Adrijana, not now. There's too much at stake. Anything you can tell me – *anything* – could help me find the man who killed Katerina.'

Adrijana bit her lip. One more push, Rose thought.

'It was Rakić, wasn't it?' She nodded her head sharply as she said it, watching for the echoing gesture in Adrijana. It never came. The girl held her eye. A tear had appeared on her left cheek. *One more push.*

She said it slowly, clearly, as a simple fact – as if she knew it for sure: 'Katerina was sleeping with Radovan Rakić.'

Adrijana's wet eyes blinked, and shimmered, and told her nothing.

A shriek of laughter burst the silence like a grenade. Rose jumped, spun to look at Sofia: the older sister's eyes were wild, her mouth thrown open, and the shrill, unnerving laughter spilled from her throat. She clutched at her midriff as if in pain.

'Sofia –'

'Radovan Rakić! Katerina and Radovan Rakić!'

Rose hesitated. Blown it, was her first thought. Sofia was closer to the edge than she'd realized. She'd taken a shot in the dark – and lost her. But a part of her brain insisted: *You weren't wrong.* It said: *Trust your instincts.* The glances exchanged, the muttered words, the set-up, the *feel* of the situation –

She'd hit a nerve. She was close, she knew it, close enough to get a reaction. It was a question of figuring out the detail – and figuring out Sofia Zrinski.

Sofia's jangling laugh stopped abruptly. The look she turned on Rose was steady and mocking.

Take your textbooks on the five stages of grief and tear them up, Rose thought. There's no second-guessing this one.

She returned Sofia's stare icily.

'Do you want to tell me what's funny?'

'What's funny is that you know nothing, police lady,' Sofia said. 'Except maybe how to make trouble for people.'

'Why were you laughing?'

Sofia crossed her arms.

'Radovan Rakić is seventy-two years old. He wears a horrible bearskin hat, even indoors, and has a grey moustache full of old food. He smokes a pipe and smells of booze, smoke and cured fish. He trades in smuggled meat and stolen car batteries. Back in Zagreb, he was a petrol-pump attendant.' She forced a grimacing smile. 'Him and Katerina. *That* is what is funny, Mrs Rose.'

Still there: *You weren't wrong, you weren't wrong.*

'Then –'

'It's his son you should be talking to,' Sofia said. She looked at Rose, at her sister, at the ceiling. Then she let out a long, whimpering sigh and dissolved into helpless tears.

The picture the girls built up, slowly, hesitantly, as the morning shaded into fast-darkening afternoon and the corridors outside grew quiet, was vivid and troubling: Dmitry Rakić, thirty-four, maybe thirty-five; raised in a tough neighbourhood outside Zagreb, did time there for robbery, intimidation, arson; hit the UK in 2002, and hit the ground running: the impetus – the demon, Sofia said – behind a sudden expansion in his father's business. Old Radovan had been in England since the war in Croatia. Unambitious kingpin of a black-economy dealership in untaxed canned goods, stolen motor parts, counterfeit food vouchers and Russian cigarettes, he found that his son had lit a fire beneath him. By the mid-2000s his Thames Valley petty-crime racket had become a trafficking empire – drugs, people, whatever paid a profit – that reached beyond Oxford to Swindon, Bristol, Cardiff, even stretches of north-west London.

Dmitry himself seemed to offer few surprises: bold, cocky, violent, ambitious. Not bad-looking, considering, Sofia said. A blue-eyed bully. Old Radovan still swaggered about the place with his chest puffed out but it was Dimi who ran things now – everyone knew it, Adrijana said fearfully.

He and Katerina had been drawn to each other for different reasons. 'She wanted to save him,' Sofia said. She shook her head. 'He wanted – well, you can guess what he wanted.'

Adrijana piped up quaveringly: 'She would never, never. With him? Never. She would rather –'

She broke off, covered her mouth with her hand. In her head Rose finished the thought: *she would rather die.*

'Was there anyone else?' she asked gently, desperate to keep the girls with her, terrified that the line might break. God, she was tired – body, brain, everything. How long was it since she'd slept? More than a day. But she had to play this out to the end. 'If there was nothing like that between her and Dmitry, was she seeing anybody else?'

Sofia – sounding as spent as Rose felt – said: 'Maybe. Maybe. A man. On the phone, sometimes – she spoke, she spoke.' Slowing, grinding word by word towards shutdown, like a tape-player with a dying battery. 'On the phone. Someone, a man – you can tell. In English. She spoke English.'

Rose kept one eye on Adrijana as Sofia spoke. The younger sister watched the floor, picked at her fingernails.

'Do you have any idea who he was?' Rose prompted.

Sofia shook her head heavily.

'No. But unless he was the devil himself, he couldn't be worse than Dmitry.'

The tears came. Not hysterically, as before, not loudly, but from deep down, deep inside – unrestrained tears, and a series of low, soft moans, dragged from the girl's gut, over and over. Without hesitation Adrijana slipped from her chair and gathered her elder sister in her arms. Rose watched the girls weep, seeing in their unchecked emotion both utter exhaustion and desperately needed release. Interview, she thought drily, terminated.

She stood, handed them her card, gave them her thanks and her condolences, and left the flat.

Once in the hall, Rose thought of what Sofia had said: that the last time they'd seen Katerina she'd been leaving the house on her way to confession. Rose leaned on the stair-rail, looking down once more into the five-storey drop. The thought of it made her feel sick: not the drop she'd come so close to taking, but the thought of a woman like

Katerina Zrinski, a good woman, a saint, walking out into the world and asking to be forgiven for her sins. Feeling guilty for what modest transgressions she might have made, never knowing that she was about to cross paths with true evil.

A monster.

A demon.

'Nitić? The big feller? He's in with Lel Phillips.' The desk sergeant shrugged. 'Been forty-five minutes or so now.'

Rose swore. There was nothing the bastards wouldn't try to take from you if they sniffed a headline in it. Nitić was *hers* – she'd got the bruises, the cracked rib, the pounding head to prove it. She grabbed a black coffee from the machine and stormed upstairs.

Hume was in the office, signing off the paperwork on a stack of crates seized from the housing block. He saw Rose coming and, putting down his sheaf of papers, raised his open hands in a gesture of mock surrender.

It didn't even slow her down: 'Guv, you have got to be bloody *kidding* if –'

'Rose, Rose.' Now one hand was held out in a 'stop' sign. 'I know what you think. You think you've landed a plum case and it's got "DI Lauren Rose" written on the nametag, and here's fucking Lel Phillips snatching it away from you. Well, you're right and you're wrong. It *is* your case, until such a time as you either solve it or fuck it up. And yes, Phillips is in there with Bernie the Bosnian – and I swear, Rose, I'll never know how you took down that big cunt by yourself, unless you fed him a fucking horse tranquillizer – but do you know *why* Phillips is in there, instead of you? I'll tell you. He took a translator in there with him, did Phillips. Waited half an hour for him to drive over from Wantage. Doesn't miss a trick, our boy Leland. But I could've told him, you don't need a fucking translator, because I could go in there myself, not speaking a word of the bloody lingo, and I could tell you exactly what he's saying. Because what that big boy's saying – as DI Phillips is at present finding out – is FUCK ALL. Which essentially sounds the same in any language.' He paused for breath, raised his eyebrows. 'And you're up here, DI Rose, because you're going to go down in the history of the force as the copper who helped DCI Morgan Hume nail the Rakić gang.' A bark of a laugh.

Rose fought for focus. Hume could throw you like that – if he wanted to, he could absolutely scramble you.

'Dmitry Rakić, guv? You've brought him in?'

'Not in person. Haven't yet had the pleasure. But uniform dug up enough in that Leys shithole to put him away proper. Him and his dad and fucking Uncle Tom Cobley and all, if we want. They brought in five of Rakić's boys on drugs charges this morning, we've warrants out for half a dozen more, and these are smart lads, not shaved monkeys like your thug Nitić, they know what the smart move is – and the smart move is to sing to the rafters. Rakić is history.' Hume chuckled, rubbed his hands together.

'And – and Katerina?'

Hume cocked a finger.

'*That* poor bloody lass is the nail in the coffin for Rakić. Every time we bear down on these fuckers they cry harassment, bleating to the papers, saying we've got it in for

Eastern European immigrants, that every time we've a cold case we haul in some innocent Serbian citizen –'

'God forbid,' Rose muttered, too tired for diplomacy.

'– but once people hear about what they did to *her* there'll be no sympathy. Carte fucking blanche, we'll have, Rose, pardon my French. Speaking of which – I've a press conference to get to.' Again the strange bark of a laugh. 'Telly news and everything. Good work today, Rose. I mean it. Now you'll have to excuse me – Mr de Mille, I'm ready for my close-up . . .'

He bustled from the room. Through the office window Rose watched him jog down the corridor, pulling on an ugly green blazer as he went, and disappear into the lift.

She closed her eyes, pinching the bridge of her nose between finger and thumb. Her body needed rest. Her brain needed sleep. Christ, she had nothing left.

But this case had to be investigated. Katerina Zrinski had to be saved from becoming nothing more than a sensational footnote in the case against the Rakić gang. Rose ran Hume's scenario through her mind: a Rakić-ordered hit, a jilted lover's revenge on Katerina . . .

But men don't display their murdered lovers in the way poor Katerina was strung up and mutilated. Neither do gangland executioners, unless they're trying to send one hell of a message. Though there was also the possibility that the sheer horror of the spectacle was itself a kind of ruse. A panicked lover or impulsive gang member's attempt to disguise Katerina's murder to look like, well, like nothing else on earth.

No, Katerina's murder was not near as clear cut as the DCI made it out to be. Once you peeked past the surface, little in the Rakićs' MO seemed to match up with what'd been done to Katerina. Hume was too smart not to see that, once he'd got bored with the limelight.

She took a slurp of the tepid coffee. It tasted vile.

At her desk, fighting to keep her eyes from closing, she leafed through her notes on Katerina's last hours. There was the church, of course; she'd call there tomorrow, find out who – if anyone – heard Katerina's last confession. *That'll be a bloody bundle of laughs.* And there was the hospital where she worked: colleagues, employers, patients to interview.

She could barely hold her head up. Her falling eyelashes blurred her vision.

'Rose!'

She jerked awake. Hume again, barging into the office, junior officers scrambling in his wake.

'Guv?'

'Rise and shine, Rose. Problem at your crime scene. The girl. We need you there now.'

Rose nodded, stood, fumbled automatically for her bag, phone, notes, car keys –

Hume snatched the keys from her.

'I'll drive,' he called over his shoulder, making for the door. 'State you're in you'll fall asleep at the fucking wheel.'

She had to run to catch him up, boot heels loud on the tiled floor.

'You're coming, guv? What about the world's media?'

Hume snorted.

'Fuck the world's media. Phillips can do it. We've got a fucking job to do.'

The figure approached Little Mouse's bed. It was not the man he now called Father. It was not dressed in black, it carried no candle. It was both less than a man and more than a man, and it seemed to make its own light. Little Mouse blinked. His sight was still poor. The figure glowed and shimmered like a flame seen through fog.

At first he was afraid. The priest spoke sometimes of wicked spirits that visited in the night. He had told Little Mouse of devils that stole a boy's breath as he slept and of the shining ghosts of the winter marsh that were the lost spirits of babies that died without baptism.

But there was no wickedness here. The approaching figure – it was so close now that Little Mouse could have reached out and touched it – emanated only goodwill, and kindness, and love. Little Mouse felt the goodness of its heart as he had once felt the warmth of a kitchen stove.

He had come to love the man he called Father. But at the same time he had learned that love was a strange and complicated thing. It was as beautiful as it was frightening.

No, this was not the man he now called Father.

As soon as the figure spoke he knew it was the abbot – the murdered Abbot Cerbonius restored, by a miracle!

'There is no need,' the abbot said, 'for you to be afraid. I am with you, as I was before, as I always have been.' His familiar voice soothed the edges of Little Mouse's mind. It was a balm on his aching body and made his spirit soar.

'I am not afraid,' Little Mouse told the abbot. The sight of the beloved figure filled his heart to bursting.

'There is hope,' the abbot said. 'Hope will always drive out fear. The treasures of the monastery, my dear child, Little Mouse – do you remember them?'

Little Mouse saw them before him as though they were as solid and real as his grubby pillow and stump of candle.

'I do.'

'Were they not beautiful, Little Mouse?'

'They were,' Little Mouse sobbed. 'But they were taken. They were taken. Desecrated. And we, their guardians, were butchered.'

'But you were restored,' the abbot said.

'But I have such pain. There is a bullet in my head. I do not see well. I am weak, and my bones hurt.'

'In time, you will be restored,' the abbot said. 'Through that same power shall we all be restored. Our treasures, Little Mouse, and our friends, my brothers – all can be made whole. With faith, all will be redeemed. You must trust in that, my dear child. You must,' the abbot said, 'trust in that.'

The figure reached out a glowing hand and pressed its palm to Little Mouse's heart. Love and joy surged fiercely through his body. Hot tears sprang to his eyes.

Chapter Four

Police tape snapped noisily and the SOCO's wide tent of plastic sheeting billowed and boomed in the fierce east wind. The blue-green grass of the field bowed low. Rose shielded her eyes with her hand. She would hardly have known it as the field she'd driven away from less than twelve hours before.

At dawn this had been a terribly, fearsomely lonely place. Now it was crawling with people.

'Christ,' said Hume, banging the car door and pulling on a shapeless woolly hat. 'It's like fucking Piccadilly Circus.'

He stomped off down the slope.

Rose waited by the car, blinking in the wind. Taking soundings.

There were uniform around the place, and SOC officers, eerie in their face masks and white hazard suits. One or two plainclothes – you could spot them a mile off, if you knew what you were looking for.

But there were others, too. Dozens of them.

Rose started down the slope. Felt a chill at the bristly touch of the tall grass on her wrists and hands. It was a reminder, one she could do without: that this field, for all its apparent transformation, held at its heart the ruined body of Katerina Zrinski.

And once again the field felt like a terribly, fearsomely lonely place.

Between where she stood and the police cordon the grass had been trodden flat in wide swathes. There were maybe fifty, sixty people gathered there. Some walked, moving in agitation or uncertainty from group to group – others stood – others knelt.

Rose could hear shouting. And – singing? Or was it that damn wind playing tricks? She turned her head. Yes, singing – an untutored choir of voices, more women than men; a tune she thought she knew, from long-ago school assemblies, though the words were lost in the wind. She guessed the words would be different, anyway, from the ones she remembered.

From here she had a clearer view of the crowd. Most were familiar from the housing-block fifth floor earlier that day; maybe not the same individuals, but the same in dress and manner – they were mourners, quiet and bowed with sorrow, heavy with grief.

Rose automatically sought out the outliers. Coppers, of course. Hume was over by the cordon, talking to a harassed-looking sergeant in uniform. And a familiar face: Stevenage, Olly Stevenage, the camera-happy student journo. He was bundled up in a pricey-looking coat and cashmere scarf, drifting on the fringes of the crowd, digi-recorder in hand, camera-bag slung over his shoulder. Looking for a rent-a-quote to hand you your front-page headline, are we? Rose thought sourly.

She noted with satisfaction that Stevenage didn't seem to be having much success.

More worrying than the snot-nosed student were the

young men she saw moving among the mourners, tough-looking, purposeful. They were the ones doing the shouting — exactly *what* they were shouting she didn't know, though she heard the name 'Katerina'. She fished out her phone, made out like she was sending a text and managed a few decent full-face snaps of some of the men. Was it likely that one of them was the killer? She knew she couldn't rule it out. A murder like this, the guy's not happy with just killing the poor woman — he has to go back, remind himself of his achievement, see the damage he's done, not just to the poor girl but to everyone who loved her. It wasn't just the killing itself that got guys like this off, it was the power that comes with it. Had the killer been beaten by his father? Spurned by girls? Humiliated by his peers? What darkness did his past hold that explained this urge to prove his 'superiority' in such a gruesome way?

Rose shook her head at the profile she'd conjured. She thought of Katerina's fine hair woven around her fingers and the black stump at the base of her pearly neck. Nothing can explain this. Not a hundred beatings or a thousand insults.

Rose tucked the phone away and started to move through the crowd. The young men, she saw, weren't just surly, naturally aggressive — there was real anger here. Christ. It wouldn't take much for this to turn very ugly, very quickly.

She saw another familiar face, over at the far end of the cordon — keeping out of trouble, it looked like. The puking PC from earlier — Ganley, was it?

A sickly look appeared on his face as she approached. He touched his hand dutifully to the peak of his helmet.

'Ma'am.'

'What's the story, Constable? Who are the goons?'

'Rakić's lads, I'm told, ma'am.' He shook his head gravely. 'They're not happy.'

Well, why would they be? Rose thought. First we blow their Leys operation wide open, and now this –

'Have we got warrants out on any of these men?' she asked.

Ganley eyed her warily.

'We have, ma'am,' he nodded. 'In the circumstances, however –'

Rose smiled sharply. That made sense: no point stirring things up here. A full-blown riot wasn't what anyone wanted – except maybe the bloody press.

'Discretion's the better part of valour, right? Okay.' She looked out at the crowd. 'Is Rakić here?'

'The younger one, yes, ma'am.' The constable gave a barely-there nod towards a man near the centre of the crowd. 'See him? Sleeve tattoos and a face like thunder.'

'Got him.'

There was a fair bit less of him than she'd expected. He was maybe five-nine, five-ten, fit-looking but not stocky, crop-haired and severe in his facial features but obviously no meathead. He was in animated conversation with a hulking squaddie-type who was twice his size across and had a good half-foot on him in height.

Heavy silver crucifix round his neck. Bold Latin cross worked into his right-arm tattoo.

Rose was sloppy and he caught her looking. She turned her face quickly away but it was too late – he was coming her way, blue eyes burning.

In the car on the way over DCI Hume had told her a couple of stories about Dmitry Rakić. About how he'd had a guy's hand cut off at the wrist for trying to stiff him on a heroin deal. How he'd gone nine bare-knuckle rounds in an underground car park with the Croatian national welterweight champ. How a pub landlord in Swindon had called him a fucking gyppo prick, and Rakić had burned his pub to the ground.

'Of course,' Hume had said, 'half of it's a load of bullshit.'

'Which half?'

He'd given her a look.

'Now that, Rose,' he'd smiled, 'is the six-million-dollar fucking question.'

Now as Rakić moved determinedly towards her she sensed PC Ganley at her side, drawing himself up to his full six-two. Saw his hand move to the butt of his baton. Somehow she didn't feel reassured.

Rakić stopped a foot in front of her. It was hard not to take a backward step – hard, but necessary. He spat into the trodden-down grass, cracked his knuckles. Unleashed a fierce burst of Serbo-Croat.

Rose kept her poker face up. Ignored the smell of his breath, the flecks of his spittle on her skin.

'You should go home, Mr Rakić,' she said.

'Bastards,' Rakić hissed.

'This isn't the place for causing trouble,' Rose said levelly. 'Start anything here, anything at all, and we'll take you in.'

Rakić jabbed his finger at her, then at Ganley.

'Police,' he sneered, showing white teeth, sharp canines. 'Fucking scum.'

Ganley shifted his weight.

'That's enough from you, pal,' he said. 'Pack it in.'

With a sharp glance, Rakić took in the constable's clean cuffs and freshly pressed uniform, his uncertain stare, his pale hand on the baton butt. Rose couldn't know what he saw in them, what these things signified to a Zagreb ex-con, but it quickly became clear that it was enough to turn up the flame under his simmering temper.

Rakić lurched forwards, went nose to nose with the young constable, baring his teeth, bunching his fists, letting rip with a torrent of fierce broken English and rattling Serbo-Croat. Rose didn't catch much of it: 'bastard', 'fuck', 'Katerina', 'murder'.

She was about to step in when, over Rakić's shoulder, she saw Olly Stevenage step from the crowd, strike a theatrical photographer's pose and raise his camera.

From behind him, the big squaddie-type folded a thick hand around his neck. Olly squawked, dropped the camera. Rakić turned – Rose heard Ganley's suppressed sigh of relief. She moved swiftly, going after Rakić as he plunged hawk-like towards Stevenage. She wasn't quick enough to keep him from tearing the camera from its strap around Stevenage's neck – Stevenage yelped, threw up a hand, wailed something about the freedom of the press and how much his new camera had cost – but she was there in time to stop Rakić kicking seven shades out of the kid, which was clearly what he had in mind.

She took hold of Rakić's hard-muscled left arm, swung her body between him and Stevenage. Disregarded the bump of his elbow against her bruised ribs. It was no time for armlocks, cuffs, batons. Instead she leaned in, hissed in his ear: 'Go. Go now. Be smart. Or I promise you, we will take you down.' She couldn't be sure how much he understood. The only hope was that the message of her words was clear.

Moved back, looked in his eyes. Their damaged intensity frightened her.

Rakić's throat rippled with the effort of containing his emotion.

'Katerina,' he said in a strangled undertone.

Hard to read, this guy. He must have cared for her, she supposed, maybe even loved her. In a violent guy, that can be dangerous. What had been done to Katerina didn't look like a crime of passion – but then, maybe what had been done to Katerina wasn't quite what it seemed.

Rose gave nothing away.

'We are investigating,' she said firmly. 'You can help by letting us get on with our job.'

Rakić spat again into the mud. The crowd's focus was on him. Rose could see him thinking fast, calculating, casing the situation. She hoped he'd seen the uniforms moving into position behind him. She hoped he was as smart as she thought he was. Violence here would cause a mess for everyone.

He snarled out a word in Croat: *brask*. Meant nothing to her. Then he was away, moving fast, shoulders hunched, back towards the lane. The crowd stirred as Rakić's heavies – more than she'd realized, maybe ten, fifteen – followed after him.

She was about to turn away when she heard Rakić yell something. Whatever it was, it sounded like he meant it.

There was a group of young women standing nearby,

looking cold, unhappy and – when Rose took a step towards them – decidedly unfriendly.

She asked them if they'd understood, if they could translate what Rakić had shouted. One, perhaps the eldest, stern-faced but beakily handsome, nodded.

'"I will kill the murdering bastard,"' she said stonily. 'And: "If he loves God so much, I will give him an introduction."'

Rose thanked them, turned away. With her hands in her pockets, hair whipping in the wind, she looked at the walls of plastic sheeting that hid Katerina's body.

Too many meanings within meanings here, she thought. Too many secrets. Too many mysteries.

She sighed. Too many bruises. Too little sleep.

'Well, this was a fucking waste of my afternoon,' said Hume, ducking under the police tape. He took a slurp from a coffee cup. 'You fuck off home, Rose. Get some rest. Come and talk to me tomorrow.' He waved a hand curtly as he moved off. 'Don't have nightmares.'

A woman from the village brought food — sausage, bread, thick root-vegetable soup. The woman's name was Olga. Little Mouse watched from the netted window of the priest's hut. He saw the priest smile — he had never seen the priest smile — and take the basket from her.

The woman was smiling, too. A kind smile. Little Mouse heard the priest ask her: 'Why did God become man?'

He couldn't hear the woman's answer. The right answer was 'That man might become God' — Little Mouse knew that. He was a good Christian. He was such a good Christian that God himself had delivered him from death.

The priest asked the woman if she feared Sheol, and if she knew of the Great Mysteries. Little Mouse could not hear her answers. He could see the priest smiling, though. He felt a pang of jealousy.

He slid from the windowsill when the priest came back into the hut. Crept back under his blanket, watched the priest as he reached up to a high shelf and took down one of his icons. Little Mouse knew it. Little Mouse had watched the priest make it. It had been made for him, he'd thought. A thigh bone hung from a thread within a cage of ribs, oiled with balsam.

The priest took it out to the woman. Little Mouse heard him say: 'It will preserve the purity of your soul. It will keep you in the heart of Christ.'

When the priest came back in he did not have the relic with him. He had given it away. It had been made for Little Mouse, to preserve the purity of his own soul. Why had the priest given it to the woman?

Little Mouse hid his tears beneath his blanket.

73

Chapter Five

5 October

Feeling out of place was part of the job. It happened every day, for a copper. You got used to it – you got so that you didn't even notice it any more. For Rose, though, churches were the worst. Here people didn't just look different and talk different – here they had different ways of *thinking*. Of feeling, too.

The Roses had never had much time for church. That was when her mum was alive. After she died they had no time at all. 'Load of old cobblers,' her dad had said – meaning church, God, religion, all of it. 'Anyone with a bit of common sense can see that.' He'd jovially tolerated his wife's every-now-and-then churchgoing – joking, 'Say one for me,' or 'Give Him my best,' as she made her way out in her good hat and polished court shoes – but after . . .

Far as Rose knew, he'd not set foot in a church since the funeral. Couldn't blame him.

She eased open the heavy door of the Queen of Peace. Katerina's church.

The entrance hall had a coat stand, a bench, a notice board crowded with posters – most in Polish, some in Cyrillic script, others in languages she didn't recognize. The air was musty, tinged with the smells of incense and floor polish. Cross between a school hall and a high-street candle shop, Rose thought. She pushed open another door, stepped into the main body of the church.

It was a newish place, red brick outside, white-rendered walls and walnut beams within. Parquet floor, pews in a dozen rows. There were a couple of people, both elderly, gathering up prayer books. She'd timed it right – just missed morning Mass.

She was glad she'd managed to grab a few hours' sleep and fix herself some proper coffee before getting here. The day before, she'd arrived back at her flat at around five; she'd headed straight to bed, aching, as wrung-out as she'd ever been – but was unable to sleep. Katerina's body. The Zrinski girls. The plummeting view of a five-storey drop. Dmitry Rakić.

At eight, sandy-eyed and sore, she'd surrendered to the inevitable. Got up, pulled on a sweater, prepared a pot of coffee. Got to work at her kitchen table.

She read and reread her notes. Dug into the files on Rakić, father and son, the files on their associates, their associates' associates. Cross-checked the witness statements, the Zrinskis, Olly Stevenage, Rob Shaw (the astronomy geek), PC Ganley. Hume had emailed her the transcript of Phillips's interview with Nitić – 'fuck all' was pretty much what it came to. There were inventories from the raid in the Leys, ancient photostats sent over from police HQs in Zagreb and Novi Sad, cuttings from court reports up and down the Thames Valley.

Midnight had found her trawling the web for information on the Croatian War of Independence, the break-up of old Yugoslavia, the patterns of displacement, immigration, dispersal –

She'd crawled back into bed at half-one. Sleep had finally arrived at around two.

Now she suppressed a yawn as she wandered down the aisle of the church. Before her, fixed above the altar, was a luridly coloured Christ, life-sized, nailed to the cross, looking down with an expression of intolerable anguish.

Rose didn't know much about religion, but she'd seen this kind of thing before. Some churches, she'd noticed, liked to place the emphasis on the resurrection of Jesus, on redemption, love and hope; others seemed to want to dwell only on his suffering.

Seemed cruel, somehow. But what did she know?

She heard raised voices beyond a wooden door that led off the right-hand transept. A man's voice, and a boy's. Rose moved quickly to the door, wincing at the resonant echo of her own footsteps, and opened it a crack. Peering through, she saw a heavy-set, dark-bearded old man in priest's garb shaking a young boy by his arm. He had what looked to be a painful hold on the kid's biceps. He was talking angrily to the kid. Not in English.

She stepped through, let the door thud closed behind her. As good a way as any of announcing her presence. The priest looked round at her, startled.

He said something in a foreign language, and then, in heavily accented English, 'This is not a public place – you cannot be here.'

'I'm Detective Inspector Lauren Rose.' Flashed her badge. The priest winced – she made a mental note of that. 'Father Florian? I was hoping I could speak to you in private.'

The priest made an impatient gesture, pointed to a door off the corridor.

'My study,' he said, not looking at Rose. 'Wait.'

She kept a hold on her irritation. Nodded coldly, brushed past the priest and the boy. A plate on the door read PRI-VATE. She slipped inside, clicked the door closed, leaned on it. Let out a long breath through her nose. Bloody *hell*. Was this how the priest always greeted visitors to his church? Was it because she was English? Because she was a woman? Because she was a copper? All three?

It was a small office, or study, or vestry, or whatever it was called. Shelves on three walls. Books in several languages: some old, with broken spines, faded titles; others newer. A desk covered with unruly papers. A crucifix nailed to the wall. A page of scripture in a black frame.

On one of the shelves a space had been cleared for a row of narrow glass bottles. They looked like a set of cooking oils – she'd something similar in her kitchen cupboard – only older, darker. The stoppers were crusted.

Rose took down the nearest. Loosened the stopper, sniffed quickly at the contents.

She nearly dropped the bottle. *The field. The grass. The cartwheel. The body. Katerina.* The smell – woody, delicate, complex. Katerina's body had had the same smell.

'What are you doing?'

The bearded priest had entered without her hearing. She replaced the stopper, set the bottle back on the shelf.

'You have some . . . *interesting* things in here, Father Florian.'

'You should not have touched that.' The scowling priest's thick eyebrows met in the middle above a narrow, pointed nose. He showed tea-brown lower teeth when he spoke. 'That is a sacred oil. You must not touch.'

Rose inclined her head slightly: 'understood', not 'sorry'. She was damned if she was going to apologize.

'What's this one?' She pointed to the bottle she had taken down – the oil with the smell of Katerina.

'Chrism.' The priest moved to his chair, shoved a pile of papers to one side, sat down heavily. 'An oil of balsam, most holy, most sacred. Used in certain ritual.' He paused. 'You would not understand.'

He fixed her with a challenging gaze. His black eyes were pink-rimmed and watery.

He stared at her, until the quiet of the room was pierced by soft footsteps. The boy the priest had been scolding skulked past them in the hall. When the lad saw Rose notice him through the open doorway his eyes widened and he took off like a shot. Looked half terrified, the poor little bugger.

'The boy out there.' She cocked her head towards the door. 'What did he do?'

The priest glared. 'He had misbehaved, of course.'

'In what way?'

'He was seen daydreaming during Mass. While the faithful were saying the Jesus Prayer the little dolt was gawping out of the window with his mouth hanging open like a fool.'

Rose laughed.

'That doesn't sound that bad.'

Father Florian lifted his brows scornfully.

'Not to you, perhaps. But for us, yes, it is bad. God asks so little of us. To disobey him in even the smallest thing – what an insult!' The priest sucked at his teeth. 'That little wretch.'

78

'Will he get into trouble at home?'

'His parents are true Christians. So I trust that he will.' He shook his head impatiently. 'Can I ask what is the meaning of this? You have something to ask me, apart from about a bottle of oil, a child's sins?'

Rose nodded, shifted gear. What'd happened to Katerina was hard news to hear, heart-breaking news. Even for this arsehole of a priest, maybe – if he had a heart.

As she opened her mouth to speak, Father Florian said: 'Katerina. I know.'

She looked at him. For the first time there was feeling in his upturned face.

'In our community word travels fast,' he said, 'and we do not keep secrets from one another.'

No. Only from us.

'I know she meant a lot to the community.'

'Yes, yes. Very much.' Father Florian nodded sombrely, spread his hands. 'But after all, we belong to Jesus Christ. He does with us what He will.'

I'm sure that's a great bloody comfort for her sisters, Rose thought with a sharp surge of contempt. It was the kind of crap she'd heard vicars say at funerals.

Back to business, then.

'From what we know of Katerina's last movements,' she said, pulling out notebook and pencil, 'she left her home in the Leys area to go to confession. That was on the second of October, around nine-thirty, ten a.m. Is that right?'

'Yes. She came for confession that day.'

'Who took her confession?'

'I did. Who else?'

She made a note calmly enough, nodded calmly enough, but something had connected in Rose's brain. Something automatic. On a murder investigation, when you found yourself face to face with the last person to see the victim alive –

Okay, they might not have had anything to do with it. That didn't matter. Something clicked, like a notch on a ratchet.

She knew to go steady.

'Tell me about Katerina,' she said. Give 'em enough rope, that was the idea. 'What was her involvement in the church?'

Father Florian, to her surprise, smiled.

'She was – wonderful. A true child of Christ.'

'Was she very devout?'

He nodded.

'Yes, very devout, very observant. But that was not all. Many will say the holy words and read the holy book and no more. And that is no sin! But Katerina – she did not only want to help herself. You understand? The soup kitchen, with the homeless ones. Missions, to London, Bristol, here, there. Wherever there were people who needed help – there was Katerina.'

He turned abruptly in his chair, fumbled in a drawer of his desk. Rose glanced over his shoulder. A dusty jumble of papers, odds and ends, scribbled notes. He took out a picture in a cheap plastic frame, handed it to Rose.

'You see. A special person.'

It was Katerina, in a group picture with a bunch of other young people. Arms around each other's shoulders, grinning in the sunshine somewhere. Nice.

But Rose saw more than just the photo. It was in a frame – so it had been on display, once, instead of crammed in a drawer. There were no other photographs in Father Florian's office, no personal souvenirs or tokens of any kind. So Katerina's picture had been the only one he wanted to see?

And he'd taken it down. Recently, too – it wasn't dusty. Why?

Because he couldn't bear the sight of it?

'You took this picture?'

'It was a gift, from Katerina. It is our church group. Volunteers.'

'It's a lovely shot.' She looked more closely at the grinning faces. Katerina stood out – for her beauty, yes, but also for her vibrancy, for the *life* that showed in her face. They all looked like good kids, Rose thought. A girl in a headscarf had her arm slung round the neck of a tall young man with an angular face; beside him, Katerina; beside Katerina, a tanned, dark-haired guy, fine-rimmed glasses and good teeth; beside *him,* a flat-featured blonde girl with cropped hair and a nose-stud –

Rose's fingers tightened on the frame. She knew Father Florian was watching her, she knew she hadn't moved a muscle in her face. But her heart was racing.

That dark-haired man beside Katerina.

'Who's this?' she asked, casually, tapping the Perspex with a fingertip. Florian craned his neck to see.

'You don't know?' He smiled thinly. 'I thought *everyone* knew Professor Brask. A most famous man, very learned. A member of our church,' the priest added proudly.

Brask. Did she know the name?

In the picture he was standing beside Katerina, on her

left. They weren't standing particularly close, but it looked like he had his hand on the small of her back.

More importantly, while everyone else was beaming at the camera, Brask was looking only at Katerina. And his smile was the widest of all.

'Is he Croatian?'

'No,' the priest scoffed. 'No, Professor Brask is an American. A visiting professor, they call it, at the university. I thought everyone knew this.'

American. Katerina had spoken on the phone in English, Sofia had said – to a man.

Rose handed the picture back to Father Florian and thanked him politely for his time. He grunted a grudging goodbye, waved a hand dismissively. She wasn't sorry to leave him to his old books and his bottles of magic oil.

She was out of the church grounds and pulling out on to the main road when it hit her. *Brask*. She *had* heard it before. Dmitry Rakić, in the meadow, as he was walking away.

He'd said that name, said *Brask* – just before he'd promised to kill the murdering bastard.

Little Mouse woke and found that he couldn't move. His arms, legs — he couldn't move! Had he died in the night? He struggled and heard the dull clink of chains at his ankles and wrists. The chill of metal bit into his skin.

He was naked. Where were his clothes? Goosebumps prickled his skin.

'Father?'

The priest loomed from the shadows. Only his mouth and chin could be seen beneath the pointed hood he wore. Instead of his usual black garb he wore the ash-grey sackcloth of the penitent. He approached Little Mouse's cot.

It was only the priest, Little Mouse knew. His — his father. And yet he could not keep from trembling.

Moving slowly, with care, as in a ritual, the priest unstoppered a vial of oil and poured a quantity into his cupped palm. Little Mouse gagged at its pungent scent.

The priest murmured verses in Latin. Little Mouse did not know what they meant. The priest went on murmuring as he smeared the oil on Little Mouse's body: his bare chest, his cuffed wrists, his forehead. He felt the oil trickle into his hair.

He could not suppress a frightened sob.

'Father!'

The hooded priest set the vial of oil aside. Went silently from the room. Little Mouse lay without moving, barely breathing. Waiting.

When he returned, the priest held a struggling chicken by its throat and feet. To Little Mouse, the room seemed distorted by the bird's noise, ugliness and fear.

He knew what happened to animals that were brought into this room.

But it was not the scalpel. Instead the priest produced from within his robe a broad-bladed knife, a ceremonial knife, its handle carved and set with gold.

A short flurry, a noise like tearing fabric, followed by the familiar iron stink of blood. Little Mouse heard it spatter on the floor, felt its warmth spill across his legs.

He closed his eyes as the priest crouched over his cot and half expected to feel the blade of the knife against his own flesh.

A scraping sound. He opened his eyes. The priest was kneeling by his cot. He was moving the blade of the gory knife against the pitted concrete floor while he murmured in Latin. The priest was writing something, Little Mouse thought.

Writing something in blood.

Chapter Six

Hume wasn't buying it.

'Come on, Rose. Everything we have points to Rakić. The two of them were in a relationship of some sort. We know what *that* means in a case like this. He's running drugs on her fucking doorstep. She finds out, makes trouble, Rakić has her killed – and makes an example of her. End of.'

End of. Hume knew better than that. Nothing in policing was ever *end of.*

'It doesn't add up, guv. There's more to this, a lot more.'

'There might well be, but that doesn't alter the bottom line. Rakić. This starts and ends with Rakić. You saw how he was yesterday. Off his head.'

It was mid-morning at the nick but she already had a dull headache and eyelids like sandpaper. She yawned, rubbed her face.

Phillips, sitting with his feet up on his desk, put in: 'I reckon Lauren would rather go and sip a cappuccino with this Oxford don than do some real police work out at the Leys.'

Mike Angler, elbow-deep in Phillips's paperwork at an adjoining desk, sniggered obligingly.

Rose sighed. Wished she'd never bloody mentioned this Professor Matthew Brask. It didn't fit with how the Major Crimes crew looked at the world. Crime, they thought, was done by criminals – by lowlifes like Nitić and Rakić, scumbags from the Leys. And most of the time they were right. The percentage game was the smart play; follow the averages, go where the stats point you.

Or to put it another way, Rose thought, just keep doing exactly what you did the last time.

But she wasn't prepared to let the averages shut out her instincts. Not now. She'd seen the professor's dopey grin in Florian's photo – seen, too, the look of hatred in Rakić's eyes and heard the fury in his voice as he'd said, no, *spat* the word: *Brask*. Like a curse. The worst curse he could think of.

There was a connection here, something real – maybe something important. She could feel it.

Hume was looking at her thoughtfully.

'What was this feller's name again?'

'Brask, Matthew Brask. He's a visiting professor in religion from Harvard. Fellow at All Souls.'

'*Brask*. I know that name. Do we know him, Phillips?'

Phillips shrugged.

'Can't think why we would.'

'I could swear we've crossed paths with a Brask. Look him up.'

'PNC check, guv?' Phillips took up his phone to dial down to the database team.

'Nah. JFGI.' Hume flipped open a laptop. Looked up, caught Rose's eye. 'Just Fucking Google It.'

Rose watched over his shoulder as he ran the search: *Matthew Brask Oxford*.

First result was Brask's page on the university website.

There was a short profile, a list of research interests, a long bibliography of publications – and a picture.

Hume drew in a breath.

'I *knew* I knew him,' he said.

Rose looked at him quizzically. Wouldn't have had DCI Hume down as a scholar of theology.

'Sir?'

Phillips, coming alongside, swore sharply.

'*That* bastard,' he said. 'Yeah, we know him all right, don't we, guv? Proper little do-gooder.'

Seeing Rose nonplussed, Hume swiftly filled in the detail.

'You know I was talking about the grief we get about "harassment" in the Leys? This bloke's responsible for a good two-thirds of it. Didn't know he was a professor, just signs himself Matt Brask on his letters.'

'And his emails, and his petitions . . .' Phillips added wearily.

'Old-fashioned bleeding-heart liberal, our Professor Brask. Thinks we go too hard on the poor old Eastern European community. Says we're targeting vulnerable minorities. Wonder if he's ever been held up in a Leys back alley with a vulnerable minority pointing a knife at his throat. Anyway, that's him – champion of the oppressed.' Hume sat back, chewed his lip. 'Maybe you should go and have a word with him, Rose,' he said. 'Shake him up a bit, see what falls out. Go this afternoon.'

'Do they work afternoons, academics?' sneered Phillips with a short laugh.

Angler looked up from his paperwork. Muttered something about getting a proper job.

*

A thin, cold drizzle fell on Oxford as Rose crossed Radcliffe Square, headed for the forbidding gate of All Souls College. A far cry from the dreary ex-polytechnic where she'd got her criminology degree, that was for sure.

In the porters' lodge a fat porter set down his racing paper to sign her in and ask who she was there to see. When she told him his pink face lit up.

'Professor Brask! Lovely feller. Tell him Maurice said hello, will you?'

She said she would, headed for the stairs. Everyone's friend, this Brask, she thought. If *that's* not bloody suspicious, I don't know what is.

It was library-quiet in the upper corridors of the college. All Souls, she knew, had no undergraduates – no students to break the silence.

Brask's office was tucked away in the north-east corner of the building (the fat porter had helpfully scribbled her a map with his bookie's biro). It seemed to take her for ever to get there – felt like miles, over deadening grey carpet, under low ceilings lined with strip lights. She'd somehow expected grand staircases and marble halls. This could have been any old sixth-form college or red-brick ex-poly. It's a place of work, after all, she reminded herself. Not bloody Hogwarts.

His office door was half open. Rose got a look at him before he heard her approach. He seemed much as he'd appeared in Florian's photo; the same thin-rimmed glasses, the same mop of dark hair. Mid-thirties, she guessed. He wore a blue shirt with a faint grey stripe and was talking to someone – she couldn't sce who. She heard whoever it was laugh softly. Caught a snatch of conversation about sport.

Music was playing quietly in the background – some kind of choral music, the kind that always made Rose think of funerals. Not so inappropriate, considering the conversation they were about to have.

She knocked on the door frame. The conversation broke off; Brask looked up, saw her. Started politely to get to his feet.

'Oh – hi there. Come in.' His expression was friendly, open. She wondered what he took her for – a fellow theologian? The provost's new secretary?

Probably not a Thames Valley DI on a murder investigation, anyway.

She pushed open the door. The man Brask had been talking to looked at her. Bald, fortyish. Didn't look much like an academic.

'Well, so long, Luka,' Brask said. 'I'll keep an eye out for the score on Wednesday night.'

The man nodded, smiled. 'You're a good man, Professor,' he said as he shuffled out, 'but not much on the pitch.' Brask turned to Rose.

'The rules of rugby,' the professor said, 'will always be a mystery to me. Doesn't keep me from trying, though.' He lifted his eyebrows in a so-how-can-I-help? expression.

Did a double-take when Rose showed her badge.

'Police? My goodness. What –'

'Please sit down, Professor. Can I sit down? Thanks.'

That was called getting the upper hand. But the real trick, she knew, was keeping it.

Brask watched her in silence as she took off her coat,

set her umbrella against the wall and took a seat on the padded bench that faced the professor's desk.

Only then did she say: 'Professor Brask, I'm Detective Inspector Lauren Rose. I'm here with – with some bad news.'

He blinked.

'Bad news? From – from back home?'

His accent was gently Midwestern, an old-movie accent, both likeable and corny as hell.

'No, nothing like that.' She watched him carefully. 'From the Leys.'

Brask just nodded. Nothing in the eyes but sincere concern, no twitch, no tremor. Good actor? Innocent man? Cold-hearted killer?

'Uh-huh,' he said, waiting for her to go on.

'We're investigating a murder.'

He raised his eyebrows at that. Not shock – you'd have to be pretty unworldly to be shocked by a murder in the Leys – but surprise, interest, again something that looked a lot like real concern. 'Gangs?' he suggested.

'We're looking at all available leads,' Rose said neutrally.

She couldn't hold it off any longer. She wondered, quickly, what there was between Katerina and this polite American. Had she loved him? Had he loved her?

She thought, How much is this going to hurt?

'We found the body of Katerina Zrinski,' she said, 'in a field north of Oxford in the early hours of the fourth of October. She'd been murdered.'

Brask's knuckles whitened on the arms of his chair. The colour ran from his face.

'Katerina?' he said, indistinctly.

A nod was all he was getting.

'I'm afraid so.'

'Oh – oh, oh, dear God.' His brow puckered and he pressed one open hand to his face, dislodging his glasses. He drew a long, wavering breath, said again, 'Oh, dear God.'

Dear God, Rose thought bleakly, had nothing to do with it.

She knew that maybe she was being pretty tough on a man who'd lost a friend, perhaps a good friend, a lover even.

But then, maybe she was going pretty easy on the man who'd butchered Katerina Zrinski.

Brask took a handkerchief from his pocket, wiped his eyes and nose. Straightened his glasses. Looked up at Rose with an expression that was difficult to read. There was something formidable in his eyes, she thought, something hard.

'All available leads, you said.' He swallowed. 'Including me?'

Rose stonewalled.

'I have a few questions,' she said.

Yes, he and Katerina had been friends. No, he hadn't seen her for a little while, a week or two perhaps.

If he was hiding something, he was hiding it well. Yes, he was nervous – Rose had made it pretty clear he was a suspect in a murder investigation; who wouldn't be? But he was composed, lucid, took time to think before each answer, wasn't obviously evasive or hesitant.

So what are you, Professor Brask? Rose wondered. A good actor? Or an innocent man?

As they cycled through the questions, Rose took in the details of Brask's office. There were no vials of holy oil, at least, no cobwebbed books. In a lot of ways it wasn't so different from the offices of her old college lecturers – only where they'd have had a holiday snap of their kids, Brask had pinned up a print of a medieval Virgin-and-child painting; where they'd have had unmarked essays strewn across their desks, Brask seemed to have been reading from a photocopied manuscript written in Hebrew.

And where pride of place in her old lecturers' offices would've been taken by a framed photo of them graduating from Hendon or receiving a bravery award, Brask had a professional-looking picture of himself in a Roman collar.

He'd been a *priest*?

No, Brask didn't have any idea why anyone would want to hurt Katerina. Yes, he went fairly regularly to the Queen of Peace church: 'I'm a professor of comparative religion,' he explained. 'I go to a lot of churches.'

There were a couple of other photos in the office. One showed Brask at a party or a dance, relaxed and grinning, with his arms around a pretty, black-haired woman. Not very priestly, Rose thought. She made a quick comparison: he was a little older in this picture than in the one with the collar. An ex-priest, then. A disgraced priest?

Yes, he had a lot of contacts among the Oxford Eastern European communities. No, he didn't know Dmitry Rakić – except by reputation.

On a bookshelf beside Brask's desk Rose saw another

photo, without a frame, worn-looking, propped against a ring-binder. A familiar photo: the same one Father Florian had shown her of church volunteers grinning in the sun. Katerina smiling at the camera, Brask smiling at Katerina.

It was right by his desk, where he could look at it every day.

She interrupted him in mid-answer.

'Were you and Katerina in a sexual relationship, Professor Brask?'

He stopped dead. Gaped at her. Worked his jaw a couple of times before getting it out: 'No! Me and Katerina, in a – No, Inspector Rose – no.'

Rose nodded evenly but she didn't deny herself the inner kick of satisfaction. *Got you.* There were still a lot of things in this case that she didn't understand, but at least now she knew one thing for sure. Professor Matt Brask was a liar.

Little Mouse couldn't remember the last thing he'd had to eat. The oat biscuit dipped in black tea? The slice of cold, boiled sausage? The bread smeared with lamb-fat?

Had that been two days ago? Three days ago?

If only he weren't so weak he might remember.

He had pleaded with the priest to feed him and begged him to release him from his chains. The priest had only shaken his head and said that he need not worry about his body, only his soul. Think of the martyrs of the True Church, he had said. Their suffering was necessary to purify their spirit. So too was Little Mouse's own suffering.

'Do you not love me, Father?' Little Mouse had begged the priest. 'Am I not a good Christian? Have I failed you?'

The priest's old eyes filled with tears. 'You are of the True Church, my son,' he said. His gravelly voice was thick with emotion. 'You are good and selfless. That is why you are so worthy. This is not a punishment but a reward.'

Little Mouse did not understand. He thought that perhaps the woman from the village would come — to free him, give him food. Make things right.

But the woman had not come.

Indistinctly, as if in a dream, the abbot had appeared to him again, a being of pure light and unequalled benevolence. The abbot told Little Mouse not to be afraid. 'Have faith, my son,' the abbot told him. The same thing the priest had said.

Little Mouse wept. The priest told him to dry his eyes. His time of suffering would soon end.

Chapter Seven

'Katerina – can you call me, please? I know you're scared; I understand why, I really do. But I have to talk to you. Give me a chance – please.'

Another:

'I just want to know what it is you're feeling. This is killing me, Katerina. I need you to tell me the truth – that's all.'

Another:

'We can't pretend this isn't happening, Katerina. It is – Katerina, it already has. Call me.'

Katerina Zrinski's voicemails, retrieved from her phone company. The voice was Matt Brask's.

She and Hume talked it through over bad machine coffee.

'I still say Rakić.' The DCI sat on a desk, scuffed shoes up on a chair, arms folded across his knees. 'Stick with that angle. If she was fucking Rakić and seeing this professor on the side, that points to Rakić – he found out, blew up, killed her. If she *wasn't* fucking Rakić, she'd rumbled his operation in the Leys and was causing trouble – he blew up, killed her, it's a gang hit. *Or* she was fucking the professor, not fucking Rakić, Rakić couldn't take it, blew up, killed her.' He threw up his hands. 'See what I'm saying?'

'I get the point, guv.' Rose shook her head. 'But Brask

lied to me. About his relationship with the murder victim! That doesn't look good, you've got to admit.'

'If you're fucking the sweetheart of a Croatian gang leader, maybe you get into the habit of not shouting it from the fucking rooftops.' The DCI slurped his coffee, shrugged. 'I'm not defending this prick of a professor, Rose. But for my money, it's our boy Dmitry all the way.'

He crumpled his coffee cup, threw it aside. 'Stick with Rakić, Rose.'

'Look, guv, none of Rakić's guys have given us a sniff, have they? I know Phillips has been leaning on them hard, and they haven't copped to *anything*. They've no idea what we're talking about.'

'Hard nuts. You know what they're like.'

Rose could've screamed in exasperation.

'Sir, I really think –'

'I'm still in charge around here, Detective Inspector. Stick with Rakić.' He stood, briefly examined a coffee stain on his tie. Looked seriously at Rose. 'You're mad at Brask because he lied to you. Remember what this case is about, Rose.'

'I thought it was about finding the killer, guv.'

'It is.' Hume nodded. 'And that means it's not about your fucking feelings.'

She was pulling on her coat, getting ready to head out to the Leys to meet a contact from the fringes of the Rakić gang, when her phone buzzed. Dr Matilda Rooke – the pathologist. Rose knew her well. Liked her.

'I was told to bump this poor girl of yours to the top of my list, Lauren.' Dr Rooke spoke slowly in a low, lugubrious voice. It was just as well – if she could speak as fast as she could think, no one would have been able to keep up with her. 'I'm getting her ready now. I thought you might like – well, not *like* exactly, but you know – to come and watch.'

'That might be helpful, Matilda. Thanks.'

'No rush, love. I'm just going to have a cup of tea before we get cracking, so you've got a good ten minutes.' The line went dead. Rose smiled. Funny how it took a woman who spent her life around dead bodies to make her feel human again.

That feeling lasted all of the fifteen minutes it took her to drive to the morgue. Once she was in Matilda's lab the deathly bleakness of this case closed over her head like an icy sea. Katerina's body, fish-grey on the slab. Katerina's head, on a nearby table. Matilda Rooke's warmth hidden behind a surgical mask and gown. The air cold, clammy.

She shivered.

She was a career copper; she'd seen dead bodies before, women's bodies, too, beaten, mutilated, lifeless in a pathologist's lab. They'd never made her feel as bad as Katerina's remains made her feel. They'd never, somehow, seemed so helpless – so betrayed.

'Now don't worry, love,' Matilda said. She was bent over a steel tray, prepping her instruments. Their aseptic steel gleamed unwholesomely. 'This is going to be horrible, but it'll all be over soon, I promise.'

Rose's mouth shaped to say thank you – but then she realized that Matilda wasn't talking to her. She was talking to Katerina. To the corpse.

She'd heard about this from Phillips, she remembered. He'd been in on an autopsy with Matilda before – that mad bag in the lab, he called her. 'Only pathologist in the world who talks to her patients.' Matilda, he'd said, called it her 'bedside manner'.

At the time Rose had thought it was just another crank story to file alongside all the others people liked to pass around about the weirdos in the path lab. Milk and sandwiches kept in the fridge next to platters of eyeballs and severed fingers. Cadavers dressed up in tinsel boas and party hats for the work Christmas do. The guy who collected thumbnails.

Some were true, some – surely – weren't. Either way, they were good for raising a smile when the job turned dark.

But seeing this now – seeing Matilda say sorry to Katerina the first time she touched the scalpel to her skin – did more than raise a smile. Rose saw the true humanity in this.

'Let's have a look at you, you poor thing,' Matilda murmured, prising apart her first incision. 'Let's see if we can figure out what they did to you.'

Rose looked away.

They'd already talked over the preliminary data, gathered at the scene. Time of death was difficult to call, Matilda had said – but from the dry condition of the severance, Katerina had been beheaded some time before she'd been taken to the meadow.

'Then there's her temperature,' the doctor had added, tapping a printout with the tip of her pen. 'She was cold, much more cold than she ought to have been. Around eleven degrees when SOCO arrived – but the outdoor temperature that night never dropped below thirteen.'

Rose had shuddered.

'It felt so much colder.'

Matilda had given her a beady look. 'I can well imagine.'

The data suggested that Katerina's body had been kept somewhere very cold for some time. Refrigerated. An image of the poor woman's body dangling in a meat locker had surged sickeningly into Rose's mind.

She still hadn't managed to shake it off.

'Is this how it happened, my love? Is this how he did it? Look here.' A lift, a professional edge in her voice indicated that Matilda was talking to Rose now. Rose leaned in, ran her eyes over the pale-grey skin.

'What am I looking at?'

'Bruises.' Matilda pointed. 'Old ones, faded, but real enough, and heavy, too. She took a real beating, didn't you, eh?'

'Enough to kill her?'

A brisk shrug.

'Couldn't say just yet. My first guess is a beating to the body coupled with strangulation.'

Rose nodded. That'd been her first hunch. But there was little satisfaction in being proved right.

'You'll have to wait for my final report to be sure,' Matilda added.

Rose nodded. *Another* report. She was already waiting for lab results on Katerina's strange hessian clothes – they were clearly handmade, SOCO had said, ruffling them cursorily as they were bagged up – and on the traces of scented oil left on her body. She'd sent uniform round to the church to get hold of Florian's vial of chrism. A chemical comparison would clear a few things up – one way or another.

The doctor's unwavering blade drew a sharp longitudinal line through Katerina's shallow navel. The flesh parted greasily. Rose did her best to swallow her revulsion. It's just – just *meat*, she told herself. Just dead stuff, not a person, not a human.

What was human in Katerina had been snuffed out of this pale carcass some time ago.

The dry gleam of bowel. Ridged tissue, pale-veined viscera.

Matilda sniffed.

'You were hungry, weren't you, Katerina? Hadn't eaten.' She probed deeper, folding back the cut skin with care, wrist-deep in the woman's belly.

After a while she looked up at Rose.

'Nothing in her stomach, barely a thing in her gut at all.' Matilda shook her head. 'She didn't starve – she's skinny, but there're no signs of serious malnutrition – but she hadn't eaten for over a day. Goodness, she must have been hungry.'

Starved. Beaten. Strangled. Frozen. And then –

The faces moved in flickering sequence behind her eyes: Rakić. Brask. Florian. Her chest constricted. I'll nail you, she thought, fiercely. Whatever it takes, I'll nail you.

She became aware that Matilda was watching her. The doctor's eyes were soft with sympathy over the severe line of her mask.

'You'll make this right, Lauren,' she said. Nodded firmly. 'I know you will. You'll do what's needed – for poor Katerina here.' She set down her scalpel, let out a sigh. 'Now why don't you go wait outside, leave me and Katerina to it?' She looked down at the disfigured body. 'It's not going to get any more pleasant from here on in, I'm afraid.'

It was over an hour before Matilda stepped out of the lab into the brown-tiled waiting area, weary-eyed and absently rubbing alcohol into her hands.

Rose set down the files she'd been rereading and looked at the pathologist expectantly.

'As I said, you'll have to wait for my report for anything really conclusive.' Matilda dropped heavily into the chair opposite her. 'But you can be pretty sure about the cause of death. And there was something else.' She lifted her eyebrows. 'Something a bit odd.'

Rose hunkered forwards.

'Okay. You've got my attention.'

'Her ankle bone, of all things. The left one.'

'What about it?'

'It wasn't there.' Her eyes gleamed behind her spectacles. 'I thought at first it was an old surgical wound, sports-injury op, something like that – certainly a very neat job. But it was new, very new.'

'There was nothing in her medical record about it.'

'No. I took a closer look. The thing had just been cut out. No rhyme or reason that I could see. Cut out and stitched up, tidy as you like.'

'Post mortem?'

'My guess is yes. Really, I've never seen anything like it.' She took off her spectacles, rubbed at her eyes. 'And as you know, Lauren, dear, I've seen such an awful lot.'

Stripped of her surgical get-up – comfy and scruffy in a charity-shop sweater, corduroys and off-white trainers – Dr Matilda Rooke looked small and painfully vulnerable. As she got up to go, Rose laid a hand on the doctor's shoulder.

'You were right, Matilda,' she said. 'I'll make this okay. I'll – I'll finish this.'

Matilda slowly lifted her head. Replaced her spectacles. Looked up at Rose.

'I'm always right, my love,' she said.

Her warm, dry hand rested on Lauren's for just a moment.

In a way it was a relief. The missing bone: it was something real, something concrete. Weird, for sure – but a hard fact, too, something she could hold on to, hang an investigation on. Too much of this case had felt unreal, hallucinatory, played out in flickering scenes from a nightmare. *This* was as real as a scalpel-edge and a surgeon's textbook; this was the work of a man, not a monster.

Rose dialled the MCU office as she crossed the morgue car park to her car. A surly DS took her orders: an urgent query to Interpol, Europe-wide, Russia, Middle East, the Balkans – anything like this in the records, anything with surgery, bones removed, oil smeared on the body, the weird handmade clothes – anything, from any time, anywhere –

Just give me a lead, she thought. Just give me a way in.

As she was fastening her seatbelt, her phone buzzed back at her. A result? Quick work. She checked the message – it was from Hume.

Just a hyperlink. Nothing more. Not that she expected a kiss or a smiley face from the brusque DCI.

She hit the link.

Oh God.

HALLOWEEN COMES EARLY TO OXFORD. The banner headline filled the screen of her phone. She scrolled, stopped – oh Christ.

Katerina. Katerina's face – Katerina's head, dangling from Katerina's crooked dead hand.

It was a grainy shot, bad lighting, an awkward angle, but there was no mistaking it; this was no fake. Rose scrolled to the byline, already knowing full well what she'd see.

There it was: *Exclusive report and picture by OLIVER STEVENAGE.*

She closed the browser. Swore viciously.

How could she have been so bloody sloppy? And just after the bollocking she'd given Ganley, too. Stevenage, the slippery little bastard, must have taken the picture on his smartphone. What had she been thinking, to confiscate the camera and not frisk him for a phone? Made her feel old as well as stupid. Spotting a pap by his camera was as outdated as spotting a journo by the press pass tucked in the band of his trilby.

The flash that set her running after Stevenage had surely been from the camera, but he must have chanced a shot with his phone first. Then it struck her, painfully, humiliatingly, that there'd been no other light at the scene – except the narrow beam of her torch. So she'd not only let him photograph the scene with his phone . . . she'd bloody well lit it for him too.

She looked at her phone and waited.

It buzzed. *Incoming call: DCI Hume.* Here we go. With a tightening stomach, she hit the button to connect.

'Sir.'

'You've seen it?'

'Yes, and I —'

'Then can you explain to me, Rose, what the *fuck* you think you were doing inviting a *cunt* of a student journalist to take *fucking* photographs at *my* fucking crime scene?'

She closed her eyes, settled in for an old-fashioned bollocking.

'You can't be any madder about it than I am, guv,' she said resignedly.

She thought she could feel the phone vibrate with fury.

'Can't I? *Can't I?* You've no fucking idea how fucking angry I can be when some fucker makes a fuck-up of my fucking murder inquiry.'

'No, sir.'

'Jesus fucking Christ, Rose.'

'Yes, sir.'

It took Hume maybe five more expletive-strewn minutes to regain his temper. The last tirade ended with a long, shuddering, sulphurous sigh down the line, and a drawn-out 'Fu-u-uck'. A silence. Then:

'We've told the university to make them take that shit down pronto. They're on it right now, or they'd better be.'

'Stevenage'll love that, sir. A chance to start crying about the freedom of the press.'

A renewed flash of temper.

'Oh, I'm sorry, Rose, what would you rather we did, give him a fucking Pulitzer prize? Jesus.' A snort. 'Pull yourself together, Inspector. There's going to be an unholy shit-storm over this and I don't intend to take it alone. The press office has already gone into meltdown. Nationals have picked up on it.'

'I'm sorry, guv.'

'You will be. Oh, and they've given him a name, too, did you know that?'

'The murderer? What –'

'"The Trick or Treat Killer". Snappy, isn't it? Clever. Likely to catch on, I reckon.' She heard him grind his teeth. 'Fucking hell, Rose. You'd better put this right.'

'I will, sir.' She swallowed, nodded. 'You'll see. I will.'

But the phone was already dead.

The priest told him not to be afraid. And yet Little Mouse was afraid.

Little Mouse understood that suffering was necessary for martyrdom. And yet in the silence of his heart he prayed for it to end.

He prayed for his hunger to be sated, if only by a crumb of dry bread or a mouthful of fatty broth. He prayed for the chafing manacles to be taken from his wrists. He prayed for release. For freedom.

'With your deliverance into Christ,' the priest said, 'the heathen will be banished from our good land. All that we have lost shall be restored.' Little Mouse wondered how a creature as lowly as he could bring about such great events. But lessons had always come slowly to him. Perhaps it was not his role to understand. Perhaps God had another plan for him.

'Your soul is pure, child,' the priest said. 'Few indeed in this foul world are worthy of sacrifice. Few deserve the martyrdom of the fathers of the True Church.' He smiled. The priest smiled at him. Despite the cold, a part of Little Mouse warmed at the sight.

'Yours will be a glorious death, child,' he said. 'A glorious death.'

Chapter Eight

6 October

It wasn't right – morally, professionally, legally – to vent your frustrations on a suspect. But, sooner or later, every copper found themselves doing it. Rose drove into Oxford with Professor Matthew Brask squarely in her crosshairs.

This isn't about your fucking feelings, Hume had said. Rose swung her car into a space, jerking the handbrake sharply. Bloody right it isn't, she thought.

It's about lying to the police.

It's about the death of Katerina Zrinski.

It's about the *truth*.

Oxford was quiet, sunk deep in October grey. A few tourists hung around outside the Radcliffe Camera. Two students in scarves and skinny jeans hurried across the square.

She was nearly too late – she saw Brask climbing on to his bike outside the gate of All Souls. He looked sullen, preoccupied.

No time for tact.

'Professor!' she yelled. A flock of pigeons, startled into flight, rose in a clatter from the flagstones. For a second they obscured her view across the square – for a second she wondered if Brask might take the opportunity to run.

A part of her wished he would. There'd be a certain

clarity in that. Things were simpler when a case came down to hunter versus prey.

But when the birds were gone Brask was still there, leaning on his bike. His hair was unkempt, his eyes weary. A weight of guilt in his face.

As Rose approached, he stood his bike against the college railings and turned to her with an imploring look.

Yesterday Rose might have taken it to be sincere. Not today.

'Inspector Rose –' he began.

'I could nick you right now,' she snapped. 'Have you chucked into the cells at St Aldate's, how would that be? I could have you booted out of your cushy job. I could have you sent back to the States like *that*.' She snapped her fingers sharply in front of his face. 'You lied to me, Professor Brask.'

He nodded, his face pale.

'I didn't tell you the whole truth. And I want you to know, Inspector, I'm sorry.'

'Sorry you lied to me, or sorry you got caught?'

'Listen, Inspector Rose, I –'

'Call after call, text after text, from your phone to hers, from hers to yours.' She chopped the edge of her hand into her palm as she spoke. 'Voicemails, *seventeen* bloody voicemails over three months. But you say you weren't in a relationship?' She felt her heart racing, bit down hard on her anger. 'I think we need to have another talk, Professor.'

Brask nodded dumbly.

As they walked back through the porter's lodge and up the stairs of All Souls to Brask's office, Rose took careful note of the way the professor carried himself. His shoulders were hunched, his head lowered. He looked defeated – hopeless and helpless.

Grief could do that to a person, Rose knew. So could guilt.

In Brask's office she took a seat uninvited and as Brask took off his jacket she quickly took in her surroundings: what had changed since her last visit – and what hadn't.

He hadn't moved the picture.

Rose had assumed he would have, after she'd left. She'd pictured him hurriedly snatching it from the shelf, cramming it into a drawer or file, thanking providence that the pushy detective hadn't spotted it.

Instead, as he sank back into his office chair, he reached for it, took it down, considered it sadly – then passed it to Rose.

'You can take this,' he said. 'It's me and Katerina, with a group from the church. Five, six months ago.'

She took it from him, turned it over in her hands. Scrawled loopily on the back, *Cardiff, 5/13*. Again she looked at the image: the smiles, the sunshine.

When she glanced up at Brask his face seemed desolate, blasted by the weight of emotion. Again she wondered whether it was grief or guilt.

She didn't see any need for kid gloves.

'You look very happy together,' she said.

Brask's mouth tightened. He looked down at the floor.

'We – weren't.'

'Weren't happy?'

He looked up.

'Weren't together, Inspector.' Brask ran a hand through

his unkempt hair. 'You asked me if we were in a relationship – and I promise you, we weren't.'

Rose snorted impatiently.

'Semantics, Professor. Twist it how you like, there was something between the two of you. You were close – closer than you let on.' She crossed her legs, tilted her head. 'Why did you lie to me, Professor Brask?'

He shook his head, grimacing as though struck by nausea.

'I – I didn't.' He met her gaze. She saw in his expression how much that took – how much it cost him. 'I loved Katerina,' he said. 'I loved her, and she loved me, but a relationship? No.'

'Explain the difference.'

'She was –' Again the sickened expression. He wiped his thumb across his lips. 'She was with that animal Rakić. She took that commitment seriously.'

'Was that a sexual relationship?'

'I don't know – didn't want to know. I never asked.'

'You'd agree it seems likely, though.'

'I – I guess.'

'And how did that make you feel?'

Brask sighed.

'It drove me crazy,' he said. He leaned forwards in his chair, pressing his hands together between his knees. 'Listen, I'm not going to lie to you –'

'Again.'

'– and I know what you're asking me and what you want me to say. Did it make me mad that she was with Rakić, that she put him first? Yes. Of course it did.'

'At Katerina?'

'No. You didn't know her or you'd understand. I couldn't be mad at Katerina, not really. She was – she was wonderful. She only wanted what was best. What was right.'

'Mad at Rakić, then.'

Brask's eyes flashed momentarily.

'My God, yes. I'm a man, after all. And that *animal* . . .' He paused. 'Sure, I was mad. But mad enough to kill? No. No.' He shook his head firmly, said again: 'No.'

And I'm supposed to nod my head and smile and simply take your word for it, Rose thought with a flicker of anger. I'm supposed to take you for a stand-up Honest Joe because you speak my language and you once wore a priest's collar.

They always said on TV cop shows that a killer never *looks* like a killer – it's never the guy you expect. That was bullshit, Rose knew. Most of the time the killer looks *exactly* like a killer, and it's the guy you think it is nine times out of ten.

Dmitry Rakić looked like a killer. He had the profile, of course he did.

That was what Brask was banking on.

But it was a mistake to forget about that one time out of ten. That time the 'normal' guy was pushed too far. That time the 'mild-mannered' guy lost control for an instant. That time when someone – anyone – found something deep inside them that no one had ever dreamed was there. The time when an Everyman became a killer.

She looked at the professor, took in his long, firm jaw, his untidy dark hair, his downcast grey eyes. His jaw was shaded with patchy stubble – he'd shaved hurriedly that morning. The fine lines of his face bunched at the corners of his eyes and thickened where they creased his high brow. A smiler, then – and a worrier.

Killers nearly always looked like killers. Nearly always.

Rose stood up, pulled on her coat.

'There's no harm in telling you you're no longer "helping us with our enquiries", Professor Brask,' she said shortly. 'You're a suspect.'

'Inspector, I –'

'The prime suspect, in fact, in the murder of Katerina Zrinski.' She looked down at him coldly. *Maybe he's still lying, maybe he's not. Only one way to find out.* Rattle him, she thought. Keep up the pressure. Don't give him an inch – don't give him space to breathe. 'You lied to me, Professor. I'm going to find out what else you're not telling me. I'm going to dig out every dirty secret you have.' With her hand on the door handle, she added: 'I'm going to blow your life wide open.'

Didn't wait for him to reply. Back out into the hall – back out into the square, the city, the teeming grey rain.

Chapter Nine

Brask pressed the heels of his hands into his closed eyes until dizzying patterns swelled behind his eyelids. Dig all you want, Inspector Rose, he thought. Find all the secrets you can, broadcast them as far and wide as you please.

I don't give a damn, he thought. I just don't give a damn.

He straightened, rubbed at his aching neck. Hadn't slept. Hadn't eaten. That morning, in meetings, he'd been barely coherent – his colleagues must've picked up on it, if any of them had been listening.

It was how the old saints lived, he thought. Starving themselves, beating themselves, always searching for new ways to make life harder, new ways to suffer.

And why did they do this?

He bent stiffly, picked up the photograph Rose had left on the bench. When he did, he saw again Katerina's smile. Felt her warmth.

To atone for their sins.

Some of the details of Katerina's death had filtered through to him – from contacts in the community, from colleagues who'd read that goddamn rag of a student paper. The thought of her suffering bit deeply, and left him aching inside. He'd found himself asking all those desperate, uncomprehending questions – *How? Why? Who? What kind of monster could* do *a thing like this?*

The answer had been right there. Rakić.

Brask knew it had been crazy to hold out on DI Rose. He stood and shook himself. He'd thought, like a god-damn fool, that to tell the whole truth about Katerina: about how she'd longed to leave Rakić, about how she'd loved Brask, about all the conversations they'd had, and all the promises they'd made . . .

At the time, he'd thought that telling DI Rose all those personal things about Katerina would have been a betrayal.

He knew better now. He knew it more clearly, more sharply and certainly the more he thought about it.

The only way he could betray Katerina now was to stand in the way of the hunt for her killer. The only way he could help her was to do all he could to make sure that the man who took her life paid, and paid hard, for what he'd done.

DI Rose, Brask realized with a lurch of self-reproach, understood that. He cursed himself fiercely for not seeing it sooner.

The sound of approaching footsteps in the hall outside made him start. DI Rose again, he guessed – must've forgotten something. Come back to give him a little more hell.

It'd be no less than he deserved, he thought grimly.

He reached for the door handle, ready for the knock.

There was no knock.

The door crashed open, the jamb splintering free, the heavy edge of the door slamming into Brask's knuckles. He grunted and stumbled back, clutching at his desk for support.

The outline of a man blocked the open doorway. The strip light behind his shaven head reduced him to a black silhouette, impossibly tall, impossibly broad. As a reflex, Brask shrank back as the man moved purposefully forwards.

The door behind him banged closed, sagged on its hinges. The light through the blind at the window painted stripes across the man's impassive face.

'Brask.'

But it wasn't the giant who had spoken. A second man, a man the professor hadn't seen until now, who'd come into the room in the shadow of his taller companion, took a step sideways and then a step forwards. This second man braced himself springily, as though for a leap, or a fight.

Dmitry Rakić. White-faced with fury. Pulsing with intent.

When Rakić spoke again he did not scream or spit but quite calmly and levelly said her name, said, 'Katerina.' The name of the woman they'd both loved.

He forced himself to look Rakić in the eye.

'They know,' he said. Fear tautened his voice. 'There's no point in this. They know it was you.'

Perhaps Rakić did not believe the lie. Perhaps he did not understand. Perhaps he did not care. He stepped forwards. Brask took another step backwards. It wasn't the threat of violence that caused him to back away: it was Rakić's eyes. They were wild and senseless. They were the eyes of a madman.

A savage undercut to the ribs ripped the air from Brask's lungs. He doubled over, felt a fist close in his hair and heard himself cry out as his head was smashed into the corner of his hardwood desk. A gout of blood from his temple fell in a spatter to the carpet. He soon followed it to the floor, face first, his body jack-knifing as a boot thumped into his midriff.

Trapped in the space between his desk and the bookcase, awaiting another blow, another boot, a knife, a bullet, Professor Matt Brask prayed.

For justice. For forgiveness. For Katerina's soul.

He did not pray for mercy – it was too late for that.

Rakić's fist thundered iron-hard into the ribs beneath Brask's arm. He gagged, tasted blood. A word was hissed in Croatian; another blow glanced off the side of his neck, slamming his head into the floor. A heavy boot on his ankle ground the bones of his lower leg. He had no breath left to scream – and besides, what good would it do?

The crunch of bones, the rending of tissue, the howl of nerve endings, the panicked flaring of neurones – what was it, beside the torture of Katerina's loss? Beside the ache of her absence?

Through a screen of blood he made out the blurred shape of a weapon – a club or a broad blade. A hand gripped his throat.

The pain, Brask thought emptily, is nothing but a promise. A promise of release. A promise of peace.

He was not afraid. The hand at his throat tightened and Brask watched the weapon descend. If this is what God wills, he thought, then so be it – amen.

The room filled with light.

Rakić's shadow lifted from Brask's body and there was noise in the room, yelling, the thump of colliding bodies. Fists against faces, knees against ribs. Brask shifted position, trying to see what was happening. He grunted at the pain and pawed the blood from his eyes.

When he could see again his eyes revealed a surprise. Rakić was on his back, sprawled in the centre of the office. A short club lay a yard from his left hand but he seemed floored, utterly winded. The man blinked red-faced at the ceiling.

By the open door, Rakić's big companion was hunched in a struggle with another man, similarly shaven-headed but barely two-thirds the size. Brask realized, fuzzily, that he knew this man: Luka, his friend from the kitchens. The pair exchanged cramped blows, grappled grimly for superiority.

And now there were other noises, from outside, from the corridor: doors banging, screams, a thickly accented cry of 'Police!'

Brask heard Dmitry's hoarse mutter: 'Fuck.' Then he watched as the tattooed Croat rolled awkwardly to his feet and limped to the doorway.

Luka was on his knees, one forearm held stiffly across his face, holding on to the big guy's wrist with his other hand, his face twisted with pain and effort.

It was a David and Goliath scenario, thought Brask as he watched the mismatched men struggle. But Rakić tugged at the giant's shoulder, yelling in Croatian, gesturing to the open door. The gist was clear: *no time for fighting – let's get the hell out of here.* With obvious reluctance, the big man stepped back and dropped his hands. Luka, his strength just about exhausted, sagged like a broken puppet.

Rakić's fury wasn't quite spent. As his hulking enforcer

lumbered to the door and peered out warily into the corridor, the Croat turned sharply, jabbing a finger at Brask.

'Kill you,' he said. The English words were thick, clumsy in his mouth, but loaded with venom. 'Make – suffer. Make – scream.' He drew a stubby finger across his throat. 'For Katerina,' he said. Then he followed his companion through the door.

Brask heard their running footsteps recede.

Alive – saved. But why? For what?

He fought to focus on Luka. Had he been hurt? The wiry man was standing now, a wavering silhouette in the doorway. Brask's tongue was thick in his mouth, his throat burning. He wanted to say thank you. He reached out a hand.

Luka nodded, raised his own hand in salute.

'I will get help, Professor,' he said.

Sirens. Police sirens, shrieking in the street outside.

Brask's head lolled on the carpet. He was faintly aware of people gathering at the doorway, and of anxious voices. He tried to lift his head, to rise –

The room spun. He heard a voice, one he knew, urgent, forceful, rising above the rest. The voice said his name. It belonged to a woman. It belonged to DI Rose.

Brask blacked out.

'You were lucky.'

Two hours later. A quiet café across the square. A college handyman was fixing Brask's smashed door jamb while a cleaner sponged his blood out of the carpet. A police doctor had tried to take him in 'for observation'. Brask had refused.

Now he sat behind a cup of tepid herbal tea, rubbed his pounding head and swallowed down the obvious retort: *I don't* feel *lucky*.

DI Rose watched him searchingly from across the café table. The smell of her espresso made his stomach turn.

'So what's your take on it, Professor?' she asked. 'This was Rakić trying to shut you up? Stop you pinning Katerina's murder on him?'

Brask shrugged, blinked slowly.

'I don't know,' he mumbled. 'I don't know what to think. I *can't* think.'

Once the pain from his head, leg and ribs had dulled, the other pain, the *real* pain, had risen up within him like a tidal surge. Flooding everything.

He'd felt a pain like this once before. He'd prayed to God, then, to keep him from ever having to feel it again.

'The alternative,' Rose said thoughtfully, 'is that you're Dmitry Rakić's prime suspect, too.'

What was the use in denying it?

'He said he was going to kill me,' he said. 'As he was leaving. He was going to kill me, for – for her.'

Rose nodded.

She was hard to shake off, this sharp-edged DI, Brask thought. She'd beaten the uniformed cops to the scene by a minute – had been halfway across the square, she'd said, when she'd heard a shout: the college porter, Maurice, yelling blue murder and waving his rolled-up racing paper over his head.

The detective appeared to hesitate. Not something Brask would have expected from her.

'Go ahead,' Brask prompted. He mustered a bone-dry smile. 'Whatever it is you have to say to me, I'm sure I deserve it.'

Rose's dark eyes were a mystery.

'I'm not,' she said.

She opened her soft-leather case, drew out a plain cardboard file and laid it on the tabletop.

Brask stared. The pounding in his head intensified. He knew, right away, what was in the file. He knew what he'd see if he opened it.

'This isn't something I can force you to do,' Rose said quietly. She slid the folder towards him. 'It's something I'm asking you to do.'

'Why?' He slid back his chair, shook his head. His pulse pounded in his head. 'Why would I do that?' His stomach churned at the thought.

Katerina. Brask knew she was in the file. What was left of her.

Rose gave a fractional shrug.

'Because you loved her. Because you have to know what happened to her – however much it hurts.'

Brask fixed her with a look.

'I thought you figured I already knew what happened to her, Inspector,' he snapped. 'Aren't I your number-one suspect?'

Rose said nothing. Just sat, watched him coolly. The folder on the table between them seemed magnified, amplified, impossible to ignore.

'I can't,' Brask said. He moved his hand – brushed the cardboard with his fingertips.

He heard Rose say: 'You don't have to.'

You know that's not true, he thought. He picked up the folder.

What did he expect? What had he imagined? In waking nightmares he'd pictured Katerina's suffering, her terror, her helplessness – but this . . .

The lank hair knotted about the dead fingers of the hand. The fragile body forced into an unnatural posture, splayed horribly on the wheel of half-rotted wood. The dark-scabbed stump of the neck.

The paper-white skin. The glassy dead eyes.

'My God . . .'

There were six pictures in the file. Pin-sharp, unforgiving. Brutal.

As Brask looked at them, he felt the world fall away – the café and its hissing machines and background pop music, DI Rose's questions and penetrating stare, the rain that scrawled on the café windows, the empty square, the grandeur of All Souls, all of it, gone.

Only his grief remained.

He closed the folder, dropped it on to the table and covered his eyes.

'I'm sorry.'

The detective's voice seemed to come from a great distance away.

The questions began their relentless chorus again: *Who? How? Why?* After seeing those pictures they were even harder to stomach than they'd been before – God knows, it had never been easy, but now even the little certainties he'd felt so sure of lay broken into pieces. How could Rakić have done this? The man was a brute, an unreflecting thug with a hair-trigger temper and violence in his blood – but he was a man, after all.

No man did this, Brask thought. Whatever did this came straight from hell.

'Tell me what you're thinking,' Rose said.

But how could he? How could he put this into words? There was a horror to this, so gut-twisting and soul-deep that he could never hope to express it.

'It's . . . unreal,' he muttered. 'A nightmare.'

'I know.'

Something stirred in the back of his mind. Unreal, yes, but – familiar? He became conscious of an unfolding sense that he'd seen this somewhere before. And not in nightmares, either. How was that possible? It's just déjà vu, he tried to tell himself. But he knew that it wasn't, that it was something more than that –

An image began to take shape in his mind. From where? Florence, Valetta, Siena? A painting in a dusty, dimly lit hall – some place a thousand miles from here. Brask's usually razor-sharp mind was still blunted by the images of the horrific crime scene, but his thoughts slowly came into focus.

He could see it now. White skin. A timber wheel. A face of aching beauty. The cruelty of martyrdom. Saintly eyes turned to heaven, oblivious to the executioner's blade.

'St Catherine,' he said, without meaning to speak out loud.

Rose blinked.

'Who?'

In his iron chains, on his sweat-soaked cot, Little Mouse prayed. To Christ Jesus, to Mother Mary, to God the Father.

To Cerbonius, his lost abbot.

He prayed to understand what was happening to him. And though he knew it was shameful, he prayed to be saved.

The priest told him that he was a good boy with the pure soul of a true believer. The man burned incense, and lit candles, and sharpened his knives.

Though he tried to be deserving, when the priest was not there Little Mouse sometimes could not help but cry aloud.

On the third night the abbot returned. Again the beloved man was a warm, glowing spirit at the fringes of the boy's uncertain sight. Again Little Mouse felt the touch of his love and his kindness, unearthly and limitless.

Little Mouse wept and told the abbot that he tried to be good and grateful, but he was hungry, he said – so hungry, and so afraid.

The abbot smiled upon him and told him to have no fear.

'Faith, my child, will always triumph over fear. So long as it is strong.'

Though he trembled on his cot, Little Mouse nodded. He gulped down tears and swore that his faith was strong and true, that he would try not to be frightened.

But he confessed that he did not want to suffer any longer. He did not want to die.

The abbot smiled.

The abbot said that he would be spared – that Christ Himself would see to it that he would be spared, if only he proved himself worthy of His mercy.

'How?' Little Mouse begged to know. 'How?'

'It is not given to us to know the ways of God's judgement,' the abbot told him. 'It is not for us to question. Strange and wonderful is the mercy of Christ. Trust in Him, my child.' Again the abbot smiled. 'Love Him, praise Him and trust in Him. Yes, you will be spared – if only you prove yourself worthy.'

That day the priest had told Little Mouse that he was to endure the martyrdom of St Erasmus of Formium, and so be delivered into the arms of God.

The monastery had many books but reading had always been difficult for Little Mouse. His favourite tome in the library was a thick and richly coloured collection containing reproductions of some of the Church's most precious works of art. This is how he learned of St Erasmus.

In the early days of the Church, Erasmus was seized by the soldiers of the heathen emperor Maximian. His teeth were pulled from his head with pincers. His skin was scoured, his hands stuck with iron nails, his eyes gouged out and his body burned upon a griddle.

Then his stomach was slit open and his insides drawn out.

Remembering this now, Little Mouse shuddered with terror. But he must be strong. He must promise the Lord God that his faith cannot be broken, no matter how hard it is tested.

Whether he must endure pulled teeth or gouged eyes, he would not fail Christ and he would not fail the abbot.

He promised the abbot that he would prove himself worthy.

Chapter Ten

It might still be him. He could be the killer. He might be the mad-man who murdered Katerina and made a nightmare of her body.

Rose walked the long stone-flagged gallery four paces behind the limping Brask.

If you really believe that, she asked herself, would you be here right now?

They'd made the short walk across Oxford to Balliol College, where, according to Brask, there was a collection of works depicting the martyrdom of the fourth-century saint Catherine of Alexandria.

'Catherine is Balliol's patron saint,' Brask had explained.

There was probably a reason why a twenty-first-century educational institution felt the need to associate itself with an Egyptian murder victim from the Dark Ages, Rose thought. She'd never understand it, but there probably was one.

She hadn't much idea about St Catherine, full stop. She knew – from childhood firework displays – that she'd died, somehow, on a wheel. That was about it.

But she went along with Brask. Not because she really gave a damn about St Catherine or the paintings or Balliol bloody College. More to keep an eye on Brask himself – on this puzzling, contradictory American academic – or priest, or art historian, or whatever the hell else he turned out to be.

Murderer?

She held on to the thought – kept it fastened as if by a thread.

She'd keep a close eye on him, watch the way he moved, gestured, fidgeted, reacted. She'd listen to the way he spoke, even the way he breathed, searching for the things he said without saying anything, and seeing the things he gave away without meaning to. Rose thought back to the Zrinski girls' flat and how their secrets had slowly unwound from them.

You could learn a lot just by sticking around.

Brask had slipped into lecturer mode as they'd trudged together along Turl Street. Probably his way of coping – his idea of something safe, familiar.

'Catherine of Alexandria is a legendary saint, not a historical one.' He'd given her a sidelong look. 'That's our way of saying she probably didn't exist. No scholars mentioned her until the ninth century, long after her supposed death. But in the Middle Ages she was really all the rage.

'According to legend, young Catherine was gifted by God with extraordinary learning, able to defeat the emperor's most eminent scholars in theological debate. When the emperor – that's Emperor Maxentius, who certainly existed and was probably a pretty nasty piece of work – began persecuting Christians, Catherine led the protests. Brave girl! Inevitably she was captured by the emperor's soldiers. And in punishment –'

Brask broke off. Cleared his throat. When he resumed, his voice had lost its detached, sardonic quality.

'In punishment,' he said, 'she was bound to a spiked

wheel. When the wheel broke – thanks be to God,' Brask put in bitterly, 'Catherine was – was beheaded.'

Rose nodded. She was glad, now, she'd agreed to come along. 'What happened to her body?'

'Borne by angels to the summit of Mount Sinai,' Brask said, fluttering a hand mockingly. Beats being borne by Matilda Rooke to a Headington morgue, Rose thought. The professor went on: 'The monastery there claims to have her relics.'

'Relics?'

'Holy souvenirs. The monks at Sinai supposedly have Catherine's head and left hand. Historically, archaeologically, it's pretty unlikely, of course – but it's interesting to those of us who study the Church.'

Crossing Broad Street, they'd passed two students, a boy and a girl, who'd both recognized Brask: 'Hey, Professor!', 'Afternoon, Professor!'

Brask didn't strike Rose as the kind of tutor who'd insist on formalities – more of a call-me-Matt guy, for all his obvious erudition. These kids, she guessed, had called him 'Professor' not because they had to but as a sign of respect.

Quite something, considering the kids *she* had to deal with. Imagine a seventeen-year-old from the Leys calling her 'Detective Inspector'.

'Students of yours?'

'I don't have any students. Too highbrow for that.' Again the wry look. 'But I know Jake and Martha from the student history society. Oh, and the classics society, too. Bright kids.'

They turned in to the gates of Balliol.

'Here we are,' Brask said with a gesture. 'Balliol – it's stood here since 1263, if you can believe it. There was a Balliol College on this spot five hundred years before my country even existed.'

But Rose had stopped listening. She was a little tired of dates and historical facts, but that wasn't what had distracted her.

Rakić's man. He'd followed them.

She'd seen him in the periphery of her vision as they'd turned the corner into the college quadrangle: a skin-headed heavyweight ducking behind a parked car. She was damn sure it was the guy she'd seen with Rakić at the meadow. From Brask's descriptions, she bet the big bruiser was also one of the gang members who'd paid a visit to the professor's office.

She'd moved her hand sharply to her jacket pocket and tugged at Brask's sleeve with her free hand.

'Sorry – my damn phone's buzzing.' Glanced at the phone, faked a reaction. 'I'm going to have to take this,' she'd said with an apologetic grimace. 'Give me a minute?'

'Sure,' shrugged Brask.

She pressed the phone to her ear and quickly walked back in the direction they'd come. She paused at the car, a knackered old Nissan, where she'd seen Rakić's man. No sign. A narrow path between buildings led off to the right. Over the road were a lifeless-looking hedgerow, more parked cars, a looming sandstone building with a gated entrance.

Nobody.

Rose sighed and dropped her phone back into her

pocket. *Bloody hell*. She made her way back up the road to where Brask waited, leaning on the college railings. He looked – no, not happier, but more alive, somehow, away from All Souls and his little office.

'Not bad news, I hope?' he'd asked politely.

Rose – with difficulty – shook off her scowl. Fact was the big skinhead had spooked her. Brask, having been on the end of one serious beating, seemed pretty stoical – strangely, unsettlingly so – about the risk of receiving another. Maybe he felt he had it coming. Christ, Rose thought – what *was* it with Catholics and guilt?

The thread tugged: *maybe he's got something to feel guilty about*. But the thought was becoming harder to keep a hold on.

'No. Nothing serious.' *I hope*. She looked up at Balliol's towers. She wasn't going to tell Brask that she'd seen the skinhead skulking after them – not yet, anyway. It was unlikely he'd be in danger while they were in the open like this. Still, she decided to stick with the professor to see if any more of Rakić's henchmen lurked nearby.

'Come on, Professor. Let's go and find St Catherine. See what she can tell us.'

Rose followed Brask into the cold gallery. She didn't need to get deep into the exhibit before an unavoidable truth became clear: picture after picture after picture told her that the twenty-first-century murder of Katerina Zrinski was insane, sick, horrifying – but not unique. According to legend, a young woman had died in much the same way, 1,700 years before.

It was crazy, surely, to think that the two deaths could be connected – but did it make any more sense to assume that the uncanny similarities were nothing more than the result of mere chance?

No, Rose realized slowly, with a disturbing certainty that solidified as she moved from painting to painting. This was no coincidence.

The wheel on which, in these paintings, St Catherine died a hundred deaths – it was the same as Katerina's cartwheel. Though the structure in the field had been rough-hewn and crudely built, something fundamental in its shape and in the darkness of its purpose marked it out clearly as a twin of these medieval torture instruments.

A 'breaking wheel' Brask had said it was called. Designed – by who, Rose wondered, by what kind of sick mind? – to dislocate the bones and muscles of the body bound to its rim.

She noticed that some of the pictures caused Brask to quicken his pace as he passed them. It wasn't hard to see why. One showed the impassive executioner gripping Catherine by her hair as he prepared to strike off her head. In others, the saint raised her hands to greet a magnificent angel, descended from broken clouds to end her sufferings and deliver her to heaven.

A seventeenth-century Spanish painting made Rose catch her breath. Here, Catherine stood upright, clothed in red – and held her own severed head in her hand. An altarpiece, the information notice said. For people to look at as they prayed.

For what? she wondered. To what kind of God?

Rose caught up with Brask at the end of the gallery. He looked a little pale.

'I had no idea this kind of art could be so gruesome,' she admitted.

'Oh, sure.' Brask nodded, slipping readily back into the role of teacher. 'People talk about violent movies and video games nowadays – they have no idea. *This* stuff is hardcore.'

They headed back down the gallery, past the row of suffering saints.

'Christianity has always had a seed of violence in its core,' Brask went on thoughtfully. 'Steeped in blood, if you like. Starting with what happened to Jesus Christ – and going on from there. Look at the Isenheim Altarpiece, from the fifteen hundreds. By a guy named Grünewald. It's an image of Christ on the cross – but it's not beautiful, it's *awful*; the body is turning green, the skin is blistered with sores . . . Christ isn't just dying, He's *rotting*.'

'But why? What's the point? Where's all the love and peace I thought these things were meant to be about?'

'It's not *about* the violence.' Brask shrugged. He made a gesture that took in the row of paintings. 'It's about your response to the horror. Your pity, your consciousness of the martyr's suffering. When Caravaggio paints Christ being flogged – and, man, it looks like it *hurts* – he wants you to feel it. He wants you to feel Christ's pain, what He went through, for – for us.'

Rose stopped, turned back to the gallery.

'Caravaggio. Did I just see that name?'

'You did. Here.' He steered them further down the room. It was a small painting, one of the first they'd passed. 'It's a copy of Caravaggio's *Catherine*. Painted in

1599.' He looked at Rose's expression, grinned briefly. 'It's a little different, isn't it?'

Rose nodded. It certainly was. *This* Catherine didn't seem to be suffering – she stood beside a cruelly spiked wheel, she carried a blade, but her expression was hardly submissive. She was beautiful. And she looked like a girl you wouldn't mess with.

'Fillide Melandroni,' Brask said. 'Caravaggio's most celebrated model.' Another fleeting smile. 'And a prostitute.'

Rose raised an eyebrow. Takes more than that to shock a DI, she thought.

'Not very saintly,' she remarked, as they moved on.

'Sainthood,' said Brask, 'is a complicated thing.'

Not for the first time Rose wondered just how much this priest-turned-professor knew about the real world, the world beyond the seminary and the ivory tower. How much it had touched him. Whether it had left marks.

She remembered the picture she'd seen in his office: Brask with his arms around a pretty, dark-haired young woman. There had to be a story there.

They didn't talk much on the walk back to Brask's office. The paintings had added a new layer to the haunting parade of images this case had imprinted on Rose's mind. As for Brask – well, who knew what was going through his head?

He'd told her there was no need for her to accompany him back to All Souls but she'd insisted. She gave an excuse about double-checking the loose ends and taking a last look for evidence of Rakić's brutal intrusion. Of course, she knew, there was no hope of nailing Rakić on an ABH charge – even now he'd be working the estates, drumming up enough watertight alibis to clear Dr Crippen. She kept a close eye out for any more of his henchmen as they made their way back to the college.

Brask's corridor smelled of disinfectant and sawdust.

'Listen, Inspector, you should get back to –' Brask began.

He stopped in mid-sentence.

His office door was open.

The repairmen could have left it open after fixing the jamb. Perhaps the explanation was that simple. But Rose's gut said otherwise, and she guessed that Brask's had as well.

She took the lead, pushing Brask back with a forearm as she moved cautiously forwards. She was sharply aware, all at once, of her aching ribs and bruised cheekbone, her wrung-out muscles and the trauma her body had been through in the last few days. If Rakić was here, spoiling for a fight – what the hell was she going to do about it?

There was no noise inside the room. No sound of movement. White wood glue gleamed on the door frame. Rose blinked as the smell of TCP grew stronger. There was another smell, too, an undertone to the disinfectant reek, something familiar –

She looked up.

She hardly had time to gasp before Brask darted right alongside her.

'What the hell?'

What the hell, indeed, Rose thought. It was suspended from the door lintel in a frame of taut brown twine. It glistened unwholesomely with grease, or oil.

Rose ducked carefully under the twine, shaking her head as she examined the thing. She tried to be as clinical as she could about it but her revulsion was instinctive.

'Bones,' she said. 'Animal bones.'

Two ribcages, bound together with leather ligatures. Brask moved to touch it.

'Don't,' Rose warned. 'It's evidence.' *But of what?*

Within the rough sphere formed by the ribcages, eight more bones – irregularly shaped but with cleanly broken ends – were knotted together in a ragged star shape.

She looked at Brask.

'Mean anything to you?'

He shrugged.

'A message, a warning of some kind?' He shook his head. 'I don't know, Inspector, I really don't. I guess one of Rakić's guys came back and . . .' He tailed off, frowning. He didn't seem afraid, Rose thought – more annoyed by being presented with a puzzle he couldn't solve.

She knew the feeling.

'Religious?' she guessed. 'A curse, or, or –'

'Black magic?' Brask smiled grimly. 'I'm not saying people don't believe some way-out stuff, Inspector. There's more diversity in the world's religions than you could fit in a hundred books. But I think it's more likely that this is somebody trying to frighten me – somebody who's watched *The Blair Witch Project* a few too many times.'

Rose could have slapped herself. She was meant to be the streetwise, savvy one, the veteran copper with her feet on the ground – and here she was being handed a reality check by a bloody theology professor. *A curse? For Christ's sake, Rose.*

She made a quick call to HQ for a team to take the – the *whatever it was* in as evidence and give the place a sweep.

'Just to be sure,' she said to Brask.

God, she was tired. The *thing* dangling from the twine reeked of blood.

It reeked of death.

Maybe it was nothing. Maybe it was a warning from Rakić or maybe it was just a joke. An early Halloween prank by a student.

Chase every clue, run down every lead, she thought. Just like you promised Katerina.

His wrists were raw from the shackles. His aching belly rebelled against the sweet stench of the chrism slathered on his skin.

The priest murmured litanies in Latin. The stropped knife blade glowed silver-black in the candlelight. Soon, Little Mouse understood. Soon the real pain would begin.

Little Mouse saw the abbot on the frayed edge of his murky sight. He knew the beloved man had come to give him strength.

The abbot told him that it was the sacred duty of the faithful to make sacrifices. The abbot told him that his suffering would be a gateway to a greater glory.

Still Little Mouse whimpered as the knife blade touched his skin.

The abbot asked, 'Would you fail your God and saviour?'

'No,' Little Mouse said. 'I will not fail my God.'

The abbot asked, 'Would you not gladly give up your life to restore the treasures of our order and the glory of the True Church?'

'I would, I would,' Little Mouse said weakly. 'I would give my life for His glory.'

The abbot grew angry, as the boy had never seen him angry in life, and spoke with hatred, as the boy had never heard him speak.

'You must resign yourself to suffering and death, child, as did the martyrs of old,' the abbot said. 'For how else is the order to be resurrected? The True Church rightly glorified? The unworthy Serb to be driven howling from our holy land?'

Little Mouse felt the sting of the knife edge. He felt warm blood spill across his jutting hip bone. The pain sang through him and as it did, it silenced his fear.

Through tears he cried out: 'I shall! I shall give all I have to give to restore the order! I shall drive out the Serb! In death or in life, by the power of my faith I shall!'

He screamed the name of Abbot Cerbonius.

He heard the clatter of the knife falling to the concrete floor.

The abbot vanished from his sight. All Little Mouse could see was the priest. The old man's hollow cheeks were wet with tears.

For a second Little Mouse was smothered in the malodorous black of the priest's robes. He felt the press and scrape of metal on his bones – and then he was free.

Free, the weeping priest declared, to stand with him against Satan and the Serb. Free to help him in his devotions, free to restore the True Church to its throne.

Little Mouse had proved his faith unbreakable, the priest told him. He had survived his trial as strong as tempered steel. He will be more than a tool of Christ: he will be His blade.

'You are free, my son.' The priest kissed him. 'Finally and truly free to do the work of God.'

Chapter Eleven

10 October

For a gangland psycho, Dmitry Rakić lived a pretty quiet life. But then, Rose reflected, his girlfriend was dead and half his mates were banged up at St Aldate's on trafficking charges – what was there for him to do? Rose popped open a packet of crisps. Went on watching his windows.

Three days she'd been on stakeout. To begin with – for the first day – she'd railed against it, knowing that sitting on her arse in a parked car was no job for a bloody DI, knowing that Hume, damn him, was punishing her for letting Olly Stevenage grab his smartphone shots at the crime scene. She'd brooded on it as she'd sat watching Rakić's flat, worked herself into a fury over it – given Angler a proper earful when he'd come to relieve her at quarter to midnight.

The unshaven DS had grunted something about 'Time of the month, is it, guv?' as he'd peeled back the cellophane on his corner-shop Cornish pasty.

By now she was settled into the job. Not happy – but focused, clear on her objectives, committed to getting all she could from her hours of watching, watching, watching . . .

Rakić did his own shopping – bog roll, milk, bread from the Polish corner shop. Plus a lot of bottles from the off-licence further up the street. He was drinking hard, it seemed, wasn't eating a lot. Had a cleaner, a trim young black girl who came on Tuesdays. She'd checked out okay: on a student visa from Mozambique, training as a nurse at St Michael's. Rakić watched a lot of TV, often late into the night. He took walks, after midnight, to nowhere in particular. Didn't seem like he was looking after himself too well; he looked unslept, dishevelled.

Guilt. Grief. Who knew?

But then, he wasn't stupid either, Rose knew. Stupid gang leaders didn't stay gang leaders long. What with Katerina and the drugs bust in the Leys – not to mention the ruckus at All Souls – he had to know the police would be all over him. Rakić was treading carefully.

The living-room light in the flat went out. The bathroom light went on. Rose sighed. *What a bloody week.*

St Aldate's might have been as full as a high-season B&B with dodgy Leys faces but it was starting to look like a lot of work for sod-all result. Rakić ran a tight ship; no one was talking. Big Nitić, the thug who'd cracked her ribs and dangled her over the stairwell, was going down for GBH, and based on the gear they'd seized from the estate they could maybe nail a handful of others on intent to supply – but these were pretty slim pickings, a poor return on a high-risk investment. And no one seemed to know a bloody thing about Katerina Zrinski.

Hume was going spare.

It didn't help the investigation that Professor Matt Brask had dropped out of the frame. His alibi, an international symposium in York over the days in which Katerina went missing and was killed, had checked out.

Yes, Rose was glad that Brask wasn't a killer. He seemed

like a decent guy and she was happy that her initial suspicions had been unfounded. But it was another avenue closed off, another dead end. She was running out of leads.

They were getting a lot of calls – that was true. No shortage of hoaxes and pranks; more trolls, time-wasters and sickos than they knew what to do with. Just last night uniform had rushed to Wadham College at half-two in the morning – a first-year student had rung 999 in a state of hysteria, reporting a severed head in his bed.

A mannequin's head, it turned out, soused in tomato ketchup.

The poor lad had been in bits. Next morning three guys from his block were all over Twitter and Facebook, crowing about the 'classic' prank. It was just 'banter', they told the WPC who'd paid them a visit.

The chief super was leaning on the university to get the little bastards slung out.

All this was against a wearying backdrop of hard-boozing students in Halloween fancy dress, gruesome fly-posters for this college's 'Murder Ball' or that club's 'Trick or Treat Social', zany Halloween-themed cocktails in the local bars . . .

And all the while young Mr Oliver Stevenage kept up a torrent of vitriol against the force, the investigation and Rose herself.

She had the latest copy of the student paper on the passenger seat. Strewn with crisp crumbs and marked by spilt coffee. It was no less than the rag deserved. Angler had brought it for her – 'Case you get caught short,' he'd grinned coarsely.

Stevenage's leader column had had her seething.

This newspaper, he'd written, *fully acknowledges the benefits –
cultural and socio-economic – brought to Oxford by the vibrant
law-abiding East European community. We hold no brief for the
far-right agenda; we are not interested in a racist witch-hunt.*

*But when the Thames Valley Major Crimes Unit investigation –
under the panicky leadership of Ms DI Lauren Rose – allows
members of an immigrant crime ring to commit perhaps the most
wickedly vile crime in Oxford's history, making no arrests in the
case and leaving the only suspect – a tattooed Balkan hoodlum – to
swagger about the streets unimpeded and unquestioned, we have no
hesitation in saying that the force is failing in its duty to our city, to
the safety of the public and to Katerina Zrinski.*

If you didn't know better, you might almost think he
gave a damn. She'd thrown down the paper thinking that
Stevenage had almost achieved the impossible: making
her want to defend Dmitry Rakić.

National press were making their presence felt, too.
Crime reporters from most of the major dailies had been
nosing around headquarters. So far Hume had kept them
away from her – or her away from them.

She shifted in her seat for the thousandth time, trying
in vain to get comfortable. Took a mouthful of tepid
bottled water and wondered whether the corner shop on
Davenport Road would be open yet.

She checked her watch: barely eight. The light of a TV
screen had glowed in Rakić's window all night. All quiet
on the Western Front.

Her phone went off like a grenade.

'Christ.' She laughed at herself, at her own jumpiness –
her dad wouldn't have known whether to laugh or cry,
seeing her startled out of her wits by a bloody ringtone.

Fumbled for the phone in her bag, hit the green button.

'Rose here.'

'Ma'am?' She knew the voice — struggled to place it. 'Ma'am, it's PC Ganley.'

That was it: the awkward copper who'd made a bollocks of her crime scene. She hardened her voice, only barely aware that she was doing so.

'What is it, Ganley? Something up with your radio?'

'No, ma'am.' His voice wavered as though on the brink of breaking. Poor lamb, she thought uncharitably. Someone steal your BMX? Beat you up for your lunch money? She'd heard Phillips say that, with some young coppers, when they said 'ma'am' they really meant 'mummy'. There was something in that.

'Then what the hell's the matter, Constable?'

'There's something — something I think you should see, ma'am.'

Rose's skin prickled.

Oh God.

'It's —' The PC paused. She heard him gulp. Then he said: 'Ma'am, it's another one. Ma'am — the bastard's done it again.'

Rakić would hear the squeal of tyres and the urgent rev of the engine but Rose didn't give a shit about that now. This had nothing to do with Rakić — oh Christ, *none* of this had anything to do with Rakić, none of it ever had — she'd known it, she'd *known* it.

The man had been under the closest surveillance for three damn days, and now another innocent person lay dead.

Rose slammed her palms against the steering wheel. That stupid, pig-headed bastard Hume! And Phillips, with his certainty, his self-satisfaction, his know-it-all sneer –

All this time the murderer had been out on the streets, out in the open, stalking his victim. This was the time they might've got him; this – when he'd broken cover, was taking risks – had been their opportunity. And where'd she been? Eating bloody crisps and watching an insomniac thug drink himself stupid in front of the TV.

It was still early, the traffic starting to build up but not yet at its rush-hour peak. She jumped a red light on the Botley Road and gunned the engine hard down the A34. PC Ganley had given her a location south of the city. A field, he'd said. A field, and a stand of trees.

When she pulled up on the worn verge of a nowhere B-road a little way east of Boars Hill, the first faces she saw were those of DI Leland Phillips and DCI Morgan Hume. Ganley had told her, with an apologetic dip in his voice, that the pair of them would be there – 'but I thought you ought to be told, ma'am,' he'd added.

It was a snub, an obvious signal that she was being side-lined. Wasn't this *her* investigation? On another day she'd have leapt out of her car spitting fire.

Not today.

Phillips was white-faced. Hands in his pockets to hide the shakes. Nothing but pride keeping his chin up. Hume, meanwhile, simply looked knackered, utterly spent – twenty years older than the dynamic DCI she'd seen the day before.

Rose hadn't time to hold anyone's hand — least of all her boss's.

'Guv. What have we got?'

Hume shook his head.

'God knows.' A drawn-out sigh. 'Fu-u-ck. Go and have a look.' He pointed over to the police cordon at the edge of the stand of spindly birches.

Rose gave herself no time to think, to wonder, to imagine. She headed off at a brisk pace across the yellow-ish sheep-cropped grass.

Phillips called after her: 'Brace yourself, Rose.'

Rose tried to ignore him. Walked on towards the shivering trees. Whatever it is, it can't be worse than Katerina, she told herself as she ducked under the twanging police tape.

She was wrong.

There was a D-shaped clearing on the edge of the wood, like an inlet cut into a coastline. Rose stood in its middle, her nostrils filled with the smell of blood. The semicircular curve of pale trees hemmed in her horizons and drew her gaze naturally towards a central point – the point straight ahead of her.

She faced it. She stared it down.

It had been a man, once. Now it was a smear of deep red with bared white teeth. Raw flesh against grey bark. Twisted hands cupped limply around the clean head of an iron nail.

Rose moved towards the thing. The leaf mould was spongy beneath her feet and smells of rot and fungus mingled with the metallic stench of blood.

He'd been skinned. He looked like a thing on a

145

butcher's counter. His blood-red flesh was dotted with small black flies. His arms had been wrenched over his head, his hands fixed to the tree trunk with a single nail. He was oddly dressed, robed in a heavy, greasy fabric – an untreated animal hide, Rose guessed. She thought of the animal bones left in Brask's office.

She took a step nearer, leaned in for a closer look –

The realization hardened quickly in the pit of her stomach: no, not an animal hide. She gulped down a mouthful of bile. It was the man's own skin, draped across his shoulders, coiled about his waist and bound in a loose knot in front like a loincloth.

A wide bolt of hessian, marked with black blood, hung round the man's neck. Its ends dangled to the floor.

Rose felt the blood rush from her head, but she steadied herself. She forced herself to lift her eyes and meet, again, the dead stare. All humanity had been flayed from the face, the nose, brows, lips torn away. And yet –

And yet there was a terrible, unbearable expressiveness in the muscles and tendons that remained. It spoke of horror. Of despair. Of pain.

She'd wait for Matilda Rooke to give the official verdict but, on looking into the staring lidless eyes of the thing nailed to the tree, Rose already knew for sure: the skin had been ripped from live flesh. Whoever had done this had done it to a living, breathing man.

She knew it, but she couldn't contemplate it. This astonishing cruelty. The inhuman horror of it. She swore under her breath and stepped back. Took a last look at the skinless skull frozen in a silent scream. Turned away.

*

Hume and Phillips talked her through what they knew.

'David Norfolk, forty-eight years of age.' Hume, slumped in the front seat of Phillips's car like a pile of dirty washing, wagged a driver's licence wearily. 'Lived locally, if this is up to date.'

'We found that by the tree,' Phillips supplied. 'Couldn't miss it, really. No accident – he wants us to know who these people are.'

'Like with your Miss Zrinski.'

Rose said: 'It's the same guy.'

It wasn't a question.

'We're running checks on Mr Norfolk,' Hume said. 'Older than Katerina Zrinski, different sex, different nationality. Maybe they've something in common but my guess is not.'

'No pattern,' Phillips put in self-importantly. He'd recovered some of his old bulletproof arrogance.

Rose murmured: 'Yet.'

They were quiet for a few moments. And Rose knew what Hume and Phillips were thinking. It was the same thing she had herself been thinking as she walked away from what was left of David Norfolk. A phrase that loomed above them as large as the horizon but no one dared utter. It was always the way. Her oldest brother, Michael, had told her about it; he'd been a DC down in Wandsworth, back in the early nineties, when some nutter had made a name for himself stabbing sex workers. Of course it was all over the papers but at HQ it was like a dirty word.

Serial killer.

The thing no one wanted to say, wanted to admit. The bleak reality no one dared confront.

Hume rubbed at his face with both hands. In front of her, in the driver's seat, Phillips was pinching colour back into his cheeks.

'What next, guv?' Rose prompted. Was she the only one with a sense of urgency? Could no one else see that it was only a matter of time before this happened again? Another innocent tortured and defiled. Another horror nailed to a wheel or a tree in an Oxford meadow.

Hume looked at her. An old man, she thought, bitterly, resentfully. A tired, beaten-up, defeated old man.

Did he understand what he'd done? Did he realize that by single-mindedly going after Rakić, by letting his own prejudices lead him by the nose . . . did he know what that had cost David Norfolk?

Of course he bloody well did. It was written all over him. Well, she hoped it made him sick.

'Any ideas, Inspector?' he said.

Rose felt her blood rise. Her stomach clenched like a fist.

Now *it's my case*. Now *you need my help*. She was on the brink of yelling in the old copper's face: *Why wasn't I called in straight away? Why did you think this was a job for your fucking boys' club?*

The radio crackled. Hume took the call.

A report from the university, Rose heard. Another body. This one on a roof.

One name, one face sprang sharply into Rose's mind: Brask. She was out of the door and running for her own car before Hume had said a word.

Little Mouse and the priest kept to the dark places.

'Christ's light burns brighter to the soul in shadow,' the priest had muttered cryptically.

Many had come to the village from the towns to the east, burned out and brutalized by the rogue Serb units. They slept in the ruins of the monastery. Little Mouse saw their pale faces at the windows. They were hungry, he understood. Hungry, wounded, sick and homeless.

The priest called them izbjeglice *— refugees.*

If his country wasn't delivered from the demon Serb, none would survive. The True Church would fail. Little Mouse understood this now.

They watched the woman, Olga, move among them. To some she brought baskets of food, just as she had brought to the priest's hut. To others she gave blankets or wood to make a fire. And where people were hurt, she helped as best she could, changing bandages, supplying medicine, all the while murmuring kind words, words of comfort.

The priest's pale eyes shone like moons as he watched.

'A saint,' he whispered, over and over. 'A saint.'

This Little Mouse did not have to be told. When he turned his head and let the image of the woman filter through the black smudges at the edge of his damaged vision, she glowed like a burning brand. A holy light. Christ's light.

A most special soul, he thought. A most special and deserving soul.

A saint.

Chapter Twelve

It felt like a cross between a train crash and a rock festival.

'Police. Move aside, please. Police. Make room.'

With her sharp elbows and her hard-edged copper's voice, Rose forced her way through the crowd of students. There was a sense of dread here, she felt, real fear in some of the upturned faces – but there were rubberneckers, too, gawping, laughing and taking photos with their phones.

She'd seen it as soon as she'd turned into Radcliffe Square: a black silhouette on the roof of the building they called the Camera, perched at an awkward, ungainly angle, like a giant crow against the morning sky.

Brask had been her first thought – but if Brask was in danger it was Dmitry Rakić who was the threat, and Rakić hadn't been anywhere near the university. She was sure of that, at least.

Then she'd thought of Olly Stevenage. He'd managed to make an enemy of Rakić, back in Katerina's meadow, but for a guy like the Croatian gang leader the kid was surely small fry, an irritant, a mosquito bite – not worth going to any trouble for.

But the killer might be of a different mind. It was anyone's guess how many people in Oxford Stevenage had managed to piss off. Maybe – not knowing who he was dealing with – he'd pushed his Trick or Treat Killer too far, too many times.

Rose reached the front of the crowd and squinted up at the unsettling shape. It was cloaked in black cloth; Rose noted with a rush of nausea that under the cloak its proportions were out of whack, the limbs misshapen, the pose unnatural, the angle of the head all wrong.

Whoever had beheaded Katerina Zrinski and flayed the skin from David Norfolk had done a real number on this poor bastard, she thought.

A paramedic balanced precariously on a roofer's ladder, trying to make his way up the domed roof to where the cloaked body was fixed. He was a lean guy, bearded, with a climber's build. In the grip of a cold, aching tension, Rose watched him fumble for a handhold. He was four storeys up, forty metres or so off the ground. One slip and he was history.

All around her the university security team were doing an amateurish job of trying to disperse the heaving crowd of students. But Rose was barely aware of the shouts, shoving and juvenile heckles. In her mind she was up there with the paramedic – with him, and with whoever was under that forbidding black cloth.

The paramedic was off the ladder now, inching his way up the Camera's ridged dome. Rose tried to zero in on him, see what he was seeing, feel what he was feeling. You think they're alive under there, don't you? she thought. Or maybe you just hope they are. Because there's always a chance, right? That's why you do what you do. You know there's always a chance. You haven't lost hope.

Rose watched the man climb, and burned with something like admiration and something like envy. She couldn't find any hope for the poor figure cloaked in black.

She glanced across to the foot of the ladder where the man's colleagues were gathered anxiously by the open doors of a backed-up emergency ambulance. An approaching fire-engine siren skirled over the hubbub. The man on the roof stayed calm, moving inch by inch. Rose could see the paramedic's mouth moving as he drew close to the cloaked figure: telling whoever was under there that things would be okay, that he was there to help.

Silence settled on the crowd as the paramedic steadied himself and made sure of his footing. The black cloak fluttered gently in the breeze. A camera clicked. Someone at Rose's shoulder murmured something, maybe 'Oh God', maybe 'Please, God'.

The paramedic extended his arm. Rose realized that she was holding her breath.

When the man, feeling beneath the cloak – for a pulse to check, for a hand to hold – uttered a loud exclamation, the crowd jerked, as one, like a startled animal. When the man yanked his hand back from the cloak Rose saw that it glimmered red with blood.

Someone in the crowd screamed; someone else swore. One of the paramedic's colleagues started up the ladder. But Rose's gaze was on the cloaked figure; she'd seen it sway at the man's touch and now she watched in horror as its balance shifted, as it see-sawed on its base, as its centre of gravity lurched –

As it slipped. As it fell.

The paramedic grabbed and missed as the figure skidded down the domed roof, painting a gaudy stripe of blood across the copper. The crowd stirred, split, broke. A tumult of voices, a thunder of footsteps, screams as the body struck the guttering in a burst of dark-pink spray – a sudden, heart-stopping silence as the body bounced, looped into the air.

There was a panicked scramble as the crowd surged back. Spinning in free fall, the body dropped towards the Camera's stone steps.

Only Rose moved forwards. Fat red spots spattered the steps. She was at the forefront of the crowd when with a sickening crunch of bone and tissue, the body hit the ground.

It barely bounced. It rolled a few inches, heavily, with a thick, liquid gulp.

It lay still – angled between steps, half-draped in blood-drenched black. The broken ends of red bones jutted out.

Rose let out a strangled noise: a sigh, a groan, a rattling cry of release.

Not a man, not a woman. A pig. A pig's carcass, nicked from a slaughterhouse, bought from a butcher, whatever –

She closed her eyes, pressed trembling fingertips to the bridge of her nose. Not another murder. Not another victim.

When she opened her eyes all hell was breaking loose. She'd thought coppers could swear, but they had nothing on the rangy paramedic, who jumped down from the roofer's ladder and spat a fearsome mouthful of abuse at the nearest gaggle of wide-eyed students. *Fucking bastard student cunts think it's a fucking joke* . . . Rose felt bodies push past her, against her, jostling for a look at the shattered carcass in its pool of blood. The clicking of camera-phones sounded like the descent of a swarm of insects. There was laughter, breaking from the silence like water from a breached dam – the wild laughter of relief and embarrassment.

Fucking Halloween.

A part of Rose told her to clear the square, secure the scene, protect the evidence. There'd been a serious offence committed here; this was more than a prank, this was a grievous waste of police time. This was a crime scene. This was no place for stupid, sniggering, snap-happy students.

But another part of her told her to just get the hell out of there. She had a *real* crime to deal with.

This was the part she listened to.

As she elbowed her way back through the milling fringes of the crowd, Rose heard a voice she knew. American accents were ten-a-penny in Oxford – tourists, visiting academics, imported postgrads – but this one was distinctive: politely authoritative, ringingly earnest. She looked over. Brask was in conversation with a confused-looking PC and the bald-headed man she'd found him talking to on her first visit to All Souls. Rose moved closer.

'– big feast, for students, very great, very expense.' The bald man was agitated, seemingly on the verge of tears. 'This pig, my pig, from my freezer. For the feast! Stolen, stolen, for –'

The young PC tried to interrupt: 'Now, sir, you say –'

'– for this *joke*,' the man wailed and wrung his hands.

Brask broke into the conversation again: 'Luka, it's all right. The college will cover the costs. There's been no serious harm done –' He glanced up, saw Rose. Managed a polite, harried-looking smile. 'Inspector! How are you?' He motioned for her to join the mismatched little group.

The young constable touched his cap respectfully as she did so; the bald-headed man gave her a grim-faced nod.

'Inspector Rose,' said Brask with a gesture, 'this is Luka, a cook in the All Souls kitchens.'

'Yes – we met briefly. Pleased to meet you.' The man's handshake was solid and brief. 'Now – is there a problem here?'

'I don't think so, ma'am,' put in the constable. 'The pig was apparently in the custody of this gentleman when it was stolen.' He allowed himself a half-smile. 'He's a bit upset about the whole thing.' Glanced over to the throng on the Camera steps. 'Not very appetizing now.'

Luka began to speak – not impressed, it seemed, by the policeman's flippant tone – but Rose cut him off.

'I'm sorry about the inconvenience to you, Mr – ?'

'Savić.'

'– Mr Savić, and the college may be entitled to a payment through the criminal compensation system. I assure you we'll be conducting a full inquiry into what happened here today.' She turned from Luka to the PC, caught his eye and nodded. *All yours, Constable.*

As she started to move away, Brask touched her arm.

'Luka,' he said, 'was the man who intervened the other day. When that animal Rakić and his thug were –' Brask

155

winced slightly at the memory – 'were giving me a beating.' He glanced at Luka. His expression was inscrutable. 'I believe he saved my life.'

'It was very brave of you,' she said to Luka.

It was another rote response. She didn't have time for this. That desolate field, that desolate thing nailed to a tree were waiting for her.

And if she didn't get a move on, Phillips would be all over it. She realized with an odd sensation that this had moved beyond office politics. It felt more like betrayal – or theft. This case was hers. Katerina, David, St Catherine, Brask and all – it was *hers*.

With another nod to the PC, she was off.

To her irritation, Brask jogged after her.

She didn't slow, didn't turn her head. She knew what Brask wanted. He wanted an update, and she had nothing. Nothing that would make him feel better, anyway. Brask fell into step with her. Together they left the emptying square and turned into Brasenose Lane. A tough character to shake off, Professor Brask, Rose thought, once he takes hold. Katerina had found that out.

'I was wondering,' the professor said, 'what progress you've made on – on the case. The St Catherine connection –'

'Dead end, I'm afraid.' She forced herself to be brusque. Maybe it wouldn't hurt to talk over the latest killing with Brask – the guy knew things. The similarities between Katerina's killing and St Catherine's execution had been interesting. And talking to Brask beat trading put-downs with Phillips. But there wasn't enough time. Interviews had to be taken while the memories were fresh, evidence had to be collected and reports pored over. There was never enough time.

They reached Rose's rain-spotted car. She gave Brask a handshake and a cordial goodbye — that was all. Climbed in and through the streaked window glass watched him walk away.

As she started the engine, she saw a silhouette stir at the edge of a dark-brick building across the street. A man's dim profile poked from a hood. It was turned her way.

Someone watching.

On reflex she bolted from the car. She was fast, but by the time she crossed the street the silhouette had slipped away. She jogged over to the building without much hope. When she reached the corner there was no one there. No trace of anything or anyone.

Rose wasn't surprised, but she sighed anyway.

She replayed the lines of the figure. She didn't have more than a half-seen silhouette to go on, but there was something about his stance, his build, his demeanour . . . He'd looked a lot like Dmitry Rakić.

Chapter Thirteen

The leafless outer branches of a hawthorn tree knocked insistently against the kitchen window frame. The stubbled field beyond was dotted with black rooks and white gulls. Rose sat at the kitchen table with both hands cupped around a cup of tea. She wished it was something stronger.

'I hope you're happy,' said Maureen Norfolk. Her heavy jaw jutted. Her eyes were red-rimmed behind thick glasses.

Rose looked down at the table.

'Not at all, Mrs Norfolk,' she said. 'Believe me. Not at all.'

'Well, why *should* we believe you? I'll never believe another word the police tell me. Three days ago we told you David was missing – three days! And what did we hear from you lot? Doing everything we can, you said. Following all available leads, you said. What a load of rubbish. Nothing but a lot of lies.'

'Mrs Norfolk, I can assure you –' Rose began, knowing she was whistling in the wind.

Helen, the elder of the family's two daughters, stabbed the tabletop noisily with a fingertip.

'Do you know what they asked her? Those policemen what came?' She made a revolted face. 'They asked our mum if our dad had been having an affair. They thought he'd run off with some other woman. That was the best they could do.'

'Our dad never would.' Alice, fourteen, was quieter, the shy one. But her voice quivered with anger. 'Never.'

'Of course he wouldn't, Alice,' Mrs Norfolk nodded. Fixed Rose with a fiercely disdainful look. 'And now they send this slip of a girl to tell us that my David . . . that my David . . .' The formidable front wobbled.

Rose looked away as Mrs Norfolk succumbed to the bitterest of tears.

She didn't blame the Norfolk women for channelling their grief into anger. How could she? Everyone had their own way of dealing with loss – she'd seen it with her own brothers and father, with the Zrinski girls, with a hundred different families down the years.

And for Christ's sake, who *wouldn't* be angry about this? An adored man, taken without reason from his loving wife and daughters. How could it *not* make your blood boil?

She'd told them that David's body had been found in woodland south of Oxford: both the plain truth and an ugly lie.

Before she'd driven to the Norfolks' small farm in Bletchingdon, to the north of the city, she'd looked up the missing-person report on David Norfolk. A farmer, small-scale, his farm the type of business that went to the wall once a week in these parts, these days – but Norfolk's holding had been run well and turned a profit. Norfolk himself came across as a stand-up citizen: didn't drink, didn't gamble, had never had an affair or a run-in with HMRC (the investigating PC had left a cynical marginal note: 'STS'. *So they say*).

More than that, he was active in the local community. Lots of kids in these farming districts left school early with not much to show for it; David Norfolk, Rose learned, had made it his business to teach reading, maths, basic bookkeeping to local kids who needed it. Helped the kids who came on to the farms with the immigrant work gangs with their English, too. Never charged a penny.

The local primary schools loved him. A field trip to the Norfolk farm was a long-standing tradition in the area: generations of seven-year-olds had been shown how piglets were fed and how spring lambs were born by the avuncular Mr Norfolk. And he didn't stop there: he made a classroom of the whole countryside, helping the kids to sketch wildflowers, find thrushes' nests and look for slow-worms in the compost heaps.

To cap it all, the man was a lector at the local church. Well, of course he was, Rose had thought, closing the file with a sigh. David Norfolk had been an impeccably, untiringly, exhaustingly decent man.

Now she sat and watched his widow weep in the kitchen of the home they'd built together.

She stood and told them softly that she'd better get going – and that she was sorry, so sorry, for their loss.

'I'll be in touch again,' she promised, leaving her card on the table.

Helen, the elder daughter, had her arm about her mother's heaving shoulders. She looked up, red-eyed. Swallowed down a sob and snapped: 'Don't bother. You've helped enough already.'

Rose nodded gravely. Let herself out.

Back on the road, thrumming south through the blustery dusk, she mentally thumbed through her case notes. She had a lead – kind of. The guy's MO: abduction, followed by murder. The Zrinskis hadn't reported Katerina missing, but afterwards they said they'd not seen her in days. The police missing-persons roster was going to be their friend if they were going to stop this bastard. A lot of runaway teens and double-crossing husbands were going to get a lot of attention from a lot of coppers.

Beyond that Rose hadn't learned much. But then that hadn't been the whole point of her visit to Bletchingdon. What she'd done – without having much choice in the matter – was act as a target, a scapegoat; she'd given the Norfolks a safety valve.

She'd come to the Norfolks' farm with the worst news in the world. Platitudes about not shooting the messenger weren't worth horseshit – the Norfolks would never forgive her for the terrible news she'd delivered to them. But these things worked in balance, she knew. The next copper to come along would get an easier ride. Especially if it was a smooth-talking bastard like DI Leland Phillips.

That was going to sting – but if it meant progress, it was a hit she was happy to take.

As she swung on to the Oxford ring road Rose plotted her next steps. One: cross-reference what the Norfolks had told her with the missing-person report; double-check everything, sniff out any hint of a slip, a contradiction, something concealed – the PC who'd scribbled *STS* had been cynical but he hadn't been stupid.

Two: chase up David Norfolk's connections with the kids on the rural work gangs. He'd have worked with local charities, education agencies. Maybe there was a link to the Leys, to the Rakić gang, to Katerina. If there was, it'd be the thinnest of threads and not a lot to take to DCI Hume. But at least it'd be something.

Could Dmitry Rakić have killed David Norfolk?

He'd been watched, day in, day out. It would have taken an almost unimaginable feat of deception to beat the stakeout – and he was a Croat smack trafficker, Rose told herself, not David bloody Blaine.

Her focus now was on ruling the Rakić gang out. And finding someone else to rule in.

When she thought of who that might be her heart seemed to falter, her skin seemed to crawl. The man who'd severed Katerina's head. The man who'd cut the skin from David Norfolk's flesh.

Who in the name of God *was* he? And what in the name of God would he do next?

'He is ill, gravely ill,' Little Mouse said. 'I fear he hasn't long. He is dying – Father is dying.'

Olga gasped and crossed herself. 'I will get my things,' she said.

'Please hurry,' Little Mouse begged.

He helped her through the half-dark of the village with her baskets of blankets, herbs and medicines. Their shadows were stretched and warped by the humming street lights.

As they went, they prayed together. Prayers to attend the release of the soul.

A weak gas lamp flickered by the door of the priest's grey-planked hut. Little Mouse pushed open the door.

'Go to him,' he urged. 'Please, he needs your help.'

The woman went inside and Little Mouse followed, closing the door behind him.

The priest sat by a guttering coal fire. He looked up from a cup of black tea. His eyes shone, and he smiled as the woman hurried to him.

'I knew you would come,' he said. 'You are such a good soul, Olga. Bless you. I knew I could depend upon you.'

The woman turned to Little Mouse with an expression of puzzlement. She opened her mouth to speak.

Little Mouse brought half a brick down hard on her head.

Chapter Fourteen

11 October

It was the wrist bone, this time.

Another cup of tasteless tepid coffee. Another late night under the blueish strip lights of the MCU office. Rose sat with her head bowed over the report from David Norfolk's autopsy.

He'd been starved.

He'd been slathered with scented oil.

He'd been draped in a cape of rough-spun fabric.

And his wrist bone, the left one, had been removed from his arm with surgical skill and considerable care.

It was all just the same as it had been in the first case. And the connection between David Norfolk and Katerina Zrinski?

There wasn't one.

She'd hammered every contact, chased every half-lead – there just wasn't one. The frustration pushed her to the brink of tears. She wanted to scream: *Why? Why them?*

The clock on the wall ticked. It was gone nine. Heating pipes clanged somewhere in the building. Rose pushed her hair away from her face, blinked, looked again at the report. The close black type was beginning to blur. *Time to call it a night, Lauren.*

No: one more read-through. One more check on the

details. She could at least do that much for Katerina and David. Rose rubbed her aching neck and flipped back through the report.

David's body had been at ambient temperature, unlike Katerina's. But in an explanatory note Dr Rooke warned against drawing hasty conclusions. The ambient temperature had been much lower on the night David's body had been placed on display, touching zero around midnight. And besides, David's body – even at the umptcenth time of reading, Rose shuddered at these words – had been denied its insulating covering of skin. It was impossible, the report stated in cold clinicalese, to properly evaluate the effect of skinlessness on heat retention in the human body; such a circumstance, it said, was apparently unknown in the scientific literature.

Lucky old scientific literature, Rose thought wearily.

The lab report wasn't yet in on the oil recovered from David's body. But study of Katerina's oil had shown it to be infused with balsam.

Just like four-fifths of the sacred oils used in Christian practice from Alaska to Ethiopia.

Rose closed the report and finished the gritty coffee, wondered if she'd be able to stay awake on the drive home.

She took the lift downstairs. The baggy-eyed sergeant on the front desk nodded a weary goodnight as she passed through the station's entrance hall to the glazed double doors that led out into the car park.

Then she froze, with one hand flat on the glass of the door. Looking out – looking out into the darkness at the pale face that looked back at her.

For a moment she was sure it was a phantom. Tangled white-blonde hair. Lifeless light-blue eyes set above flat Slavic cheekbones. It was Katerina. Oh God, it was Katerina.

Rose shoved open the door. Winced at the bite of the October wind. Blinked.

A small hand closed on her upper arm.

'Inspector,' said Adrijana Zrinski. 'I help you. I tell you. I help.'

Katerina's younger sister looked as though she hadn't slept in days. Maybe she hadn't. Rose sat her down in a 'soft' interview room, stood a cup of sugary tea on the table in front of her. Adrijana stared unseeing through both tea and tabletop. There were indigo-blue shadows under her heavy-lidded eyes.

Rose checked a yawn. Whatever Adrijana had come here to tell her, there was no use in trying to force it. Even if it took all night – sleep could damn well wait.

She asked the girl gently where Sofia was, if Sofia was okay.

Adrijana gave her a hunted look.

'Sleeping,' she said. 'Very worry, very trouble.' She shook her head. 'Does not know. Must not know.'

'I won't tell anyone you came to see me, Adrijana,' Rose promised.

The girl nodded, sipped her tea.

'Before,' she said, after a moment – then stopped.

Rose leaned a little closer to her across the tabletop. 'Before?' She was careful to speak quietly, slowly, without the least hint of urgency. It wasn't easy. 'Before you came to this country?' A shake of the unkempt blonde head. 'Before Katerina went missing?'

A nod.

Rose sat back. Let the silence do the work. Adrijana fidgeted with trembling hands. Her pale face looked taut, smudged with sleeplessness. But there was determination in there, too. Rose had noticed it the first time they'd met. The girl looked frail but she had a seam of iron underneath.

Then she said: 'A thing. In our home. A – a thing was left. We found.'

A chill of anticipation rose up Rose's spine as Adrijana reached into the folds of her outsized tracksuit top and drew out something wrapped in a supermarket carrier bag.

'Someone left it in your flat? You don't know who?'

Adrijana shook her head again. She began to unwrap the thing in the bag. Rose watched intently as she drew it out; it was an elongated ball, maybe the size of a pineapple, covered in a sheet of newspaper.

Already Rose knew what it was – before Adrijana peeled back the grease-marked paper, before her nostrils filled with the smell of old bone.

It was a cage of animal ribs, fastened with leather thongs. A boiled-clean fragment of bone tied in the middle.

In the creased newspaper Rose saw a tangle of greasy twine.

She looked at Adrijana carefully.

'Where did you find this?'

'Window. Window of our home.'

The girl had been holding the thing in her lap. Now she put it on the table and drew her hands quickly away, as if she badly wanted rid of it.

'Have you ever seen anything like this before?'

Adrijana shook her head firmly.

'Never,' she said. 'Never. Is – *creepy*.'

You're dead right there, Rose thought. She rubbed her eyes, took a good look at the structure. As far as she could see it was just the same as the artefact left in Brask's office – the *Blair Witch* thing, she'd come to think of it as.

'Why now, Adrijana?' she asked. Tried to smile encouragingly, felt the dryness of her tired skin. 'Why did you wait till tonight to show me this?'

Adrijana shrugged nervously.

'Was our business, Sofia say. Not for police.' She caught Rose's eye fleetingly. 'Sofia very worry.' Adrijana looked away – thinking darkly of something, of her lost sister perhaps, or of Sofia, racked by anxiety and grief. 'Then I hear on the news. A murder, another murder.' She gave Rose a frank look. 'And I think, maybe same man. I think, man who kill Katerina kill again.' A brief, disgusted gesture towards the bone-thing on the table. 'I think maybe clue. I think – I think maybe help you stop. Stop him.'

The effort of speaking and the emotion stirred by what she had said showed clearly in Adrijana's glimmering blue eyes. She started to say something else – please, Rose thought – but her pale lips folded inward and tears spilled down her cheeks.

Rose leaned forwards, took the girl's hand. It felt tiny

and cold. She murmured what she hoped were comforting words: 'We'll do all we can; we won't let you down.'

So many tears, she thought. All this sorrow, all this hurt – and still no answers in sight.

Rose sorted out a car to take Adrijana home, then walked her down to the front office and waited with her while the car was brought around. She saw the girl off with more reassurances and sincere thanks for her help. She'd made desultory small talk with the desk sergeant, then grabbed a pallid-looking sandwich from a vending machine on one of the landings.

Now she sat dead-tired in the interview room and looked at the off-white bones gleaming unpleasantly in the low lighting.

The first of these things (no, she corrected herself – the second) had been left with Brask to spook him, they'd assumed. An elaborate calling card from the Rakić mob. So did this mean that they'd been trying to spook Katerina, intimidate her, threaten her? She'd got used to the idea that Hume and Phillips's gang angle was way off-beam – now she was thinking again.

It'd be easy enough, she realized, to ignore this new information, or to warp it to fit her pet theory. But it was a detective's job to be flexible, to alter course mid-investigation, to tailor the theory to fit the facts. Not the other way around; *that* was just lazy police work. That, she thought, was what Hume and Phillips had done – and now David Norfolk and his grieving family had paid mightily for it.

So say Katerina's murder *had* been a revenge hit, say

Rakić had staged the display of her corpse to make it look like something else, something it wasn't. She turned the hypothetical set-up over in her head.

The Norfolks hadn't mentioned any threats, any weird bone-things. So had David Norfolk just been a red herring? A feint to throw them off the scent? Maybe he'd been picked at random – picked, in fact, just *because* he had no links to the Rakić gang.

It was a hell of a thing to brutally torture and butcher an innocent man just to avoid the suspicion of murder. Was Rakić really that far gone?

Was anyone?

Rose knew all too well that the question was rhetorical. Its answer was strewn all over her desk and the front pages of every newspaper in the country.

Well, it was a theory. And the bone artefact Adrijana had brought her was unmistakeably evidence. It was also – at 10.45 at bloody night – more paperwork.

Rose chewed down the last of her flavourless sandwich and got to work. She carefully bagged the thing of bones, the greasy twine and the paper they had been wrapped in. Logged the evidence diligently in the files: times, dates, names, circumstances. Wrote out an explanatory note, ordering chemical analyses on the oil, the twine, the bones, the leather – hell, why not, the newspaper too. Told them to run a comparison with the thing left in Brask's office. Took the lift down four storeys to forensics, left the whole lot on the deserted desk of the head lab tech.

Ignoring her thumping headache and her heavy legs, she trudged back up to the interview room. Popped out the tape of her interview with Adrijana, dropped it in her pocket – she could listen to it on the drive home.

Home. It felt like a long way away.

Then back in the lift, g'night to the sarge, out into the car park –

It was empty, cold, lit with flat white light. She took a deep breath and exhaled a long day's worth of stale station air. Christ. Christ, this was tough.

But then, she told herself, so are you.

You've had to be.

Something about the clammy-cold night, the desolate car park, made her think of her first murder case in CID. She'd been a DS then, newly transferred from uniform at the Met. Thought she was a hard nut. Got *that* knocked out of her pretty quick.

Mary McTiernan had been found under a rhododendron bush beside a train-station car park. She was thirteen. Rose hadn't been leading the case – it'd been Morgan Hume's, just a DI back then, and he'd worked round the clock to nail the bastard who did it – but it had given her sleepless nights all the same.

It hadn't just been the long hours – though God knew there'd been plenty of those, on the streets, on the phones, in the interrogation rooms, in the labs and the morgues. No, the thing that had got to her, that had wormed under her skin, dug itself deep into her unconscious and left her wide-eyed in the small hours, was the sense of helplessness – the feeling that there was nothing anyone could have done to save little Mary McTiernan from what had been done to her. She'd realized that she was always going to be chasing, always going to be one step behind.

Bad things – the very worst things – were always going to happen. By the time they reached her, the most she could do was clear up the mess. That's what the job was. She examined the broken pieces and sorted out who was to blame, but nothing was ever going to make the victims caught in the wreckage whole again.

And the thing was that these messes – the murders, and crime and catastrophes – they never stopped. Being a cop was a parade of horrors as senseless as they were endless.

After the Mary McTiernan case was all over – they'd put the guy away for life, and he'd hanged himself in Parkhurst – she'd talked to Hume about it. Hadn't opened up all the way, of course, just hinted at her unease, her self-doubt. Hume hadn't been unkind, but his message had been clear as a bell: get tough, quick – or get out.

And now here she was. Still here, after all. She sighed, ran a hand through her hair. It felt greasy, uncared for. Yet another thing she hadn't allowed herself time to worry about.

She was unlocking her car door when, deep in her coat pocket, her phone buzzed. A call.

Ignore it.

It can wait.

Don't pick up. Don't pick up. Don't don't don't –

'DI Rose here.'

'Inspector, it's Matt Brask.'

Rose tensed. The same old cornball Midwestern accent but compressed to a hoarse whisper, and tightened by fear or pain.

'Professor? What's the matter?'

An agonizing pause. Brask's breathing. The noise of him working saliva into a bone-dry mouth.

'There's – there's someone here. In my house.'

Oh Jesus.

'Do you know who?'

'No. Just noises. Someone moving.'

Rakić. Had to be. Christ, she should've insisted on a security detail for the stubborn bastard. Rose felt a sickly surge of dread.

'Tell me where you are.'

Brask gave her an address in the Jericho district. The panic in his voice was palpable, but he was keeping a lid on it – just.

'I'll be there soon. I'm leaving now.' As she spoke she was dropping into her driver's seat, firing up the engine. She felt nauseous, like she'd taken a shot of strong espresso on an empty stomach. That was adrenaline – that was fear. 'Professor, if you can, get out of there. Can you hear me? Get out of there.'

A silence, then the line went dead.

On the first day she had begged for medicine to soothe the pain in her head.

On the second day she had begged to be released from the shackles and for food.

Now she lay still. Her breathing was shallow, her skin damp with sweat. There was a grey smear of ashes on her pale forehead. Her black-lashed eyes were closed; her lips were slightly parted. Her dark-chestnut hair was a lank coil on the dirty sheet. The air of the hut was thick with smells of incense, oil, wax and excrement.

'You are bound for a greater glory, miss,' Little Mouse had reassured her. 'You are to be reborn in Christ.' But she had not understood.

The priest had taught him well. The necessary rites had been conducted and the blade was sharp.

He had not enjoyed killing the hen – she had struggled in his arms and he had felt her heart beating in fear. But the hen's death, too, served a higher purpose. Little Mouse had daubed the bird's blood on the concrete floor beneath the bed.

The priest now stood at the foot of the bed, intoning the Latin litany.

Little Mouse parted the robe of sackcloth in which they had dressed the woman. He thought of the glorious martyrdom of St Erasmus. His eyes filled with tears at the beauty of it.

It was a fate that might have been his, he knew. But the Almighty *had intended for him a different path. He was Christ's servant. He was the Lord's blade.*

He drew the knife blade across the woman's belly. She woke from her fevered dozing and screamed. The fine red line scored by the blade swelled into a glossy belt of blood.

She screams because the body does not want to release the soul, Little Mouse thought. The body is a blind thing. Soon she will see — soon she will see the light. Again he drove the blade through the skin. The cut he made bisected the first to make a cross.

He put his hand wrist-deep into the woman's hot, roiling belly. Blood slopped over his feet. Shrieks rang in his ears. He thought: This is not like when I killed the hen. That was a practical matter, a necessity. This is something greater — O, far greater, and far more magnificent!

Little Mouse's spirit soared.

Though he knew that this was the most solemn and the most sacred of rites, though he knew that in this moment he was in the very presence of Christ, as he drew out from her gut a fistful of the howling woman's intestine, Little Mouse began to laugh.

Chapter Fifteen

Wade Street was a thickly shadowed curve of tall Victorian red-brick terraced houses, lined with parked cars and the odd ragged sapling. Rose parked a hundred yards from Brask's address. Yes, she could have done it by the book. She could have forwarded Brask's call to dispatch, but for her money, Rose thought she was a sight better than whichever pair of wet-behind-the-ears constables happened to respond to Brask's call.

She was quicker by herself. Better by herself.

She grabbed her baton from the glovebox, jumped from her car and loped warily towards Brask's place. About twenty yards short she spotted a figure in the shadows outside Brask's address. The sight of it made her pause.

After a moment's watching she let out a breath: it was Brask. Shivering on the pavement in pyjama bottoms and a short leather jacket. Alive. Safe.

He looked up at her approach.

'Is he still in there?' was Rose's first question.

Brask nodded stiffly. It was a cold night, dank and bone-chilling.

'I think so,' he said. 'He got in through a window – the noise woke me up. It sounded like he was coming up the stairs, but he must have ducked into one of the other bedrooms up there. I got down the stairs and found the hall window open. That's when I called you.'

'Is there a back way out?'

'The kitchen door – or a jump out of the upstairs windows into the bushes if he was desperate . . . and there's a skylight. Opens on to the roof.'

'Okay.' She moved out into the road, scrutinizing the narrow-fronted house as she went. Steep stairs. Lots of windows. Lots of outs. She flexed her legs and arms almost unconsciously. She jerked out her baton to its full length, took a limbering-up backhand swipe through the air.

Over her shoulder she said to Brask: 'If you see him come out the front, yell.' Then she quickly closed the distance to the house. The front door opened quietly, which was something: she'd been braced for an ear-splitting gothic creak – it was that kind of place, and that kind of night. The hall was dark and deserted. Rose closed the door softly behind her and paused at the foot of the stairs.

Waited. Listened.

A noise – the slightest of noises. Might've been a mouse under the boards. Might've been the next-door neighbour rolling over in bed.

Rose cocked her head, held her breath.

And again, a rustle, from inside this house, definitely, and from this floor – down the hall, one of the back rooms. There was a kitchen there, she already knew (her mind raced: *knives, cleavers, flames – no place for a fight*); and there was another room, adjoining the kitchen. Must be small, she thought, picturing the dimensions of the building. A study?

A small room meant not much space for throwing a punch or swinging a baseball bat.

And no stairs to be dangled over.

Rose edged down the hall. The door of a room on her right at the far end of the passageway was open.

Another noise.

If the intruder was the big Croat she'd seen at Katerina's meadow and again at All Souls, this was going to be over very quickly. Maybe she'd stand a chance if it was Dmitry Rakić. Rakić wasn't a big man, and besides, he'd be too smart to do a real number on a copper. Maybe.

She hesitated a yard from the door. The small noises went on, intermittently. They were the sounds of a person at work, hurried, perhaps, but careful. Meticulous even.

Whoever he was, he hadn't heard her approach.

Rose moved forwards into the open doorway. Yes, a study: desk, office chair, dully gleaming PC screen, bookcases, a winged armchair – and a crouched figure in the furthest corner. Hidden by shadow. Was it Dmitry Rakić? The figure was roughly the right size and build, but she couldn't say for sure.

Rose's nose wrinkled involuntarily. A musty, familiar smell.

She lifted her baton and charged forwards.

The back of the man's neck was her target. Aim carefully, hit hard: job done.

Never quite that easy, though.

At her first step the man whirled. He straightened like an uncoiled spring and raised an arm defensively. He was hooded, dressed in black.

Rose crashed through his attempt to block her and brought the baton whistling down. He writhed, grabbed – got lucky. His hand, broad and sinewy, closed around the shaft; he yanked it with astonishing strength. Rose's thumb twisted backwards. Her baton fell with a clatter to the floorboards.

Shit.

She lunged for the man's neck and tried to wrap an arm around his throat. He made a gurgling grunt, jerked his head forwards. With his hood pulled low and his chin forced down into her forearm, there was nothing to see of his face but a jutting white nose.

'*Police*,' Rose hissed.

The man squirmed and braced his feet against the bookcase. She said it again: '*Police*.'

He bit her. She felt his teeth tear the skin of her arm.

Rose swore savagely – then swore again as the man broke her grip, scrambled free and made for the door. She lunged after him, following the sound of his panting breath.

Her grasping hand closed on his sleeve. She hauled and felt his arm crash against the edge of the heavy dark-wood door. She renewed her grip and pushed, the arm bent backwards.

The man's animal cry of agony ran through Rose like a knife blade. She felt his hand close in her hair and bunch into a fist. There was a moment of fierce pain as her scalp felt as if it was about to be ripped open – then the side of her forehead crashed into the weighty brass doorknob. The last thing she heard was the sound of his fleeing footsteps.

A dark blur in an off-white oval resolved itself into a face. A saw-edged baritone hum became a voice.

'You're all right,' said Brask. 'Inspector? You're all right.'

She pressed a hand to her head. No blood – just a banging pain behind her eyes. She was getting used to that. The bright light in the room made her nauseous.

She sat up and looked around.

'Where is he?'

'He got out the back way.' Brask put his hand on her shoulder. 'You were out cold. Take it easy.'

'Did you chase him? Did you see him?'

Brask gave her a look.

'I was a little more concerned about the police officer lying unconscious on my study carpet.'

Rose shook her head. *Civilians.*

'Come on. Let's get you on to the chair. Easy now.' He took her elbow and helped her to her feet. The room spun gently.

'Oof.'

'I know. You must've taken quite a whack, Inspector. We ought to get you to a hospital.'

'How long was I out?'

'Can't have been long.'

'Then I'll be fine. No hospital.' Rose hated hospitals. She'd hated them since she was five years old.

'But you –'

'*No hospital.* What happened?'

'I heard a bang, came running. The back door was still swinging. A minute, not much more.'

She sighed. Tried to think past the ache in her head.

In a voice heavy with meaning, Brask added: 'He left something.'

Rose looked up and followed the professor's gaze to the wall behind her.

It wasn't quite like the others. It was a thing of bones, but elongated, more like a crude figure than a cage, and it was dressed with feathers, black feathers – a crow's or rook's maybe. Again the bones were greased and held in place by leather thongs.

It lay on a shelf of the bookcase. Oil had pooled on the fine-grained wood.

'Any significance to these books?' Rose asked, squinting at the embossed spines.

'Not that I can figure. They're not in any order – I haven't gotten around to arranging my books properly since I moved in. Besides, I don't think he meant to leave it there – you interrupted him, remember.'

'Right. He was probably planning to string it up like before.'

'I can't say I like his idea of interior decoration. It's a heck of a thing.'

'Uh-huh.' She put her hands on her hips. 'Look, Professor. It's time to start taking this seriously. Whatever this is supposed to mean – it's a threat. You've been beaten up; now your house has been broken into. The bottom line is you're not safe. I'm going to put a security detail on you.'

Brask leaned on his desk, spread his hands.

'How can I let you do that? I know how it is, Inspector – you're way underfunded, stretched too thin as it is. You just don't have the resources. How can I justify you going out of your way to protect me when the maniac who killed Katerina is still out there?'

Rose gave him a calculating look.

'We have a watch on Dmitry Rakić,' she said levelly.

'Yeah? What about his goons?' Brask asked, pointing to the artefact of feathers and bones. The professor shook his head slowly. 'Anyway, I heard the news reports. I know about the second killing, that poor farmer.' He caught Rose's eye and held it. 'It's not Rakić, is it? I mean, I know the guy's a psycho, a real nut, but . . .'

Rose stonewalled.

'We're looking at all the angles,' she said. Carefully – feeling the world lurch – she got to her feet. 'Come on. We're getting you out of here.'

Brask looked surprised.

'It's a little late for a hotel.'

'You can stay at mine, on the sofa.' She raised a hand to forestall Brask's reply. 'No arguing, Professor. Getting yourself killed won't help us find this guy. I want you out of harm's way. Go and get dressed.'

On the doorstep, heading out, Rose stumbled, caught herself, gripped the door frame. Took a long, steadying breath. Saw Brask watching her with concern.

She threw him her car keys.

'You'd better drive,' she said.

Brask fixed a pot of strong coffee while Rose moved around the small flat, picking up discarded clothes, shifting stacks of binders and papers, tidying away Chinese takeaway cartons, empty mugs, unwashed plates. It felt like she was hardly ever here . . . how the hell had she managed to get the place in such a mess?

'Don't have many guests,' she muttered apologetically. Also, she thought, I'm a slob.

'Don't worry about it.' Brask handed her a pungently steaming cup. 'You have a lot of more important things to worry about. You've had a heck of a time lately, Inspector.'

Don't I know it, Rose thought. Her thumping head and sore limbs reminded her of it every time she moved.

'Listen,' she said, sinking into the spare chair, 'I'm going to call you Matt, and you're going to call me Lauren. I'm too bloody tired for anything else.'

Brask smiled: 'Sure.'

She sipped the potent coffee. Closed her eyes for a moment, let the world settle into place. But it wouldn't quite settle right. How could it?

A late-night interview with a victim's sister. Two weird bone sculptures. A break-in and a fight. Just another day on the Thames Valley beat, she thought wryly. It didn't matter how tired she was, she wasn't going to get much sleep tonight. Police work could do that to you: leave you utterly exhausted but at the same time buzzing, wired, keyed-up.

She glanced at Brask. He was staring into space – looked almost as knackered as she felt.

'What do you know about the murder of David Norfolk?' she asked.

The professor blew out a breath, rubbed at his brow.

'Not much. Only what I read in the papers. A family man, right? A farmer. Worked with charities. Seemed like a good guy.' He looked at Rose searchingly. 'The reports said he'd been – mutilated?' A pause. 'Was it . . . was it like Katerina?'

Brask's a part of this now, Rose thought. He's involved, deeply involved – and that means he's here to stay.

This was a guy who committed to his causes, she knew. A fleeting thought struck her: it must have taken something serious, something big, to make him leave the priesthood. From what she'd seen of the professor she didn't think it was in Brask's character to give up.

But that was a conversation for another time.

'Can I tell you,' she said slowly, 'what was done to David Norfolk?'

Brask set down his coffee cup. Sat forwards. Nodded.

'Go ahead,' he said.

She tried not to leave anything out, tried to remember every detail of that terrible scene in the birch wood. The thick iron nail in the grey bark. The bolt of hessian that fluttered in the breeze. The nightmarish robe of skin. And the body – the dark-red, blood-red body of the farmer, flayed cruelly bare, frozen in unimaginable anguish.

Brask listened carefully, grimly expressionless.

When she was done – finished, spent, empty – Rose prompted: 'So – what do you think?' She thought of the grim medieval images of poor St Catherine. 'Do you know what it might mean? The scenes are so elaborate. There must be a reason the killer's going to so much trouble. What's the message meant to be? What's he trying to do?'

Instead of responding, the professor reached for Rose's laptop, which was open on the coffee table. With his jaw set, he tapped in a search term. Spun the laptop to show Rose the screen.

She flinched. Couldn't help it.

The screen was filled with image after image of men bound, stripped and having the skin cut from their flesh.

'The martyrdom of St Bartholomew,' Brask said. 'One of the great themes in medieval art.'

Rose scrolled slowly through the pictures.

'Maybe our man fancies himself as an artist,' she murmured. A few names she'd heard of were showing up on screen – Michelangelo, Bronzino – along with a lot more she hadn't. The paintings were visceral, powerful, grotesque.

'Do you want to know the story?'

Rose grimaced. 'No. But tell me anyway.'

'Bartholomew was one of Christ's Apostles – we also know him as Nathaniel. We don't know a lot about him, but according to tradition he travelled widely in the east: Persia, Mesopotamia, maybe even India.

'He's said to have finished up in the kingdom of Armenia, on the Black Sea. He converted the Armenian king to Christianity and destroyed all the idols in the temple. The king's brother, in a fury, had him seized, beaten and –' he made a weary gesture towards the images on the screen – 'executed.'

'By being skinned alive?'

'Uh-huh. Actually there's quite a tradition of flaying as a punishment in that region. In Mesopotamia, eight hundred years before Christ, rebel leaders captured by the emperor were often skinned alive. And if you know your Greek mythology –'

'I don't.'

'– then you'll remember it features there, too. Apollo

flayed the satyr Marsyas for daring to challenge him. There are dozens more examples. Everywhere from medieval France to Aztec folklore.'

'Christ. What a way to die.'

'Quite a martyrdom,' Brask agreed.

Rose looked at him.

'I think you're going to have to talk me through that, Matt,' she said. 'Martyrdom – dying horribly for a good cause, right?'

Brask shrugged, nodded.

'Kind of. I can only give you the Catholic take on it. The ancient martyrs are hugely venerated within the Church. These were the guys who, in the first centuries after Christ's death, endured all kinds of persecution – in the Roman Empire and elsewhere – for their faith. We're talking around two hundred and fifty years of victimization and torture.'

'But the idea is that martyrdom gets you fast-tracked to heaven?'

'It's – complicated.' Brask grinned. 'Everything's complicated in the Catholic Church. But yeah – a person who is designated a martyr is considered to have been accepted into heaven.'

'So it's not all bad,' Rose remarked drily.

'That's one way of looking at it.'

They both stared at the screen. A dozen despairing faces stared back at them.

An hour later the coffee pot stood empty and Rose and Brask were side by side at the kitchen table, leafing through the files sent over by Interpol.

You're in deep now, Professor Brask, she'd thought as she'd dug out the folder from her briefcase. No going back.

These were the old cases that bore a resemblance to Katerina's murder: major mutilations, pseudo-religious imagery, bone extraction. She'd asked for a broad sweep and the Interpol researchers had obliged. The file was a horror movie.

Rose thought – no, *knew* – she'd got used to it, grown hardened to violence and bloodshed and death over her years on the force. But this was something else. These crimes populated the nightmarish outer fringe of what humanity was capable of. They represented the kind of horrors that were well outside her scope of experience – or at least they *had* been, until some monster delivered them right to her doorstep.

The crime-scene photos showed limbs hacked away. Organs cut out. Faces and genitals mutilated. Victims sawn open like joints of meat prepared for cooking.

Almost all women, Rose noted bitterly.

At her side, Brask had grown pale, his cheeks hollower, his brow creased – but he worked on; he was on to something, he reckoned. The fates of the martyrs, the executions of the early Church. There were some resemblances here, he'd said – 'Echoes, tributes, homages, call it what you like.'

'We'd call them copycat killings,' Rose said.

'Look here.' Brask had pulled out three files from the pile he'd set aside. 'From north-east France, back in 2005. Cold cases. Horrific stuff – but kind of familiar.'

His voice was heavy with meaning; Rose didn't quite see why. She swiftly scanned the printouts.

'I don't see it,' she said. She tapped the top sheet with her pen. 'This woman was cut into pieces, completely dismembered. That's not how our man works.' *So far.*

'They all were. Three victims. No' – he moved another page on to the pile – 'make that four. All cut into a dozen pieces. Not our guy's MO at all, I know – and the lab in Rheims got nothing from examining the body parts.' He looked at Rose. 'But I think I know why. Look here.'

He fished a sheet of photographs from the pile. Rose bent over and stared at them. Black-and-white crime-scene photos. She'd looked at them once already: twelve pieces of a human body, twelve lumps of neatly butchered meat, laid out on a stone-flagged floor. Police tags and tapes marked the distances and angles.

She was no good at guessing games.

'What am I supposed to be seeing?'

'There's no reason you should see it – no reason anyone should, unless they knew what they were looking for.'

Rose turned to Brask. *Unless they thought like a psychopath.*

'So what is it?'

Brask angled the sheet of pictures.

'It isn't easy to see, with the camera position where it is – but there's a pattern here. Look. Imagine the body parts are points on a chart.'

'Join the dots, you mean?'

'If you like.' He traced a fingertip across one of the photographs. 'From here – to here – to here –'

'Matt, for God's sake –'

'– to here – to here . . . Do you see?'

She was about to say *We're wasting our bloody time here* or *This is getting us nowhere* or *I could be doing some* real *police work right now, Professor* –

– when she saw it.

A figure. A human body, mapped out in body parts like a constellation drawn in stars. Arms outstretched.

'What the hell?'

'*Art.*' Brask said the word sharply, ironically. 'I know it, I know this shape, this figure. The arms held out like that, the tilt of the head, the position of the legs.' He shook his head, looked at Rose. 'It's St Peter – St Peter, the father of the Church, who was crucified upside down because he declared himself unworthy of suffering the same punishment as Christ.'

Rose was sceptical. She squinted at the grotesque outline in the pictures.

'How can you possibly know that? It could be anyone.'

'Caravaggio,' Brask said stonily. 'I've looked at the painting a million times. It's Caravaggio's *Crucifixion of St Peter.* It's one of my favourite Renaissance pieces. Or used to be.'

Rose had been leafing through the autopsy reports on the four victims. Now her mouth went dry.

'Matt.'

'And in *this* one the outline suggests the dying pose of St Paul, in the nineteenth-century painting by –'

'*Matt.* Look. Look here – and here – and here –'

A portion of bone had been removed cleanly from the victim's forearm . . . The body showed clear signs of a recent surgical

189

operation to remove the first bone of the left thumb . . . The victim was missing a portion of vertebra . . .

The wording was different in each report but to Rose the meaning was plain.

To Brask, too.

'This can't be coincidence,' he said. 'And did you take note of the causes of death? Stoning. Burning alive. These aren't twenty-first-century homicides, Lauren.' He looked at her gravely. 'These are martyrs' deaths.'

But Rose had stopped listening. She was staring at the first page of the first file – the crime report, the call log from when the first grisly mosaic had been found laid out on the floor of a Saint-Dizier basement.

The date-stamp in stark black type: 4 October.

'Katerina was found,' she breathed, 'in the early hours of the fourth of October.' She snatched the second file from Brask's hand, tore through to the relevant page. Her pulse thundered in her temples.

'Lauren, what the –'

'Tenth of October.' She let the file drop, looked at Brask. 'The body of David Norfolk was found on the tenth.'

Brask's jaw dropped as he reached the same conclusion Rose had just come to. She was already reaching for the third file. Whatever the date on it was, Rose thought desperately, it was more than a clue, now.

It was a deadline.

There had been no answer, no sign. Little Mouse and the priest had prayed daily, together, for hours at a time, their voices echoing hoarse and strained in the fetid dark of the cottage – and yet they had still not been delivered.

Still the Serbs ravaged their land. At Osijek, at Dakovo, at Slatina – still Karadžić's infidel legions spilled Croat blood, raped Croat women, defiled Croatia's holy places.

It had been a week since Little Mouse had buried the body of the woman deep in the mouldering earth of the forest. A week and no sign of deliverance.

Sometimes the priest would weep. Sometimes, Little Mouse thought darkly, it was as though the priest was losing faith.

On the seventh night after the woman's martyrdom the Abbot Cerbonius appeared to Little Mouse in a burning vision. The abbot told him that his work was not yet done – that, after all, the soul of one woman was a small thing indeed, balanced against the destiny of Christ's kingdom and the restoration of the holiest of orders.

Their homeland, their monastery and the venerated Order of St Quintus itself would not be resurrected by a single conjuring trick, the abbot said. Little Mouse felt in his blood the abbot's indignation. The sacred treasures of the order will not be restored by piety and prayer alone.

'There must be new relics, Little Mouse,' the abbot said. 'There must be new treasures.'

Chapter Sixteen

12 October

Nine days. Nine days to stop it happening again.

The date-stamp on the third killing in the French murders was 21 October. Rose put down her tea and reread the old report from 2006. It was pretty sketchy. She needed more. Chasing up the French police authorities was top priority.

It was nearly ten. Christ, she had needed that sleep.

She looked up at the sound of Brask's footsteps in the hall. When he appeared in the doorway she laughed – and shocked herself with the freshness, the sheer spontaneity of it. It felt like something she hadn't done in a long time.

Brask blinked at her stupidly. During the night his wiry dark hair had knotted itself into a drunkenly towering up-do, a listing mass of unkempt curls whose waving split ends brushed the door lintel.

'Sleep well?' Rose asked.

'Uh-huh, thanks.'

'I wasn't talking to you. I was talking to the small mammal that made a nest in your hair overnight.'

Brask lifted a hand to his scalp and smiled ruefully.

'I guess I've gotten used to waking up alone,' he said. He shambled into the kitchen. 'Should I cook breakfast?' he called. 'I feel it's the least I can do.'

Rose stood, suddenly awkward. *Got used to waking up alone? You're not the only one, Prof.* It was a long time since she'd had a man in the house overnight. Self-consciously she followed Brask into the kitchen.

He was standing in front of her open refrigerator, one hand on the door, shaking his head in mock dismay. Or real dismay, for all she knew.

'It can be hard to keep up with shopping, the hours I work,' she said defensively.

Brask smiled.

'You don't say? I'd assumed the delivery guy from the stale-cheese-and-half-jar-of-mayo store must've only just left.' He closed the fridge door with a whump. 'Sorry. You know I'm only kidding. My place is hardly any better. Do you have anything edible in this apartment at all, or should I go out for groceries?'

'There's bread.' Rose shrugged. 'And, um, jam. In the cupboard by the cooker.'

'Breakfast,' grinned Brask, 'of champions.'

They settled into a thoughtful quiet as, sitting elbow to elbow again at the table, they worked their way through a pot of tea and a stack of toast with raspberry jam. Both preoccupied, both looking ahead. The twenty-first of October. That was the deadline for the discovery of the next body. Nine days.

'Can I ask you something?' Brask said after a while.

She eyed him warily.

'Personal or professional?'

'Professional.'

'Go ahead.'

'These cases. This killer.' Brask's look was intent, serious. 'Have you ever seen anything like it?'

Rose shook her head emphatically.

'Never. I mean, I've been a copper a long time, I've seen a lot of blood, violence, murders, my fair share of X-rated stuff. But this.' She blew out a breath. 'It's something else. It's not just all in a day's work. It's – well, it's the kind of thing a murder detective has nightmares about.' She returned his look. 'Okay. Your turn.'

Brask smiled.

'Only fair, I guess. Personal or professional?'

'I – I'm not sure.'

'Consider me intrigued. Shoot.'

Rose took a slurp of tea.

'Your picture, the picture in your office.' She spoke cautiously, inching forwards as though on weak ice. 'You, in a – a dog collar, do you call it? You as – as a priest.'

Brask looked at her solemnly, then nodded.

'Halloween, 1997,' he said. 'Quite a party. And your question is, where did I hire the costume?'

Brask held the deadpan for a moment – then let rip a deep-chested laugh. Jesus, this guy can be as corny as his accent, Rose thought. Couldn't help but laugh along, though.

'No, it's true, I admit it,' Brask went on. He spread his hands earnestly. 'And I guess I shouldn't kid about it. It was – is – a serious thing. I was ordained into the Church. I wore the Roman collar. A real commitment. Meaningful.'

'But you –' Rose hesitated, let the sentence hang unfinished.

'Broke my vows? Deserted the Church? Turned my back on God?' He cocked an eyebrow wryly. 'Yup – I did all those things. To a greater or lesser extent.'

'Why?'

His smile grew distant, inscrutable.

'The usual story.'

'A woman?'

'Do you have to sound so surprised? Yeah – a woman.' He swallowed, rubbed his upper lip. 'And I lost her, too.' When he looked up at Rose his dark eyes were intense, almost fierce. 'Drunk-driver, Fremont, Ohio, July, 2006.' Looked away, shook his head. Rose thought he was going to say something more – but he only frowned, and shook his head again, and picked up his mug of tea.

Grief and loss, blood and death. They ran through both of their lives, Rose reflected, like a black thread through coloured cloth. Small wonder he had taken the loss of Katerina so hard.

For the thousandth time Rose saw the face, Katerina's still, white face, in her mind – she saw the whole scene all over again: the cartwheel, the black blood, the stitched skin. Images of David Norfolk's ruined red body soon followed. Last came the crime scenes in bleak monochrome from France. So many victims. So many flavours of pain.

All from one monster.

'Do you believe in evil, Matt?' she asked, in a quiet voice. It sounded ridiculous as soon as she'd said it. Imagine asking that in the police canteen, she thought. Imagine asking Phillips or Angler. Imagine asking DCI

Keith Rose of the Metropolitan Police – aka Dad. God, you'd never live it down. She could imagine the derisive laughter. Coppers didn't trade in good and evil.

For a lecturer in comparative religion at All Souls, Oxford, though, this was his meat and drink. Brask didn't laugh. His brow creased and he set down his drink.

'I do,' he said. 'In abstract – as a force, for want of a better word, in human society. We do terrible things to each other, inhuman things. I think these things are the signatures of evil, its footprints, the marks it leaves. But do I think humans can *be* evil?' He shrugged one shoulder. 'I'm not so sure.'

'That sounds pretty subtle.'

Brask smiled.

'I didn't go through four years at the seminary for nothing. But listen.' He ran a hand through his tangled hair. 'When Hester died – she was visiting her folks in Fremont, driving from the airport at Sandusky, a pickup truck lost control on the freeway . . . when she died, man, I believed in evil that day. And I thought it had a human face: the face of Larry P. Mickelson – see, I still remember his name. I mean, of course I do. How could I forget it: the lousy drunk who drove her rental car off the road and didn't even stop to see if she was all right.

'My God, I hated that man.' Brask's face was grim. 'He embodied everything that I thought evil: selfishness, greed, cowardice, basic disregard for human life, for his fellow man. What could be more evil than that?

'Then I saw him in court.' His lip curled in a bitter smile at the memory. 'And I saw what Larry P. Mickelson truly was. He wasn't Satan, wasn't a monster. He was just an asshole.' Brask showed his teeth briefly. 'You understand me? He was a dumb guy, not much education, not much of an upbringing. A wreck of a guy, I saw there in court. Scared, stupid, ignorant. And you know what, I believe he was sorry for what he did.'

'That hardly makes it all right,' Rose butted in. 'Drink-driving is unforgivable.'

'It's appalling, awful, a terrible crime to commit.' Brask nodded. 'But I'd say it's half an inch short of unforgivable.' He measured the distance with his thumb and forefinger. 'And I look back on my life, times when I've been stupid, selfish, reckless, times when I've made terrible mistakes – and I think, *thank God for that half an inch*.'

Rose shook her head.

'This is a bit too abstract for me,' she said. 'People are defined by what they do. Murders don't commit themselves. Murderers –'

She broke off. But Brask had guessed where she was heading.

'Can I forgive the man who murdered Katerina – like I forgave the man who killed my Hester?' Something in his face and voice acknowledged that this wasn't just academic discussion any more – that they were face to face with the reality of evil. 'One thing I know,' he said slowly, 'is that he's not the devil. He's a man – a sick man, a man who's done things beyond the reach of any recognizable morality – but still a man.' He met Rose's eye, seemed like he was forcing himself not to look away. 'This will sound crazy,' he said, 'but when I look at the photographs of Katerina, of her body, the crime scene, I see something more than murder. There's – a kind of *care* there. Attention, observance. I dunno, Lauren, it's nuts, but – I see a kind of tenderness.'

He was quiet for a moment, then stood abruptly and began to collect up the tea mugs and crumb-strewn plates. Muttered something about getting to work.

Rose sat silent, watching him tidy up. Her gaze wandered back to the photos strewn across the tabletop.

It's not nuts, she thought. I see it too.

The cold of the previous night had yielded to a mild, moist morning of milky sunshine and sputtering winds. As she and Brask left her apartment building in the west of the city, Rose felt – for the first time since 4 October – that the day had promise.

Yes, there was work to be done, hard, serious work; there was still a killer on the loose in Oxford, for Christ's sake. And nothing could shake the chilling grip this case had taken on her heart. Maybe nothing ever would.

But she finally had a solid lead. She finally felt like she could begin to see the way forward, the way to get justice for Katerina and David Norfolk and bring the Trick or Treat Killer's murders to an end. Yes, she felt less lost this morning. Less threatened. Less afraid. It was a good feeling, amid the darkness.

It lasted all of two minutes.

'What a happy couple!'

She spun, startled, and found herself looking into the broad, sneering smile of Olly Stevenage. He waggled a smartphone under her nose. 'Here you go, Ms Rose. Smash it, if you want. Drop it down a drain. I've already uploaded the goods to the Cloud: a dozen hi-res pictures of you and the professor here leaving your flat together – very obviously,' he added, with a mocking up-and-down glance at Brask's rumpled sweater and cords, 'in the same clothes you were wearing last night.'

Rose felt Brask's hand brush her coat sleeve – the merest of touches, enough to say *Take it easy, don't make this worse.*

'Good to see a new generation being brought up in the best traditions of British journalism,' she said bitterly. 'Should I be grateful you didn't go for an up-skirt shot?'

'It's called *reportage*,' Stevenage said.

'It's called gutter journalism, more like,' cut in Brask. 'Who the hell are you? What are you doing here?'

The young man flicked back his hair and self-importantly presented a press card.

'Oliver Stevenage, *Oxford Times.*'

'That paper,' Brask said heavily, 'has quite a tradition – and a fine reputation.'

'It's got a bright future, too,' leered Stevenage. 'We'll be the talk of the national media when we break *this* story.'

Rose knew it was coming, knew Brask was too naive, too unschooled in these things not to set Stevenage up with the ugly punchline the little rat craved. She tried to hurry him along, get him to the car, but he stood his ground. With a bewildered expression he said: 'Wait, Rose.' Then to Stevenage: '*What* story?'

Stevenage held his fingers at right angles to frame an imaginary headline.

'*Trick or Treat Killer probe police chief leaves Oxford love-nest with prime suspect* – how does *that* sound?' He sniggered nastily. 'Enough to get you booted off the force, would you say, Inspector?'

Brask made a strangled noise in his throat.

'I'm not going to justify any of that bullshit with a denial or an explanation,' Rose said sharply. She stepped closer to Stevenage. She had a handle on her anger – but she wasn't going to let Stevenage know that. 'What I'm going to do instead is assure you that if you run that headline – or anything like it – I'll nail you. I don't care what for. I'll find something. I'll nail you, and you'll be out of this university, out of this city, for good.'

The kid had some nerve – she had to give him that. He didn't take a backward step.

'I don't need a headline,' he said. Rose could see he was fighting hard to keep the querulous tremor from his voice. 'I don't need to write a thing. What's that phrase? "A picture says a thousand words." I publish my photos this morning and within an hour I'll have the world's press eating out of my hand.' He leaned down until his beaky nose was inches from hers. His breath smelled of coffee and onions. 'It's hard to see how you could have bested this, Ms Rose,' he said. 'Short of inviting Dmitry Rakić round for a three-way, you two really couldn't have made this any juicier.' He laughed, skipped back to the kerb, climbed nimbly aboard a parked-up scooter.

Brask shouted: 'I'll be speaking to the vice-chancellor about this, Mr Stevenage.'

The scooter's engine drowned out Stevenage's reply but Rose didn't have to be an expert lip-reader to make it out: *oooh, scared*.

They watched him drive away, revving the little engine triumphantly.

'Puerile little prick,' Rose spat. She breathed out hard through her nose, looked up at Brask. 'If it's any comfort,' she said drily, 'you're no longer our prime suspect.'

Her anger had subsided to a dull, helpless exasperation – tinged now with embarrassment at Stevenage's remarks. *Love-nest?*

'I'm sure he won't dare print . . . what he said he was going to print,' Brask said uncomfortably as they climbed into her car. 'It'd be libellous – defamatory – whatever you have over here.'

'You don't know much about the British press,' Rose snapped.

'It was not enough,' Little Mouse told the priest furiously.

He held in his quivering hand a two-day-old newspaper he had found blowing through the street. It brought more news of the barbarians — of the heathen Serb still rampaging unchecked through their godly land. Thirty-seven killed, the paper said, at Kutjevo, and two churches burned to the ground.

The priest's awful pale eyes were filled with anxiety. He looked so ancient — so withered and worn.

'Father.' Little Mouse shook him by the shoulder. 'It was not enough!'

In a weak, arid voice: 'Were we wrong, my child?'

'Wrong? No. Our hands were guided, Father. We were in Christ's command. I felt it.' He hesitated. 'Didn't you?'

The priest's scabbed head wobbled in a vague nod.

'The woman was a deserving soul,' Little Mouse insisted. 'We conducted the rite. It was a true martyrdom, Father. And yet our land is not free, the order not restored —'

He looked at the priest. Hunched and snivelling in the shadows, he seemed to Little Mouse diminished, weakened.

Little Mouse's vision flickered. In the blurred periphery of his sight he saw the abbot and in the depths of his soul he heard the abbot speak.

'The path of the righteous,' the abbot said, 'is a hard path to tread. Not everyone has the strength. Many fall by the wayside.'

And yet all have a part to play.

Little Mouse looked again at the newspaper headlines: slaughter, pillage and fire. Saw again the monastery of St Quintus consumed by flames. Smelled the burning. Heard the screaming.

Many fall by the wayside, but Little Mouse swore to himself that he would not be one of them.

'It was not enough,' he told the priest.

Chapter Seventeen

18 October

Rose's phone was ringing piercingly. It jerked her from sleep into a sombre grey morning. She blinked, checked the clock. Barely seven.

Say what you like about journalists, she thought, you can't knock their work ethic. The last call the night before had been at 11.45. *No rest for the wicked.*

When nothing appeared on the *Oxford Times* website the morning Olly had surprised them coming out of Rose's flat, she'd dared hope that they'd scared him enough to drop it. She checked the site the next morning and then the next . . . nothing for three days. She'd almost thought the matter was done with. In the meantime she'd interviewed David Norfolk's farmhands, close friends and charity contacts. She'd visited all of the children he'd met through his tutoring – including several who lived in the Leys. After hours criss-crossing the countryside on her way from one emotional interview to the next, all Rose knew for sure was that the world had lost one good man.

No new suspects.

No new leads.

No answers.

Then, on the morning of 15 October, Olly's headline

finally appeared, blaring in twenty-four-point font at the top of the *Oxford Times*. It was precisely what Stevenage had said it would be, except with a couple of exclamation marks added for good measure.

The little shit had been holding out for the print edition.

DCI Hume had done his best and the Thames Valley press office had been blitzing their contacts on the nationals but it had done no good. Stevenage had been right: once his 'story' had gone online and the tabloids got wind of it, no force on earth could have kept it under wraps.

She'd read the piece. She'd had to – and anyway she'd had Hume bellow every word of it down the phone to her within ten minutes of it going live. Leland Phillips had spent the day sending her choice extracts by text message.

Late-night tryst . . . looking tired but happy . . . exchanging warm, intimate smiles . . . no attempt to conceal . . . shameless . . .

Rose had had to change her phone number twice that day. Hadn't worked. Everyone from the lowest tabloid slime to the top broadsheet crime correspondents to reporters on the evening news had been on her back.

Now she checked the caller ID, recognized the number of a hack from one of the hang-'em-and-flog-'em right-wing papers, hit the 'off' button. Crawled from bed.

Focus, she told herself. It's about Katerina. It's about David Norfolk. Focus.

Today was 18 October. If the killings followed the same pattern as the ones in France, that meant they had three days to go.

Showered and dressed, with coffee brewing, Rose pored over the new information Interpol had pulled together for her. The email with the zipped files had been sent over to her just after 1 a.m., UK time. Did no one in the world sleep any more?

Here was the full works on the four French killings from ten years before. All the case notes, transcripts, tech reports; all the cold leads, dead ends, wrong guesses. Mostly in French. Rose had a dictionary propped open on the desk beside her; with this and a half-remembered GCSE, she found she could pretty much make sense of it.

Of the words, anyway. The deeds the words described remained beyond her grasp.

A few weeks ago, she thought wearily, this kind of stuff – countless unpaid extra hours, liaison with overseas forces, in-depth case research – would've earned her a gold star and a shedload of brownie points from DCI Hume.

Now it was all that was keeping her from being kicked off the case. That and Hume's pride: the idea of admitting that he'd blundered in putting Rose in charge, she guessed, was too much for the pig-headed old copper to stomach.

But he had a breaking point, she knew. With the constant barrage of venomous press coverage – not to mention Phillips dripping his poison in the chief's ear – it surely couldn't be far off.

Again she remembered the date, the deadline. Wondered who, how, where. Tried to blot out the thought of some poor woman shivering in a locked cellar, tied up in a car boot or the back of a van, who knew –

They'd been keeping a close eye on the missing-person

logs. She and Hume had drawn up a shortlist, strictly off the record. Three people on it: three missing persons with no obvious reasons for going AWOL, no history of mental illness, no financial problems, no love affairs or dirty secrets anyone knew about.

Susie Canning, vicar's daughter, fifteen, missing from her home in Banbury for just under a week.

Craig Rotheray, health-club entrepreneur, twenty-nine, reported missing by his fiancée four days ago.

And Caroline Chaudry, a medical student.

The force had ripped Oxfordshire apart looking for the three of them. Not a sniff.

Rose had had a word with Hume about going public, putting out a statement warning that the killer was likely to strike again. Hume – as she'd known he would – had dismissed the idea. 'Enough fucking hysteria around as it is,' he'd said in exasperation. A cynical part of her guessed that Hume was more worried about everyone finding out just how little progress the force had made on the case. What exactly could they say, after all? *There's someone out there, we don't know what he looks like, what his name is or where he is – but take care, or he might kill you.* How would that sound? Hume wasn't much of a one for focus groups and community engagement but he knew a PR disaster when he saw one coming.

Rose returned to the reports. Sighed. Flipped through the French dictionary.

This was Murder Three. *No*, she reminded herself: it was the murder of Emilie Jourdain. A person, more than a number. The pictures had showed a pattern of body parts laid out on the dusty tiles of a derelict library.

As she cross-referenced the words in the dictionary she scribbled her loose translations in the margins of the report.

Souris. Mice.

Température ambiante. Room temperature.

Décomposé. Decomposed.

She paused. Her mind lurched into a higher gear. She scrabbled through the paperwork for the crime-scene photos. Here they were: the butchered body parts, dark slabs of meat laid out on the chessboard floor tiles. They were, she saw now, a little shabby, ragged-edged where mice, rats and stray cats had gnawed and worried at them. And they lacked the gloss of fresh meat: the camera flash showed only a dull, dead, matte grey.

Décomposé.

Murder Three, Rose realized with a thudding sense of dread, had gone wrong. Maybe a security guard called in sick, maybe a builder forgot to show up.

No one had found this until 21 October. But it had been there, waiting – for how long?

The other victims had been found soon after their deaths, but the state of this body suggested Murder Three had been undiscovered for days after its presentation. That meant that the timeline Rose was working from was wrong. She grabbed for her phone, to call Brask, Hume, Phillips, anyone – to tell them that time was running out, that it was later than they'd thought.

It went off in her hand, rattling through its shrill routine of descending bleeps. She swore violently, cursed Olly fucking Stevenage and the fucking vultures from the press . . .

But it wasn't the press. It was PC Ganley, calling from a stretch of fallow land outside Oxford. His voice was broken in a way that by now seemed almost familiar to Rose. It wavered, thick with horror.

Chapter Eighteen

Brask sat at his computer in the stark light of his anglepoise lamp, a stack of notes at his elbow, books piled on the floor, a dozen tabs open in his web browser.

No sense in lying in bed, he'd finally figured, when it was clear that sleep had given up on him. He'd dropped off for a couple of desperate hours around two, been up since five and at his office in All Souls since six. Researching, working. Now he leafed through a stack of printouts of the Interpol files. The clock showed seven-thirty.

In his own eyes he seemed foolish, delusional.

You're not a cop, he told himself. You're an academic playing at being a private eye.

He'd looked up at his own photograph on the wall. The hair forcibly combed into a side parting, the grin boyish and toothy above the Roman collar. Hardly Humphrey Bogart.

But it helped. Thinking through the case, trying to find Katerina's killer – it helped *him*.

And he'd hardly realized that he needed helping.

He'd drawn out a rough chart on a page of his notebook. Across the top there were four dates, the dates of the four French killings. In the columns lists of names. Saints' names.

Most people, he knew, thought of saints' days – if they thought of them at all – as just footnotes on the calendar, scattered thinly through the year and scarcely regarded. Send your lover some chocolate on St Valentine's, get drunk on stout on St Patrick's Day – that was about it.

But in the Catholic Church the calendar was dense with saints' days. Each was rich in history, tradition, meaning; each one *mattered* to someone, somewhere.

They found Katerina on her cartwheel on 4 October – and on the same day ten years previously, in the crypt of a church in Rheims, they'd found a young woman's body parts arranged into a coarse likeness of the body of the crucified St Peter.

That day, 4 October, was the day of St Ammon, of St Francis of Assisi, of St Petronius, of St Peter of Damascus, of St Hierotheus, of St Quintus.

In Brask's notes the name of St Quintus was underlined in red.

He'd done a little digging. Quintus wasn't much known among western Catholics – he was an obscure martyr from the sixth century, killed at the court of a Frankish king. In the east, though, he was more widely venerated, thanks to the influence of the Orthodox Church. There was even, he'd discovered, an Order of St Quintus, founded somewhere in the north-central Balkans. One of its central figures was an Abbot Cerbonius.

The feast of St Cerbonius fell on 10 October. The day they found David Norfolk. Could've been a coincidence, sure. For all they really knew, this whole damn case – Katerina's wheel, David Norfolk's mutilation, the dates, the French killings – could've been nothing but a run of macabre coincidences.

Facts were what they needed.

Now, squinting, leaning close to the monitor, Brask scrolled through a series of blurred scans from an English-language Croatian newspaper. They were dated from the early 1990s – the height of the Yugoslav Wars, when the country was falling apart and Sarajevo was in flames.

What happened at St Quintus hadn't had much coverage in the west – certainly not in the States, as far as he remembered. But the facts were all here, scanned and posted to the web by a Croatian blogger whose handle was Nikad Zaboraviti. He'd googled the name, only to find that it wasn't a name; it was Croat for *never forget*.

No one knew, it seemed, just how many people had been killed by rogue Serb units at the monastery of St Quintus the night it was attacked. Dozens, maybe hundreds. As he read through the muddy, close-set type of the news reports, Brask's own words on the subject of evil came back to him. *The signatures of evil. The marks it leaves.*

He read about what the soldiers had done to the Croat women who lived in the shadow of the monastery. He read about what had been done to the children caught trying to escape the slaughter.

Men aren't capable of true evil? God, Rose must have thought him such a fool – such a *child*.

Still, though: even the soldiers who ravaged the village, raped the women, shot down the fleeing children, pillaged and burned the monastery were only men. Not devils. Only men.

Remember this, Matt, the professor told himself.

The destruction of the monastery of St Quintus had had wider repercussions for the Church in the Balkan region. It had been thought safe, secure; the village in which it was situated wasn't a military target, had no strategic value. So the monastery had been used as a store-house. A treasure-house. Ancient artefacts from churches across Croatia had been crated up and shipped to the brothers of St Quintus – so as to be safe, it was thought, from theft, fire, war.

In one terrible night the brothers had learned that their safety was a cruel illusion. None had survived the butchery.

Brask hadn't been able to dig up an inventory of the treasures held at the monastery. It wouldn't have been common knowledge, of course. Maybe he could dial up some old contacts. Someone somewhere must know; no institution on earth had a longer memory than the Church.

The treasure could have been pretty much anything: paintings, icons, statues, chalices, illuminated manuscripts, relics.

The last word struck him with a new force. *Relics*. Fragments of the True Cross. Strands of hair. The bones of saints.

Katerina's missing ankle bone. Norfolk's taken wrist bone.

Brask checked his watch. Nearly seven. Rose would be up. This was hardly the big break in the case they needed, but it was something she should know about. It was 18 October already. They didn't have time to ignore any leads.

He reached for his phone, then froze at a sharp noise from behind him. A draught stirred his papers. He turned.

Dmitry Rakić stood in the doorway. He held a gun, and the gun, black and unwavering, was pointed at Brask's heart.

This man, a liar. This woman, a whore. This man greedy, this man selfish, this man cruel.

Is this why Christ has forsaken us? Little Mouse wondered. Are there no deserving souls among us?

He prowled the late-night street. The priest had told him not to go to the village again but he had come anyway. In the ruined square men sat around an oil-drum fire, drinking, getting drunk. A thin woman and her young daughter picked their way through a burned-out shop, foraging, thieving.

Not a single soul glowed with the holy light Little Mouse sought. The light that encircled the vision of the abbot — the divine light of Christ.

He watched two scrawny children run by. Street children. He watched one trip the other mischievously, watched them tangle, fight, heard them swear disgustingly.

'Damned,' he murmured. 'All of you — damned.'

A hand fell heavily on his shoulder. When he turned he saw the cavernous face of the priest looking down at him.

'Father!'

The priest struck him fiercely, back-handed, across the mouth. He spat foul words from spittle-flecked lips: wretched child, miserable boy, disobedient, strayed from Christ . . .

The ranting priest loomed above him but Little Mouse's gaze was drawn to another figure. From a higher, further, better place, the abbot was smiling upon him.

'What you seek, my beloved child,' the abbot said, 'stands before you.'

Little Mouse blinked. The priest still shouted. He still looked decrepit, used-up. But Little Mouse saw something he had not seen before. Something new.

The priest had changed. He was the same mortal man, his flesh no less withered, no less wasted. But beneath his wrinkled skin, behind his half-blind pale eyes, he shone with an unmistakeable light.

Little Mouse groped on the ground for a stone. When he found one he swung it with all his strength at the old priest.

The man toppled unconscious to land at Little Mouse's feet.

The night was dark, but the old man, he shone.

Chapter Nineteen

The sky was sunless, sullen, a blanket of ominous grey. It was just after eight and barely light. Rose climbed from her car, flexed her shoulders wearily. She wondered what to expect. Warned herself to be prepared for anything.

They'd shut the crime scene down tight, this time. As if they've done it before, Rose thought bitterly. A decisive sergeant had taken charge: the hazy meadow was closed off with police tape and uniformed constables lined the meadow edge, grim-faced and ankle-deep in nettles.

Rose sought out Ganley in the line.

'Constable.'

'Ma'am.'

The young policeman seemed to have aged a decade in the past two weeks. Rose gave in to an old copper's habit: the darker the mood, the more pressing the need to joke.

'No puke on your shoes today, Ganley,' she said. 'I'll take that as a good sign.'

'No, ma'am.' Ganley didn't smile. 'It's me what's changed. Not him.'

Him.

Rose thanked the young officer for his call before moving off into the field. Grey skies, a bare Oxford meadow . . . It felt like a recurring nightmare.

There was a sluggish, low-lying mist here that she hadn't noticed on leaving her flat. Off the river, she supposed; she could see the stooped willows that marked the riverbank half a mile to the west.

And there was this *smell* – it put her in mind of a summer barbecue.

She stopped suddenly. Her hand flew to her mouth and she gulped down hard on a throatful of vomit.

She knew without any doubt what she was going to see beyond the glimmering police tape. For the first time she wondered if she'd be able to bear it – after Katerina, after Norfolk, after everything.

It's your *job* to bear it, Rose, she told herself angrily. She pushed on through the wet grass. With every forward footstep she heard it, insistent, relentless, like a thumping heartbeat: *Do your job, do your job, do your job.*

The WPC at the tape looked as sick as Rose felt. Rose knew her slightly. She liked her: a solid, smart young constable, transferred from inner-city Birmingham a year or two back. No shrinking violet, well able to hold her own in an argument – or a fight, come to that.

'Is it as bad as I think it is, Constable?' Rose asked her, masking her unease as she ducked below the cordon.

The WPC shook her head. When she spoke it sounded as though she was winded from a body blow.

'No, ma'am,' she said. 'It's worse. It's much worse.'

This guy's put the wind up the entire force, Rose thought as she moved cautiously onward. She'd never seen anything like it.

The Trick or Treat Killer.

There's never *been* anything like it, she thought.

Up ahead, just beyond a patch of scrub and gorse, a dark-brown patch had been burned in the grass. Circling wide, moving past the scrub, she saw that the patch was the leading edge of a round, ragged scorch mark, maybe eight feet across, and that at its middle was the killer's latest victim. Murder Three.

We knew it was coming, Rose thought. We knew it was coming and yet we couldn't stop it.

She put herself in a place beyond shock, beyond horror, because that was where she had to be to do her job. She had to look on the blackened corpse with a clear, clinical eye. Thinking analytically, logically, didn't make you a robot or a psycho or an ice-maiden, didn't make you any less human; Dr Matilda Rooke had taught her that.

The victim sat chained to a crudely made iron chair in the middle of a rising column of white smoke. The chair stood in a pit in the middle of a heap of coal, some still dark grey, some spent and white, some still glowing a hellish orange-red.

Watery fat glistened in yellowish puddles around the soot-blackened chair legs. The body was a dark husk. Hair burned off, eyeballs boiled away; skin charcoal-black and creased with blood.

White teeth framed a withered tongue. Another silent scream. Another scream born in unimaginable suffering and enduring through death – another scream that would haunt Rose's nightmares.

The stench was almost overpowering.

Rose looked down. There was a pool of porridgey sick by her feet. Mike Angler, she guessed. Over the phone

Ganley had told her that the stout DS had been down with DCI Hume first thing to view the scene. Angler was a boozer – and this was no sight for a man with a hangover.

Hume was there when Rose returned to the open meadow. He stomped towards her through the grass, blue-black bags under his gleaming eyes, mud on his trouser cuffs.

Rose got straight to the point: 'Which one is it, sir?'

'Chaudry's ID was on the scene.' The DCI's voice sounded as tired as he looked. 'The state of her, there's no way to confirm visually. We'll have to wait for Rooke to get her on the slab before it's official. My money's on Chaudry, though, even without the ID.'

Rose nodded. She was glad she'd seen the body before she knew that. It was hard to be analytical, hard to see with a clear eye, when you knew that the charred carcass had a name, and a face, when you'd seen her smiling out of a dozen missing-person bulletins.

'Why's that?' she asked.

'Build's all wrong for the bloke, Rotheray, he's six-foot-some, and that poor bastard over there can't be more than five-six.'

'How about Canning?'

'Canning turned up last night. Ran off to Norwich with some old fucking pervert. Back with her family now, all tears and apologies.' Hume sighed, crossed his arms. 'So it's Chaudry.'

Caroline Chaudry. Just twenty-one.

'I knew it,' Rose said – without meaning to speak. Hume heard her.

'Another fucking hunch, Rose? Christ. Fat lot of fucking good those have done you so far. Nostra-fucking-damus you aren't.'

'No, guv.'

'Stick to police work.' He looked at her frankly from under his scruffy eyebrows. 'It's what you're good at.'

'Yes, guv.'

'Keep me posted.'

He walked off across the field, back towards the lane. She could see Angler waiting by the DCI's car, propping a cup of coffee on the car roof.

Caroline had been a medical student at Oxford, gifted, by all accounts, even by the university's high stand-ards. Grew up in Bradford – big family in the suburbs. Spent her gap year in Angola, working with a health charity.

Kind, charitable, loyal, generous with her time, well liked . . .

Rose *had* known, whatever Hume said. Caroline Chaudry had just felt right.

She thought back to what Brask had said last week – about evil, about how evil is somehow something men *do*, but not what they *are* . . . Bullshit, she thought angrily. This guy, whoever he is, maybe he's not Satan, not the devil – but if he's not evil, through-and-through, down-to-the-bone evil, then I don't know what is.

Funny, she thought. Brask was a priest, a Catholic bloody priest – shouldn't he be the one preaching hellfire and calling down damnation on the wicked?

And shouldn't she, the seen-it-all veteran copper, be

the one dealing in shades of grey? The one explaining how the world was more complicated than it seemed, how ideas of 'right' and 'wrong' weren't really so straightforward?

But no. In the kind of old-school nick where she'd learned the ropes, bad guys *were* just bad guys – or villains, nonces, wrong 'uns, psychos, smackheads, scumbags. Walk into a Met section house preaching rehabilitation and you'd get short shrift.

Coppers of her dad's generation had a pretty uncomplicated sense of morality, she reflected. Right now she felt that Professor Matt bloody Brask would benefit from a good dose of that sort of common sense – even if it made him sick.

She was alone in the middle of the meadow, halfway back to her car, when a call came through from dispatch.

Emergency at the university. College of All Souls.

Chapter Twenty

Rose had said that Rakić was smart.

Brask had thought he was an animal.

Now the Croatian gangster looked out of his mind.

'Dmitry. Take it easy. Take it easy, now.'

The Croat's piercing eyes were bloodshot and heavy-lidded, his chin dark with stubble, his clothes obviously a few days old. But his grip on the gun was rock steady.

'This,' he said, 'is for Katerina.'

Brask raised his hands. This is what comes of playing at policemen, he thought disgustedly. 'Don't. Please.'

'You. You kill her. My Katerina.' Brask could see a vein pounding in Dmitry's heavy right biceps.

Brask shook his head urgently. 'No. No. Not me. Dmitry, believe me – I'd never hurt Katerina.'

'Liar.' The man took a pace forwards across the office threshold. Again: '*Liar.*'

On campus in broad daylight, waving a gun around, making no attempt to hide, even to be quiet: this is a man, Brask thought, with nothing left to live for. A dangerous man. *No*, Brask corrected himself. Rakić had always been dangerous. Now he was a bomb ready to blow.

Brask heard a shuffling noise in the corridor outside. Rakić heard it too and, wild-eyed, turned sharply, levelled the gun at whoever had surprised him. Brask couldn't see who was there but he heard a gasp followed by a low whimper.

'Don't shoot, Dmitry!' Brask cried, leaping to his feet.

Dmitry cocked the gun.

Between Dmitry and the door frame Brask could now make out the stunned, sheep-like face of Professor Sir Harold Warde-Fowler. A great authority on English religious sects of the mid-seventeenth century. Ninety-two years of age and, unfortunately for him, an early riser.

Rakić was sighting the gun right between the old scholar's eyes.

'Dmitry!' Brask yelled. 'Dmitry!'

The Croat looked round. A glaze seemed to lift from his eyes as he abruptly remembered why he'd come to All Souls with a loaded gun and a heart full of helpless rage. The gun swung again through the stale office air.

Brask backed away. He couldn't take his eyes off the gun but he could hear – *oh, thank God* – Warde-Fowler's footsteps retreating down the corridor.

'Shut the door, Dmitry,' he said. 'Come in, shut the door – and we can talk.'

'Not here,' snarled Rakić, 'to *talk*. Here' – he shook the gun in Brask's face – 'for *this*.'

Brask's face felt numb, his legs weak, his gut achingly hollow. How, he wondered, is a man like me supposed to face death? Without protest, without regret, knowing this is God's plan? Am I meant to just *accept* it?

Maybe he would have, before. The last time Rakić was there, Brask hadn't given a good goddamn for his own life, hadn't cared whether he died or lived, hadn't felt afraid, because – God forgive him – he couldn't see how dying could be any worse than living in a world where Katerina was gone.

Things were different now. He'd stopped weeping, stopped regretting and second-guessing. Instead he'd started *doing* something. He was involved in the hunt for the killer now, deeply involved. DI Rose needed him – which meant Katerina needed him. It wasn't much to live for, wasn't much to fight for. But it was enough.

I do *not* accept it, he decided. I do *not* give up. He eyed the unwavering gun barrel.

He'd been playing at being a cop and he knew how a cop would fight: a straight right to the villain's jaw, a decisive blow to knock the miscreant out cold. You're not a cop, Matt, he thought. You're a priest – or near enough. And you know there's more than one way to fight.

'Tell me about Katerina, Dmitry,' he said, battling to keep his voice calm. Pretend it's just a seminar with a student, he told himself. Just a chat over a cup of coffee. 'You knew her better than I ever did.'

Rakić bared his teeth.

'*You* did not know her.'

'Tell me. Talk to me.'

Beneath his t-shirt, Rakić's chest was heaving. His pale face was spotted with red.

'What for? What point? Talking not bring her back.'

'In a way,' Brask said gently, 'it might.' He met Rakić's rabid stare. 'Remembrance is how we ensure that the people we lose never really leave us.'

He saw Rakić shift his grip on the butt of the gun.

'I not lose Katerina. You took her.'

'Someone took her. I don't know who. It was a cruel and terrible thing to do.'

'Then why?' Rakić blinked. 'Why? Tell me! Why take her, why take Katerina?' He moved forwards and kicked the door closed behind him. He leaned his back against the door, as if exhausted, and maybe he was. The gun was still levelled at Brask, but it no longer seemed the focus of Rakić's intent.

'I can't tell you why, Dmitry. I don't know why.'

'Katerina a saint. Never hurt anybody. Who would hurt her? Make her – suffer?' His voice faltered. The gun bobbed. 'She was perfect.' He grimaced. Brask could see clearly the fierce battle Rakić was fighting with his emotions. 'A perfect thing. For me, in my life. So much stupid, ugly, bang-bang, money, drug. And then – Katerina. A perfect thing.' He looked at Brask. 'When she go – nothing. For me, nothing.'

The Croat blinked again. But Brask saw that it wasn't enough to keep back the tears. They glimmered in his pale eyelashes.

'Tell me *why*.' Dmitry jabbed the air with the gun.

Why? Countless men of God had spent lifetimes asking that question. Brask wondered if any of them had ever really found an answer.

'Katerina,' he said cautiously, 'had great religious faith. Do you think God –'

The muscles of Rakić's tattooed forearm tightened.

'*God!* That *govno jedno*. Fuck him. *Jebi ga*. Fuck your God.' Rakić's brow was furrowed and beaded with sweat. 'Katerina, she believe, good girl, good Christian. Always in the church. Always pray. And your God, he let this happen for her? To be killed? Crucify? Her head . . .' He bit his lip. 'Your God is a piece of shit.'

'Dmitry, I know –'

'You know nothing.' The gun wavered. Rakić rubbed his face with his free hand. 'Katerina. This man now, his skin? Cut off? What is this?' He looked Brask in the eye. The madness, Brask saw, had drained away. Now there was only the weariness, the dullness, the deadness of loss. 'What sort of God?' Rakić threw up his hands. 'What sort of God, hey? What sort of world?'

Brask had no answer. No one did. He felt the nausea of an adrenaline crash climbing in his chest.

Sirens screamed, somewhere outside. Warde-Fowler's doing, no doubt.

Rakić slumped on to the couch by the door. The hand that gripped the gun went limp at his side.

'I love her,' he said, wiping a thumb across one wet eye.

'I know,' said Brask.

One last flash of anger. '*You?* You don't know. You . . .' He tailed off. Gave a broken-down shrug. 'Maybe you do. Whatever.'

'I didn't kill Katerina, Dmitry.'

The Croat looked at him appraisingly, his lively eyes narrowed. Rose was right, Brask thought. Not dumb. Razor-sharp – but hurting beyond all tolerance.

'No,' Rakić said at last. 'No. Not you.'

'Not me, Dmitry.' Brask swallowed. Brushed his eye with his cuff. 'I loved her too.'

Rakić dropped his gun. It thudded dully on the floor as the gangster's face contorted. Brask saw his own pain reflected in the man's tortured expression. He couldn't bear it; he buried his own face in his hands, shoulders heaving.

Neither of them moved when a loud knock rattled the door. At the third knock Brask called out hoarsely: 'It's okay.'

The handle turned and DI Lauren Rose stepped cautiously into the room. Looked curiously at the two men. We must look like wc've been having a therapy session, Brask thought.

'You all right?' she barked at him.

He smiled sadly.

'I will be,' he said.

Chapter Twenty-one

'What'll they do with him?'

Rose had arrived ten minutes ahead of an armed police unit. She'd watched with Brask as two gun-toting officers, severe in their smart caps and flak jackets, led Rakić away in cuffs. Now they sat in Brask's office drinking instant coffee from the college kitchen.

'I doubt that firearm was licensed.' Rose shrugged. 'He'll do some time for that, I reckon, with his record. Beyond that, it's pretty much up to you. Will you press charges?'

Brask shook his head.

'No. I can't see the point in it.'

The guy takes you hostage at gunpoint in your own office and you don't see the point in prosecuting? But Rose said nothing. Just watched him. He seemed calm, weirdly so. Not that she expected him to have a fit of the screaming abdabs or a full-blown PTSD episode. But it was something, how he spooned the grainy coffee into the cups without the faintest quiver in his hand.

He just seemed sad – terribly sad.

'How about Professor Warde-Fowler?' Brask asked.

'The old guy who phoned in the report? He's as bad as you, Matt.' She shook her head. 'You academics. Said he didn't want any trouble, wanted to be left alone. He was very polite about it, though.'

Brask managed a smile.

'He would be. But I think what he really wants is to be allowed to retreat to the seventeenth century and stay there.'

Rose laughed. Then she leaned forwards, looked at Brask questioningly.

'Listen, Matt – do you want to get out of here? You've just been through a hell of an experience in this room. It might not feel like it yet, but –'

'No.' He spoke decisively. 'No, I'm not going anywhere. I'm fine. Actually, there're some things I have to tell you. I've been doing research.' He leaned over, took up a sheaf of papers from his desk.

Rose nodded and shifted her mental focus. If Brask said he was fine, she'd have to take his word for it. The case was what mattered now.

'More medieval art?'

'More medieval religion. But much more than that. Listen . . .'

Rose snapped open her notebook and took shorthand notes while Brask talked. He really *had* been doing some research. A bloody civil war. A Catholic treasure trove. A forgotten atrocity in a Balkan backwater. This was all getting much bigger than she was prepared for.

When Brask paused for breath Rose broke in: 'Matt. Slow down. The Croatian War of Independence was, what, about twenty-five years ago?' She remembered it only dimly from the reports on the six o'clock news. Bullet holes in concrete and thin faces behind barbed wire. 'These relics, or whatever they are – they're long gone now. Scattered across Europe or destroyed outright. Who knows?'

'I know.' Brask made a face. 'I can't make much sense of it. But the bones taken from Katerina and Norfolk's bodies, removed so carefully, with such delicacy – I'd say this guy's collecting relics.'

'And that's our only link?'

'That and the dates. The feasts of St Cerbonius and St Quintus.'

Rose lifted her eyebrows.

'It's not much, Matt.'

'I know it. But can we afford to ignore it? It's three days till the twenty-first, Rose. We're running out of time.'

She looked at him sharply. Took a second to twig: of course – he didn't know. She drew a breath.

'We were wrong, Matt.'

He looked puzzled.

'Wrong? About what?'

'The date of Murder Three, in France. Remember?'

'Of course. The file said October twenty-first. That was the one with the body parts arranged on the floor of the library. How were we wrong?'

'We assumed that everything went to plan for our guy. We assumed that all the bodies were found when he *wanted* them to be found.' Swiftly she explained about the decomposed flesh, the body parts left for three days to be chewed on by vermin.

Brask frowned sceptically.

'You seem pretty certain about this,' he said. 'How can you be so sure?'

'Because,' Rose said, 'the charred body of Caroline Chaudry was found at a quarter past six this morning.'

*

Rooks cawed in the tall oaks beneath a pewter sky. The air was cool and damp, the shingle path spotted with shallow puddles of rainwater.

At Rose's insistence they'd left Brask's office and come out into the grounds of All Souls. She'd felt too cramped in there, too confined – it was a bad place to talk about what they had to talk about. When Brask had started telling her about old torture methods she'd felt the windowless walls begin to close in. She'd needed fresh air, to wash out her airways, to take away the terrible, long-lingering burned-meat stench of the meadow that morning.

'The ancient civilizations of Europe were very inventive in finding ways to torment Christians,' Brask said now as they walked the winding path behind the towering college buildings. 'Fire was always popular. Not much effort, maximum suffering.' His voice was heavy with contempt. 'A man named Perillus the Athenian, for instance, invented the brazen bull: a hollow model of a bull, cast in bronze. There was a door in the side, through which the luckless Christian was pushed.

'Then the door was bolted and the bull was heated over red-hot coals – slowly.' He looked sideways at Rose. 'The victim's echoing screams were meant to sound like the bellowing of the bull. And the smoke of the burning body issued from the bull's nostrils, like steamy breath.'

'Jesus Christ.'

'It's said St Antipas and St Eustachius both perished in the bull. But at least justice was done in the end – if you like your justice Old Testament-style.'

'Perillus came to a bad end?'

'Uh-huh. Shut up in his own brazen bull and roasted to death.'

It was hard to know what to say. More platitudes about man's inhumanity to man? No – she was sick of philosophy. And she couldn't think of a copper's jet-black joke to break the mood.

'Jesus Christ,' she said again.

'Leaves you lost for words, doesn't it?' Brask shook his head. 'It's hard to imagine that scale of indifference to human suffering.'

'Not as hard as it was two weeks ago,' Rose said darkly.

She asked about the specifics of Caroline's death: the iron chair, the glowing coals.

'It was pretty common in the days of the early martyrs,' Brask said. 'The iron chair was kind of a thrift-store brazen bull. A lot of Christians were tortured and killed in that way.'

'And they were alive throughout?'

'Yeah. Sometimes they died quickly – the chair would be red-hot before they were chained to it – and sometimes slowly. More often than not the chair would be spiked, too.'

'This is where you rattle off a long list of Catholic saints killed this way.'

Brask smiled without humour.

'Well, St Lawrence, St Dorotheus and St Macedonius all suffered something similar – roasted on a gridiron. But St Blandina is foremost among those martyrs condemned to the iron chair. She was a slave girl, according to legend, in the second century. She was martyred before a baying crowd at Lyon, in France. Fifteen years old.'

'*According to legend*,' Rose stressed.

Brask tilted his head.

'Sure. Blandina's legend may be false – she may not have even existed. But these things surely happened to someone. People did these things to each other, just because of the things they believed. This *happened*, Lauren – just as surely as what was done to Caroline Chaudry this morning.'

They walked on in silence.

Rose had never had much time for ancient history. Wasn't it a byword for irrelevance, after all? *That's all ancient history now.* She'd never been hit by its full force, its vivid reality – until now.

Real blood, real pain, real wounds. Was that how Brask saw it all? The ordeal of a slave girl in a Roman amphitheatre, the agony of a martyr as the flaying knife slid beneath his skin, the suffering of a carpenter stretched on a wooden cross –

Perhaps, to Brask, it was all as real as Katerina's pain, or David Norfolk's, or Caroline's.

As real to him as the death of a young woman on an Ohio freeway a decade ago.

As real, Rose thought with a lurch, as a thirty-six-year-old woman dying from cancer on a hospital bed twenty-eight years ago.

'All Souls' Day,' Brask said suddenly.

She looked up at him.

'What?'

'That's when the fourth body in France was found. November second. All Souls' Day.' He met her enquiring gaze. 'That's when you'll find the next victim.'

'Unless we stop him.'

Brask nodded. They'd come to a halt in the lee of a yellow-lichened stone wall.

'You have to get the word out,' he said urgently. He took hold of her arm. 'Warn people. It's the only way.'

'A recipe for mass hysteria is what it is.' She pulled away. 'And warn them of what? Bogeymen? Things that go bump in the night? We've got nothing, Matt. And people here are already on the brink.' *Even the police.*

'Can you blame them? They need to know. We have to tell them what we know.'

'How can we?' She shook her head in exasperation. 'Matt, what could we possibly say that wouldn't make things worse? You wait till word gets out about poor Caroline. Wait till you see what our friends in the press make of that, on top of everything else. *Then* tell me what we need is more panic.'

'But we have to do *something*,' Brask protested.

'We do.' Rose wrapped her coat tighter, looked up at Brask with a wintry smile. 'We have to stop the bastard.'

Brask nodded vaguely, but he looked unconvinced.

Little Mouse would never have thought the priest had the strength to scream so loudly.

He had anointed the old man with the necessary oils.

He had spoken the litany.

He had asked the priest to pray with him – but the priest had refused to pray. The old man only begged to be freed, to be spared.

Little Mouse had lifted the priest from his bed. After days without food the man was only scraps of bone, leather and hair bound in stinking sackcloth.

Little Mouse had tied the wrists of the priest to a branch of an ash tree a day's walk from the village.

He'd taken the iron claws from their burlap sack. These were fine things and he was proud of them. He had scrubbed away every spot of rust and greased the metal with balsam oil. The edges of the hooked blades were stropped and keen.

It was at this point that the priest, hanging from the bough by his stringy arms, began to scream. Began, and – as Little Mouse buried the bladed claws in his abdomen, ploughed away the flesh, drew out the blades, wiped them clean and ploughed again – did not stop.

For all the screaming, no one came. In this part of Croatia people had long since learned to ignore far-off screams. In all the hours Little Mouse worked and the priest screamed no one came.

Finally the priest hung motionless and silent.

'*You have found the heaven you longed for, Father,*' Little Mouse cried, his face drenched with sweat and tears. '*By the grace of Christ, you are saved.*'

Still no one came.

Chapter Twenty-two

26 October

DCI Morgan Hume was a sly old dog. He'd found a middle way. Rose was still officially heading the investigation – that is, as far as the press and the chief super were concerned. But in reality?

'Hello. Ken Randall here. I live in Iffley, run a little tea shop there, quite a successful one as these things go, but anyway, this probably isn't relevant, but I mentioned it to my wife, Mary, and she said, "Ken, that could be important, you have to call that police hotline we saw on Meridian" – so here I am, and the thing is, it's probably nothing, but I was leaving the golf club the other night, Tuesday, it would have been, it's just outside Littlemore, not Iffley at all really, and I saw these young lads, young men more like, Asian-looking, in what d'you call them, those hooded cardigans, and it wasn't so much what they were *doing* as how they *looked*, if you see what I mean . . .'

Managing the tip-off hotline. An appeal had gone out on the local news: cue a deluge of calls from hoaxers, busy-bodies, lonely pensioners, conspiracy theorists ('Yes, but have you *checked* the alibi of the Earl of Oxford?') . . .

All while DI Leland Phillips strutted about the place as de facto head of the murder team with DS Angler following in his wake like a pageboy.

One upside of this was that it gave Rose head-space and – in the rare moments when the bloody phone wasn't ringing off the hook – time to herself. Time for research. Brask had been helpful: he'd given her a stack of books and a list of obscure websites with .hr web extensions ('hr' for *Hrvatska*, he'd explained: Croatia in Croat).

She'd been learning all about the St Quintus massacre.

There were good reasons why no one remembered it. News reports during the wars had focused on the atrocities of the marauding Serb forces among the Muslim Bosniaks, at Srebrenica and elsewhere – they focused, as they always did, on the greatest horrors. There was only so much mass murder you could cram into a teatime TV news bulletin, Rose reflected grimly.

And so few people knew what was done in Croatia.

As Yugoslavia tore itself bloodily apart, the Orthodox Serb units, punching through the Croatian border to the west, targeted Catholic Croat communities, Catholic churches. In 1991 the monastery at St Quintus was burned to the ground and the neighbouring community viciously brutalized. No one had counted the dead. Maybe a hundred, maybe more.

Rose had followed a trail of URLs to an obscure decade-old report from the International Criminal Court at The Hague. She printed off the spotty PDF, flipped through. St Quintus was mentioned here and there: in a footnote, an appendix, low down in a long list. It was almost lost entirely in the dense, tightly spaced columns.

Among several photographs, there was one that stuck with her.

Someone had obviously thought it striking enough to

be included in the report but hadn't been able to figure out where it belonged. It was dated, and captioned 'near St Quintus monastery, Croatia', but that was all. Nothing else in the report — lists of POWs taken at Sarajevo, an account of the discovery of a mass grave near Hrasnica — seemed to belong to it.

She squinted at it. Couldn't figure it out, couldn't make sense of the overexposed monochrome.

She looked again, more closely. Wished she hadn't.

The phone began to ring again but she ignored it. It was hard to believe that the photo really showed what it seemed to show.

A bleak, sunlit, rocky landscape of low shrubs and scattered boulders.

A tall tree, alone among the rocks.

A man tied by his hands to a low-hanging branch.

The high contrast of the photo tested Rose's eyes. The man was hardly more than a silhouette, a stark figure of black and white. Sunlight gleamed on his bald head. His scrawny arms looked like black ropes.

His bare torso tapered weirdly inward at the middle, above the waist, like an apple chewed down to the core. Rose might have thought it was an oddity of his build, a physical deformity, had the photograph not clearly shown the sun reflecting white from the exposed bones of his ribcage.

Three ribs on each side showed starkly against the bloodied skin. The flesh of the man's trunk had simply been ripped away.

Another Serb atrocity? But the date on the photo was four weeks *after* the sacking of St Quintus.

Rose tucked the page with the photo into her file. The image of the man tied to the tree remained, though: burned into her vision like the after-image of a bright light. It was horrific, haunting – but, more than that, it was somehow familiar.

The phone began to ring again. She swore under her breath. Here we go.

'Thames Valley Police, murder investigation hotline.'

'Ah, *finally*. You really ought to answer more promptly – it could be important.' A well-spoken, teacherly voice. Retired public-school headmaster, Rose guessed.

'Do you have some information for us, sir?'

'As a matter of fact, I do. It all began on Thursday afternoon. My basset hound, Charlemagne, normally such a mild old fellow, suddenly began barking furiously at our next-door neighbour, a chap named Goldthorpe...'

Rose propped her cheek on her hand as the man rambled on.

You could hardly blame people for losing the plot, she thought. This case was reducing hard-as-nails coppers to blancmange. Take a psychopathic murderer, throw in a few blood-curdling newspaper reports, give the whole lot a good shaking: result, a collective nervous breakdown for the population of Oxford.

'... now, I don't know much about this chap Goldthorpe, but my wife's close friend Henrietta Craw-ford, who lives three doors up on the other side, tells us she has good reason to believe that ...'

Thing was, no one felt safe. Normally killers like this had their favourites – they murdered women, they murdered rent boys, they murdered lone hikers or wealthy pensioners.

But a Croatian immigrant from the Leys, a middle-class Bletchingdon farmer, a university student from Bradford – what was the pattern here?

No one could make sense of it. And confusion fostered fear.

The door opened. Rose looked up to see Evans, the baggy-eyed desk sergeant, jerking a thumb towards the cells and mouthing: 'Another one.'

She rolled her eyes, made a with-you-in-two-minutes gesture. Evans nodded, disappeared.

'. . . and what you have to understand, you see, is that Charlemagne really is a tremendously good judge of character, and . . .'

'Sir, what you've told me is very helpful. I'll add a note to our case file – and, on behalf of the whole Thames Valley force, I'd like to thank you for your public spiritedness in calling us today.'

She hung up before the man could reply. Almost sounded sincere that time, she thought. You're getting good at this.

She grabbed a watery black coffee from the machine before heading down to the cells. Another one. Terrific. That'd be, what, the fifth in two days?

For some of the local nutcases, it turned out, the phone wasn't good enough. They preferred to waste the police's time in person.

'Wouldn't tell me what exactly he wants to confess to,' Evans explained as he led the way into the station's custody unit. 'Just said he wanted to speak to a senior officer on the David Norfolk case.'

He led her down to a cell at the farthest end of the unit, snapped open the communication grille.

Rose peered through.

A middle-aged man in grey jeans and a blue jumper out at the elbows. Wild grey-black hair and a weak chin thick with white stubble. He had his feet up on the bench. Seemed to be talking to himself.

'Seems about par for the course,' Rose murmured.

Evans grinned, shut the grille.

'Count yourself lucky, ma'am. DI Phillips had an hour yesterday with a chap reckoned he was a werewolf.'

'I'm not counting my chickens, Sergeant. We don't know what this one thinks he is yet.' She smiled wearily. 'Interview room five. I'll be there in a sec.'

The room was the usual set-up: scuffed tiles, hard seats, rank BO smell and humming tape recorder. The sergeant half asleep beside her.

At least today the conversation was a little different.

'I ate her face, first of all. Fried up in beef dripping.'

'Mm. Okay.'

'I really did, you know. Write it down. I cut her face off her head and fried it and ate it. With bread and butter.'

'No brown sauce? Fascinating.'

The man's weak chin quivered with indignation.

'It's no laughing matter, this, Inspector. I'm giving you the confession of the century here, on a plate. You oughtn't to make fun.' His lower lip poked out. 'I've had it with people making fun.'

'You want to stop talking bollocks then, Frank,' Evans rumbled.

Francis Ryan John O'Neill gave Rose a goggle-eyed look.

'Here, Inspector, is he allowed to talk to me like that?'

'Depends, Mr O'Neill. Do you want us to arrest you for wasting police time?'

O'Neill shook his head so that the loose skin of his ropey throat wobbled.

'*I'm* not wasting anyone's time. It's *you* that's wasting time. I'm the Trick or Treat Killer, d'you see? I am him, and you ought to put me away before I kill again.'

Rose glanced to her right to see that Evans was scribbling a note behind his hand. She read it quickly, nodded. Frank O'Neill had been in this very nick, drunk and incapable, on the nights of the first two murders.

Okay. They'd done their duty as by-the-book coppers. Now it was time to get shot of this clown.

'With the first one I sucked the marrow out of her bones, d'you see, and . . .'

'Mr O'Neill, I've had enough. Interview terminated, two-oh-eight p.m.' She reached across, shut off the recorder. 'Now, Frank, I'm going to have Sergeant Evans here escort you off the premises. He'll be very polite and decent about it, because he's like that. But if I ever see you here again, day or night, drunk or sober, I'll do the job myself – and I'm not half so polite. You'll go stumbling back to your hostel with my boot print on your arse. Do you understand?'

Now it was Evans's turn to get the goggle-eyed look.

'Here, Sergeant, is she allowed to talk to me like –'

'Come on, Hannibal,' Evans sighed, rising to his feet. 'Let's get you out of here before DI Rose goes proper feral on you. She'll make a meal of *you* with bread and butter if you don't watch it.'

O'Neill was led from the interview room shaking his head sadly.

'You know,' Rose heard him say, 'I used to have such respect for the police. Such respect . . .'

The door banged shut behind him. Rose leaned back in her chair and sighed. That was the thing: half of Oxford was giving the force grief for not having caught the killer yet, while the other half seemed hell-bent on wasting time and resources that should have been ploughed into the manhunt.

Then there were the likes of that piss-artist Frank O'Neill, who did both.

Halloween wasn't helping, either. Not with a city full of students just looking for an excuse to take the piss. Every detail leaked from the investigation quickly found its way into sick jokes in the union bars and fancy-dress routines on the city pub crawls.

The victims' rough cloth clothing had been the latest. She'd driven past a fancy-dress hire place on the edge of town that was displaying a bloodied mannequin dressed in ragged hessian in its window. Headless, of course.

She'd gone in and torn the owner a new one. He'd promised to take it down, but it was a drop in the ocean. Come the night of Halloween there were going to be some real horrors out on the streets – and nothing the police could do about it.

What happened to a ghost made from an old bed sheet and a pumpkin with a candle in it? Rose wondered. Nothing like a student town for making you feel old.

She didn't feel any need to rush back to the tip-off hotline. Instead she found an empty office on the third floor and looked over the autopsy report on Caroline Chaudry.

It was a sign of how far out in the cold she was that Hume hadn't even bothered to send her a copy. She'd had to talk Matilda Rooke into sending one straight to her, in direct breach of the unit's protocol. Rooke had obliged: 'I know you'll look after the poor girl,' her email had read.

'I'll try, Matilda,' Rose had replied, and she meant it – if looking after Caroline meant tracking down her killer and stopping what had happened to Caroline happening to anyone else.

It was too late to do anything more.

The report was a rigorous analysis, a rational, hard-headed breakdown of all the information the pathologist could scrape together.

Thanks to Brask, she finally had some predictions she could test against these facts.

He had a theory that the guy was a relic-hunter, a bone-collector – that they could expect the latest victim to have had a bone removed.

Check. Caroline's lowest rib had been taken out. But that didn't tell Rose much: she already knew that was part of their man's MO.

Brask had said that the 'iron chair' was often spiked, to increase the victim's suffering.

Check. Once the body had been prised from the chair the two-inch metal spikes had been evident. As had the puncture wounds.

He'd said that the martyrs were shown no mercy.

Rose turned to the paragraph detailing the cause of death.

Check. Caroline had been burned alive.

She threw down the report. For once she couldn't hold back the tears.

Rose sat in the dying afternoon light that filtered in lines through the slatted window blinds and wept for all of them. For Caroline, for David, for Katerina. Her phone buzzed in her pocket: Brask. But Rose couldn't speak to even him right now.

She wanted to make some kind of vow, swear a solemn oath: *By all that's holy, I'll catch this murderer! On my mother's grave, I swear your deaths will be avenged!*

But what was the point now? She glanced up at the wall calendar: 26 October.

What was the point in making promises you couldn't keep?

Chapter Twenty-three

She'd taken another look at the photo of the hanging, mutilated man from the International Criminal Court report – looked as closely as she could bear and discovered something she hadn't noticed before. She wasn't entirely sure what it meant. It was something odd. Something that could make all the difference . . .

Still chewing it over, Rose had straightened herself up in the station toilets, pulled herself together – *turn it on, turn it off* – and was heading back to tip-off hotline purgatory. The DCI had caught her on the stairs. She'd never seen him like this. Hume was lost-the-plot furious.

'*You*,' he'd croaked. His face was a dangerous purple. His jaw clenched and dark brows bent into a forbidding V.

Rose had had a bellyful of DCI Morgan Hume lately. The evening before, shuttered in an office in the MCU suite, he and Leland Phillips had worked on her for two hours, hammering home their take on the case: Rakić, Rakić, Rakić.

And making it increasingly clear that it was their way or the highway.

Rakić had a motive, they'd said. Rakić was in love with Katerina – *madly* in love (Hume had pointedly stressed the 'mad').

'Feelings like that can do strange things to some men,' Phillips had said, tucking his thumbs in his pockets and affecting a worldly air, 'if they don't know how to handle it.'

Katerina had threatened to leave him for Matt Brask, Rakić had flipped, it all ends up with an ugly scene in an Oxford meadow. End of.

'*End of?* What about Norfolk and Chaudry?' Rose asked.

'He got a taste for it.' Phillips shrugged. 'Pegging out the Zrinski girl in the field was a cover, misdirection to throw us off his scent – maybe that was what he told himself. But deep down he knew he got off on it. So he did it again. And again.'

Rakić had had the opportunity. Yeah, he had alibis left, right and centre, but so what? His type always did. They carried alibis around with them like business cards. But what sort of jury is going to take the word of a bunch of well-dodgy Leys faces in a case like this?

'He was under our own surveillance when Norfolk was abducted and murdered.'

'Under *your* surveillance for most of the time,' Phillips said. 'And you have to admit, Rose, you haven't exactly had two firm hands on recent events, have you? Not too much of a stretch to think Rakić gave you the slip, is it?'

With difficulty, Rose subdued the impulse to fly across the room at the smirking DI.

'He's violent,' Hume said. 'Has a hell of a record.'

'Colourful one, too,' Phillips put in. 'You ought to read it, if you like horror stories. He's not squeamish about hurting people.'

'But that's his business,' Rose had said, knowing how weak it sounded.

Phillips had laughed in her face.

'Oh yeah, here we go. Proper Croatian Ronnie Kray, is he? Only hurts his own, loves his old mum.' He'd smiled patronizingly. 'He's a scumbag, Rose. Plain and simple.'

A scumbag, and a nutcase. The episode at All Souls had proved that.

'Bursts in on your pet professor in broad daylight waving an illegal handgun,' Phillips summed up, 'and when uniform pick him up ten minutes later he's sobbing his eyes out and goes along with them gentle as a lamb. Do those sound like the actions of a sane and well-balanced man?'

'He's grieving,' Rose protested.

'He may well be,' Hume countered. 'He may be very sorry Katerina is dead. But that doesn't mean he didn't kill her.'

Rose had asked, if Rakić was such a nut, so out of control, how come he hadn't let anything slip – not the least hint – in interrogation.

'You've had him in there hour after hour, I know you have,' she'd said. 'Giving him the full works. His brief's filed three complaints already. How come you haven't got anything out of him, if he's so flaky?'

At this point Hume's eyes had slid sideways to Phillips. The DI had shifted uncomfortably in his seat, his face reddening.

'I will,' he said, with a confidence it was obvious he didn't feel. 'Don't worry about that. I will.'

For all their cajoling and bullying, their distortion of the facts and their sixth-form debating-club tactics, they hadn't changed Rose's mind. But they'd made her worry.

This case wasn't going to be about convincing a jury. First she had to get Hume and Phillips to change their minds. She had a feeling this would be a much harder task. In the meantime resources and manpower would be tied up trying to implicate Rakić while the real Trick or Treat Killer was still on the loose.

Rose knew that she and Brask were on their own for now.

'Downstairs. Now. Move it.'

She followed the DCI down the clattering stairwell with a feeling of dread growing in the pit of her stomach. What now? Hume could have a short fuse, but still, it must be something big, to push him over the edge like this. Must be something bad.

The DCI barged through the swing doors into the MCU office. It was crowded: looked like the whole unit in there, plus a few from regular CID. What the hell?

The crowd of coppers formed an untidy semicircle around a TV set. CCTV, she thought at once. Someone's caught the bastard on camera.

But that would hardly explain Hume's temper tantrum.

There was an image paused on the screen. Not what she'd expected: it was the face of a TV host, the presenter of a tabloid current-affairs show on one of the low-rent regional channels. Quentin something. Slick hair, whitened teeth, ferrety eyes. He was known for keeping a close eye on the force's activities: more than once a lowlife booted out of the nick's cells on Monday morning had found himself blinking in the studio lights of this guy's show on Tuesday afternoon.

'Guv, what's going on?'

Hume yanked out a spare chair, practically shoved Rose on to it.

'Sit,' he barked, 'and watch.' Snatched up a remote control. 'This went out on local telly at half-one this afternoon.' He hit 'play'. The screen lurched into life.

The host was introducing a panel discussion. The topic of the day scrolled across the bottom of the screen in sensational capitals: *OXFORD'S TRICK OR TREAT KILLER: IS POLICE INCOMPETENCE PUTTING LIVES AT RISK?*

'Oh Christ,' Rose muttered.

Beside her, Hume gave a stiff nod.

The camera cut to the panellists. First was a red-haired woman in black-framed glasses, around Rose's age, maybe a little older. She was introduced as 'a bestselling author and leading criminal psychologist'; Rose had never heard of her. No 'Dr' before her name, either. An opportunistic quack, then, jumping on the bandwagon to try and flog a few books. Nothing for Hume to get wound up about.

Next in line was a face she knew. She'd been half expecting to see it since she realized what this was all about. Olly Stevenage.

He was done up in a stiff collar and tie, trying and failing to suppress a shit-eating grin. This is his big moment, Rose thought sourly. His chance to crap all over us – no, me – in front of a live studio audience.

As the audience applauded the student hack she leaned over to Hume.

'This guy's a nobody, guv,' she hissed. 'A troublemaker, a shit-stirrer. You're not really going to take any notice of what he says, are you?'

Hume didn't take his eyes off the screen.

'It's not *him*,' he said heavily, 'you want to be worrying about.'

A familiar voice broke from the TV speakers as Hume hit the volume: 'Thank you for having me on your show, Quentin.'

Rose looked back at the TV. Her jaw dropped open. Brask!

Her mind raced. What the hell was he playing at? It made no sense, no sense at all. Apart from anything else, she'd thought Matt Brask at least had a little dignity. What was an All Souls theology fellow doing on a downmarket daytime TV show?

She was aware that half the room was looking in her direction. Leland Phillips, standing by the wall on the other side of the office, treated her to a supercilious smirk.

'Guv, I didn't know anything about this,' she whispered urgently to Hume. 'I promise you. I had no idea.'

Hume's thunderous expression suggested that he couldn't care less what she knew or didn't know, and didn't give a damn for her promises. He jerked the remote – whizzed through the 'psychologist's' opening remarks.

Hit 'play' to hear what Stevenage had to say. Rose breathed a silent prayer – not that she thought it'd do much good.

'. . . absolute, unqualified, unforgivable dereliction of duty,' Stevenage was saying. 'As the viewers will know, I've been tracking this case very closely since day one, and in my dealings with Lauren Rose' – *here it comes* – 'I've found her to be aggressive, secretive, manipulative, obstructive, untrustworthy and – if I may be frank, Quentin – not really very bright.'

A ripple of muted laughter stirred the room.

But Rose wasn't laughing.

Neither was Hume. He whizzed the recording on. Matt Brask's earnest face reappeared on the screen.

'I know DI Rose pretty well,' he said.

More laughter. Rose felt herself reddening. Thanks, Matt, she thought fiercely. Thanks a bloody bunch.

'I've never found her,' the professor went on, 'to be anything other than utterly professional and completely dedicated. She's hugely competent and fiercely intelligent. I think people ought to know that.'

'It's gallant of you to say so,' smarmed the host.

'Not at all. It's the simple truth.' Brask shifted in his chair. 'But Quentin, may I say something more? I believe there's something else the viewers ought to know.' He glanced uncertainly at the camera.

Rose froze inside. Oh God. He wouldn't. He couldn't.

Quentin the host was doing his serious face.

'Go ahead, Professor Brask,' he said.

'I've been doing some research,' Brask said, 'and I've – I've figured something out about how this man, this murderer, operates. There are – religious elements at play in these killings.'

That information was strictly need-to-know.

'Interesting,' the host frowned. 'Go on.'

Rose felt frantic. She itched to grab the remote, make it stop, make Brask shut the hell up – to smash the TV, tear out the DVD from the player, something, anything –

But it was too late for that. Always too late.

'The victims are abducted approximately three days before they are killed,' he said gravely. 'That's how the man the press calls The Trick or Treat Killer does it, that's what he always does. For, as I say, religious reasons.'

'Can you elaborate on these religious elements, Professor?' the host put in.

Brask nodded.

'I can, to some extent. The details of the murders point to associations with certain martyrs of the early Catholic Church. Extrapolating from this, Inspector Rose and I have gained some insight into when and why these murders take place.'

'And what' – the focus of the shot tightened as the host spoke – 'have you learned?'

Brask turned his sincere gaze fully to the camera.

'I have very good reason to believe that the next murder will happen very soon.' He took a deep breath; Rose was holding hers. 'I have very good reason to believe,' Brask said, 'that someone – and my gosh, I wish I knew who – will be abducted on Halloween. And that on All Souls' Day, November second, that person will be killed.'

Cue chaos in the TV studio.

Cue fury in the MCU office. Rose heard Angler's shout: 'For *fuck's* sake!' Someone angrily booted over a chair. Doors banged, phones buzzed. The air was filled with expletives, strung-out, overworked coppers cursing Brask's name, and hers, too.

This was going to cause mayhem. It was going to throw Oxford into panic. It was going to cripple the investigation.

Hume flicked off the recording. Turned to her with an ominously blank expression.

'My office,' he said. 'Now.'

It was a betrayal. There was no other word for it. Rose might not have had a theology PhD but she knew a Judas when she saw one.

She understood, of course, that Brask had only done what he thought was right. She knew that he wouldn't have done it lightly or without thinking carefully about the consequences.

But in a way that only made it worse. He'd known, he *had* to have known, what his statement, live on TV, would mean for Rose – and he'd done it anyway.

A betrayal.

Rose sat silent in Hume's cramped, clutter-strewn office as the DCI unloaded. A fucking disgrace. A fucking outrage. Turned the biggest fucking murder investigation in the city's history into a fucking French farce. And so on.

'If you were a bloke,' Hume seethed, 'I'd break your fucking nose and kick you the length of fucking St Giles'.'

Rose lifted her chin.

'Go ahead, sir,' she said. 'Wouldn't want people saying I got special treatment.'

'You'd better do as she says, guv,' Phillips put in, 'or she'll have you up for sex discrimination.'

The smug DI had come along for the ride. He was perched on a desk in the corner, enjoying the fireworks.

But Hume wasn't in the mood.

'I can do without any smart fucking remarks from you,' he snarled, with a fiery look. Then to Rose: 'What were you thinking?' He shook his head. 'I mean . . . I mean . . . I mean, what the *fuck* were you thinking?'

He ticked off the charges on his stubby fingers. She'd been told to steer clear of Brask, to concentrate on police work – and here they were, seemingly thick as thieves. She'd let that little toerag student journo make a bloody fool of her, of Hume, of the whole fucking force. Worst of all, she'd obviously disclosed highly sensitive, highly confidential information to a man with no official connection to the case at all.

'No, hang on.' Hume corrected himself. 'I mean to a man' – he widened his eyes in mock wonder – 'who two fucking weeks ago was your prime fucking suspect!'

Rose looked at the floor. Christ, she felt stupid. She'd *been* stupid. What had she known about Brask, after all? That he was polite, and supportive, and sincere. That he was intelligent and knew things she didn't.

That he wasn't a copper. Wasn't Hume or Phillips or Angler.

'I trusted him,' she said helplessly. 'He was – he was helpful, sir.'

In the corner Phillips snickered like a schoolboy.

'I *bet* he was,' he said archly.

Hume snorted, planted his hands on his hips.

'It was amateurish, Rose,' he said flatly. 'I wouldn't expect a fucking junior PC to behave like that. You let me down – let us all down.'

'I know, sir,' she said. Wondered where this was headed. She was hanging by a thread, she knew that much. She'd done more than fuck up the investigation; she might just have fucked up her entire career.

She made herself meet Hume's eye. 'I'm sorry, sir. You know I am.'

'Yeah. Yeah, I do.' The DCI looked at her thoughtfully. 'Worked with your old man a couple of times, Rose. He was at the Met, I was a DI in Watford. Liked him. Good copper.' Sighed, turned away. Shuffled some papers on his desk. 'I'm not going to say "we look after our own" or any of that bollocks,' he said over his shoulder. 'Because that's not true: if one of our own fucks up badly enough, he – or she – is out on his arse. We're not the fucking Freemasons.' Turned to face her again, hands propped against the desk edge. Still red-faced, still breathing hard. 'The reason I'm not going to kick you off the force is nothing to do with that. It's because of what I've seen in you before today. And it's because I don't believe any daughter of Keith Rose can be as much of a fucking moron as you've made yourself look this week.'

Rose winced. That felt like a low blow.

Hume moved behind his desk, sat down wearily. Put on a cheap pair of reading glasses and picked up a file of papers.

'You're off the case, of course,' he added, looking at her over the lenses. 'And on indefinite leave until I say otherwise.' Flipped open the file.

'Sir, if you'd just let –'

'Now fuck off out of it, Rose.'

He said it like it was an afterthought, Rose remembered later. He broke her life into pieces like it didn't mean a thing.

As he walked back to the village through the barren, stony scrub, something gnawed at Little Mouse like a parasite. A vacancy; something missing, something left undone.

As he walked, weary in body and soul, he prayed — and his prayer was answered.

He saw his beloved abbot up ahead, an indistinct, deep-glowing figure in the washy white sunlight.

'It is not enough,' Little Mouse shouted, and heard his words echo among the trees.

'The order,' the abbot told him, 'needs more than blood. Think of our treasures — the lost treasures of St Quintus. You must restore them,' the abbot said. 'When they are restored, then shall we all be reborn.'

Little Mouse threw up his hands.

'I cannot paint pictures, Father Abbot,' he cried. 'I cannot work with gold and silver. I am no prophet, to write new sacred texts.'

The abbot said nothing. And in the silence Little Mouse saw the truth.

The relics.

He turned and ran back to where he'd left the body of the priest, his father, dangling from the ash tree.

As he ran, he heard the abbot's voice. It chimed like a bell amid the boulders and gullies. It told him what he must take, what he must preserve, what he must keep safe so that the order might return to its former glory.

When Little Mouse reached the priest's body he drew from his pocket a small, keen-edged knife. Folded out the blade. Steadied the hanging body with a firm one-handed grip on the bare, damp ribs. Reached up with the knife and carefully pared away the priest's right ear.

The work done, Little Mouse held the ear in his hand. It was grubby, rough with dead skin. It was holy. A relic. Little Mouse's soul sang.

This would be the first. 'There will be more,' Little Mouse promised the abbot. 'Wherever I must go, whatever I must do, there will be more.'

Chapter Twenty-four

27 October

Brask was in the All Souls refectory, talking with a group of colleagues over cups of coffee and a plate of biscuits. He looked up at Rose's approach. His face creased in anxiety, but he stood and gestured around the table.

'Inspector Rose, please join us,' he said. 'This is Professor Kingston, visiting from Edinburgh, and this is Dr Lionel Jessop, who –'

Rose let fly with a string of expletives that made Dr Lionel Jessop spill his milky coffee on to the tabletop.

Into the stunned silence that followed she said: 'We need to talk, Professor Brask. In private. Right now.' Turned a bleak smile on Brask's colleagues. 'It won't take long. I'll let you have him back shortly.'

Though I can't guarantee he'll be in one piece.

She marched Brask wordlessly out of the refectory – he walked stiff-backed, as if being escorted at gunpoint – and turned sharply into the first vacant office they passed. She slammed the door behind them.

Brask turned, lifted his hands.

'Lauren, I –'

'You can stick with "Inspector Rose", Professor. And you can start by telling me why I shouldn't run you in for obstructing a police investigation.'

'There's –'

'Have you *any* idea how irresponsible you've been?'

'I've –'

'You've made our job impossible. You've made the killer's job a damn sight easier. You've put God knows how many innocent lives at risk. All for the sake of your precious bloody conscience. Well done. I hope you're happy, Professor Brask.'

She threw down her coat, yanked out a chair, sat down.

'I'm sorry,' said Brask. 'I called you. More than once. Left voicemails. The last thing I wanted to do was blind-side you with this.'

She had got his messages, but too late for it to do her any good. Besides, when he'd left them it was clear he'd already made up his mind to go public with everything. He'd been calling to ask for her forgiveness, not her permission.

She couldn't look at him. Checked her phone instead. Fourteen messages, nine voicemails. Every crime journo on every paper in Europe seemed to have her number. Time for yet another change – but that was the least of her worries.

'You're not sorry,' she said. 'Admit it. You're not sorry at all. You think you did the right thing.'

'You don't have to say it with so much contempt,' Brask said defensively. 'Doing the right thing might be a dirty word on the police force, but –'

'Don't you *dare*.' She stood, pushed her face close to Brask's. 'Don't you even dare try and pull that on me. Are we perfect? No. Are you? Do we always get it right? No.

261

Do you? *Everyone* on this force is busting a gut to catch this bastard. And now you not only go out of your way to undermine the biggest manhunt in Oxford's history, you've got the fucking brass neck to lecture us on morality!'

Brask's face was pale, his mouth a tense, hard line.

Eventually he said: 'I got you in trouble with your boss, obviously.'

She had to turn away. The alternative was a right hook across Brask's jaw.

'As it happens,' she said, through clenched teeth, 'you did. You sold me out without a thought. But you know what? That's nothing. That's nothing beside the harm you've done to this investigation.'

'People have a right to know,' Brask insisted.

'To know what? That you've got a theory? Every nutcase shouting on the street corner, every mad bastard sending me long letters in green ink has a bloody theory. They don't all go on the bloody evening news and cause mass bloody hysteria!'

He looked at her grimly.

'You know I'm right.' Brask straightened his shoulders. The look on his face was withering. 'You want me to say sorry? All right.' He nodded stiffly. 'I'm sorry I spoke the truth without running it by your press office first. I'm sorry I did the right thing without regard for office politics in the Thames Valley Major Crimes Unit. I'm sorry I put the safety of innocent people before your career prospects.'

'Oh, you sanctimonious *prick*.'

'I made a judgement call, Inspector.'

'Based on what? Your extensive experience of murder investigations?'

'Oh, please, tell me, how was this one going before I came along?'

'Before you came along and lied to the police?'

'You needed my help, Rose.'

'I *trusted* you.' She stopped, conscious of her reddening face, of her voice on the brink of breaking. She had to admit it to herself: she was more than angry. She was hurt. Drew a breath. *Steady.* 'I trusted you,' she said again, 'and you betrayed me.'

Brask kept up his straight-backed poker-up-the-arse stance.

'I'm truly sorry,' he said, 'that you feel that way.'

There was a noise at the door, behind Rose. She turned. A moon-faced woman, middle-aged with golden-brown hair knotted in an untidy bun, peered uncertainly around the door frame.

'I, um, think I booked this room? For, um, the seminar on . . . on . . . on Images of the Visitation, and . . . and –'

Brask, recovering his temper with a visible effort, held up an apologetic hand.

'Of course, Dr Helpmann,' he said. 'We'll be done very soon. If you could just give us five minutes –'

'No need,' Rose interrupted him, snatching up her coat. 'We're done here.'

'But Inspector –'

'We're done, Professor.'

She pushed past the worried-looking Dr Helpmann and out into the corridor. Brask called after her, something she didn't hear, didn't want to hear. She was conscious of being watched curiously as she hurried through the college: by two academics loitering by a water cooler, by a librarian wheeling a trolley of books down a corridor, by the fat porter, who looked up from his paper as she passed.

Well, that's that, she thought, as she passed out into the college courtyard, pulling on her coat. You're on your own again, Inspector Rose.

Chapter Twenty-five

29 October

She'd tried forgetting, tried thinking about other things, tried keeping busy. She rejoined the gym; cleaned the flat; started reading books she'd set aside ages ago for when she had a bit of spare time; called up a couple of old school friends and talked about their fulfilling jobs, their happy marriages, their wonderful kids . . .

It hadn't worked. How *could* she forget? Someone out there – a *good* person: a charity worker, a food-bank volunteer, a legal-aid lawyer, Christ, who knew? – was going to die. They'd be tortured and then butchered – and who was going to stop that happening? A burned-out DCI and an arrogant, out-of-his-depth detective? A do-gooding Yank theologian?

No.

The flat was a tip again. Takeaway cartons were piled on the kitchen counter and there was an unwashed wine glass, pink with dregs, on the table. Three dark-stained coffee cups were set on the carpet. There were papers everywhere.

Rose had thrown herself back into the case. They could suspend her but they couldn't stop her working.

The Interpol reports, the documents from The Hague, the crime-scene photos, printouts from websites on

Balkan history, classical art, Catholicism in south-eastern Europe, anything, everything . . . covered virtually every surface in her kitchen and living room.

Now she slurped down cold coffee and peered again – her vision fuzzed by strain and sleeplessness – at the photograph in the old report from the International Criminal Court. The man hanging from the tree in unforgiving black and white. The man whose flesh had been ripped away, whose ravaged ribs glinted in the sunlight.

She felt like she'd been gazing at the terrible image for ever. Since the day of her suspension she must have looked at it a thousand times – and each time her certainty grew. It wasn't insomnia or stress skewing her judgement. It wasn't her eyes failing her. It wasn't a trick of the light.

The Trick or Treat Killer cut away body parts, didn't he? As keepsakes maybe, or – as Brask theorized – to collect them as modern-day relics. The murderer's sick way of playing out whatever religious psychosis infected him. She blinked, refocused.

The picture was nearly twenty-five years old, for Christ's sake – and from a country hundreds of miles away. A different world.

And yet –

It was right there, on the page. In black and white.

'His *ear*,' Rose said again. 'He's missing his ear.' She'd noticed the mutilation just minutes before Hume had unceremoniously dumped her from the case and sent her on her merry way, but the sudden onslaught of his fury had driven the revelation from her mind.

'I have the picture in front of me as we speak, Inspector

Rose. I cannot see the mutilation you describe.' The man spoke fluent, polished English with a faint Dutch accent.

'Look closer. It's hard to make out because of the high contrast.'

A long pause on the line.

A gentle, apologetic clearing of the throat.

'His right ear is missing,' the archivist said.

Finally.

'*Yes*. Ear removed, torso ripped to pieces. A record must have been taken, surely. Some kind of report, a mention in despatches.'

'Possibly. Possibly.' He made a dissatisfied little noise. 'But at the time, Inspector, the situation in eastern Croatia was *very* disorganized.'

That was one way of putting it.

'Can you say whereabouts it was found? Where it was in relation to the monastery of St Quintus?'

'Ah, well, the monastery's location is on record and well-attested: a village called Niza. But the body . . .' He tailed off in disappointment. 'Very disorganized,' he said again.

The staff at the International Criminal Court had been helpful; a couple of calls had got her through to this man, an assistant archivist specializing in material relating to the Croatian War of Independence. It seemed like a nightmare job. There were stacks of documentation: reports, transcripts, written orders, press cuttings, inventories, troop numbers, casualty lists, material from the peace negotiations, depositions from the post-war prosecutions. All of it in a state of chaos.

What was that old line? Truth is the first casualty of war. This guy would have disagreed: the first casualty of war was efficient organization of paperwork.

'I will look into this matter for you, Inspector Rose,' the man said, his reedy voice firm with determination. 'I will find all the facts I can.'

Rose thanked him, wished him good luck. Hung up.

She put the kettle on and, leaning on the kitchen counter, leafed again through her printout of the ICC report, looked again at the dead man hanging from the black tree.

A victim, Rose was convinced, of the iron claws.

She'd done some research of her own.

The iron claws went right back to the days before Jesus's birth, to the sacred Hebrew Books of the Maccabees. Soldiers of the tyrant Antiochus, Rose had read, had tormented a Jewish youth because he refused to eat forbidden meats: 'They ripped out his muscles with their iron claws,' the ancient text read, 'and tore his flesh all the way up to his chin.'

The boy was a Jewish martyr, though; Catholicism was the thread – the only thread – that linked together Katerina, David, Caroline and the monastery of St Quintus.

Rose had continued her search.

Grisly medieval paintings. Catalogues of witch-hunts and Inquisitions. Eye-watering accounts of emperors' bloodthirsty circuses.

She'd found what she was looking for in third-century Rome. St Tatiana, a deaconess of the Early Church, was tortured on the orders of Emperor Severus Alexander. The most terrible of the punishments Tatiana suffered was being raked with iron claws, which ripped the flesh from her upper body.

Angels descended to heal Tatiana's wounds and transport her to heaven.

Rose thought back to the figure in the photo strung from a tree. No healing angels there. Must've turned up after the photo was taken.

She set the report down, rubbed her eyes. What the hell was she *doing*? A twenty-five-year-old massacre. Torture in ancient Rome, saints and martyrs, obscure Hebrew texts . . . Hume was right. This wasn't police work. Meeting Brask had knocked her way off course.

But what was she supposed to do? She was off the case and out of the loop, barred from any contact with the Zrinskis or the Norfolks or Dmitry Rakić. Even Leland Phillips wasn't taking her calls. The orders from the top were clear: leave the case alone.

But the case wouldn't leave *her* alone.

Brask could've helped. He'd have known about the iron claws, St Tatiana, all the stuff it'd taken Rose hours to dig out.

The professor wanted to help, too. He'd left half a dozen voicemails on Rose's phone, apologizing, explaining, offering to do whatever it took to set things right. It was all a little familiar, Rose'd thought, listening to the messages. She'd heard that same sincere, earnestly pleading tone before – on Katerina's phone.

Katerina had never had the chance to call him back.

Rose didn't have the inclination. After what he'd done she was seriously not in the mood for Brask's well-meaning intrusions.

All this stuff, though, from the Yugoslav Wars, from the Early Church. Okay, it was obscure, maybe kind of tenuous, and the thought of standing up in court and setting it out before a judge – 'You see, m'lud, it all begins with the ancient Hebrew Books of the Maccabees . . .' – made her want to laugh and cry at the same time.

But it fitted. It felt right.

She heard DCI Hume's mocking jibe: *Another fucking hunch, Rose?*

Yeah, well. If she was off the case, Hume wasn't in charge any more.

She picked up the phone, ready to bother the fussy assistant archivist with yet more enquiries about a little-known monastery and long-forgotten corpse – and then stopped mid-dial. To a copper used to asking direct questions, going through the ICC records office felt unsatisfying, third-hand, like a long-range game of Chinese whispers. Was there a way to cut out the middleman?

The Abbot of St Quintus and the one-eared dead man were long gone and weren't going to be helping anyone with their enquiries any time soon – even if it was Halloween.

Christ – Halloween! Sunk in her research, Rose had almost forgotten about that. The night before she'd stopped at a corner supermarket to pick up bread, tea and a bottle of wine, and had had to pick her way through rack after rack of plastic merchandise in lurid pumpkin-orange. In the student quarters of town the fancy-dress partying was already underway. She'd passed one kid passed out drunk on a park bench near Magdalen, his pissed-up mates dousing him with joke-shop blood. The local paper had run a story on a third-year Classics student who'd jumped into the Isis in full Dracula costume and nearly drowned. Real fun and games.

Over-excited kids, drunk teenagers and a city in the grip of serial-killer hysteria . . .

And it was only going to get worse. She had to *do* something.

She put down the phone and moved to the kitchen table, where her laptop hummed softly on standby. She fired it up. New browser window. Quick search: *flights to Croatia*.

Chapter Twenty-six

31 October

Mass graves. Bloodied bodies. Shelled-out towns. The old reports from The Hague had painted this part of eastern Croatia as a hell on earth.

But now, out of the car window, bathed in clear, cold, late-autumn light, it looked almost like heaven.

Rose turned to her translator and driver, Dragan.

'Is the whole country this beautiful?' she asked.

'Yes,' Dragan said simply. He moved the hired car up a gear, nodded with satisfaction. 'Most beautiful country.'

The villages they passed through were picture-book pretty, set in expansive landscapes of stone and river, forest and sky. As Rose watched, a dark crowd of thousands of starlings rose from a stand of bare trees to perform a dramatic flight over the road, furling and unfurling like a black flag waving in the wind.

So strange that only twenty-five years ago this was a nation in the grip of civil war. Twenty-five years ago this soil was soaked with blood and this countryside was in flames.

Twenty-five years ago a man was tied to a tree and his body was stripped of its flesh.

Twenty-five years later, Rose wondered, had his killer returned?

She thought of the Interpol files from France a decade before, the terrible monochrome pictures of dismembered corpses strewn across dusty floors. Had he ever, in fact, gone away?

'Not far,' Dragan said, gesturing as a road sign flashed by.

Niza. The town nearest to the tree from which the man's body had been strung. Would anyone there remember? Would anyone care?

Rose was counting on it. Niza was her best shot at getting to the dark heart of this case.

A mile or so later they swung on to a side road and followed its winding course up into starkly handsome hill country.

'Many monasteries in the hills,' Dragan said conversationally. 'Higher you climb, closer you are to God.'

Another sharp turn off, into a swaying tunnel of overhanging trees, and then a steep, straight climb to where a whitewashed gable end marked the western edge of a small huddle of buildings.

Dragan revved noisily up the slope, swung the car into a bare tract of land that seemed to serve as a car park. He killed the engine and slapped the steering wheel with finality.

'Here we are,' he said, beaming behind his blackout sunglasses. 'Welcome to Niza.'

Rose smiled uncertainly.

She'd come to like this beefy, uncomplicated Croat. He was a good translator – he'd spent four years in England, working variously as a taxi driver, hospital porter, trucker's mate and nightclub bouncer – and knew every inch of this part of Croatia. He was maybe thirty-five, forty. He thought fast, learned quickly and spoke without thinking.

And he smiled a lot. Even when Rose had explained who she was, what she was doing in Croatia and what her interest was in Niza, he'd smiled – smiled and said, 'No problem.'

A hard man to faze. A hard man full stop. Reminded her of some coppers she'd known.

They climbed out of the car. It had been mild enough down in Slavonski, to the south-west, where her connecting flight from Zagreb – a wind-buffeted hundred-mile hop in a twin-propellered rust bucket – had set her down. Up here, though, it was blustery and stingingly cold. Rose shivered.

Dragan, who seemed comfortable in his tracksuit bottoms and tatty hoodie, stretched extravagantly and said: 'All right, boss. What now?'

She zipped her coat, checked her pockets for notebook and pen.

'Now,' she said, 'we do some old-fashioned police work.'

Twenty-five minutes of door-to-dooring around the village reminded Rose that people – whatever their nationality or language – really aren't so different underneath.

No one likes talking to coppers.

She'd shown the picture of the dead priest to maybe seventeen people. Her in-built persistence coupled with Dragan's straight-talking charm had earned them maybe five half-useful answers – plus a nice collection of suspicious looks, frank refusals, slammed doors and Croat go-fuck-yourselves.

'Nasty memories,' Dragan had shrugged after a middle-aged lady had threatened to set her dogs on them. 'A long time ago, but nasty, still. Painful. No one wants to be reminded.'

'Don't people want justice?'

'Some, maybe. Twenty years ago, ten years ago, maybe. But it's just a word now, justice. The trials go on and on. War crime. Milošcvić, Karadžić. Me, I'd sooner forget.'

But *someone* has to remember, Rose thought.

As they crossed the deserted village square, Dragan said he knew the butcher in the village; he'd done a little business with him, he explained vaguely. Poached venison, Rose guessed – though from what she knew of Dragan it could have been anything from used car parts to smuggled small arms.

'Old man, this Karel, very, very ancient,' he said. 'Knows everything in Niza. Knows nothing *outside* Niza – but in Niza, everything.'

The butcher's shop was a small place, with no display window at the front, just a faded wooden sign and a rickety fly-screen. They squeezed inside to find themselves in a terracotta-tiled space, just big enough for the two of them, framed by an L of glass-fronted counters.

The air was suffused with the smell of blood.

Dead rabbits and dusty cured hams hung on hooks from the ceiling. Along the counter, heavy cuts of dark-red meat were crowded artlessly into the chiller shelves. For Rose, the sight was almost overpowering: these last few weeks she'd seen enough raw flesh and exposed white bone to last a lifetime.

A slightly built old man stood at a bloodstained

chopping block behind the counter. Half turned away from them, he pulled fistfuls of feathers from a scrawny partridge. He seemed unaware of their presence until Dragan cried: 'Karel, you old hound! Put down your breakfast and talk to us.'

The man turned, still holding the half-plucked partridge by the neck. *Very, very ancient* was about right, Rose saw. The man's face was like a crumpled brown paper bag. But his dark, deep-set eyes were clear and quick. At the sight of Dragan, his face broke into a grin.

He said something in Croatian and extended a hand that was stained red past the wrist by years of butchery. Dragan shook it vigorously. The old man, with a questioning glance at Rose, said something that sounded like *'supruga'*. Whatever he'd said made Dragan laugh.

'He wants to know if you are my wife,' the translator explained with an amused look. Another burst of Croatian. She heard the word 'Oxford': Dragan said it twice, with emphasis, proud as a new undergraduate of his tenuous association with the ancient city. But he might as well have said Addis Ababa or Saturn for all the recognition that showed in the old butcher's face.

Then the butcher spoke animatedly, with excited gestures, the half-bald partridge swinging haplessly from his fist as he talked. Dragan nodded with the pained look of a man trapped in a conversation he is too polite to bring to an end.

When Karel paused for breath Dragan murmured to Rose: 'He is filling me in on all the village gossip. This guy. Russia might invade, America might sink beneath the sea, and this fellow would still speak of

Lizaveta Handzel's divorce and Martin Krasić's new pick-up truck.'

Rose smiled.

'I know the type.' She took the photo of the man and the tree from her pocket. 'Show him this. See what he remembers.'

Karel the butcher seemed to be about to unleash another volley of Niza gossip – but when Dragan placed the photo on the countertop he fell silent. His smiling mouth narrowed to a furrowed crease.

Dragan rapped out a question and the butcher nodded.

As he began, hesitantly, to speak, Rose nudged Dragan.

'Translate as he goes,' she murmured. 'I don't want to miss anything.'

The burly Croat nodded. What followed wasn't easy to keep track of – the two men speaking over one another, Karel thoughtful and slow, Dragan brisk, professional, concentrating hard – but Rose managed. By the end of the brief exchange she felt, for the first time in a long while, as though she'd taken a step forwards.

Karel remembered. He remembered the horror that had run like a flash flood through the devastated village when the mauled body was discovered. Despite the years of bloodshed, the killing of the priest had shocked the village to its soul.

'Priest?' Rose put in sharply.

The word sent a reel of images across her mind's eye: Brask in his dog collar, Father Florian and the Church of the Queen of Peace, the ancient martyrs, the Oxford murders – the twisted religion that drove the Trick or Treat Killer.

Yes, Karel said, the man was a priest. Or had been, once. He'd been defrocked, long ago, before he'd come to Niza. Nobody knew why, Karel said, but out here, nobody cared much for what was 'official'. The man knew Latin, said Mass, wore a priest's collar and crucifix: he was a priest.

He lived out in the woods, by himself. Didn't come to the village much. People said he was crazy, but then people were always saying that about someone. And anyway aren't all priests crazy? Why else choose a life without women? The wizened butcher shook his head. No way for a man to live.

'Would anyone else remember him? Is there anyone else we could talk to?'

A shrug. Maybe. There was an old woman who lived not far from the priest's place. She'd surely remember him well enough, if they could get any sense out of her. She was the widow of old Matić, the ironmonger, who'd caught tetanus from a rusty nail and died, although that was a long time ago, before this last war, and before their daughter ran off with some young fellow, or so people said –

Dragan broke off with an apologetic look at Rose.

'And so on,' he said. 'More local gossip.'

'Could we go and see this woman? Can he tell us where to find her?'

Dragan passed on the question and the butcher, hands waving, poured out a long stream of complicated directions. Even in English Rose felt sure she'd have struggled

278

to follow him – but Dragan absorbed the information impassively, nodded and turned to Rose: 'Shall we go?'

'Did you get all that?'

'Uh-huh.'

'Then let's go.'

They thanked the old butcher, who smiled – perhaps less happily than before – and wished them good luck.

Rose was glad to step out of the shop's smothering fug of blood. On the walk back to the car she breathed the cold upland air gratefully.

'Quite a guy, huh?' Dragan chuckled as he clambered back into the driver's seat and banged shut the door. 'What a character.'

Rose nodded. Quite a guy indeed. He'd given her her first solid lead in days: she wouldn't forget him in a hurry.

If the villages they'd passed through on the way to Niza were scenes from a fairy tale, this, Rose thought, was where the witch lived.

The roof sagged and the gutters were thick with moss and lank yellow weeds. The brick walls looked damp-eaten; the bent iron drainpipe was crusted with rust. Off-white bracket fungus jutted from the timbers.

Beyond the smeared, uncurtained windows Rose could see nothing but darkness. 'Someone *lives* here?' she muttered as she eased open the stiff metal gate.

Dragan shrugged, eyeing the tumbledown cottage with unease.

'That's what the butcher said.'

'An old woman living all alone in this place? Christ. Poor thing.'

Dragan said nothing. He seemed spooked. Rose had assumed the guy was bombproof – but then she knew that everyone has their hang-ups, their weaknesses; everyone comes to a tipping point sooner or later.

If a sixteen-stone Croat bouncer was scared of a harmless old biddy, who was she to make fun?

She knocked loudly on the cottage door.

Shuffling noises came from inside.

'Stay behind me if she turns violent, Dragan,' Rose murmured. 'And remember, little old ladies can smell fear.'

The big translator scowled. *Gotcha.*

Rose wiped the smirk off her face as the door opened hesitantly inwards. She knew the drill here. Be polite, be open, be confident. Speak up. Accept a cup of tea when it's offered. Try not to look bored. What you want will be in the detail, the incidentals, the stuff they don't think is important.

The face that poked out from behind the door was narrow and pale-skinned, framed by stiffly pinned grey hair – a good-looking woman she'd have been, once. She had plastic-rimmed glasses and when she opened her mouth her ill-fitting dentures clacked.

'Jesi li ovdje o Olga?'

It didn't sound like 'Yes?' or 'Hello?' Rose glanced at Dragan, who shifted his feet uncomfortably.

'She wants to know,' he said, 'if we've come about Olga.' He shrugged.

Olga? Rose thought quickly back to what the butcher had said. *Before their daughter ran off with some fellow . . .*

Dragan spoke curtly to the woman. *Engleska*, England.

Policija, police. The woman blinked slowly, drew open the door, muttered something indistinct.

'She says to come in,' Dragan said unhappily.

Rose gestured. 'After you.'

They followed the old woman into the cottage.

Mrs Matić directed them to a little room where they waited as she puttered away in the kitchen. After a few minutes she brought them cups of a bitter, mould-green herbal tea. The old woman settled into a bony armchair whose upholstery was worn to a dull shine. Rose perched on a three-legged stool while Dragan squatted on the carpet before an unlit wood stove that was grimy with old ash. Everywhere were the smells of disuse and decay.

'Jesi li ovdje o Olga?' the woman asked again.

'Tell her,' Rose said quietly, 'that we don't know anything about Olga. Tell her we're sorry.'

When Dragan did so the woman wobbled her head, said something in a high, querulous voice. '"Sorry" butters no parsnips,' Dragan translated. 'Mr Matić will be very angry when he learns that you still have not found our daughter.' He gave Rose a wry look.

So Mrs Matić was a little confused. Living alone here in the woods with only the memories of a dead husband and runaway daughter to keep her company, Rose couldn't blame her. They'd just need to be patient and show the poor woman a bit of understanding.

Besides, this could work in their favour. Mrs Matić, it seemed, lived in the past. The past was what Rose had come all this way for; memories were all they had to go on.

Rose produced the picture of the dead man tied to the tree. Dragan asked the question.

Mrs Matić looked at the picture and turned a sharp, bird-like look on Rose. Rose saw the foul green tea quiver in her teacup.

'Does she know who he was?' Rose urged.

At Dragan's repeated enquiry the old woman set down her cup and rose to her feet. The sunken hollowness of her face seemed to deepen but a sort of sorrowful clarity came into her dim blue eyes.

For a moment Rose thought she was about to ask them to leave.

'*Prati*,' the woman said. Rose didn't know the word but the woman's stiff rheumatic gesture was clear enough. *Follow*.

The old woman shuffled around the back of her arm-chair, towards the far end of the room. There must have been a window in the far wall, but if there was, its light had long been blocked out by the heaps of accumulated belongings. Old furniture, mildewed books, newspapers tied with string, a rack of women's clothes.

Rose had seen this sort of thing before and knew what it was about. Olga. The missing daughter.

A part of it was pure attachment, a desperate clinging to the things of the past, as if by association they might conjure the spirit of the departed: *as long as we have the bed Olga used to sleep in, the records she used to listen to, the books she used to read, we still have Olga.*

The other part was to do with hope.

When Olga comes back, what will she think if I have thrown away all her good dresses?

Rose found herself thinking of the Zrinski girls, Sofia and Adrijana. How long would they hang on to Katerina's things? How long would they keep Katerina's room just as it was? When would they delete her number from their phones? When, if ever, would they stop half expecting their sister to walk in through the door?

Her dad had kept a wardrobe full of her mum's dresses for years, after. Never looked at them, never touched them. All sheathed in dry-cleaners' dust covers but there, all the same.

It made Rose want to weep.

She followed Mrs Matić into the shadows with Dragan sloping along behind like a sulky schoolboy. The old woman led them through a narrow passageway between stacks of worm-eaten dark-wood furniture. The carpet beneath their feet was worn through to the weave. Many footsteps, many times a day.

Where the passageway opened out Rose saw that the rear window of the room was not only blocked out, it was boarded up. The darkness here was no accident.

And nor was the light: three sweet-smelling wax candles flickered on the floor, by the wall. They illuminated a photograph in a black frame, covered by a cracked pane of glass.

A portrait of a young woman.

Olga.

Rose came alongside Mrs Matić and gently touched her shoulder.

'I'm sorry,' she said. There was no need for Dragan to translate.

The old woman's shoulders shook.

Olga had been a nice-looking young woman, perhaps in her early or mid-twenties. Dark hair, indigo eyes, a laughing, open-mouthed smile. Wouldn't have been the first pretty country girl to take off with a persuasive young man. Rose thought of Susie Canning, the vicar's daughter who'd gone missing the previous week in Oxford for the same reason. Then she thought of Caroline Chaudry, whose absence had occurred under far more sinister circumstances.

She heard Dragan mutter behind her: 'What has this to do with the dead man?'

Fair point. *Focus, DI Rose.*

'Ask her if Olga knew the priest,' she told the translator.

Mrs Matić shuddered before she answered that yes, yes, Olga knew him. The priest was an old fool, sick in the head, and Olga had sometimes taken him food and medicine. She cared for everyone in the village, Mrs Matić said, everyone who was hungry, cold, ill – everyone who needed help.

'Was Olga a religious girl?'

Yes, of course – a very good girl, a good Catholic girl.

Sounds familiar, thought Rose.

But that was not why she helped the priest. She helped everyone: Bosniak Muslims from the south, Orthodox Serb refugees from the east. Everyone.

Again the old woman turned the fierce, bird-like look on Rose. Was it the thought of the Serbs, the men who'd ravaged her village and burned down the monastery?

'Does she think the Serbs took Olga?' Rose asked gently.

Everyone said she went off to the city with David, the railwayman's boy, Mrs Matić said. But that was nonsense. David, like so many boys, was in a mass grave somewhere and nobody wanted to admit it.

Olga was killed.

'By the Serbs?'

A tight-lipped shake of the head. No. The Serbs have done many terrible things – but it was not the Serbs who killed Olga.

Rose tried to catch Dragan's eye, to tell him, with a look, to go steady here, to tread carefully. But he was already replying to the old woman, and now the old woman was snapping back at him. Dragan frowned, shook his head.

Rose didn't want to butt in – she was aware, more than ever, that she was an outsider here, a stranger. But whatever thread had been spun here was fragile and threatened to snap at any moment.

'What's she saying?' she interrupted at last – but Dragan ignored her. He was growing red-faced, through anger or embarrassment.

Mrs Matić talked on, making clawed gestures with her hands.

'Dragan –'

The big translator swiped a hand through the air: *Enough.* Looked at Rose. A vein bulged in his temple.

'We are leaving,' he said. He turned and ducked back into the corridor of old furniture.

Mrs Matić watched him go, then with a slight start looked up at Rose as if laying eyes on her for the first time. The woman frowned.

Again the wavering question: *'Jesi li ovdje o Olga?'*

'I'm so sorry,' was all Rose could say. 'Thank you – I'm so sorry.'

She went after Dragan.

'What the bloody hell was that all about?'

He was getting into the car, sunglasses on, heavy jaw set. She jumped in beside him, fizzing with anger.

'I *said*, what the bloody hell was that all about? What did you think you were playing at?'

'Crazy old bitch,' Dragan muttered. 'Nothing but a lot of crazy talk. What do you expect? Crazy woman living in a crazy place like this?'

He reached for the ignition key – but Rose snatched it from its slot and pocketed it smartly.

'We're not going anywhere until you explain what the hell happened back there. What did she say to you? Insult your mother, slag off your football team, what?'

Dragan sighed. Pushed his sunglasses on to his forehead, rubbed at the side of his nose.

'Okay,' he said. 'I'll tell you what she said.'

'Please do.'

'Then I will explain something to you.'

'All right.' *Because what woman doesn't like having men explain things to her?*

'Good.' Dragan pressed his hands together, nodded. 'Okay. She said that the priest, the dead priest, took in a boy, a refugee boy, thirteen, fourteen years of age. He had been badly hurt in the massacre. Perhaps the priest saved his life. He lived with the priest, in his cottage.'

Rose shook her head in irritation.

'Why didn't you tell me that? Can't you see that could be relevant?'

Dragan gave her a level stare.

'The old woman did not say it,' he said, 'like I have just said it.'

Christ.

'Then tell me how she said it.'

'Very well.' He sniffed, wagged a finger. 'But remember, we are not all like this. Croatia, we are a modern country. Remember this. We are not backward peasants in broken-down houses. We have Wi-Fi, smartphones, Twitter. We take selfies, drive Toyota Prius.' An ironic smile. 'We are not scared of the dark, Inspector. Because we are east of Berlin you think we are all fucking Borat. We are not.' He wagged his finger again. 'We are not.'

He let out a deep-chested sigh. Subsided.

Rose smiled. 'Okay. Understood.' She let the smile fade. 'Now tell me what she said.'

She found bodies, animal bodies, cats, dogs, Dragan said, in bracken near the priest's cottage – not long after the refugee boy arrived. Their bones had been pulled from the flesh. One day, after Olga had been out in the village, she came home with a strange thing, a horrible thing, made out of greasy bones. Olga would not say where it had come from. But the old woman had known.

'Strange,' Rose said. She was careful to keep her voice neutral. No sense in jumping to conclusions.

Dragan nodded uncomfortably.

'All this stuff about the refugee boy, though,' he said. 'The old woman said that it was just what the priest told the villagers – that it was not the truth.'

287

'Then what was the truth?'

'A crazy story.'

'*Dragan.*'

'All *right.*' He slapped the dashboard in irritation and glared red-faced at Rose. 'She said that the old priest had brought a demon into his house. All right? She said that the priest raised the demon as his son. That the demon had devoured her daughter, Olga – and that in the end the demon had devoured the priest, too.'

Dragan shook his head, pulled his sunglasses down over his eyes.

'Wasting time on a mad old hag's bogeyman stories. This is how police work in England?' He held out a meaty hand for the car key. 'Can we go now?'

As they drove away, Rose stared out of the car window but saw nothing of the world beyond. Her thoughts were elsewhere. A thing made from greasy bones, given to the girl just before she disappeared. Like the one left for Katerina. Like the one left for Brask.

A demon? No.

But a damaged, lonely young man, scarred by the war, cut off from the world and raised in isolation by a zealous priest –

Someone had taken the girl, Rose thought. Someone had slaughtered the priest.

A cold feeling of horror uncurled in her stomach.

Chapter Twenty-seven

To her surprise Rose found, amid the ruins of St Quintus, that she had a mobile signal. She dialled quickly before she lost it. Brask. Yes, he was the arschole who'd wrecked her investigation – but he was also the last person to have found a greasy structure of animal bones on his doorstep.

The last person still alive anyway.

Voicemail. *Bloody hell.* She left a quick message, asking him to call back ASAP.

She needed to speak to a copper – someone reliable, clear-thinking, effective. Phillips and Angler were out. Ganley? Too young, too shaky – a good constable but, right now, a bag of nerves. Instead she dialled Pete Conners, the tough ex-Met PC who'd been with Ganley that first night, that night in the meadow when they'd found Katerina.

He answered on the second ring. *Thank God.*

Conners sounded a little puzzled, a little wary at first, but he agreed to do as Rose asked: call in on Matt Brask, see if he was okay, keep a keen eye out for anything not right, anything suspicious. Before she rang off Rose asked him how things were in Oxford.

'Bloody awful, ma'am,' Conners said cheerfully.

She thanked him, put away her phone. Looked around at the place in which she stood – at the rubble, the derelict foundations and the scorched earth that had once been the monastery of St Quintus. Rose had seen photos of the old monastery before it was destroyed. It had been, if not majestic, at least impressive. Now it was little more than stray piles of stone being slowly reclaimed by the forest.

'You have some strange ideas about how to spend a holiday,' called Dragan. 'First the mad old woman, now this.'

The big translator had regained his usual unflappable good humour. He was sitting on a tumbledown wall, playing a game on his phone.

'It's not a holiday.'

'I thought English women were fun.'

'Did you meet many women like me when you were in England?'

He looked up at her, narrowing his eyes in the low sun.

'No,' he said, after a moment. Shook his head with a half-smile. 'No. None.'

He went back to his game.

Rose wandered the ruins. Anxiety began to wheedle its way into her brain. The jigsaw puzzle, she felt, was slowly coming together, and she had the sense she wasn't going to like the picture it showed her. The priest, the refugee boy, the missing girl – and this place. St Quintus. Where men lived among the bones of saints.

She touched a hand to the sandstone of a stricken archway. Such an ancient place – and yet ruined so recently. It had the feeling of a castle destroyed by Vikings or Yorkists or Cromwellians, by siege engines or cannon in a long-gone past. Not by the shells and guns of vengeful Serbs, barely twenty-five years ago.

She took her hand away from the stone. The death is fresh here, she reminded herself. The destruction is new. Modern. *Ours.*

Checked her phone. Nothing: no word from Brask, no word from Conners. Rose chewed her lip. Couldn't shut off her rising unease.

They'd left the car in a lay-by at the south side of the monastery site. Circling the area to the west, Rose found that the place wasn't quite as derelict as it had at first seemed. Beyond the ruins of the north-west tower there was a small, fenced car park and a memorial to the murdered monks. The memorial was an off-white standing stone, engraved simply with the date of the massacre, and a series of weathered information panels.

She took a look. The boards featured printed text in Croat, English, Russian and German, sketching out the background to the destruction of St Quintus. There wasn't much in it that Rose didn't already know. She'd read pretty much everything ever written in English about St Quintus, about its history, its status as a valued Catholic reliquary, the high position of Abbot Cerbonius within the Balkan Church – and its destruction, amid blood and fire, on that terrible October night.

She did find something new here, though: pictures, colour photographs of the brothers of the order. The first board showed her the face of Abbot Cerbonius, an intelligent-looking man in late middle age, broad-shouldered and silver-haired, smiling slightly crookedly into the camera. For what it was worth, Rose thought that he looked like a good man. But she knew that it wasn't worth much.

The other two boards displayed photographs of life in the monastery interspersed with text. There were robed brothers at prayer, monks brewing and gardening, the abbot saying Mass, staff busy in the kitchens, a wiry-haired monk reading to a class of children. Rose snapped a quick photo of each image. The quality would be dismal – the images had already been faded by sun and rain – but you never knew.

These images made her think. They forced Rose to see the murdered brothers as men of flesh and blood, not just bit-players in a historical tragedy. They made it hard for her to look at the blackened, crumbling stones of St Quintus and not imagine flames leaping to the dark sky, the clatter of automatic weapons, the growing terror of the monks gathered within their burning home.

She thought of brothers executed on their knees before the chapel altar.

Of children shot down as they ran from the carnage.

Of the torn-out heart of an ancient order.

Rose hadn't yet figured out the whole story. But somehow, that night, a monster was born at St Quintus.

Her phone buzzed in the quiet. Brask?

No: Conners.

'Any news?'

'Nothing good, ma'am.' The constable's voice hissed and doubled on the long-distance line. 'I called his college. Professor Brask's not been seen all day. Missed three meetings, one of them pretty important – something to do with funding. Need the details?'

Rose's stomach plunged as if she was falling from a great height. The ruins of St Quintus were gone. Croatia was gone. For a moment there was only Rose, the constable's words ringing in her ears, and the swelling blossom of terror in her gut. She struggled to find her voice.

'N-no – thank you, Constable. But I want you to go to his house – the address is on file.' She swallowed, gulping down her nausea. 'It's important. I want him found, Conners.'

Rang off. *Oh Jesus.*

DI Phillips had called Brask a proper little do-gooder. Maybe someone else had him pegged as a saint.

Images of blood and fire flickered across her mind.

Saints die as martyrs. Martyrs suffer.

When you find his body, Phillips, Rose thought as she raced back to the car, you won't be able to say you weren't warned.

Chapter Twenty-eight

Brask's hand closed around the grip of his baseball bat.

Once again he'd been woken by a noise somewhere in the house. Something out of place: a window breaking? A latch giving way? He'd been dreaming – a confused, messy dream of dark meadows, old paintings, monochrome photographs, half-forgotten faces –

On opening his eyes, it had taken him a moment to get oriented. Wakefulness. A dark room, the furniture nothing but dim outlines. He was alone. A storm outside. He was in England. Oxford. What day was it?

What was the date?

Again the out-of-place noise. A kind of scuttling, too substantial to be a mouse.

He'd lain still. He'd listened to his own shallow breathing, the too-fast beating of his own heart, the wind at the bedroom windowpane and footsteps – he was almost certain that's what they were – in the hallway downstairs.

That's when he'd reached for his bat.

It had always been with him, the bat, a reminder of home, of the little-league baseball he'd played back in Ohio, of America's great national pastime. Sentimental? Maybe, but what the hell? And as far as methods to dissuade unwanted late-night visitors went, a baseball bat was hard to beat.

Now, hearing the faint, creaking footsteps – *were* they

footsteps? – mount the staircase, he hefted the bat and felt further from home than ever before.

'Hello?'

It came out sounding funny, croaky. No spit in his mouth. He swallowed, climbed out of bed. The floorboards were cold under his bare feet. With the bat cocked over his right shoulder, he moved to the door.

Flicked on the light. Waited. Didn't breathe.

No more footsteps. No sounds at all except for those of the storm raging outside.

He eased open the bedroom door and slipped out on to the landing. The bat knocked loudly on the door frame. *Dammit.* He quickly hit the light switch, blinked in the glare. Nobody.

Dmitry Rakić was in jail. But Rakić had friends – a lot of friends.

Brask moved along the landing to the stairwell. The window rattled in the wind. Blowing a gale out there. It's an old house, he told himself. Old houses creak in the wind – like ships. He paused again to listen. Yes: nothing but the small protests of an old roof, old rafters, old boards, old window frames.

He flicked off the landing light, went back into the bedroom. Leaned the bat against the wall in a nook by the bed.

A scream sounded over the noise of the wind. A woman's scream – out in the street.

Brask dashed to the window, threw aside the curtain, pushed up the sash. The cold was like a slap across the face. He leaned out. The street seemed to tremble as tree branches swayed in the storm.

'Hello?' he called.

A woman came running. A young woman, sprinting from the shadows, a young woman in a miniskirt, knee-high boots, a cape and a witch's hat. She screamed again. Racing behind her were two young women and a man dressed in black gowns – academic gowns, Brask noted with a grin – and white *Scream* masks. One had a rubber axe. All were completely oblivious to his presence.

He watched them run yelling out of sight and pushed the window closed. Halloween. You had to love it. *Finally*, he smiled to himself, the Brits are getting into the spirit of it – the young ones anyway.

Nothing on earth more American than Halloween, Brask thought as he turned back to his bed. Now he really did feel at home.

He glanced over to where he'd propped his baseball bat.

It was gone.

The curtain stirred, a floorboard creaked. A muscular arm locked around his throat.

Chapter Twenty-nine

1 November

Rose pushed ninety on the M40 from Heathrow and her little car juddered with the effort of it. On the passenger seat her phone blinked slowly as it tried to download a file of high-res jpegs from the assistant archivist at The Hague.

She cursed them both, the car and the phone. While she was at it she also cursed the commuter traffic, the hold-ups at Heathrow, the hours of waiting at Zagreb, the high winds at Slavonski that had kept the rattletrap plane stalled on the runway for forty-five minutes . . .

Why was everything so fucking *slow*?

Everything except the clock. That seemed to hurtle forwards; time seemed to be in free fall. Every minute was a minute she couldn't afford to waste. Every second was the second that could save a man's life.

Matt's life.

She dialled Matt's number on the hands-free for the tenth time. Still no answer. Reception had been so spotty in the Balkans that she had not yet heard what Conners had found at the professor's flat. There was still a chance Brask was laid up at home with food poisoning or a hangover. There was still a chance that he was okay.

Rose swung out into a barely-there fast-lane gap and

rocketed past a dawdling white van, ignored the irritated flash of an Audi's lights behind her.

She called Hume.

'Rose.' The DCI's voice came over in an urgent bark. Rose got ready to do some fast talking. She'd been so busy playing planes, trains and – she accelerated past a lorry on the inside – bloody automobiles she hadn't had the chance for a proper debrief with Hume. She'd done her best to fill in the DCI by email and she'd hoped Conners had filled in some of the gaps. She only hoped it had done the trick. 'Tell me what I need to know, Rose. We've no fucking time to waste.'

Rose could've wept with relief. Hume was finally onside.

'It's not Rakić, guv, not the gang. But it *is* from Croatia. A woman out there remembers, her daughter was given one of them in the early nineties.' She paused – but there was no sceptical sigh this time, no 'But that was twenty-five fucking years ago . . .'

'One of these bone things,' she went on. 'Weird things, animal bones, knotted into shapes. There was one at Katerina's place, one in Brask's office. And –'

Hume cut her off.

'We found one in Caroline Chaudry's halls of residence.' A stiff, awkward pause. 'Weren't you told?'

No, I bloody wasn't. But this was no time to air a workplace grievance.

'It's the Trick or Treat Killer,' she said, with certainty. 'He makes them; they're a sign, part of a kind of ritual – I don't know exactly, it doesn't matter. But it means that Matt Brask is next on his list, and if –'

'Brask's been taken,' Hume said grimly.

She'd known, of course she'd known – all the facts had pointed that way, all her instincts had said so. But it still hit her like a body blow.

'How?'

'At his place, looks like. Forced entry, signs of a struggle. I've not been over there yet but your boy Conners said it looked like Brask put up quite a fucking fight. Furniture knocked over, window put through.'

Good for you, Matt, Rose thought. I hope you made him suffer.

'So,' said Hume, 'it's your call, Rose. What next?'

'Send a team to clean out the Norfolk farm, guv, top-to-bottom search. There'll be a bone thing there, somewhere.'

'That's not going to help Brask.'

'Maybe he got clumsy,' Rose said. 'Left us a print or other trace we can use to find the bastard.' Rose pushed her car ahead of a lumbering HGV, dived on to the city slip road.

'That'd be a fair bit of luck.'

'I'd say we're due some luck, wouldn't you, guv?'

There was a brief pause before Hume said: 'Listen, Rose. I'm not much of a one for apologies but –'

'Then why break the habit of a lifetime?' She jumped the roundabout lights, cut sharply across three lanes of traffic. 'Don't apologize, don't thank me. Just help me find this bastard before he – before he does it again.'

Had she ever spoken to a senior officer like this before?

She'd never been on the track of a serial killer before.

Hume said: 'Let me know what you need.' Rang off.

Ten minutes later Rose slewed into a parking space opposite her flat, ditched the car at a forty-five-degree angle from the kerb. She checked her phone as she jogged across the road: still a few minutes to go till the damn files downloaded.

The flat was as she'd left it. A half-empty coffee cup on the kitchen counter, laptop open on the table. No one lying in wait. No weird Croatian bone structures anywhere.

She grabbed the case file from her carry-on bag, woke up the laptop. There had to be something, something in the data, something someone had said or done, a detail, a whisper – something to tell her who this guy was, and where. Something to lead her to Brask.

As she was spreading her papers across the table her phone pinged softly.

Download complete.

In his email the fussy Hague archivist explained that these were pictures found in a file confiscated from the Serbs; an unofficial kill-list, he called it, a file on prominent Catholics in the north-eastern provinces of Croatia. In the troubled weeks before the massacre the Serb troops had tramped from village to village taking names and pictures. It was all about intimidation, Rose supposed. Echoes of Nazi Germany – or Communist East Germany, come to that.

The archivist had sent her pages regarding the staff of St Quintus.

She scrolled through the photographs. Not much information for each entry: just a face, and – if the goons had been especially thorough that day – the person's name. You got more than that from a police mugshot.

Some faces she recognized from her earlier research. The Abbot Cerbonius glowered gravely at the photographer. A man who knew wickedness when he saw it. Other faces were half-familiar: was this wiry-haired monk the teacher from the information panel in the car park? And this boy —

Rose stopped scrolling. This boy.

She stared at the photograph. The boy stared back at her.

She dropped her phone, started scrabbling through her papers. She was sure she'd seen that face before, but when? *Where?*

Add in some lines on the brow and around the eyes and mouth. Add twenty-five years. Take away his hair. Take away his innocence.

Rose dug out her copy of the photo she'd been given by Father Florian, Katerina's priest. There they were: Katerina Zrinski, Matt Brask, the rest of the church volunteers, grinning in the sunshine.

Hanging back a little, off to one side, part-hidden by someone's shoulder . . . An uncertain smile, a bald head, the same face as that Croatian boy. A face she knew. *But from where?*

There were more photos on her phone. Rose ran frantically through the messily filed albums. There'd been so many new faces in these last few weeks, new places, strange circumstances. She'd kept snapping as she'd gone along. Good habit for a copper to get into.

Finally she found him. He'd been in Radcliffe Square; the agitated cook whose pig had been stolen by the student pranksters. This was the man who'd also stepped in to stop Brask from being beaten to death by Dmitry Rakić. In fact, she'd seen him that very first time she'd met Brask: the bald man had been in his office. The two of them had been talking about rugby. *Christ*, he must have been keeping his eye on Brask since the very beginning. And all right under Rose's own fucking nose . . .

Brask had known his name, spoken to him as a friend . . . a *good man* the killer had called him.

Good enough to be a saint.

Good enough to be a martyr.

Rose glanced again at the face staring back at her from the phone.

He was the Trick or Treat Killer.

Chapter Thirty

A downstairs flat in a two-storey house, on the edge of a newish west-Oxford housing estate. Most of the houses had Halloween pumpkins in front of them, but not this one. Rented through an agency for the last few years. Neat lawn. Drawn curtains. Could've been anyone's.

This was the place the Trick or Treat Killer called home.

Once Rose had connected the photo of the boy from St Quintus to the photo of the cook from Oxford all it took was a call to the University Contract Services to match a name with that face.

Luka Savić was his name, and today the Thames Valley police force was going to pay him a visit he wasn't likely to forget.

'Take it apart,' growled Rose.

The Firearms Response sergeant rapped out an order. There was a splintering thump as the back door went through. A few seconds later Rose saw flashlight beams play over the curtains. She waited. Didn't dare breathe.

No shots.

The sergeant, Munro, waved forward the rest of his unit. They deployed swiftly, silently, across the front of the house. Rose heard the lock on the front door pop.

Munro was muttering into his comms headset. He nodded, turned to Rose.

'Ground floor's clear, ma'am,' he said in his clipped Glaswegian accent. The second unit of armed officers were filtering in through the front door. 'Standing by.'

No nasty surprises then. Yet.

She took a second to compose herself. She was so close, so damn close to pinning down the man who'd caused so much misery, who'd put so many people through hell. A part of her, pent-up and raging, was ready to tear his home apart with her bare hands.

But this thing wasn't over, not by a long way. Luka had Brask. And Brask's life depended on Rose making the right calls – on Rose doing her job.

She turned to Munro and nodded.

'Let's go.'

Up the green-tinged stone path into a bare, carpeted hallway. Shop-bought religious prints on the right-hand wall. No real smell to the place; that was odd. Three officers stood, guns cocked, by the door that opened into a small living room. Flashlights glimmered in the gloom inside. Someone coughed softly.

The atmosphere was hair-trigger tense.

'Let's get some light in here,' Munro snapped. At his gesture two officers ripped down the cheap blue curtains. Grey late-afternoon light flooded a nondescript room. Another religious print on the wall, a bookcase stacked with clutter, rosary beads hanging from a hook on the chimney breast. A metal crucifix nailed to the wall above an unplugged TV.

There was a sofa and chair that looked hardly sat on.

This is his flat, Rose thought, moving slowly through the room, but it's not where he *lives*.

Her heart was galloping.

Two doors opened to the right. The first led into a small, magnolia-washed bedroom. The FR boys had done a number on it: the single bed was overturned, a wardrobe door off its hinges. A carved dark-wood crucifix on the wall had taken a knock and hung at a crooked angle.

'Nice work, lads,' Munro murmured, taking it in with a glance. 'Thorough.'

One of the officers nodded, touched his cap with a grin.

The kitchen, too, was plain, clean, normal. Save, Rose noted, for the splintered back door. She turned to the officer who stood in the doorway.

'Anything in the fridge?'

The officer grimaced.

'Nothing you'd want to eat.'

Rose's stomach lurched. She thought of missing ankle bones and severed ears.

'How d'you mean?'

'Old food, ma'am. Bottle of milk that's been there for weeks. Bit of green sausage. Kept his bread in there, too, the weirdo.'

It'd be a turn-up if that was the weirdest thing they found today, Rose thought.

She walked through the narrow kitchen, splinters from the door crunching under her feet. Beyond the tall fridge, half hidden by a plywood plank, was another door. A cellar door. Bolted.

The sudden knowledge – call it instinct, call it intuition – rose up in her like a shark through dark water: *This is it.*

There was no doubt in her mind. Whatever was down there, it held the key: to the murders, to Luka's madness, maybe to saving Matt Brask's life. Whatever was down there, it was what Rose had come here to find.

Munro had followed her into the kitchen. She gave him a look.

He nodded. 'Barkley, in here with the cutters,' he shouted sharply.

The officer, young, black-bearded and athletic, ducked through the crowded kitchen and readied the heavy-bladed bolt cutters against the padlock.

There was a blood-curdling clatter of guns being cocked. The feeling of bodies tensing, senses sharpening, minds shifting up into a new mode of operation. The door had clearly been locked from the outside but no chances would be taken with this one. Rose backed out of the room as the FR team moved silently into formation.

Barkley cut the lock and the men surged into the darkness beyond.

Brace yourselves, boys, Rose thought, her gut tight. Christ alone knew what they'd find – what was waiting for them down there. She steeled herself for shouts or gunshots, but she heard only the officers' footsteps and Munro's sharply clipped commands. She edged into the doorway, looked down. Blinked at the acrid smell that rose up the dank stairwell.

Scented oil. Burned wax.

Munro's face appeared at the foot of the stairs, grave and lit from below by a flickering glow.

'No one here, ma'am,' he called up. It was clear from

his voice, though, that there was something she needed to see.

PC Ganley with puke on his shoes, trembling at the edge of Katerina's meadow. DCI Morgan Hume, beaten down and haggard after finding David Norfolk. The tough ex-Brum WPC guarding the cordon where Caroline had been burned alive, looking like she'd tasted poison.

And now Sergeant Munro, beckoning her down into the darkness. All these coppers – good coppers, good men and women – bringing her a new kind of hell each time.

She started slowly down the steps. We're into the end-game now, she told herself. We're going to put things right, we're going to stop this – all of this.

Munro moved aside to let her step into a wide, low-ceilinged cellar. The other officers had gathered into a loose group and Rose overheard snatches of their muttered conversation: *Nutter . . . Batshit crazy . . . Creepy as fuck, man . . .*

They'd killed their dazzling flashlights and now the cellar was lit only by low-burning candles. Lots of candles. Hundreds of them, arranged in heights and valleys like a range of flickering mountains.

Rose pulled out her own torch and ran its narrow beam across the damp-eaten brick walls.

Felt her chest constrict as she took in the sight. 'Oh, bloody hell.'

'Yes, ma'am,' Munro quietly agreed.

There was part of a wall for each of them, for each of the Oxford victims. Maps, photos, charts, calendars, duct-taped to the brick. Some of the photographs were blurred and obviously snatched from a distance, others had been taken from disturbingly nearby. Rose peered closer. The maps were looped and dotted with marker pen, tracking movements, predicting routes. Spidery timetables logged the victims' activities over periods of hours, days, weeks. Charts of scrawled lines drew together the names of the victims' friends, families, colleagues, neighbours.

In a way it was disturbingly familiar.

'Looks like he'd have made a good copper,' Munro remarked.

That was it. Looked like a bloody incident room. Who else watched people so closely? Who else dug so deep into the lives of strangers?

Only the walls of incident rooms weren't decked with crosses made from brown-tinged bones. The walls of incident rooms weren't plastered with medieval images of bloodily martyred saints. The walls of incident rooms didn't carry anatomical diagrams showing how the skin can be pared from a human body, how the blood vessels of the neck can be severed and tied.

It was terrifying. There was so much madness here, so much power. It wasn't just that Luka did what he did, Rose thought – it was that he *could*. He could do it, with the knowledge he'd built up, the skills he'd learned, the twisted courage that drove him, and there was nothing anyone could do to stop him.

Till now, perhaps. We're closing in on you, Luka, she thought.

Tried to make herself believe it.

Rose panned her torch slowly around the four shadow-blackened walls. One for Katerina Zrinski: a painful lump swelled in Rose's throat as she let the torch beam linger on the photos. Katerina grinning in the church doorway. Katerina, hair tied up, leaving her flat in the Leys. Katerina kicking a football around with some local kids. She'd been so full of life.

Rose moved the torch beam on. One for David Norfolk, one for Caroline Chaudry.

One for Matt Brask.

They might have got him already, she thought, as goosebumps crept up her arms. There's a team hitting the All Souls' kitchen right now – Luka might already be in custody and Matt might be all right.

'Have you seen the shrines?' Munro pointed downwards. 'Proper confused, this boy.'

On the concrete floor, behind the banks of greasy, glimmering candles, more photographs were propped against the brickwork. They were blown-up full-face shots, as close as a stalker could really get to a formal portrait, framed in wood or brass. Prayers or blessings – in English, Latin and what Rose now knew to be Croat – were scratched into the walls.

The floor gleamed dully with a thick ledge of dirty wax – rendered from Christ knew where, but evidence of candles kept burning on and on, day after day.

Rose thought back to the old woman's gloomy cottage in Niza, the candles at the shrine to Olga Matić.

She shone her torch on the portraits. Yes, there were Katerina, David, Caroline; then there were other faces, faces she didn't immediately recognize. One, a middle-aged black woman, wore a nurse's uniform in unfamiliar colours. Then it clicked for Rose: these were the French victims, the killings from a decade before.

'You've got a long memory, Luka,' she murmured.

There was no portrait of Matt Brask. Not yet.

She swept her torch beam round to the wall papered with data on the missing professor. She knew this wasn't going to be easy.

There was Matt's life, stripped down to dates, times, the streets he walked, the people he knew. Interlocking lines of ink on a map charted his routes from home to All Souls, to the churches he visited, the libraries and archives he used in his work. There were press cuttings about his work with the immigrant communities, even a clipping from a US local paper: *FREMONT WOMAN KILLED IN DRUNK-DRIVE HORROR*.

And there was DI Lauren Rose. A short slash of black ink linked her to Matt in a stark spider chart. She was struck by how few other names there were: a couple of academics, three Brasks from back home, a handful of names grouped under the heading '*crkva*', 'church' – and Katerina, of course.

Brask didn't have many people in his life, Rose realized.

And right now he had no one but her.

She tried to set aside her worries about what he might be going through, what he might be thinking, feeling, suffering. She tried to blot it out and focus on the job in hand. Tried to be nothing but a copper.

Tried and failed. A dozen terrible scenarios, blood-drenched and black as night, played out behind her eyes.

In one she pictured Luka, hollow-eyed and intent, drawing out a small, blood-smeared bone from Brask's carefully sliced flesh –

A relic.

Rose shook away the thoughts and swept her torch beam back towards the shrines. The bones – the wrist bone from David Norfolk, the ankle bone from Katerina, Caroline's rib – they weren't here. This struck her as strange. Shouldn't they, the relics of Luka's saints, be here in pride of place? Set up at an altar or behind glass or something?

Unless he was keeping them somewhere else. Not here, and not at his work in the All Souls' kitchens. Some third location.

Could be anywhere, Rose thought in bitter frustration, anywhere in this damn city, anywhere in this damn country – Christ, he could have been shipping them back to bloody Croatia for all she knew.

But working in the dark was part of the job. You could never know everything. You just had to keep on, keep on – digging, looking, thinking – until you knew enough.

Her drifting torch beam picked out one of the medieval prints Luka had duct-taped to the wall. An unfamiliar one. She checked back: yes, Katerina's wall had a garish depiction – a photo of an old stained-glass window, she thought – of poor St Catherine, lashed to the wheel and waiting for the decapitating blade; David's a print of a Renaissance painting she'd seen before, of St Bartholomew, flayed down to the muscle, with his own skin folded over his arm like a bath towel; Caroline's a horrible woodcut of young St Blandina, roasting slowly to death on the iron chair.

The print taped up on Matt's wall showed a stripped young man bound to a wooden post. His white body was disfigured by savage wounds and from each wound jutted the shaft of an arrow. The young man's head drooped limply on to his shoulder.

'St Sebastian,' came Munro's voice from behind her. 'Christ's pincushion.' When Rose turned to look at him he smiled awkwardly and shrugged. 'Catholic school.'

She looked back at the picture and the agony in it struck her hard. She thought of the puncture wounds, the cruel arrowheads buried deep in the man's defenceless flesh. Shuddered.

This is what Luka has planned for Matt? A martyr's death by a hundred arrows?

Nausea gripped her stomach. A kind of claustrophobia seized her chest and ramped up her heart rate. She couldn't stay here. She needed air, she needed light. More than anything, she needed to *do* something.

She'd always thought she could take pretty much anything, if she had to; DI Lauren Rose could stick anything the world could throw at her. But this feeling of helplessness, utter helplessness . . . this she couldn't stand.

She told Munro to sit tight in the flat. She passed SOCO on the stairs. Then she was off and running.

Leland Phillips's deep-red Audi was swinging up on to the pavement outside the house when Rose broke from the front door into the quiet suburban dusk.

He was out the car almost before it had come to a standstill.

'Hold on,' he called to Rose across the car roof. 'News from the college.'

No smart remarks, no supercilious smirk. This was Lel Phillips when the chips were down. A copper, after all.

Rose jogged over.

'Anything?'

'No trace.' He shook his head gravely. 'Our Luka wasn't in today, wasn't in yesterday. We know he has a car, know the reg: we've got tech going through the number-plate recognition logs from CCTV across Oxford.'

'That's a start.'

'Uh-huh. And there's something else. At the Norfolk farm –'

'Bones?'

'In the barn. One of those bloody weird bone things. No one found it before because it wasn't where they keep the livestock   it was buried in straw, over in a corner. Turns out Norfolk used to sleep there sometimes, if he'd a sick animal.'

Rose blew out a sigh.

'So now we know.'

'Looks that way. The bones are warnings, or blessings – Christ knows with this guy. If you get one, you're on his list. Hey.' Phillips cocked his head and squinted at her. 'Rose, you couldn't have known he'd come for Brask. They don't teach weird fucking occult symbolism at that ex-poly you studied at, do they? It's done with. Come on.' He ducked back into the car.

Rose paused, her hand on the door pillar.

Phillips leaned across.

'Rose? Get in. I'll drive you back to the nick.'

The farm, the Norfolk farm. There was something about it, something stirring in the back of her mind. Where had it been, Bletchingdon? Way out to the north.

'No,' Rose said.

'No? What –'

'Come inside. There's something in the cellar. You need to see it.' She began to walk back towards Luka's house. 'The answer's in there,' she called over her shoulder. 'I know it is, I bloody know it is. I just don't know where.'

Phillips followed her into the house and down the stairs to the cellar.

Rose shooed SOCO out of the dank room before they could get fully set up. Okay, a crime scene was sacrosanct, she knew that – she remembered the bollocking she'd given Ganley, that first night. But to wait for all *this* to be dusted, logged, bagged, filed, run through the labs and written up –

They just didn't have time. Brask didn't have time.

'So what am I supposed to be seeing?' Phillips asked after taking in the sheer insanity of the room.

Rose motioned Phillips to her so that they stood side by side in front of a local Ordnance Survey map Luka had taped to the wide back wall of the candlelit cellar.

The white-coated SOCO techs sat impatiently around the foot of the stairwell as Rose and Phillips frowned over the map.

'I don't know yet.'

'Great.'

Rose pointed.

'The red cross he's marked on the map, here – that's All Souls, the chapel of All Souls.'

'Okay.'

'God, religion, the Church – it's at the centre of Luka's delusion. Always has been.'

This was true all the way back to St Quintus. Back to Croatia, where he killed Olga Matić and the reclusive priest. Back to France, where he murdered four people, just as he aimed to do here.

France. Rose dug into her briefcase and pulled out a sheaf of notes and an A3 map of the middle-sized market town where the bodies of the French victims had been found.

'Wouldn't say this is the time to plan a holiday, Rose.'

'All Souls is important to Luka,' Rose said as she scoured the map. 'He marked the chapel with a red cross and he's planning to kill Brask on the second of November, All Souls' Day. But it's not just a murder for him, it's a ritual, it's a –' She stopped and stared at the map.

'Église Toussaints,' she said, reading words off a label on the map.

'You mean Église Toussaints.' Phillips rolled the French syllables pretentiously round his mouth. 'Translates as "Church of All Saints", of course.'

'All Saints and All Souls,' Rose said. 'What are the chances?' But she already knew. Chance had nothing to do with it.

Phillips made an unconvinced noise.

She checked her notebook and began to mark the map

with biro circles in the four places where the French bodies had been found. To the south, in a factory, to the west, in a derelict library, to the east –

How could she not have seen it?

'Rose, your hand is shaking,' Phillips remarked. 'I can't read the bloody map.'

Her eyes snapped back to the plan of Oxford on the wall.

To the north, the meadow in which Katerina Zrinski's body had been found, decapitated and pinned to the timber of a broken wheel. To the south, the grove of grey-barked trees where a dog-walker had stumbled across David Norfolk's skinned corpse. To the east, the stretch of field where they'd found all that Luka had left of poor Caroline Chaudry.

'A cross,' she breathed. She was faintly conscious of a flickering feeling of elation, of hope. Hope was danger-ous; she stamped it down. *Focus.* She jabbed the French map with her forefinger. 'He's drawing a cross, look, four miles out to the library, four miles out to the factory, four miles to the north, where the woodland was, and six miles out to the last one –'

Phillips was ahead of her.

He slapped his hand on to the left side of Luka's map of Oxford.

'We go west,' he said decisively. 'That's where the bas-tard's taking him.'

Rose looked up. Again that weak surge of hope, low in her chest.

Hope was for amateurs. *Look at the facts, Rose.*

'Or that's where he's taking his body,' she said.

Chapter Thirty-one

'I – I thought we were friends.'

'We *are* friends, Professor Brask.' Luka's pale face loomed out of the darkness. 'That is why I do you this service. That is why I deliver you to your true destiny.' The man's bloodless lips curved in a childlike smile. 'You do not see it yet. You will, in time.'

Brask closed his eyes.

He ached inside, felt hollowed-out by hunger. His head throbbed unceasingly. Fear stirred the nausea that roiled in his lower belly.

He didn't know where he was. He remembered the fight in the bedroom – Luka's unrelenting strength, the clatter of the furniture going over, the jagged pain of his elbow crashing through the bedroom window as he tried to wrench himself from Luka's grip. The last sensation he recalled was that of suffocating, chemical-stinking darkness.

He'd woken up here. A featureless place, from what he could see. Hard-edged and utilitarian. An institution of some kind. It smelled stale.

He couldn't move.

By now the skin of his wrists and ankles was raw from the unkind pressure of the manacles that bound him. When he moved, he smelled the old-iron odours of blood and rust. He no longer bothered to struggle – the pain was too great, and his energy was too low.

Twined with his hunger, his pain, his fear, was his guilt. Luka. Kind of an oddball in the church group. Kind of an oddball at the college, too – though they said he was handy in the kitchen. But Brask had taken the time to get to know him. Treated him, for Christ's sake, like a *friend* . . .

And all along he was the very killer they'd been hunting.

How could he have been so blind?

A draught from the door rippled the low candlelight in the room and Brask shivered. Even *that* hurt. He'd awoken to find himself stripped naked, save for a few bolts of untreated cloth about his hips and shoulders. Had he ever felt so vulnerable before? Or so alone?

He had. Just once. After Hester.

That had been in another bleakly lit institution: Fremont Memorial Hospital. A cloying antiseptic smell, a curtained-off cubicle. He remembered the doctor's voice, low, regretful, but still matter-of-fact, still businesslike – telling him that Hester wasn't going to pull through.

He'd felt stripped bare, as if by a raging wind; utterly exposed and completely abandoned. There had been fear then, too. Doubt. Dread. He hadn't known how to go on. He hadn't known how to survive.

Back then, Brask had prayed to be saved. Rescued. Redeemed. But there had been no miracle. The healing that came had been slow and painful – and was still, he knew, not yet done. Perhaps it never would be.

Brask prayed again now.

He prayed to the God that had deserted him after Hester's death. The God that had stood by and watched Katerina, David and Caroline die at the hands of a maniac.

Brask prayed for a miracle.

He cried out at the touch of a punishing cold on the skin of his chest and heard Luka's soft laugh. Opened his eyes to see the man holding a pail and cloth.

'Do not fear, Professor. It is time for the cleansing of the outer flesh. With this blessed water' – he dipped his fingers into the pail, rubbed his wet fingertips together – 'I shall rinse away the dust and filth of the world.' Dunking the cloth, he added: 'A necessary first step, most necessary.'

Brask swallowed painfully. First step? And what were the second, the third?

What was the last?

The iron chair. The flaying knife. The breaking wheel. Who knew what awaited him? Only Luka.

He gasped as Luka washed the ice-cold water across his ribs and belly. His chest heaved, his back arched and the skin of his wrists screamed. He pulled in an aching breath and bit down on his dry lower lip.

Luka's cloth moved relentlessly over his body, stripping away his body heat. The man was murmuring to himself – in Latin, Brask made out after a moment.

'Luka – talk to me. Tell me . . . tell me *why*.'

Luka thoughtfully wrung the cloth out over the pail.

'For nearly twenty-five years,' he said softly, 'I have wandered. An exile, Professor. Outcast. A seeker – a seeker after Truth.'

'And you think you've found it in me?' Brask shook his head grimly. 'I don't have the truth, Luka. I don't have any answers.'

'I *have* found the answer. You, Professor, are only a part of it.'

Brask tried to ignore his own pain and nausea. He tried to think.

'We're all a part of it, Luka. God's plan includes us all, doesn't it? God judges all our actions – yours, too.'

Luka smiled, ran a hand over his shaven head.

'I am such a small thing,' he said. 'A tool only. I do the work I must do, but I am not so important. Not like you, Professor.' He showed his tea-coloured teeth in a grin. 'Not like you.'

Brask let his head fall back on to the hard bed, closed his eyes. Despair swelled in his throat. How could he negotiate with such insanity? How could he find a way in?

But finding a way in to Luka's madness, he knew, was his only hope of finding a way out of these chains. It was the only way out of this room. His only escape from the fate Luka had in store for him.

Luka muttered, as if to himself: 'The relics are almost ready.'

Brask looked at him. Luka returned the look. Though middle-aged, the man seemed like a boy. There was shyness in his eyes, but a sort of pride, too. Like an embarrassed schoolchild who wants to show you the good marks he's gotten for his homework, Brask thought.

'Relics?'

'Of the worthy ones.' Luka nodded. 'They are needed, you see, to restore the order. Restore the brothers and' – he smiled, tapped his temple – 'the abbot.'

'Worthy ones? And you yourself judge who is worthy?'

Luka looked shocked.

'No!' He crossed himself jerkily. 'I would not, Professor,

I would never presume. Only the Lord God may judge the worthy ones.'

'You speak with Him?'

'He talks to me,' Luka said, 'through the holy abbot.' Again he made the odd gesture towards his temple and then to his left eye. Then, leaning hopefully forwards, he said: 'Would you like to see?'

Brask hesitated. What new horrors would Luka show him? Could he bear it? He was so tired. So scared. He didn't know if he could take it.

He forced a smile.

'Yes, I would, Luka.' He nodded. 'I'd like that very much.'

And in the end it was such a small thing, a mundane thing – a tray of seven or eight mismatched glass jars, scrubbed clean of their labels, each with a small surgical specimen inside, bobbing gently in a preserving solution –

Still it was the most horrible thing Brask had ever seen.

An ear. A small bone. A finger. There was no blood, no gore, but Brask felt his face pale as he looked at them. Stolen things, things taken from others' bodies. One of these . . . these *relics* had been taken from Katerina. He thought of her living body, the softness of her skin, the strength in her slender limbs.

He looked at the things in the glass jars and bit down hard on his revulsion.

Why? For what? For *what* had these things been done, these horrors perpetrated, these sufferings inflicted? A maniac's dogma? One man's iron-hard certainty that he, he alone, knew the truth – that he alone had heard the eternal word of God?

It wasn't a new story. Brask had read of it, and even seen it himself, time after time: Caesars, suicide bombers, cult leaders, Pharisees, inquisitors, hate-preachers –

Whatever they called themselves, they'd always sickened him. Now they outraged him.

'They are very beautiful. Do you like them?'

Luka was looking at him with a hopeful expression. Brask swallowed. Jesus, he was tired. The despair thickened in his throat.

So much of the world's pain was caused by people who thought like Luka. There was so much pointless bloodshed. So much joy snuffed out.

He met Luka's eye.

'No, Luka, I don't,' he said. 'I don't like them at all.' Again he let his eyes close, let his head fall heavily to the bed. 'Get them out of my goddamn sight,' he said.

The silence that followed was as smooth and cold as ice.

He's not a schoolboy, Brask told himself. He's not a sick child. He's a grown man. He's a murderer, a cruel, cold-hearted murderer, and he killed Katerina.

In a taut voice Luka said: 'It is time for us to pray.'

Brask mustered the energy to open one of his eyes a slit. Just enough to meet Luka's gaze.

'Go fuck yourself,' he said.

Chapter Thirty-two

A good day to be a crook in Oxford. Looked like Hume had pulled in every copper in the Thames Valley.

Rose had said as much to the rumpled DCI.

'Bad day to be a fucking serial killer,' he'd growled back.

Rose had never seen the nick so busy, so buzzing with purpose. Uniform swarmed downstairs, crowded the corridors. There was a strident racket of phones and printers. Bulletins came in every half-hour from the SOCO guys at Luka's place. Team by team, officer by officer, Hume laid out his trap.

The force was targeting a district of Oxford four miles west of All Souls. A high-impact, rapid-response, low-noise strike on the suspect: that was the plan. Plainclothes were out in force, unmarked surveillance vans covering all approaches to the area. Munro's FR unit were on standby.

'A fucking rat couldn't sneak through the cordon we've set up,' Hume had said with bleak satisfaction.

'He's going to be twitchy, guv,' Phillips had warned.

'Nah. That sort don't get twitchy. Too busy wanking over the Book of fucking Deuteronomy or whatever it is he does. Rubbing himself down with chicken blood.' Hume had looked at Phillips, then at Rose. 'Everything we can do, we've done,' he'd said. 'It's all in place.'

'We'll nail him,' Phillips had agreed.

Rose had nodded, vaguely, unconvinced. She'd envied them their confidence – and it worried her, too. *A rat couldn't sneak through,* Hume had said. But the thing was, a rat wouldn't try. Rats are smarter than you think.

And even if Luka did fall for it, it still might be too late for Matt Brask. David and Katerina had both been killed before they'd been moved to where they'd been found, to their point of the cross. Rose didn't care whether they took Luka alive or if one of Munro's boys shot him down in the street; she didn't give a damn.

But if they lost Matt . . . she didn't know what she'd do.

A copper wasn't supposed to let things get personal. *Turn it on, turn it off.*

Well, maybe she couldn't turn it off this time.

Now she sat at her desk, rereading the logs the tech team had compiled from their CCTV sweep. Hume, Phillips and Angler had gone on ahead, out west, to the temporary command centre north of Hutchcomb's Copse. She'd said she'd join them later – just wanted to check a couple of things.

Rose was glad that Hume and Phillips were on board. And she was thrilled at how quickly Thames Valley had kicked into gear for this. Thing is, when you move that fast you're likely to miss something. Some detail. And today a detail could mean the difference between Matt living and Matt having his chest lanced by a quiverful of arrows.

The tech guys had earned their overtime on this. Rose knew they had. When she had gone down to the tech suite with Hume's orders they'd been confident. 'We'll find him,' the team leader had nodded briskly. 'Don't worry.

We've got good visuals, we've got his car details. If he's been out there, any time, anywhere, we'll have him on camera.'

Rose had been sceptical.

'These are pretty rural areas,' she'd said doubtfully. 'Nothing much but fields, trees and the odd barn. How much CCTV coverage can there be?'

The look the lead tech had given her had been almost pitying. She'd felt two inches tall – no, she'd felt five years old, a naive little girl.

'CCTV is *everywhere*,' the tech told her.

And yet Luka still hadn't been found.

The tech suite was deserted now. Everyone had been seconded to surveillance, Rose guessed. They'd be rigging up their gear at Hume and Phillips's temporary HQ out west.

While she loaded up the video files she managed to get Leng, the tech lead, on his mobile. Interrupted him setting up shop in the command centre.

'He just wasn't there,' Leng said, against a faint, humming backdrop of chaotic activity. 'Simple as that. The car's registered as on the road; it's a knackered old blue Renault, and the cameras near his house and work picked him up a few times – we ran a couple of searches to check we weren't on the wrong track altogether. We've got him filling up with petrol, even got him doing thirty-six in a built-up – but nothing in the target sites.'

Not only had they failed to spot Luka out west, Leng told Rose, but as far as the log showed, Luka hadn't driven anywhere near any of the crime scenes on the dates of the previous murders.

'Was anyone spotted near the other scenes around the time of the murders?' Rose asked. She knew she was grasping at straws but it killed her to have so many loose ends when any one of them could make a difference. 'Any vehicles near the scenes more than you'd expect? Or hanging around at odd hours?'

'Dozens,' Leng said bluntly. 'I'll mail you the list. But it's a long one.'

She hung up, grabbed a machine coffee and cued up a few minutes of footage from near the north Oxford site, without much hope, knowing that six guys had burned up hours of overtime scrutinizing these files – she wasn't going to find anything new.

It was footage from the dashboard cam of a patrol car doing the rounds about closing time, the night before Katerina's body was found. Probably Ganley and Conners. Rose whizzed forwards, watching the dark streets rush by in double-time. The odd drunk student weaving along the pavement. Pizza-delivery scooters, city taxis. The patrol car was heading out of town. Keeping out of trouble, Rose thought drily. *How'd* that *turn out for you, lads?*

On an unlit B-road beyond Summertown, the car passed a white van coming in the other direction. A Citroën Berlingo, newish. The camera clocked it at 29 mph.

Only one sort of van driver does 29 mph at quarter to midnight on an open road, Rose knew: one who's too pissed to drive legally but sober enough to know he *really* doesn't want to get pulled over.

Of course, there were other reasons he might not want to get pulled over. Something dodgy about the van, say.

Or something dodgy *in* the van.

She rewound the footage. Froze it at the point where the van passed by. No decent visual on the driver: half a white face in the shadow of a low-pulled baseball cap. She made a note of the van's registration.

It wasn't much of a lead. Could just've been some bloke half a pint over the limit, after all. Or even a decent, law-abiding motorist.

Rose allowed herself a smile at that.

She called up the spreadsheet Leng had sent over and opened it to find thirteen close-spaced pages of vehicle details. She Ctrl+F'ed the van's registration number.

It was there.

The hair on her neck prickled.

She called through a PNC check on the van.

Registered, the operator told her, with Oxford University Contract Services.

She felt her heart rate quicken, but checked herself. It could be nothing. Twenty-two thousand students kept those guys busy. Throw half a brick anywhere in Oxford and you'll hit someone who works for the university.

Leng answered his mobile on her third attempt.

'We're at full tilt here, ma'am,' the tech lead said with a hint of impatience.

'This is – might be – important. I'll clear it with the DCI, okay? I need you to run another sweep through the plate-recognition log.'

'Another? We were *very* thorough, ma'am. That car wasn't out there.'

'Not that car. Another one.' She read off the van's reg. 'I don't need a full report, I just need to know when and where it was last seen. Can you do that?'

Leng sounded reluctant.

'We can try. But DCI Hume –'

'Thanks, Leng. I'll be waiting for your call.'

Rang off. Dug out a number for University Contract Services.

A surly-sounding man answered her call. They'd already had police all over the ruddy place, he told her, resentfully. Causing bother. Upsetting the students. Luka hadn't been in for a couple of days – he'd already told three different coppers that.

Rose tried to keep her tone civil. Fairly civil.

'This is a murder investigation, sir. I'm sorry that the Thames Valley Police isn't prepared to cut corners for your convenience. Now the quicker you give me the answers we need, the quicker we can let you get back to your very important work.' She took a breath. *Easy.* 'What vehicles did Luka have access to out of hours? University vehicles?'

After a sullen pause the man said: 'Well, most of 'em. He'd only a standard licence, of course – if you can call it a licence, what they get given out there in Poland or wherever – but he could drive any of the transits, Hiluxes, fridge vans, whatever.'

'At all hours?'

'He was kitchens. Kitchens work funny times.'

Something he'd said had snagged in Rose's mind. She rewound.

'Fridge vans?'

'Refrigerated vans.' He said it slowly, like Rose was an idiot. 'For fetching veg and meat from the suppliers. Now, if you've no more questions –'

No more questions, and no time for this. Rose hung up.

Katerina's core temperature had been way down, hadn't it? She'd been severely chilled.

Refrigerated.

Her phone buzzed in her hand. Voicemail. Leng had called back with the data from the logs while she'd been talking. Fast work.

'There's a recent spot, Inspector.' The tech lead sounded harassed. Hume must've been running them ragged out there. 'A petrol station in the east of the city – here's the postcode. Hope it helps.'

Rose ran a quick check.

Yes – yes, it helped.

It pulled everything into focus, narrowed the weird geography of this case to a single point.

It meant that for the first time Rose was one step ahead.

It meant that she could save Brask's life.

The petrol station was on the same street as the Church of the Queen of Peace. Where Luka went to Mass. Where Katerina went. Where Brask went.

And ten cross-town miles from where Hume, Phillips and the best part of the Thames Valley Police were waiting for their man.

Chapter Thirty-three

Her heart was thumping as she walked cautiously past the lichen-green stone gateposts of the church; she'd left her car further up the road. If Luka was there, she had no intention of giving him advance warning. Night was already falling – no, it was rising, swelling from the ground, gathering in the shadows and corners of the car park. Above, the sky was clear, a deep bruise-indigo.

She wished she had an idea of what to expect. If he was here, would she have to give chase? Would she have to fight?

Or was she going to be that just-too-late copper again, with nothing to do but pick up the pieces, file the report and identify the corpse? Yeah, and then sit back and wait for the next one to show up.

She moved closer to the square-bodied red-brick church.

Light showed behind the stained glass. Someone was here.

There was a white Citroën van in the car park.

Luka.

Swiftly she dialled through for backup. Everything they could spare. She'd tangled with this guy once, at Brask's place, and come off the worse; she wasn't keen on a rematch. But who knew how long it'd take uniform to get across town?

Matt could be dead already.

She circled the church and found the rear entrance: an inconspicuous wooden door with a wire-reinforced window. It wasn't locked.

A trap. Had to be, didn't it? What kind of kidnapper leaves an entrance – and, more to the point, an exit – unlocked? Unless they want company.

But there was no way Luka could know she'd tracked him down. No way.

She paused with her hand on the door, listening for the sound of sirens. Nothing: nothing but the mutter of traffic, the sound of the wind in the roadside poplars. The same wind she'd heard whistling through the terrible meadows Luka had made such horrors of. *Christ.* In her mind's eye she saw the agonized faces of David Norfolk and Caroline Chaudry, the lifeless eyes of Katerina Zrinski.

Not again. Never again.

She pushed open the door.

This was the warren of offices in which she'd spoken to the parish priest, Father Florian.

She made her way along the fusty-smelling corridor and past the priest's study. She walked softly and kept her breathing shallow. The heavy dark-wood door that led into the church was closed. She stood with her shoulder against the wood. Gathered herself.

Eased open the door. It moved ajar with almost miraculous silence. She was behind the altar, to the left. Ahead of her a row of pews receded into darkness.

No lights on. There was a reek of incense and the glimmer of candlelight. It felt a few degrees colder than in the corridor.

Someone was speaking. Rose strained to hear. Latin?

The door closed softly behind her. She crept forwards. As she approached, she saw that candles were lit along the floor in front of the altar rail. The balusters of the rail kept her from seeing more but there was someone there . . . someone kneeling.

Again the voice, speaking in a strange language. No, not Latin. European, Rose thought, Croatian, maybe?

She wondered what the Trick or Treat Killer was praying for. Strength? Forgiveness?

When she moved beyond the altar rail she saw him, on his knees in the weak candlelight, hands pressed together. His voice had a curious resonance in the high-vaulted church. Before him, yellow-tinged incense smoke leaked from a burning thurible. He rocked back and forth as he prayed, his dirty grey beard brushing the parquet floor.

Father Florian.

Rose sucked in a breath. She remembered the priest's hostility, his words about everyone being subject to Christ's plan. The chrism, balsam oil, in his study.

She stepped forwards, letting her shoe heel ring on the floor.

The priest looked up at her sharply.

He opened and closed his mouth, drawing out strings of saliva from his loose lips. Finally he found words: 'No – not here, not permitted.' The man clambered, wincing, to his feet.

Rose held out her badge as she approached him. She was pretty sure he wouldn't remember her: just another damned unbeliever, just another foolish woman.

He peered short-sightedly at her credentials. Scowled.

'Hm. Well.' His watery eyes challenged her. 'This is a very sacred time. Really you should have made an appointment, madam.'

I thought all were supposed to be welcome in the house of God, Rose thought. But she kept her words to herself. There was no time for a philosophical discussion.

'I'm looking for Luka Savić,' she said quickly. 'Bald man who attends your church. Has he been here?'

'I know who Luka is,' the priest replied high-handedly – as though he claimed association with a prince, Rose thought, instead of a sick-in-the-head serial murderer.

'He's wanted in connection with some very serious offences.' She watched the priest closely as she talked. It was hard to read much in his deep-lined face and dark, pink-edged eyes – much, that was, beyond dislike, disgust and bitterness. 'We have reason to believe that he's been here very recently, that indeed he might still be here. We believe he's extremely dangerous. That's why we're here.'

She was sure to use *we*, and to put as much into it as she could, as if there was a SWAT team waiting out in the corridor and a helicopter gunship hovering overhead. Okay, this was only a decrepit priest, and not much of a threat if he turned nasty, but still, the illusion of backup was reassuring somehow.

Made her feel less alone. Less vulnerable.

But she'd have felt a whole lot safer if *real* backup had got its arse in gear.

Florian frowned at her, his lower lip quivering within his grubby beard.

'Luka?' he said.

'*Yes*. Have you seen him? He's a dangerous man and lives are at stake.'

There was a pause. Then the old priest laughed.

'Luka! Dangerous!'

Rose's fists clenched. Priest or no priest, this old bastard was asking for a smack in the mouth. A holy man, a so-called man of God. The kind of man, she sourly supposed, who claimed to be concerned with *higher things*.

'I didn't ask you for your opinion,' she said. 'I asked you if he was here. Has he been using this place?'

'Luka uses the kitchens of this *church*, madam, to prepare food for the poor. Luka gives much of his time to supplying our soup kitchens. For the needy, you see.' Florian spread his hands and smiled unpleasantly. His palms, Rose saw, were slick with oil. 'He is a good man, a most holy soul.'

'Where are the kitchens?'

'A separate block.' The priest made a vague gesture. 'Outside, out at the back.'

'Tell me where exactly.'

He lifted his whiskery chin.

'I will lead you there,' he said.

You won't lead me anywhere.

'Sir, you're in great danger,' Rose said insistently. The priest gave her a belligerent look – because she hadn't called him 'father', she guessed.

'I am quite safe, madam. This is my church, *my* responsibility,' he said. 'Besides, the kitchens are locked.'

'This is police business, sir. *Urgent* police business. We've no time to waste. Please give me the keys.'

'My business is Christ's busi—'

'For God's sake, this is *important*,' Rose shouted.

Florian tottered backwards, grabbed at the altar rail for support. Blinked at her in disbelief.

It was as though she'd slapped him. Hell, she almost had.

'Give me the keys,' she repeated. She felt her hands curl into fists, her cheeks hot. Whatever fear she'd had was gone, burned away by her fury. She held the priest's damp gaze. '*Now.*'

Florian tried to straighten his crooked back.

'I go,' he said stiffly, 'to get the keys.'

He moved unsteadily off towards the door Rose had come through.

'Please hurry,' Rose shouted after him.

It made no difference: Florian shuffled arthritically to the door, pulled it open with difficulty and disappeared into the back rooms.

Left alone in the dark church, in the dying light of Florian's candles and with the sickly smoke of the smouldering incense curling about her feet, DI Lauren Rose prayed.

For the foul priest to come back quickly.

For backup to get there so that she wouldn't have to confront Luka alone.

For Matt to be alive. For Matt to be okay.

She felt like a damn fool praying, she who'd never prayed to anyone or anything in her life before, but she prayed anyway.

She spun around sharply at a soft noise from the door. There was Florian, shuffling forwards, holding a bunch of silver keys. Instinctive, gut-level dislike rose up in her again. This priest ... She took a second, as he came towards her, to rationalize her loathing of the man. Christ, he embodied everything she hated: unearned privilege, misogyny, dogma and superstition, authority based on nothing but a silver cross, a mouthful of Latin and a set of grimy vestments.

He shook the keys.

'For kitchen,' he wheezed. The old man seemed to be getting older and slower before her eyes.

'Which way?'

He pointed along the nave, towards the most distant corner of the church.

'Side door.'

'Give me the keys.'

Florian glowered from beneath his unkempt brows.

'*My* responsibility,' he said.

A man's death is going to be your responsibility, Father, Rose seethed silently.

'Quickly, then.' She stalked impatiently up the aisle, cut right, ducked into the gloom of an anteroom. She came up against a door washed pale green with peeling paint. It was bolted. She slammed the flat of her hand against the wall in frustration.

Doors she couldn't open, languages she couldn't understand, codes she couldn't crack.

But no one else was going to put an end to this, she knew. No one else was going to stop Luka in time to save Brask. Besides, she'd made a promise, to Katerina, or Katerina's memory – and, for Christ's sake, this was her *job*.

What the hell was keeping that bloody priest?

She began to turn, to see where Florian had got to, when a bone-cracking pain broke against the base of her skull.

A flash of phosphorous-white.

Her forehead smashing into the door.

That was all.

Chapter Thirty-four

Rose awoke and the world swam. She turned her head and vomited on the floor.

Where? What?

The pain in her head was unbearable. It was more, so much more than a headache. It screamed, pounded and tore at her nerves.

Luka must have been hiding. He must have seen her arrive and been waiting for his chance to attack her. All that time he'd been lurking in the dark while she talked to the old priest and . . .

The old priest. Had Luka attacked him, too? Was Father Florian yet another victim Rose was responsible for?

Christ, her head hurt.

And it wasn't just the pain. She felt as though she were drowning in a dense fog of oily perfume. She gagged, coughed. The smell was all too familiar. Katerina. The bones. Balsam.

She squeezed her eyes shut. Tried to think – tried to block out the pain, block out the fear, and *think*.

The floor was painfully hard under her hip, knee and elbow. She could see now that the tiles she lay on were red. She definitely wasn't in the church. So where the hell was she? And how long had she been here?

What light illuminated the room was faint, tremulous. In front of her there was a stained white-papered wall and a dusty skirting board. She shifted her position, to try to get a better look at her surroundings.

Steel counters. A grease-spotted intake rising to the ceiling. A faint, bitter odour of fried onion.

She must be in the kitchens, Luka's kitchens, in the annexe to the church.

She was in Luka's kitchens.

Panic surged in her chest.

This was most likely where he'd beaten and decapitated Katerina and flayed David alive, and Rose couldn't move her arms or legs.

Her wrists were tied behind her back, her ankles bound tightly together. She struggled, jerked – felt not an inch of give, not the slightest sign of weakness. They felt like old fibre ropes, with none of the smooth feel of nylon, but they were well tied.

She subsided. She'd seen Luka's handiwork before, after all. The bastard was nothing if not thorough.

Best to save what strength she had. It wasn't much – but it was all she had.

When she rolled on to her left side the light pushed a spike of pain through her eyes, into her head. Candles, more candles, two dozen or more. These weren't the grubby tallow of the ones at Luka's shrines but tall, brightly burning pillar candles of blood-red wax. Their light was agony to her pounding head. She clenched her jaw and rolled away.

But it wasn't just because of the bright flames . . .

Beyond the candle flames she'd glimpsed a vision as from a gallery of medieval art: a man, stripped bare, bound with his arms behind him to a post, a dark-wood pillar that ran from floor to ceiling. He looked bloodlessly pale. His skin gleamed with oil and his head lolled to his chest. Lit from below, sacrificial, terrible.

St Sebastian the martyr.

Professor Matt Brask.

'*Matt!*'

Rose was surprised to find she had the breath in her lungs to call out his name. She managed to squirm on to her back. Above her, a bare grey light bulb, ancient polystyrene ceiling tiles and a wavering circle of candlelight.

'Matt? Can you hear me?' She steeled herself to turn her head back towards the light, towards Brask; again the fierce light jabbed at her and her vision blurred. All she could see of the man bound to the post was the dark spot of his head.

It was moving.

'Matt!'

'Katerina?' His voice was slurred, broken, but still Brask's. He was trying to lift his head.

'Matt, it's Inspector Rose – it's Lauren.' She blinked, winced. 'Where – where is he?'

'Get out.' Brask spoke like a man trying to make himself heard in a hurricane or a snowstorm. The words were indistinct but the terror in them rang like steel on stone. 'Lauren, get out – it's not safe, Katerina, my darling, it's . . . it's not safe – he's coming . . .'

Rose wondered what Luka could have done to Brask to reduce him to this state. Then, in her head, she heard Matilda Rooke's kind, sad voice: *You were hungry, weren't you, Katerina? Hadn't eaten . . .*

The man hadn't been beaten, poisoned or drugged.

Just starved half to death. Barely an ounce of strength left in his body – and he'd used it, not to cry out for help but to try and warn her. To try to save her.

Her and Katerina.

'Hold on, Matt,' she called. She heard the fear in her own voice. 'Just hold on.'

There had to be a way of getting free, getting out. Had to be.

There was a row of stripped-back steel counters running along the wall beyond the circle of candles. This is a kitchen, Rose thought hurriedly, so there must be, what, knives, cleavers?

No way of knowing where they were. No way of getting to them, with her ankles tied. No way of using them, with her wrists tied. No way. No use.

Think, Lauren. Think.

Again she heard Brask's broken voice, thick with dread: 'He's coming . . .'

Soft, barefooted steps sounded on the tiles behind her head. The effort of craning her neck made her want to scream.

A silhouette. A man's dark shape against the inferno of candles. Him. Luka.

'It is almost time,' he said.

He sounded grave, solemn – but there was the tautness of intense emotion in his voice, too.

Luka padded across the tiles to the edge of the circle of candlelight. He lowered himself to the floor in front of Rose and crossed his legs.

'I want,' he said, 'to explain.'

Rose looked at him and he met her gaze without

hesitation. Her gut tightened nauseatingly. He had child's eyes. They were the haunted eyes of a damaged boy in the worn face of a forty-year-old man. She could see the gleam of perspiration on his shaved scalp and in the pit of his throat.

There was a smear of black on his brow. Ashes.

He wore a robe of hessian. Sackcloth, just like the fabric that had clothed Katerina, cloaked David and now swaddled Brask's waist.

Luka, she saw, was a penitent – in his own eyes, at least. A miserable sinner, seeking redemption.

This was his idea of redemption?

Rose's body stiffened as a fresh wave of pain ran like a harrow through her head. Holding her head up was too much; she let it fall to the hard tiles, grunted and closed her eyes. Her hands, bent under her body, ached with cramp.

She listened to the thunder of her own heartbeat.

Then Luka spoke again.

'I want you to understand,' he said. 'I want – I want you to *see*. Because I understand you, Lauren Rose. I know that you are afraid and I know why. I want to take away your fear, and take away your pain.'

Muscle spasms shook her shoulders. *Then untie my fucking hands.*

'What I do,' Luka said, like it was his job, like he was a quantity surveyor or a lab technician, 'is enable the truest expression of God's love.'

Rose felt sick.

'Martyrdom.'

'*Yes.*' She could hear the smile in his voice. 'Professor

Brask has taught you well. Through martyrdom, the elect – the deserving ones – enter into the shining glory of Christ's kingdom.'

Rose opened her eyes again, to look at Luka.

'All you do is cause pain and hurt,' she told him. 'Suffering, Luka, is what you enable.'

He nodded seriously.

'That is a part of what I do, yes. The road to salvation is a hard one to travel. But I believe that – in the end – the blessed ones I lead along that road are grateful to me.'

Rose laughed harshly.

'You *believe*? You mean no one has ever said thank you?'

Luka frowned, compressed his lips into a stern line.

Then he said: 'You should be happy. If Professor Brask is your friend, you should be glad that he is to be saved.'

'I guess I'm not a very good Christian.'

Luka shook his head.

'Indeed you are not.'

'Then where *do* I fit in, Luka?' She struggled to sit up, to meet his eye. 'I see what part Professor Brask plays in all this, but what's my role here? How does kidnapping a policewoman fit into Christ's plan?'

Luka's eyes narrowed.

'The Devil places many obstacles in the path of the righteous,' he said.

'Then I'm an agent of the Devil?'

Another sombre nod.

'You do not even know it – I see that. It is often this way. You think you are on the side of good. Perhaps even on the side of Christ. But you do Satan's work.'

He rose to his feet, lithely, an athletic man in spite of his slight frame.

'Now there is work to do,' he said bluntly. 'The last martyr must be prepared.'

Rose watched as he moved to the ring of candles. Brask, she saw, was quite still. Luka took a tray of jars from the kitchen counter and set it with a gentle clink on the floor. He made the sign of the cross and murmured to himself – a blessing, a benediction, Rose supposed.

She heard him say '*pater*', 'father'. Then 'Cerbonius'. The long-dead abbot of St Quintus.

Luka's religion – or whatever the hell you wanted to call it – was a thing of chaos, Rose saw, a monstrous creation, a chimera pieced together from the shattered wreckage of a traumatized boy's mind.

She squinted at the jars. They shimmered with reflected candlelight but inside she could see dark shapes suspended in clear fluid. In one, the outline of what may have been a finger bone. In another, what looked like an incisor tooth, the long root broken off halfway.

The relics. Body parts from Katerina, David, Caroline, the victims in France. She made a quick count. Eight of them – and a ninth left empty.

Eight?

Three English victims so far. Four in France. And yet eight relics?

She narrowed her eyes, peered again at the relics. In the smallest jar, a flattish, uneven shape floated horizontally, like a dead fish. It was an ear.

The stark black-and-white image flashed into her mind. For a moment she'd forgotten the priest: the old priest who was carved up and hung from a tree in a Croatia convulsed by war. The priest who was missing an ear. The priest, Mrs Matić had said, who raised a demon in his house, loved it, nurtured it, until it devoured him.

Eight relics then. The ninth would be taken from Brask.

'*Luka.*'

The cry escaped her almost without her meaning it to.

He turned to her, his face a shifting map of dark hollows in the candlelight.

'What we do is sacred. There must be no more interruptions.'

'Father Florian called the police,' she improvised desperately. 'A firearms team is on its way.'

Luka shook his head slowly.

'Father Florian is a most righteous man,' he said. 'He will do nothing to stand in the way of Christ's work.' He glanced briefly at Rose. 'I am sorry he had to strike you. But the wrath of God was within him.'

Florian! Florian, the first link in the chain. The old man *knew*! He'd known from the start.

Rose tried to hide her dismay. She could have stopped it all that very first day, that first bloody day; she could have pulled Florian in, leaned on him, made him talk. By Christ, she'd have *made* him talk, if she'd had any idea what he knew. Then he'd have led her to Luka.

That would have saved David Norfolk and Caroline Chaudry.

It would have saved Matt.

'The police *are* coming,' she managed to say. 'They'll have this place shut down tight, Luka. They know you, know all about you. You won't escape.'

Luka went on fiddling with his jars.

'Escape,' he murmured, 'is not a part of the plan.'

Rose struggled for words, something to trap Luka, outwit him, confuse him, make him see the madness in what he was doing.

She fought against saying the words that rose in her throat. Help. Please. No.

'Luka, talk to me.'

'There is nothing more to say. Now I speak only to God.'

Rose wished Brask would wake up, produce a smart argument, a theological paradox or a clever moral theory to cut through Luka's insanity. Because what hope did she have on her own? What was she, but a career copper with a copper's education? Not much of a reader, certainly no scholar and not a religious bone in her body. She'd never believed, never had much time for airy guesswork about God and the afterlife, never set much store by what people called 'faith'. Rose had learned to stand on her own two feet, to trade in facts, to face the hard realities of every day full on and fearless. She'd never had anything to fall back on – except the truth.

The one thing, maybe, that Luka was afraid of.

'It won't change anything,' she said sharply.

Luka had been on his knees, unwrapping something tied up in a sheet. She guessed what it was from the shape of its long, taut curve through the fabric. Now he paused, looked at her.

'It won't change anything,' she repeated. 'Whatever you do, to me, to Brask, it won't . . . it won't bring Abbot Cerbonius back.'

A spasm of anger passed over Luka's face.

'You do not say his name.' He stood. Rose saw that his hands were quivering.

'He's gone, Luka.' She kept her voice level, detached, cold as concrete. As hard as the facts themselves. 'Nothing can bring the abbot back. All the killing, all the blood and bones – it won't help.' She drew a deep breath. 'The abbot is dead in the ground. Gone. Gone for good.'

Luka's lips curled in a grimace.

'And you say you are not Satan's thing.'

'It's the simple truth.'

'So says the Father of Lies.'

'I think you know what's real and what isn't, Luka,' Rose insisted. 'The abbot is dead, the monastery burned to the ground, the relics are dust – you know these things.'

'No.'

'That's why you hide. In your "religion". Say the holy words, block out the truth. Live in the past, try to pretend what happened didn't happen. You say escape isn't part of the plan but that's not true, is it? Escape is what all this is about. Escape is all you want. Escape from what happened at Niza, what happened to you.

'And now you try to drown the truth in blood, the blood of innocent people. But underneath it all – you know what's real. You know what you're hiding from.'

'*No.*'

Luka turned his back to her, dropped again to his knees. He threw aside the tangled sheet.

The fine-grained wood of the bow shone in the candle-light. Rose saw the glinting steel tips of half a dozen arrows. Luka, his hand trembling, thumbed the bow-string gently and it sang a soft bass note.

'It isn't real, Luka!' Rose shouted, her self-control snapping. 'None of this, it's not true, it's not *real*!'

Luka picked up the bow and a long-shafted arrow. Turned the arrow over in his hands. Its point was barbed and savage-looking. He stood, the bow in his left hand, the arrow in his right; he handled the weapons expertly, with confidence.

The shadows of his movements flickered across the tiles.

'You will find,' he said softly, 'that it is real enough.'

In a single movement, fluid and well practised, he stood, turned, nocked the arrow to the bowstring, drew with a soft grunt of effort, aimed and fired from point-blank range.

The arrow point plunged into Matt Brask's body.

Brask screamed, his head jerking up.

For a moment a fine mist of blood darkened the air over the shimmering fire of the candles.

Chapter Thirty-five

Rose felt sure that the sound of the arrowhead puncturing her friend's muscles and splintering his bones would stay with her for ever.

Now the words she'd been fighting all spilled from her at once: '*No!* Stop! Please!'

Luka might as well not have heard her. He squatted, took up another arrow, felt its balance in his hands. The first arrow, Rose saw, jutted grotesquely from Brask's upper chest, below the shaded angle of his collarbone. Brask was groaning, a terrible noise that bubbled with blood. He stopped when he saw Luka's right biceps flex, saw Luka again draw back the bowstring. That's when Brask stopped groaning and began to beg.

Luka ignored him. *Now I speak only to God.*

This time the barbed steel buried itself in the thick muscle of Brask's thigh.

Brask cried out, his voice cracking. A gout of blood spat from the broken flesh, splashing across the tiles. Rose looked away, she couldn't help it. When she looked back she saw that the shaft of the arrow, stuck inches deep into Brask's leg, was quivering, quivering to the rapid beat of Brask's heart. The professor was breathing heavily, in gulping, terrified sobs – but he was conscious. He was alive.

There was no colour, no blood in his face. He was drenched in sweat – surely slipping into shock.

Luka paused to murmur something to himself, a prayer, in what sounded like Latin.

Rose hoped it was a long one.

Between the ranked red candles she watched the blood pooling darkly at Brask's bare feet. Christ, she felt so *helpless* . . .

Then: *Think like a copper, Rose, for God's sake.*

Then: *No – think like a Rose.* She thought of her dad, her brothers. The Rose police department, people called it. Policing was in their blood, going way back. They were a type: hard-headed, good-natured, unflappable, resourceful. Proper coppers.

Not her, though. An outsider from the off. Always loved by the family, always wanted, but a girl – a misunderstood minority in the Rose household. Her dad hadn't wanted her to go into the service. Not until he'd seen how damn good she was anyway.

Her brothers had been supportive, in their own way, as best they could. Even though that meant a lot of piss-taking – all the way through from college to Hendon to the Met to the Thames Valley – she'd never doubted that they cared for her, that they meant well.

But they never understood. Not really.

She'd had to scrap harder, work longer, think faster and be smarter than the lot of them. She'd taken twice as much bullshit for half as much reward. She'd proved herself as a copper ten times over.

So no, she thought, correcting herself again. Don't think like a Rose. Think like DI Lauren Rose.

Luka was selecting another arrow from the bundle, still murmuring, still praying, as Rose rolled on to her front and began to squirm forwards across the tiles. Her cramp-ridden body shook with the effort. The hammering in her head grew more insistent, more violent. She crawled on, towards the light, towards the candles.

She was aware of Luka turning an arrow over thoughtfully in his hands, saw the play of light on steel. Composing himself, she guessed, preparing himself for the final acts of this 'ritual'.

She could hear Brask's breathing, harsh and shallow. Could anyone live through something like this and not die, whether from blood loss, shock or internal injury? She didn't know. All she could do was keep going. Keep fighting.

She crawled on. One inch at a time. One twisting, aching, agonizing inch at a time.

Then she stopped and lay on her back, trying to control her breathing and slow her shuddering heartbeat. Lay bathed in the candlelight.

Her stomach muscles burned and her scrabbling knuckles scraped on the tiles as – slowly, slowly – she bent her body into a sitting position.

Behind her she heard Luka bring his prayers to an end.

'Don't,' she heard Brask say. His voice was weak, a half-voice – and yet she could hear the fear in it.

From Luka there was only silence.

'For God's sake,' said Brask, 'for Christ's sake, Luka, my friend –'

If she forced her arms up, twisting the muscles of her shoulders, the joints of her elbows, Rose could lift her bound hands perhaps a foot from the floor. It was beyond painful.

But then she learned another lesson in pain. The bow-string snickered, the arrow punched into flesh and Brask screamed, a throat-tearing animal howl that reverberated nightmarishly around the tiled room.

She didn't, couldn't look round at her friend. She tried not to think about him or his pain and terror. She tried not to wonder where the arrow had struck him or whether he could survive another wound or more blood loss –

Instead she concentrated. She ignored the spasming of her muscles and the protest of her twisting elbows and *made* herself lift her hands.

Set her bound wrists upon the burning candle wick. Bit her lip and waited for the fire to take hold.

She could hear Brask's shallow, rough-edged breathing. She could hear Luka murmuring another prayer. She could smell, over the pervasive stench of balsam, her own flesh burning, charring, crisping in the candle flame.

Over it all – over and through it all, within it all, engulfing everything in a scalding flood – was the astonishing pain.

With every endless second that passed Rose told herself she couldn't take it. And yet she did. The blistering of her skin, the searing of a thousand nerve endings, the soft-hissing cauterization of her exposed flesh. And that smell: it reminded her, sickeningly, of that terrible morning east of the city, the discovery of Caroline Chaudry's body – the finding of her roasted remains.

Tears wet her cheeks and bitter blood from her deep-bitten lower lip filled her mouth. She would not give in. She would not let Matt die. She would not let Luka kill again. She would not be beaten. She would not give in.

Luka prayed on, an obsessive background murmur riding the rhythms of her agony.

Then he stopped praying.

And Rose smelled burning rope. It was giving way.

One more second. Two more seconds. If she took her hands from the flame and the rope still held – Christ, how could she bring herself to put them back there, to plunge herself back into this hell? She wasn't sure she could.

Her head pounded; a grey mist began to thicken in her vision. She had never imagined such pain. It was more than anyone could take, surely, too much for anyone to bear –

Yet she bore it.

Make sure, make sure. The words thumped in her head like a mantra. In her mind's eye, though, she saw Luka drawing back the bowstring, aiming the vicious arrowhead – where? Brask's gut? His face? His heart?

She slumped forwards, felt her hands slip – oh Jesus, the relief – from the flame. And then, with every ounce of strength left in her ruined muscle fibres, she forced her wrists apart.

The half-burned rope seemed to yield thread by thread.

Rose struggled, grimacing as she fought to drag her trembling, scorched hands through the nooses of rough-fibred rope.

She half heard Brask gasp: 'No.'

The rope fell away.

Rose spun, lurched upwards into a smear of light and a fog of pain. Luka stood before Brask, face to face to fire the killing shot; bow poised, arrow notched, he was a dark shape, a blurred target. The arrow point was a bead of silver light. It was pointed at Brask's throat.

Rose's ankles were still tightly bound, her senses dulled with pain, but she flung herself forwards through the shining wall of candles.

Luka – absorbed in his grim ritual – was late to react. He threw up his right hand and the arrow clattered to the tiles. His knuckles crashed against Rose's cheekbone. She grunted, threw a blind punch, connected with nothing.

As they tumbled together to the floor, Luka's bow tangled between his arm and his falling body. Rose fell across the tightly drawn bowstring. She felt it bite into the flesh of her neck and the sharp sting of it as it snapped.

Luka gaped at the ruined bow and then wailed like a lost child. He shrieked something in Croat.

Rose noticed before he did – a split second before – that the fallen arrow was resting on the tiles within reach of Luka's left hand. She grabbed for it.

Luka dropped his elbow hard on to her outstretched forearm, driving between muscle and bone. Rose screamed – then rolled, jerking back her head as Luka swiped the arrow past her face. With a snarl, he shifted his grip and stabbed downwards. She was able to twist aside just in time. The keen edge of the arrowhead scored a line down the side of her neck.

Rose was scrambling to get back to her feet when Luka's knee landed heavily on her chest. Her head knocked hard against the tiled floor.

'You broke it,' Luka sobbed. 'You – you ruined it. You ruined *everything*.'

The arrow was still clenched in his fist.

'No, Luka.' Rose shook her head, disoriented. 'No.'

'You did, you *did*.'

The man's knuckles whitened on the arrow's shaft. Lauren raised her hands, turned her face away and braced herself.

This was how it had ended for all the others, for Katerina, David, Caroline. Luka's face was the last thing they saw. Luka's voice was the last thing they heard – save for the sound of their own screams. When Lauren was gone it would be Brask's turn . . .

As Luka's arm swung down, his weight shifted; the pressure on her chest lifted, just a fraction – but enough.

With a scream of effort, Rose wrenched her body to the left. The arrow point ripped into her shirt, scraped painfully through the flesh of her armpit. Reflexively she slammed her arm down, sideways, and felt her elbow strike bone. The bone shifted horribly under the impact.

Luka fell away, wailing, clutching at his right cheek. As Rose struggled to rise, he rolled and staggered unsteadily to his feet – then he bolted, hared to the door, the soles of his bare feet slapping on the tiles.

Rose started to struggle with the ropes binding her ankles, her copper's instincts kicking in, adrenaline spiking, ready to run, to chase –

Then she saw Brask. His pale body sagged motionless, lifeless, in the ropes binding him to the pillar. Bloodied arrows jutted horribly from his upper breast, his thigh, his hip. From the chest downwards his pale body was awash with blood.

Rose felt empty – hollowed-out inside.

Dead, she thought, for a second, her mind reeling. *Lost*.

Like all the others. Only this was worse, so much harder to bear.

With raw-red fingers she finally ripped loose the hard knots in the old rope. Kicked her feet free. Stumbled into the ring of candlelight. She reached for the pulse in Brask's throat.

Nothing.

Then something — almost too faint to feel, but yes, something under her numb fingertips, the weak, insistent kick of a heartbeat.

Brask stirred, tried to lift his head.

'Go . . . go after him.'

'Don't try to speak. Don't try to do anything.'

Every second counted now. Rose tore loose Brask's ropes from the wooden pillar, lowered him carefully — her every muscle protesting — to the cold floor. She tore off her sweater and pressed it to the wound bleeding most heavily, where a shaft jutted from his hip.

Brask groaned in pain.

'Shush,' she said briskly. 'It's okay. You're going to be all right.'

His body was slick with blood and pungent with balsam oil. That stubborn pulse just about kept going, kept fluttering. He struggled to keep his eyes open.

And still he found the strength to urge her to leave him, to go after Luka.

'He'll . . . do it —' Brask broke off, swallowed painfully. *'He'll do it again.* Someone . . . someone else.' His hand momentarily tightened on her wrist. 'Lauren. Stop him. Go.'

She looked down at him. His face was slack, his skin

waxy. Was he going to make it? Had he already lost too much blood? Christ, how was she meant to know?

This was the copper's life. One impossible call after another. She thought of Phillips, Hume and the rest camped out over at the copse. All that effort, all those resources – to save how many lives?

The human mind just wasn't built to make those decisions, Rose thought bitterly. She smoothed Brask's sweat-damp hair, muttered something reassuring and meaningless. Never mind the human heart.

Through clenched teeth Brask again said: '*Go!*'

Rose went.

The door Luka had gone through led to an unlit flight of stairs. Luka had carried her – or dragged her – all the way down here, Rose realized uneasily. A disturbing thought: she'd been so powerless, so vulnerable.

It made her think of all the other limp, dead-weight bodies Luka had hauled through fields and ditches, in and out of his meat van, up dark stairwells and through shadowed backstreets. Of the things he might have done to her – if only she'd been *worthy*.

She took the stairs two at a time. Her body felt stretched, punished, warped out of shape; her scorched wrists seethed with pain, but at least the adrenaline had blunted the edges of it.

Upstairs was another suite of starkly functional rooms, probably used for parish meetings or as a place to feed the needy. There was nothing here but the stagnant stink of neglected washing-up and a loose coil of rope on the floor. She crashed through the outer door and into the car park.

It was dark now. Faint light from the street picked out the outline of Luka's parked van. Rose could hear the distant skirl of a police siren or two, maybe three. *Finally.* But they'd be too late to do anything but pick up the pieces.

She whirled and swore to herself. The back wall, out into the road, through the gardens of the adjoining houses, Christ, he could have gone anywhere . . .

The church was an angular black shape against the violet city sky.

He's in there.

Rose knew it, as surely as she knew anything. This was what Luka did when he was frightened, panicked, lost. This was where he went. He ran home to his God.

She went in the front way, through the heavy, iron-studded door and into the entrance hall with its fluttering posters for community days out and free English lessons. The sickly-sweet smell of Father Florian's incense lingered in the church.

It was darker in here than outside. Almost pitch-dark, save for the candles that flickered by the altar rail.

She crept down the left-hand side of the nave. Running had been easy; moving steadily, keeping control, reawoke the bone-deep pain in her arms and legs. Her head still pounded from the priest's blow.

Luka was on his knees before the altar. His stringy white arms were outstretched and his forehead was pressed to the floor.

As Rose moved forwards, she could hear him, praying, begging, in helpless tears. She couldn't make out what he was saying; he seemed to slur from one language to

another, Croatian, English, Latin. The odd word registered: *sorry . . . forgive . . . sinner . . . saints . . .*

And one word more than any other, repeated over and
over: *Why?*

Rose took another step towards him.

Luka stopped praying and swallowed down a sob.

Slowly he turned his head towards her.

Chapter Thirty-six

'*You.*' His voice was steeped in hatred and hoarse with grief. '*You.*'

'Luka Savić, I am arresting you on suspicion of the murders of Caroline Chaudry, David Norfolk and Katerina Zrinski, of the kidnap and attempted murder of Professor Matthew Brask, and –'

It all sounded so inadequate, so weak, in this place, beside the horror of Luka's crimes.

Luka was already on his feet and backing away as Rose spoke, holding up his hands, shaking his head.

'Not now, not here,' he said. 'Sanctuary. I must not be stopped. I am so close. House of God. Sanctuary.'

'I don't think so, Luka.' Rose moved forwards, maintaining the distance between them at six, seven feet. 'You have to answer for Katerina. For David. For Caroline. It's called justice.'

Luka's lip quivered.

'I – I delivered them.'

'You *killed* them, Luka. Doesn't your God have something to say about that? You put them through suffering I wouldn't wish on any living thing, and you killed them.'

'I purged them of their sins,' Luka whimpered. 'I – I mortified their flesh, and –'

'It's over, Luka,' she said softly.

She'd been sizing him up, readying herself mentally for the next move. Yes, he'd overpowered her down in the kitchen basement, but she'd been in shock, in terrible pain, with her ankles bound. Now – well, now she still felt like hell.

But at least this was face to face, on level ground.

He wasn't a big man, after all. Perhaps five-six, five-seven. A few years older than Rose, she guessed, but that wouldn't count for much. He wasn't muscular, but he wasn't skinny either; he seemed as hard and resilient as wire. Plus, Rose thought, he's crazy, a fanatic. There was a strength in that, she knew, that she'd be a fool to underestimate.

Forget his child's eyes, his tears, whatever horrors are buried in his past, she told herself. This guy took down David Norfolk, a farmer in his physical prime, a good man but tough as old boots. Caroline and Katerina were far from defenceless either.

Whatever else he was, this man was a killer and a predator.

She tensed, ready to make her move.

'I will not fight,' Luka said. 'Not here. Not in this place of Christ.'

Rose kept her guard up, held herself on the balls of her feet.

'Good. Then you'll come with me.'

The expression on Luka's face shifted like the surface of a sea in a storm. His mouth gaped and tears again shone in his dark eyes.

'I was so *close*,' he cried again. 'Only one. I needed only one – to complete my work, the abbot's mission . . .'

He was talking about those relics again. Rose felt her temper start to stir.

'Do you think your God gives a damn about a scrap of bone from a dead man?'

The tears still came, but unforgiving iron entered into Luka's gaze.

'You understand nothing.'

'So you've said. But I understand you well enough, Luka.' She took a pace towards him – he didn't back away. This was it. 'Come with me.'

He was almost within arm's reach. A weeping man-child, small and pale in ill-made sackcloth, trembling in the shadow of the altar's monumental iron cross.

'Come with me,' Rose said again. Then she lunged.

She was expecting him to run and slip out of her grasp once again. She wasn't expecting him to step in, pivot on his left foot and deliver a punch of crippling power to her lower ribs. As she doubled over, she cursed herself for a bloody idiot.

He's not a broken kid. He's not going to run sobbing into your arms.

He'll do to you what he did to all the others. Remember that.

Now that he'd thrown her off balance, Luka did run.

The punch had given him a few seconds' start, but Rose, quickly scoping the layout, second-guessed him and cut off the space as he veered left, towards the exit, towards escape. She drove herself forwards with a hand on the corner of a pew and swung herself into his path, forcing him to shift direction. He skidded, turned awkwardly, slipped beyond her reach –

Feet pattering on the wooden floor, he vanished like a ghost into the darkness behind the altar.

Rose, gulping achingly for breath, clawed her way along

the altar rail and followed him into the gloom, where she found a metal spiral staircase twisting upwards to a mezzanine floor.

At its base, one hand on the cold iron newel, she paused.

Luka was up there, waiting, knowing that she'd follow him. He knew this place like a rabbit knew its warren. On the other hand, Rose had no damn idea what to expect. He was out of his mind, right on the brink, pushed by trauma and madness to a point where he was capable of anything.

But she was a copper doing her job. So what choice did she have?

She gripped the newel and began to climb.

There was a little light up here, at least. A semicircular window of plain glass let in the dull orange glow of a nearby street lamp. Rose climbed slowly, letting her eyes adjust. This place would've been for what? A choir? For members of the congregation? Brask would know –

– but Brask was downstairs, barely conscious, barely alive, hurt, alone, terrified . . .

Rose couldn't afford to think about him right now.

The mezzanine stretched the full width of the building, a broad balcony of smooth, dusty boards that overhung the echoing space of the church to a distance of perhaps twenty feet. A decorative wrought-iron rail marked the far edge.

Rose scanned the space. A stack of hymn books set against the wall. Three metal-framed chairs heaped on top of one another. A spatter of white bird shit from an old pigeon's nest in the eaves.

And Luka. He was backed into the far corner of

the mezzanine. The dull light gleamed in his wide, wet eyes.

Rose stopped dead. In the silent church she could hear his breathing: fast, shallow, panicked – that and the runaway gallop of her own heart.

'There's nowhere to go, Luka,' she said. The words rang from the dark beams above.

Luka's voice came from the gloom, a gabbled incoherent whinny: '*Jedini*. The only one, only one, to redeem, to restore . . . *blagoslovio oca*, gone, lost, *mrtav* . . .' He stuttered to a halt.

'No more,' Rose said. She did her best to sound strong, but she felt weak, so weak, inside.

'One more,' he said.

'No.' She began to cross the mezzanine. The boards bowed beneath her feet. 'Luka? This ends here. There's no point any more. No point in going on.'

Luka twitched.

'One more. One more and I will be with my brothers again.' He grimaced, nodded. 'With my blessed father.'

For a moment she was sharply conscious of Luka's madness. His strength. Her own pain. Keenly aware of the long, dark drop to the hard church floor and of what would happen to Matt Brask if she took on Luka and lost. And in this moment Rose hesitated.

Luka pounced.

He came for her throat, his sinewy white hands outstretched and a wild, desperate look in his eyes that had nothing to do with God or Christ.

His right thumb dug deep between the tendons of her neck. The fingers of his right hand bunched to a tight, wrenching fist in her hair. She blocked the swing of his left hand and replied with a jabbing elbow that glanced off Luka's jaw.

He grunted and snarled something in Croatian. His free hand snaked through her flailing defence. Rose thought he groped for her throat or her face but what he found was her ear. His long fingernails dug into her skin.

She swore fiercely and kicked out. Luka evaded her boot and tightened his grip. Rose felt blood running down her collar. Felt her skin about to rip like paper, like he was trying to tear her ear from her head . . .

One more?

She thought of the ghastly glass jars, the sick souvenirs looted from innocent bodies. Luka's relics.

Fuck that!

She slammed her head forwards. Luka recoiled. Rose – with a splintering rush of pain – felt the left side of her forehead connect with the bridge of his nose. His blood spattered her face.

He reeled backwards, across the groaning mezzanine boards, both hands pressed to his shattered, bleeding nose. He mouthed indistinct syllables: roaring, blood-filled noises of pain and fury. Rose went after him. She grabbed a fistful of his sackcloth garment and tried to pin him against the wrought-iron rail, but he twisted, squirmed, like a man having a fit.

She took two hard blows to her head and shoulder from Luka's hard-knuckled fists. These pushed Rose disorientingly backwards. She swung off balance and then felt the ornate iron edge of the rail press into the flesh of her lower back.

She could see the dying light of the candles at the altar rail, deep in the darkness so far below.

'*You.*'

She turned back to Luka, whose blood-splashed face was six inches from hers, whose strong fingers dug like iron nails into her upper arms. He shook her like a dog worrying a rat.

'You broke it, you spoiled –'

'No, Luka.'

'I was so close, so, so –'

'*No.*' Rose tried to shift her body and dislodge the hard point of the rail from the muscles of her back. 'Not me, Luka.' She thought fast and desperately. 'He didn't let it happen, did He? Your God – your beloved God, He saw what you were doing, and, Luka, He *stopped* it – didn't He? He didn't want you to do it. He didn't want you to kill those people. He didn't want you to kill Brask –'

She gasped as Luka, with a grunt, jerked her harder against the rail; she thought of the vertiginous drop into the church just inches behind her. 'He didn't want you to kill *me . . .*'

There was a crash from the front of the church that made the mezzanine shake. Flashlight beams broke the darkness of the pews below. Shouts sounded as dark figures moved down the naves and aisles.

Munro's FR team. Finally.

A hissing noise broke from Luka's throat. He, too, was staring into the darkness beyond the rail, at the probing flashlights. His grip on her arms grew tighter.

There wasn't going to be another chance.

Rose braced her back against the piercing iron and,

grimacing at the pain, forced one foot forwards. She gripped the rail with one grasping hand and drove the full weight of her body against Luka, turning as she did so and bringing up a hand as Luka's grip loosened to seize the sackcloth collar of his vestment –

And now it was she who held him fast, by his collar and his left wrist, against the rail.

And now, bloodied, tearful, he looked like a broken boy again.

'Don't move,' she said, emphasizing the words with a tug on his collar. 'Don't even try.'

Luka shook his head dully. His eyes were blank.

There was more shouting and then the noise of boots on metal. The mezzanine shook with heavy footsteps. Someone was coming up the spiral staircase.

'I'm okay,' Rose called over her shoulder.

Another reassuring lie.

Luka mumbled something and glanced backwards at the drop.

She looked at him. 'What?' she asked.

'One more.'

She let her bitterness surface. 'One more stolen fragment of flesh, Luka? One more mouldy bone?'

His eyes gleamed.

Oh Christ.

'One more soul,' he said.

She braced herself for one last, desperate lunge from Luka. She prepared herself to counter the force of his shoulder driven into her chest. She was ready to heave him back – but instead of a fresh assault Luka's body suddenly went limp. The balance between them lurched, like a game of tug-of-war when one side suddenly lets go. He stumbled like a drunkard back into the rail, his centre of gravity at a tipping point.

Rose snatched for his wrist. Her fingers grazed his sweaty skin and felt it slip away.

Luka fell.

Rose heard a shout from below. An alarmed clatter of boots. Then this *noise* . . .

It sounded, she thought in confusion, like the noise of Luka's arrow entering Brask's body. A thick, raw noise, a stomach-turning crunch of bone, flesh and iron.

She darted to the rail and looked down. Saw him, lit by groping flashlights and the sputtering candles.

She looked away. In the last few weeks she'd seen enough blood to last her a lifetime.

But as she stared, trembling, into the darkness of the church's roof space, the image of him lingered before her eyes. Luka's arms and legs had been thrown out, as if in celebration or release, his body a pale star glowing against the dimness. His robes had been torn away. His eyes were open, his mouth agape in something like a smile. The iron cross of the altar jutted from his chest in a bloody wreckage of smashed ribs and spilling guts. His lips had been moving, saying something, something she couldn't make out, over and over.

It was Munro she'd heard climbing the stairs. He moved towards her uncertainly.

'You okay, ma'am?'

Rose stared at the sergeant.

'Fucking hell, no,' she said.

'Are you hurt?'

She grimaced.

'Nothing that won't mend.' She looked at the grim-faced Scot. 'Is he dead?'

Munro peered over the railing and made a grimace of his own. He nodded. 'He is.'

Rose returned the nod, not knowing quite what she meant by it.

'What – what was he saying? Did they hear what he was saying?'

Munro frowned. 'Ma'am?'

'His lips were moving. As he was – after he landed.'

Munro touched his earpiece. Muttered the question: 'Were there any last words?'

The reply buzzed promptly back; Rose didn't catch it.

'What was that, Sergeant?'

Munro cleared his throat softly.

'He said, "Father."' He looked at her curiously. 'Does it mean something?'

'Does anything?'

'Ma'am?'

She sighed, rubbed her eyes.

'Never mind. No – I don't know. Was that all he said?'

'Aye. I don't suppose he had time for much more.'

Some people, Rose thought, would say that Luka was free now – free from his madness and his hurt. Some would say that, at last, he was with his lost father, the abbot, and with his murdered brothers of the Order of St Quintus.

Some would say he'd cheated justice.

Some would say he'd burn in hell.

It was all the same to Rose. To her, all that mattered

now was that he was dead and gone – it was time to worry about those left behind.

'The annexe,' she said quickly to Munro, moving towards the stairs. 'In the basement – Matt, Professor Brask, he's . . .'

She trailed off at the sight of Munro's face. Grave, sombre. A face with bad news behind it, a face that went with 'I'm sorry to have to tell you . . .' or 'There's no easy way to say this . . .'

'I know, ma'am,' Munro said. 'We already found him.'

Chapter Thirty-seven

A scattering of dull stars showed over Oxford. SOCO's high-intensity lighting rigs cast long, sharp shadows on the concrete.

'Does it hurt?' the paramedic had asked.

She'd wanted to reply, *Compared to what?*

'Not really,' Rose had lied. She'd flexed her hand, testing the soreness of her bandaged wrist. It had still felt raw, scorched, damaged. The burns would leave scars, she knew. 'Thank you.'

'You're welcome.' The medic was young, female, with thoughtful eyes and gentle fingers. Maggie she'd said her name was. She'd been sitting beside Rose on the church steps when the ambulance crew had brought Brask out of the annexe.

Rose had tried to see beyond the hi-vis bodies crowded round the rattling gurney, through the urgent chaos of blankets, drips, tubes. She'd caught only glimpses: Brask's bloodied skin, Brask's wild dark hair.

Then he was gone, hoisted briskly into the back of the ambulance.

'They'll do everything they can,' Maggie had said. 'I know we always say that. But it's true, they will. All these horrible deaths . . . they've made us as sick as anyone. The guys'll do whatever it takes to prevent another one.'

Rose had nodded moodily.

Now, alone on the steps, she tugged her blanket around her shoulders and thought about Professor Matt Brask.

Brask was a man of God. Okay, he was more complex – subtler, deeper, more curious, more troubled – than your usual parish priest. But he was a man who looked for meaning.

Would he find any meaning in this? Rose wondered. In all this pain, all this suffering, all these wrecked lives?

Or would he go to his grave asking why?

She thought back to her first visit here, to the Church of the Queen of Peace. Thought of the garishly gruesome painted Christ suspended over the altar: the red of the blood, the dark-pink of the scarified skin, the terrible grief in the down-tilted face.

If they can find meaning in that, Rose thought bitterly, they can find meaning in anything.

She ran a hand through her hair and blew out a sigh. How could anyone make sense of what Luka had done?

There'd be an investigation, of course. A senior Thames Valley officer throws an immigrant off a balcony – how could there not be? And the press'd be all over it like blowflies. She'd come through it all right, she supposed.

Aside from anything else, it seemed so surreal: this case – tortured saints, medieval paintings, ancient monasteries and all – being soberly dissected by men in suits in a wood-panelled committee room . . . it felt *wrong*.

At first glance it seemed that Luka's crimes didn't belong in our time. Didn't belong to our world. It'd be nice to think so, Rose thought. But take a look at the court reports. Read through the 999 call logs. Pick up a bloody newspaper. Who are you trying to kid?

A tall figure moved out of the darkness.

'Word from the hospital,' said Leland Phillips.

Rose looked up sharply and tried to kill the shoot of hope that sprang up in her chest.

'Go on.'

Phillips adjusted the sit of his trousers and settled himself on the step beside her.

'He lost a lot of blood in there,' he said. 'But there was no damage to anything important. The arrows missed all the vital organs.' He gave Rose a nudge. 'Your professor's a lucky boy. *Damn* lucky. It'll be a hell of a recovery, but he's going to be okay.'

She wanted to weep. She wanted to hug Phillips. Christ, she could have kissed the supercilious bastard.

Instead, through a knackered half-smile, she said: 'Not lucky.'

'Huh?'

'He wasn't lucky. Luka knew what he was doing. If he'd wanted to kill Brask, he knew where to aim.'

'So he was, what, just tickling him for fun?'

'He was keeping him alive, Phillips. He needed Matt to suffer. He'd have killed him in the end, of course – but the suffering was the main thing.'

There was a silence.

Phillips said: 'Fu-u-uck.'

'Yep.'

The DI reached into his jacket, drew out a hip flask.

'Let me guess,' Rose said as he unscrewed the cap. 'The finest vintage Armagnac?'

Phillips smiled thinly.

'Pisspot Scotch, actually. It's Angler's. I took it off him

and gave him a bollocking for drinking on the job.' He upended the flask and took a mouthful. 'Christ. Here.' He passed it along. 'You look like you need it.'

She didn't disagree.

'Steady there,' Phillips murmured as she took a long, burning swig. 'Don't want you going all *Prime Suspect* on us.'

Rose coughed, laughed. The noise echoed in the dark church car park.

'Listen, Rose,' Phillips said after a moment. There was the slightest note of discomfort in his voice. 'You did what you had to do in there, all right? Killing the mad bastard. You didn't have a choice.'

She looked at him.

'It – it was an accident.'

Phillips tilted his head.

'From your point of view, maybe. But the way I read it, he wanted it to finish that way. He *needed* you to do what you did.'

'There was nothing else I could've done.'

'I know that. Like I said – he didn't give you a choice.' He shrugged. 'The man wanted to die. Who knows since when. Since last week? Since twenty-five years ago? Since always?' He put a hand briefly on Rose's shoulder. 'He wanted to die; he's dead – it's over.'

She shook her head emphatically.

'No. Not over. Florian, the priest – Florian's still out there.'

Phillips made a dismissive gesture.

'We've an all-points alert out across the city. He's a seventy-year-old priest with a limp and a strong Eastern

European accent. How far is he going to get?' He sniffed, spat on the concrete. 'It's over, Rose. Done with. You can get on with your life.' Gave her a smirk. 'Such as it is.'

He stood, smoothed his jacket.

'Keep the flask. Angler drinks too much anyway.' He frowned judiciously at the dressing on Rose's wrist. Blood was already seeping into the off-white cotton. 'You need to get to A&E with that. Get it sorted out properly.' Another dry look. 'Plus all those other injuries you're keeping to yourself, you brave little soldier.'

She nodded, smiled. Her head throbbed. Her ribs ached.

'I'll drive myself there,' she said. 'Once I've got my head together.'

'Okay. Then fuck off home to bed. You look like you've not slept in six weeks.'

'You're not far wrong.'

'Take it easy, Inspector.' Phillips flipped her an ironic salute and disappeared into the gloom. A minute later she saw the headlights of his Audi flare, watched the big car purr through the gates and pull out on to the main road.

Luka was still on her mind.

All this to justify a decades-old death-wish? All this to find a way, a reason, to die? It was insane – but then, so was Luka.

There was belief behind the things he did. For Christ's sake, surely there *had* to be. To tear the skin from a living body, to throw a young woman in the fire and watch her burn, to butcher a woman you knew, had worked with, *prayed* with –

There was something behind that stronger than madness. There was faith.

She stood, stretched her legs, flexed her back and winced as a ripple of pain passed through her body. She kind of hoped the hospital would want to keep her in overnight. A fistful of painkillers and a long lie-down on clean white sheets – it sounded like something she could really use right now.

Her car was parked by the road, outside the gates. She wondered, as she unlocked the door, if she'd have the strength to work the pedals.

She started up the engine, put the car into gear, pulled away from the kerb. Left the Church of the Queen of Peace behind her.

Didn't look back.

Epilogue

Nine months later

'*Policija gadovi*,' the man snapped, shaking his head with a lemon-sucking expression. '*Policija može pojesti govno.*'

Rose glanced across the makeshift office at Adrijana. Adrijana looked awkward.

'He says – something about the police.'

'I gathered that much, Jana. What exactly did he say?'

'He said police are – bastards? And that the police can . . . "eat shit".'

Rose grinned, shook her head. Same old, same old.

'Tell him,' she said, 'that we'll send an officer round to speak to him this week.' She made a note. Then to the man: 'We'll get it sorted, Mr Blažević. You have my word on that.'

Adrijana rattled off the translation. Mr Blažević scowled, shrugged, nodded.

'*Dobro*,' he grunted, getting rheumatically to his feet.

Dobro, 'good'. It was the best she'd had so far from the old bugger. She gave him a well-practised smile.

He grumbled something as Adrijana helped him on with his anorak.

When he was gone Rose stirred two teabags in the steel pot and asked Adrijana what he'd said. Adrijana laughed.

'He said it was no use trying to flirt with him,' she said.

'Fair enough,' Rose said drily. 'Out of my league, I guess.'

Mr Blažević was eighty-four. His on-going problems with a mob of local youths – empty booze bottles in his vegetable patch and, when he'd complained, a dog turd through his letterbox – were just one of a hundred issues that had been brought to Rose's weekly sessions at the Leys. Building bridges, that was the idea. Letting the local immigrant communities know that the police were on their side.

Some – like Mr Blažević – took more convincing than others.

It was an eye-opener anyway. Problems with employers. Problems with asylum applications, visa applications, citizenship applications. Problems with crime, drugs, trafficking.

Okay, she was a copper, not a social worker. There was only so much she could do. But she was there and she was listening. That was something. And it was a damn sight more than any other DCI had ever done.

At his leaving do Morgan Hume had told her to play down the 'soft stuff' if by some miracle she managed to land an interview.

'They don't want airy-fucking-fairy touchy-fucking-feely bridge-building,' he'd said, slurping at a glass of orange juice. 'They want to hear about *cracking down*. They want fucking Robocop, Rose, is what they want. Law and order. Start banging on about community policing, they'll take you for a soft touch.' He'd given her a look of amusement tinged with respect. 'And I know from bitter fucking experience that that's the last thing you are.'

She'd thanked him. Could've argued, but it was his leaving do after all – and it didn't seem right to start a row with a guy who was headed for a triple heart bypass.

'Fucking *ill health*,' he'd declared to the MCU one

January morning, storming in out of the drizzle. 'Fucking *pension.*'

Then he'd shut himself in his office for the rest of the day.

It had been hard to picture the Thames Valley Major Crimes Unit without Hume at the top. But things were changing. Leland Phillips was already gone – to the Met, a DI post in the financial crime division. Had enough of nutters, he'd said.

Rose had wished him well. The MCU didn't bring out the best in everyone. Phillips had done okay when the pressure was really on.

And in the end, that had left her, Rose, staring at a nine-page application form and wondering if she *really* wanted to be Detective Chief Inspector Lauren Rose.

Turned out she really did.

Hume's advice had made sense, in a screwed-up sort of way. Play it tough, be the hard-but-fair copper, don't let them see any sign of weakness. 'That goes double with you being, y'know, a woman,' the old DCI had added. 'They'll be expecting a fucking wimp. Don't give 'em one.'

Her dad told her much the same thing.

Knowing who she was up against didn't make it any easier. No Phillips, true, but a Cambridge grad with five years as DI in Edinburgh, a Met DCI moving sideways, another DCI who'd been making headlines as an 'enforcer' in Bristol . . .

It had kept her awake for a few nights before the interview. And it had taken her quite a while – longer than it should have, she thought later, exasperated with herself – to see the obvious.

She wasn't DCI Morgan Hume. She wasn't DCI Keith

Rose. So she went into the interview and talked about community engagement, offender rehabilitation, partnerships and problem-solving.

They'd offered her the job on the spot.

It was her passion, they'd told her afterwards, that had made the difference.

Now, in the makeshift office at the bottom of a Leys housing block, she settled into one of the second-hand chairs and sipped her cheap tea.

'We will see him again next week,' Adrijana predicted, 'Mr Blažević. I think he likes us.'

'*You* might see him next week. I can't make it.'

'Then Matt –?'

'Uh-huh. It's Matt's turn to flirt with Mr Blažević.'

Adrijana giggled.

The youngest Zrinski girl had been in on the project from the start; the door of the Zrinskis' flat had been the first Rose had knocked on after securing her DCI's stripes. She'd needed someone local, someone to help her establish trust with the residents of the Leys, if her diplomacy drive was going to get off the ground.

Adrijana was smart, a quick learner and understood what the people in the housing blocks were going through – because she'd been through it herself, and a hell of a lot more besides. It helped that she had a teenager's elastic capacity for new languages. She could help Rose out with everything from Estonian to Romanian.

'How's Sofia?'

'Doing good.' Adrijana, her mug of tea cupped in both hands, nodded. 'Her boss at the supermarket is very happy. Maybe permanent job.'

'And Dr Levinson?'

'He says she makes very good progress.' A shadow passed across the girl's expression. 'It's very hard.' She looked at Rose. 'It hurts, Lauren.'

'I know, Jana.' She reached forwards to lightly touch Adrijana's arm. 'She's lucky to have you.'

'And I am very lucky to have her also.' She gave a brittle smile. 'So.'

They'd both of them been through hell, Rose knew. With help, they were finding ways to carry on. One-on-one psychotherapy, grief counselling, victim-support groups – an awful lot of airy-fucking-fairy touchy-fucking-feely, she thought wryly. And it was working, little by little, week by week, but it was working.

Rose sometimes went to see Maureen Norfolk and her girls on the farm out at Bletchingdon. The place was still an open wound. Raw, angry. It was hard, she knew, for them to see her. Maureen wasn't going to consider her a friend any time soon. Didn't matter, though. Rose knew there were things there she could help with – and as long as she knew that she'd do whatever she could.

And she'd spoken on the phone to the Chaudrys in Bradford. They were a big family, the parents successful second-generation Gujarati Indians, seven kids all high-achievers, students, lawyers, scientists – and all of them broken into pieces by what had happened to Caroline. It was easy sometimes, Rose knew, to think that the loss was less when the family was big. But she knew that the mathematics of grief didn't work that way. Caroline's murder had torn a hole that could never be mended.

Mr Blažević was their last visitor of the day. When the

teapot was drained Adrijana bounced up, wished Rose a good day, grabbed her bag and went. She had a date, she said, with a young plumber's lad from the next block along. 'Ukrainian. Seventeen. Very *buff*.' Rose smiled as out of the window she watched the girl hurry along the sunlit footpath, bright in a green vest top and yellow cord skirt. *God's gift to the charity shop, that girl.*

She had a quick tidy – rinsed the mugs, put away the thick-as-your-arm file of Mr Blažević's complaints – and checked her phone. Twelve calls. Christ. *Back to it, DCI Rose.* She locked up the office and headed back to her car.

The Leys was no place to leave your car when everyone in a four-mile radius knew you were a copper. It was a bit of a banger, but Rose liked it with its paintwork and four tyres intact. She'd got into the habit of parking up a couple of miles short of the Leys, towards town, and of walking through the estates – whatever time of day or night it was.

It was sobering to think that Adrijana walked these under-lit paths between the bleak, hard-edged housing blocks every day. But it gave Rose a connection with the place. She'd known a lot of detectives lose touch with the streets when they hit DI or DCI level. This way she gave herself no choice.

Besides, it was simply good policing. Any mug could cruise by in a patrol car and see this was a bloody tough area; everything about the Leys said so, in a voice you could hardly ignore. Walking the paths gave Rose a chance to listen out for the whispers.

It tested her nerve, too. She didn't like to admit this, even to herself. She didn't like to think that her nerve ever needed testing.

But despite the summer sun, Oxford had been a dark

place for her since the Trick or Treat murders. She saw ghosts everywhere.

It could have been worse, she reflected as she passed through the shadow of Dmitry Rakić's old housing block. Rakić was history: banged up for eighteen months for his gun-waving appearance at All Souls, he'd been transferred from HM Bullingdon up to Wakefield in Yorkshire to keep him from pulling any strings from behind the prison wall. Wakefield had done for him. There were some real villains in that place, Rose knew. One of them had pushed Rakić too far. The Croat had stabbed him to death in the exercise yard. Twenty-five years. She didn't expect to see Dmitry Rakić again.

She didn't expect to see Luka again, either – but that didn't stop her spying his face half hidden in the bustling town crowds, his stringy figure forever lurking on the edge of her vision, his broken, blood-spattered body in the darkness when she closed her eyes to sleep.

An autopsy had revealed a bullet lodged deep in the murderer's brain. Rose guessed that it was a goodbye kiss from one of the Serbs who'd destroyed St Quintus so many years ago. Had it been this brain damage that sent Luka so deep into his religious psychosis? Rose didn't know – never would. But she wondered about it all the time.

Yes, she was going to be stuck with Luka for a while yet. But then, every copper had a ghost or two. It went with the job. Some coppers she'd known had seemed to collect them, like old coins or postage stamps.

At least she knew beyond doubt that Luka was dead – unlike Father Florian.

The thought of the shuffling old priest made her shiver.

A city-wide sweep hadn't found him; there hadn't been so much as a sighting since, despite appeals in the papers.

Rose had wondered, at first, if Florian had had friends who might have helped him hide – helped him leave the country, even. Florian had helped Luka; what if Florian, in his turn, had had helpers, accomplices? She'd found herself imagining an underground network of them – who knew how many more Florians? How many more Lukas might be out there?

Phillips, though, had been dead sure that Florian had pegged out in his hiding place – that he was lying dead in a storm gutter or a drainage ditch somewhere. 'Good bloody riddance,' he'd said, theatrically dusting his hands together.

But he and his cocky certainty were gone now.

So no Phillips and no Hume, but Mike Angler was still there. The dim DS was too bone idle to ever go anywhere else. Conners had finally made sergeant, over in uniform. She sometimes still saw PC Ganley gangling about the place.

And then there was Matt Brask.

For now he still walked with a stick.

'I'll miss the gravitas it gives me,' he'd said, only the night before, when he and Rose had met for a catch-up in an Oxford pub. 'I think a professor *should* look venerable. Right?'

She'd laughed and said, 'Yeah, sure, why not?'

'Though I still think they ought to have given me a staff,' he'd added, setting the stick against the panelled wall of the booth and sliding awkwardly into the bench seat. 'You know, like Moses. Ow.'

'Hip still sore?'

'A little. But in a month or so, they tell me, I'll be leaping around like a spring lamb.'

The jokes didn't quite disguise a subtle change in Brask since All Souls' Day, since that night in the Church of the Queen of Peace. It was true, he *did* have more gravitas, but the walking stick had nothing to do with it.

Brask, Rose knew, had never been an ivory-tower academic. He'd never tried to cut himself off from the real world of human hardship. His break with the Church, the loss of Hester, even his work in Oxford with the Leys communities – this was a guy who'd always fronted up to the real world. He'd had to.

But what he'd been through with Luka was different. Had it made him harder, tougher, more distant? Rose had watched him, in the pub, chatting with the barman as he fetched in their drinks. No – no, quite the opposite. If anything, the new Brask reached out to people even more readily than before.

If Brask had been a different kind of character, what Luka had put him through might have kept him from ever trusting anyone again. And who could have blamed him? But Brask seemed to have found the capacity – somehow, somewhere – to welcome the world into his life, without conditions. He hadn't got harder. Just stronger.

It made Rose think of her walks alone in the dark through the alleys of the Leys, that need to test herself, push herself.

Brask had slid her glass of red wine on to the tabletop in front of her and worked his way back into his seat.

'You're all right taking tomorrow's open-door?' He'd sipped his bitter and made an apologetic face. 'I know you're snowed under, but I have to fly out to Bologna first thing tomorrow, for a conference.'

'Such a hard life. Yeah, that's fine. But you know I can't make the week after? Meeting with the council. "Problems" with traveller communities. Going to have to knock some heads together.'

He'd laughed, called her a militant do-gooder.

Then she'd remembered something Lel Phillips had emailed her about the day before. Subject line: *KARMA*.

'I heard something about an old friend of ours,' she'd told Brask.

'Mm?'

'A trial at the Old Bailey. Three tabloid journos up for phone hacking.'

'Oh, don't tell me –'

She'd nodded, not bothering to hide her satisfaction.

'Olly Stevenage. Suspended sentence, and two hundred hours of community service.'

'Couldn't,' Brask said, 'have happened to a more deserving fellow.'

Ambitious young Stevenage, according to Phillips, had dropped out of his Oxford degree course in February; on the strength of his scoops in the Trick or Treat Killer case he'd landed a job at one of the downmarket red tops. Acquired some bad habits and got run in when a hacked-off celeb went to the police.

The thought of Stevenage scrubbing graffiti and picking up litter went some way to restoring Rose's faith in the justice system. Christ, she thought, it was almost enough to make you believe there was a God . . .

The conversation had turned back to the Leys. It always did, somehow. They'd talked for a while about the poverty, the problems, the crime, Mr Blažević's complaints . . .

In the middle of the conversation – halfway through denouncing the state of the accommodation provided for asylum-seekers – Rose had broken off abruptly. Looked frankly at Brask.

'Can you imagine Morgan Hume talking like this?'

'Nope.'

She'd rubbed her eyes wearily.

'Am I still even a copper, Matt? I mean, with all this.' She'd taken a slug of wine. 'Sometimes I wonder what I'm even *doing*.'

'You're keeping people safe,' Brask had said without hesitation. 'You're helping people make the right choices. You're looking after people.' He'd slapped the table with a grin, making their drinks jump. 'Of *course* you're a god-damn cop.'

Now, as she left the Leys and walked sore-footed through the suburbs, she felt the heat of the day weighing heavily on her.

Her car was parked in a residential street of well-kept semis, not far from the football ground. Up ahead, a grey tabby cat slunk across the road and slipped into a hedge-row. A blackbird burbled in a scrubby hawthorn. Midges fogged the air.

Rose's car stood alone, half on and half off the kerb, next to a bank of dull-green nettles and the side wall of someone's garage. She slumped into the driver's seat. For a moment she thought: Christ, this car needs a new air freshener. It smelled like something had gone rotten, started to ferment.

Then instinct kicked in. It was a smell she knew. Her gut recoiled. Her body tensed.

The church cellar.

Brask's office.

Katerina's body.

The bones.

Balsam oil – Father Florian's sickly sacred chrism.

She turned her head to the passenger seat, not wanting to see, not wanting to believe.

The oil had seeped into the upholstery, making a black stain. In the declining sunlight of late afternoon the greased bones gleamed.

A small cage of ribs, knotted about a single bone. The single bone was broken in the middle. Its splintered ends made her think of Luka, impaled and spreadeagled on the cross.

A short thong of cracked leather fastened the cage to a larger construction, just the same except for its size – and the bone in this one was not broken.

Something moved on the edge of Rose's vision. Her eyes flickered to the rear-view mirror . . .

THE END

He just wanted a decent book to read ...

Not too much to ask, is it? It was in 1935 when Allen Lane, Managing Director of Bodley Head Publishers, stood on a platform at Exeter railway station looking for something good to read on his journey back to London. His choice was limited to popular magazines and poor-quality paperbacks – the same choice faced every day by the vast majority of readers, few of whom could afford hardbacks. Lane's disappointment and subsequent anger at the range of books generally available led him to found a company – and change the world.

'We believed in the existence in this country of a vast reading public for intelligent books at a low price, and staked everything on it'
Sir Allen Lane, 1902–1970, founder of Penguin Books

The quality paperback had arrived – and not just in bookshops. Lane was adamant that his Penguins should appear in chain stores and tobacconists, and should cost no more than a packet of cigarettes.

Reading habits (and cigarette prices) have changed since 1935, but Penguin still believes in publishing the best books for everybody to enjoy. We still believe that good design costs no more than bad design, and we still believe that quality books published passionately and responsibly make the world a better place.

So wherever you see the little bird – whether it's on a piece of prize-winning literary fiction or a celebrity autobiography, political tour de force or historical masterpiece, a serial-killer thriller, reference book, world classic or a piece of pure escapism – you can bet that it represents the very best that the genre has to offer.

Whatever you like to read – trust Penguin.